PRAISE FOR
STELLA ATRIUM

"The plot has everything a reader could want. Action, adventure, humor, romance. . . . Atrium's beautifully descriptive style sweeps us up and carries us into this new world. We are invested. We need to know what happens next . . ."

—Rabid Readers Review

THE BODY POLITIC

BOOK II OF THE TRIBAL WARS

STELLA ATRIUM

Stella Atrium Writes
3023 N Clark Street
Suite 762
Chicago, IL 60657

Ordering Information:

Quantity sales. Special discounts are available on quantity purchases by corporations, associations, and others. For details, contact the publisher at the address above.

Orders by U.S. trade bookstores and wholesalers. Please contact Stella Atrium Writes: ADMIN@STELLAATRIUM.COM

Printed in the United States of America

ISBN: 978-1-958959-04-6

ARRIVI DUCHY

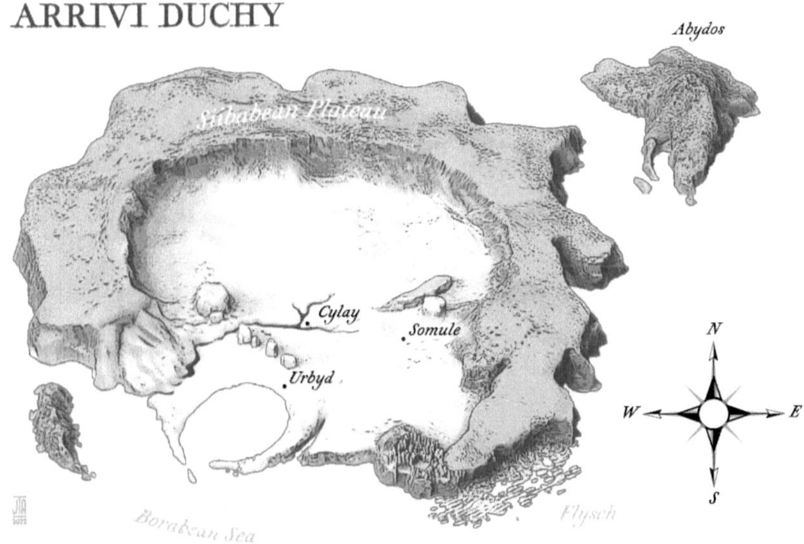

For the reader's convenience, a glossary of character names with relationships, and a separate glossary of locations and terms, are found at the end of this book.

PART ONE

Brianna Miller in Pear-ass now resides
Who saved the gouleps out of bondage
Star traffic for Somule Gems she guides
Who jumped back while warriors did make
For Uburu a safe passage

Far distant from our stars and dreams
Far distant from the sisters of Arim
Enrich the gouleps, but at what cost
To home and hearth and husband?
She who is promised to Dacupitte, anon

ONE

from Brianna Miller

I LEARNED ABOUT THE SELF-TORCHING FROM THE EVENING NEWS in Paris. Footage of the public suicide ran repeatedly while armchair experts crowded talk show segments. The way it ran was: on Dolvia, a woman wearing a traditional Arrivi gown plus a sky-blue burka entered the plaza in front of the governor's mansion in Cylay. She sat cross-legged on the brick street across from the ornate gate before splashing gasoline onto the burka and setting herself on fire. The repeated news footage showed the bright and angry flames, the shearing clothes and blackened skin, and the exposed skeleton while the orange conflagration cooled.

Kyle Rula had honored tradition by wearing the body veil that was still required in the towns controlled by Karl Wyley. She had made no speeches and left no manifesto. No banners displaying her face were paraded through the streets. Rather, she had protested oppression under the tribal leaders' rule by exercising her right to die as she chose: death by fire in the public square.

Immolation, they called it.

I sat in the Paris apartment above my nightclub and reread the online message. The curtains were drawn against the sunlight, and I wore a robe and camisole. My trade was conducted mostly after sunset after all. My hair hung between my shoulders, and I pushed an errant section aside before I watched the news clip again, searching the crowd for a familiar face. Hakulupe Le or the convent gouleps risked prison and torture if they stood with this sister of Arim in silent allegiance. Rabbenu Ely was an unforgiving leader.

The Company still had a stranglehold on travel through the wormhole. Tariff barriers at both ends of the wormhole had slowed trade. Information came in bundles, sometimes delayed for a full week. Our Somule Gems online chatter was data-mined by interested parties. Packages were diverted and opened and delayed at whim.

Posited in the future tense, the message was dated four days before the incident, common standard time. "Kyle Rula will rob the desert of one. Come home. Hakulupe Le." Was Dolvia my home? Was Dolvia anything like the savannah I had left more than a decade ago?

There was a quiet knock at the door. Cool air from the hallway and a shaft of light announced her entrance before Laura crossed the wide oriental carpet. "Pardon me, Brianna," she said in French. "Two men wait to speak with you."

"You know I don't entertain during the day."

"These are different. Dressed western, but they have Westend ID papers."

"Shoes?" I asked. You could peg a person by the shoes they wore.

Laura shrugged. "New, also their suits are new. One has black hair tied at his neck. The other has—"

"Rufus? Surely not." I pulled the silken robe across my chest, an instinctive gesture. "Have them wait twenty minutes while I dress, then show them in here."

Rufus was the younger son of Kyle Rula and the Mecukoo warrior Cyrus. For Rufus to have arrived in Paris on this day, he must have been traveling at the moment of his mother's self-execution. Perhaps he had made peace with her in Mecukoo style, condoning her act.

Had Rufus come to collect me for the journey home?

I dressed in a business suit with a long skirt. I brushed back my hair, allowing it to cascade down my spine. The rich weight of my tresses had secured the return of many clients after the novelty of having a Dolviet woman had passed. The flesh trade had not made my fortune though. I viewed my social liaisons as personal politics, an avenue into French and European government circles that only a working woman can secure.

Another soft knock. Laura peered around the door, and a shaft of amber light spilled into the room. I switched on a big lamp behind the sofa and crossed to receive my tribal cousins. I hoped my Arrivi language skills were not too rusty.

I reached to shake hands. Rufus was age 28 and light-skinned like his father, with a narrow nose. When our palms met, a battle scar across the back of his wrist was visible. I was certain there were many more.

"Hiki, Rufus. Melinga."

"Melinga. May I present Kyros rabbe Sudl, a cousin to Karen Osborn?"

Kyros hesitantly extended his hand to shake. He was perhaps 35, taller and stouter. I had to assume Kyros had spent his tender years herding erriv with Southeast Arrivi, too old to have tolerated attendance in Hakulupe Le's classroom. His wife and academy-trained children had likely participated in rice cultivation. This trip through the wormhole, disembarking in Beijing and traveling on to Paris, must have been a wonder to him.

I could not resist having a little fun at Kyros rabbe Sudl's expense, maybe because Laura stared with her mouth agape. "Kyros is a woman's name," I said in Arrivi.

Kyros shifted his weight and stared at the floor.

"There was a woman named Kyros," Rufus said. She was his grandmother. "There was a man named Brian."

Rufus had not changed much, and he put no strain on my dormant language skills.

"Laura, would you bring tea?" I asked in French. I gestured to the long dining table. "Please, won't you have a seat?"

Rufus pulled a chair away from the table so it faced out. He sat with a straight back and hands on his knees, which were spread wide apart. Kyros stood at his shoulder. Their postures told me everything. Each wore an arm amulet, a glassy topaz stone trapped in a binding cord and tied around the big muscle of the right arm, indicating that they knew a time of mourning.

"About your mother—"

Rufus was silent, raising his chin slightly with folded lips.

"A moment of karsci," Kyros quickly said, "that changes hearts."

"Heartstone for you and Lynus," I said.

"You have inherited the fortress by Kyle Rula's hand."

"I robbed you of your birthright?"

"Mekucoo don't require a library." Rufus glanced around at the apartment's furnishings and exchanged looks with Kyros. "Your riches are Dolvia-derived."

"I developed the shipping channels, so the convent residents prosper."

"A rich woman is just a target."

I sighed. I had set aside tribal logic, forgetting how numbing and exclusive it could be. I had a life here in Paris, a position and a name, however tainted. Why return to a war-torn desert where women were granted no voice? Where you had to light yourself on fire to get noticed.

"Dacupitte sent this." Rufus drew from his pocket a gold bracelet fashioned into acacia leaves placed side by side—the traditional Arrivi engagement bracelet to be augmented at the wedding celebration by a similar necklace. Dacupitte was called Pete, the 45-year-old father of legions, and my supposed betrothed on Dolvia.

I only chuckled. "Dacupitte assumes much."

"It is seen."

I had never held with tribal prophecy, especially this claim. "That was a convenient vision offered to bolster Pete's leadership status."

Rufus blinked. "You question second sight?"

"I question everything."

Rufus considered that. After a long moment he said, "How sad for you."

A knock came at the door. Laura entered with a silver tray laden with a tea service. I allowed her to pour. Rufus barely noticed her heaving bosom as she drew close. Kyros frowned at her sweet smile. How to keep them distracted while I made a few plans?

"Surely you will want to view parliament," I said in English. "And tour some industry while you're here. Also, there are—"

"We leave the day after tomorrow," Rufus pronounced. "Your jump back number is already secured."

"But you cannot—"

"You are an employee of Somule Gems. You are being recalled."

"Deported, you mean."

"A Softcheeks word."

Softcheeks was the common tribal label for Earth corporate officers who had disembarked generations ago with their well-armed security forces and mining equipment and arrogant manners. Perhaps I had one trump card, though, that Rufus had not anticipated. "Laura," I said in English. "Ring up Daniel Chin. Inform him I cannot keep our appointment tomorrow as I am being railroaded out of town."

Rufus squinted. "Daniel Chin? Of the Company?"

"I entertain many travelers here, a clearinghouse for Westend news."

"Then you know what he is."

"I know what each of you are."

"And you—" Rufus gestured slightly, probably wondering how personal my relationships were with the Han Chinese executives.

"My dealings are more than you can know," I said in a bare whisper.

"Or want to know. You have done well, but now a new season is upon us."

"On Earth, people designate the seasons rather than being ruled by them."

"A new Dolviet season is upon us," Rufus corrected.

"Surely a short delay won't—"

"You will come. That is all."

Perhaps I would come, but not because Rufus pronounced it, and certainly not because of Pete's paltry gift. Perhaps I would greet Sarah at the savannah convent and take vows and become a welfare minister and raise gualareps and teach Arrivi women a non-suicidal means of protest. Perhaps I would visit the fortress and give reverence at the Canyon of Buttes and . . . and go home.

But not today. Today I would have a little fun.

"Laura," I said in French. "Have rooms made up for our guests. Have a meal served and some music, the full treatment."

She giggled and gestured that they should leave with her. "Laura," I added. "Our Dolviet friends have some English."

"Won't you come with me?" she said in English with a lilting accent.

Kyros blinked. He had not expected to understand her words.

"I can see to your comfort," Laura added.

"We have rooms already," Rufus said in Arrivi.

"Laura," I said in English. "Have their hotel send over their luggage and papers and charge the bill to my personal account." Laura gestured again that they should leave with her.

Rufus hesitated.

"Surely you won't refuse my hospitality," I said, "after you have traveled so far?"

Laura stared with question. Rufus stood and showed an open hand gesture before walking out, while Kyros only stared. Laura giggled again and scurried after them. I was fairly certain her efforts would soften their resolve.

I sent messages that local Somule Gems managers should visit for brief meetings and issued additional orders for the other managers along our overland travel route. I called the banks and made wire transfers. Detailed instructions were already resident with my lawyers; the most immediate was that they should not know each other. I called several clients with explanations, claiming that it had been a pleasure. To each I recommended a club employee who may succor his loss in my absence. I called a seamstress and had certain garments altered for travel through Consortium customs. The show was not closed, just changing venues. Perhaps my conversations were extra fun because I knew I would not be back this way.

Colored light streamed through the stained glass window and fell on my gloves where I sat in a sanctuary pew in the Lutheran Church. The parable depicted in the window mosaic was the woman at the well, the one whom Jesus had called out for having several husbands. Behind me, somebody dropped a hymnal, and the noise reverberated against the high columns. I saw Petra Mitterand and Heather Clark enter from the side where they had been conferring with the pastor. I knew my answer just by looking at their postures.

Petra was the grown daughter of Pierre Mitterand, my sponsor for travel through the wormhole more than a decade ago. His part of the pox cure had made him rich. His later investment in Somule Gems, which I managed, had made his family rich for generations.

Heather was the daughter of General and Billie Hartley, mother to three children, and married to a pilot who had risen to the rank of colonel here on Earth. Heather was a minor investor in Somule Gems, mostly encouraged by Petra, and a supposed friend to me. Her dark hair framed a pale complexion, the eyes cynical in a patrician mask. The two women approached quietly, hesitating a few paces from me.

"He said no," I said, "because of the club."

Heather looked away, but Petra sat next to me, her narrow skirt on the edge of the pew. "It's not the club. Heather told him you're leaving that life behind."

"When I think of all the money I contributed while here," I said. "I placed fourteen young people from the orphanage. Who else has—"

"It's you," Heather said. "You must confess and be baptized."

I chuckled through the bitterness. "I have always loved this big empty room. Now it seems as empty as the pastor's heart. After today, Somule Gems has no more business with Earth religions, here or throughout Westend."

"And you decide that?" Heather asked.

I graced her with a level look. "You are free to tithe from your share. Several managers who were church orphans will return to Paris seeking work. I'll send them to you, Heather."

Heather made a sour face. "Why so dramatic?"

Heather had recently reappeared in my life after the news that deposits of silicide had been found on the savannah of Dolvia. Heather's daughter waited in the vestibule, dressed fashionably and staring at a game on a handheld device. "Can we go now?"

Heather turned to me. "I tried with the pastor. I sincerely tried."

I forced a smile. "I will deliver your gifts to General Hartley. Thank you for your time." I waited with arms crossed and feet planted wide apart while Heather and her daughter left.

Petra sighed softly. "She asked me why you dislike her."

"Remind her that actions have consequences."

"She doesn't remember an infraction that set you against her. What was so unforgiveable?"

"Nothing. None of it has meaning."

We walked down the steps to the waiting limousine. The rain had stopped, but the eaves still dripped, and people hurried along the pedway. I had often heard clients complain that Paris was humid, but I treasured the dewy mornings and frequent patches of fog. I looked across the skyline of the stylish graystones and the spreading oaks that thrived in the moist climate. The south suburbs were overbuilt in a riot of styles made possible by new materials gained through intra-solar asteroid mining, but this borough held landmark buildings and restrictions on skyline additions. Because so many young people had gone adventuring to space colonies, there was room in Paris for all those left behind to enjoy reasonable rents and space in parks on lazy afternoons. The talent had ventured offworld, but good living still resided here.

Petra waited by the car's open door, her eyes bright with sympathy. She knew the price I was paying to meet the demands of my tribe. We settled into the plush seats. While the car glided along the wide boulevard, Petra began again. "You have managers for the club, at least?"

"The operations are separate and serve different talents than, um—"

"You could just hire some managers. Not every person must be handpicked after. . . ." Petra made a wide gesture with her hands. "After you see the light in her aura."

"I need people I can trust while I'm on the other side of the galaxy."

"You want a battalion of destitute infantry with no family, fanatically loyal because you plucked them out of poverty."

"That principle sounds better each time you complain."

The limousine sped away from the center of the borough and finally slowed in the circular drive of an aging mansion that had been converted into a private hospital. The sky was crowded with fat clouds heavy with moisture. I was hoping the rain would dissipate before this interview concluded. I had too many errands to be delayed by a downpour.

We were greeted on the front steps by the manager and two nurses with a show of concern for my friend who was sequestered there. We were led to a solarium where brooding light from the overcast day created shadows on the path, one I had followed many times before, to a serving table where Pierre Milleraud sat in a wheel chair. He suffered from a debilitating bone disease contracted in Africa, where he'd overseen vaccination programs using a variation of the pox cure. Pierre had been cut low by a disease here on Earth after he had weathered the virulent threats to his health during a doctor's residency on Dolvia's savannah. We had noted that irony in more than one of our talks, and the price adventurers pay for service in Westend.

I paused a moment to steel myself for our greeting. Time was a loop, I cautioned myself, and I often only understood events long after they had passed. "Hello, Pierre."

"What a rare treat." His shoulders were hunched, and the transparent skin seemed stretched on his emaciated skull. "And Petra too." He reached a blanched and bony hand to receive her kiss and hug. "This is a red-letter day. Sit and tell me what's new in the world."

I removed my jacket in the humid room while Pierre ordered tea from an attendant. I took a wide-brimmed hat from the back of a chair and tried it on to ease the glare from the banks of windows. I fingered an orchid near the table and sniffed for its perfume, but there was none.

"Your news must be serious," Pierre said behind my back.

"Kyle Rula is dead," Petra said. "Brianna has been recalled to the savannah."

He blinked twice, his breathing regular and shallow. "You could tell them no, Brianna. They should be accustomed to resistance from you."

I kept my back to him. "I have seen this world. I have accomplished my goals."

"You have accomplished much. What is your purpose today?"

"Just . . . hello and goodbye."

"Um-huh."

I turned to confront his curious expression. "You hold certain rights for import—"

"I knew it!"

"You cannot use them now." I stepped closer. "Once inactive, they can be bought at auction. Do you want the licenses to go to the Bryants?"

"I can sell them to the Chinese," Pierre said.

"Is this a negotiation?" I asked.

"From the moment you walked down that path."

We chuckled together. We had negotiated together since I was nineteen. "My enterprises can export the silicide," I said. "We have the expertise, the equipment, and managers I can trust."

"You would have to mine the silicide on the flats of Arim," Pierre said. "The sacred flats. There's no guarantee enough exists to justify the costs, even if you gain tribal permission."

"I know the risks. I need to secure the licenses before I leave."

"How soon?"

"Tomorrow."

Pierre chuckled. "Tell me, if you were not being recalled, would you have waited until I drew my last breath?"

"I would talk to your heirs, to Petra."

Pierre lifted his chin as his eyes drew into a narrow squint. Petra shrugged with a sly smile. I knew that Pierre had already settled many affairs, facing his mortality, so now he was just marking time. "I may linger here and delay your plans," he said.

Petra placed a hand on his arm. "Brianna cannot stay. You cannot use the licenses."

"Petra wants what is best for the family," I added.

He sighed and waited as two servants brought a tray with the tea. We remained silent until their footfall was no longer audible on the path.

"Today, I brought something to trade," I said. "You remember Kyle Rula and the blood sample she supplied to Dr. Greensboro one day? The HeLa cells?"

Pierre saw Petra's questioning look. "HeLa cells are immortal," he explained, "and can be grown in a lab. They were named after a woman on Earth whose cells were used to map the genome. Some time ago, Kyle Rula provided the blood sample we used to develop the pox cure. But Kyle Rula never agreed to provide additional samples, and we kept the source a secret for her protection."

"Kyle Rula who just died," Petra guessed. "The one who set herself on fire?"

"Immolation," I said. "A beautiful word for such an ugly death."

"My condolences," Pierre said. "You were related as I recall."

"She was my aunt, but my blood is, um, diluted by Softcheeks blood."

"Your arrogance is the same as hers," Pierre noted from behind his teacup.

"Kyle Rula had two sons," I added, "Rufus and Lynus, by Cyrus the ketiwhelp killer. Rufus is in Paris today." The tension in the room jumped immediately, but they both held onto their silence. The hanging orchid trembled with the stirring air.

"Of course, there is no guarantee." I pulled a vial of blood from my skirt pocket. I held the narrow tube to the fluctuating natural light. "The blood of Cyrus may overwhelm Kyle Rula's contribution. Rufus was raised on Mekucoo land, not on the flats of Arim with its old water pools. This may be a placebo."

"We can have it tested," Pierre said.

I shook my head slightly in the negative. "A fair trade, a one-time offer good for the next hour only. The blood of Rufus for the import licenses, which you were prepared to sign over anyhow."

Pierre ducked his chin, his eyes glistening with avarice. "How do we know it's even his blood?"

"Because you know me," I said, "and I guarantee it's his blood. Rufus did have the pox as a child."

Petra leaned forward to add her counsel. "Father, we should wait for—"

"There's no need to wait," he said. "Brianna just attached her word, and so her reputation, to the claim. Nothing is more import-ant to Brianna Miller than her reputation."

I placed the vial on the table. "Petra is right; the blood has not been tested." I reached again into my skirt pocket. "However, I did bring this letter of intent, which requires a signature from each of you. And once again, the secret of origin is included in the agree-ment, for the safety of Rufus while we travel. Do you want to take a moment?"

Petra unfolded the single page and read the paragraphs intently. Pierre placed his teacup gently on the saucer. "You will get what you came for, as you always do. My liaison with your scheming ways has proven more profitable than knowing Dr. Greensboro or any Dolviet leader."

I shrugged slightly. "You take a risk on the quality of the blood sample. I take a risk on exporting the silicide using the dormant licenses. On Dolvia, we call this a fair trade."

Pierre nodded to his daughter, so she signed the page. He also signed and passed it back to me. He sat back as though the effort was exhausting. "Take my situation here as fair warning, Brianna Miller. Riches are not security. In Westend especially, all you will have is your reputation."

"Then I will be certain to write my name large so security follows."

We shared the tea and some moments of reminiscing. Petra decided to stay for more talk with her father, so I said goodbye there. Goodbye forever.

When I walked down the steps of the sanitarium, a second limousine was waiting in the circular drive. Petra's chauffeur was standing by the hood, flanked by two Chinese men in silk suits with panda logos on the breast pockets. I walked to the second car. A window rolled down at my approach.

Daniel Chin leaned forward to show his face. "Take a ride with me."

"Mr. Chin, starting today we are on opposing sides of many business concerns."

The window rolled up, so I walked around the car and got in next to him, the smell of an acrid perfume fairly slapping me in the face. A spattering of raindrops decorated the car's polished hood as we left for the short drive back to the club.

Daniel Chin was listed in more than one index as one of Earth's twenty richest men. He had Westend experience from thirty years ago when he had served as the prosecutor in a famous trial in which my father had been the defense lawyer. Daniel Chin was not chatty but had a wicked sense of humor and more business acumen than my other mentors. And he was my most valued personal client at the club.

"Dr. Mitterand agreed to sell the licenses," Daniel Chin stated flatly in perfect French, as impeccable as his English.

"He was waiting to make some grand gesture."

The rain came down strongly, and the chauffer switched on the windshield wipers for a muted click-clack sound.

"My people have been in negotiations with him for months," my host said. "Mitterand was only waiting for you to visit. Brianna, we already own the rights to export from Abydian land. The larger deposits of silicide are there. Allow me to provide equipment and expertise and access to the shipping channels."

"I will take your offer to my people, of course."

"You make the important decisions. Don't be coy." After a moment, he added, "I can block your jump back number."

"I must leave so another can take my place. I will provide her with letters of introduction."

"There is no other like you."

"How gallant. Will you visit the club on occasion, just to keep the managers in line?"

"My pleasure."

"And perhaps you will jump back?" I asked.

"My curiosity about regions beyond the wormhole has waned, a young man's adventure."

"Is there someone I should greet for you? Perhaps carry a message?"

He smiled indulgently, showing wrinkles around his eyes. "You know the extent of your wealth, of course."

I showed an open palm gesture. "I draw a modest salary as a middle manager in a large corporation."

"In Paris you may live quietly, but on Dolvia your fortune will raise the volume of your voice. Don't let them see you stumble."

At the club entrance, I exited the car and walked under an umbrella held by his bodyguard. I stood under a dripping eave. Daniel Chin didn't bother to wave as the long car entered the traffic among a cacophony of reflected lights.

We held a club party, of course. Any excuse to extend invitations to longtime clients without concrete promises. The club was at street level with a bright main floor and many private rooms. Behind the rows of liquor bottles was a sizable fish tank where exotic saltwater varieties swam lazily back and forth. The decorations were retro, with a dance floor and reserved mezzanine stations to cater to the wishes of key-holders who wanted to watch the action below. I attended late for perhaps forty minutes to share a glass of champagne. I was there to present Celeste, just in from the wine country and eager to learn more about Paris. Also, please meet dark-skinned Sherry who joins us from the sub-Sahara and speaks a little French. Oh no, I could not possibly consider your offer for my time tonight with so many responsibilities. A gift of jewelry? For me? Farewell, my sweet.

Fat stinking bastards, and with no prowess; Earth's most enduring dichotomy. Only Daniel Chin had displayed stamina in that area. Of course, I never offered the compliment. He would have taken the remark as empty flattery.

Laura handed me several messages, a frown clouding her bright face. "You took me off the streets. I owe you everything."

"And you will manage the club until I return."

"You will not return."

"But you'll manage this as though I'm about to return."

"You taught me how to run the business. You did not have to do that."

"Of course I had to," I said and patted her flushed cheek. "I knew this day would come and that you would be of use to me."

"Your words are harsh, but your heart is soft." It sounded lovely in French.

"Let's keep that a secret, shall we?"

At the celebration, Rufus stood apart. Since Daniel Chin was not in attendance, Rufus disregarded my earlier claim. Warriors only trusted their visceral senses, their most debilitating foible.

In a mezzanine alcove, Kyros rabbe Sudl indulged himself by tasting several buffet dishes. He would not dance and did not know any modern ditties to sing along to, but he spoke kindly to each dancer as she came offstage. I knew that Kyros would entertain late night guests after Rufus feigned exhaustion and went to his rooms alone. Men were so simple.

I joined Rufus. "Won't you taste the food at least?"

"When you chose to jump back here," Rufus said in English, "Kyle Rula wondered out loud what would become of you. But this?"

"I took these women off the streets. I see to their health."

"I learned a new word here in Paris: expatriate." Rufus spat out the syllables with phlegm. He brushed my shoulder roughly as he passed. I had been separated from tribal logic for so long that I could only admire it. Rufus blamed me not for my businesses, but for my absence from Dolvia's savannah during a difficult time.

TWO

TRAVEL WITH RUFUS AND KYROS RABBE SUDL WAS AWKWARD those first days. "You take insult too easily," I told Rufus after he turned to challenge a hotel manager, who drew back with surprise. Finally, the warriors allowed me to take the lead while they assumed positions as my bodyguards. Their exotic looks, perhaps accentuated by the western suits, garnered envious looks from stylish ladies ensconced behind their own entourages.

Overland channels for traveling to the jump back station in Beijing were not uniform. The infrastructure among the former Slavic states was sorely crippled. Chinese enterprises had first arrived in the post-democracy provinces with technical assistance. Only later did the Company bureaucracy of educated technicians form a superclass for the ethnic backwaters, where paper money had no value and political parties were suppressed.

The monorail followed the ancient Silk Road through mountain passes and across desert plains. In connecting cities, security at the rail stations was mostly local enforcers dressed as Blackshirts and commanded by Company executives in silk suits with round mandarin collars. The enforcers left us alone, but not because of Rufus's warrior demeanor or Kyros's friendly gestures. Rather, we were spared because of the special stamp in our passports, a Company stamp I had secured from Daniel Chin by way of a porcelain-faced and exquisitely tailored male secretary who had made a special trip to my Paris apartment. I worried how the stamp's presence might affect our reception in Westend where Consortium troops managed security.

The Chinese were not the only national group that had prospered. Many inventors and engineers had labored under the Saudi flag more than a century ago because the Saudis could afford R&D investment. South Africans were also players, due mostly to the domestic minerals they could exploit to get offworld, much like Great Britain and Spain had once felled their forests to build sailing ships sturdy enough to command the oceans. But education of the masses was lacking among these groups, and independent thinking had been squashed. Soon enough, the Americans had imposed new ideas about how to build stations in space using nickel or iridium from asteroids, and the husbandry of offworld water, and growing vegetables on rice paper.

Children were born in space and never visited Earth, venturing farther afield with each blended generation. Certain colonies were abandoned for the next asteroid boom station. But the Chinese had exclusive rights to wormhole travel. Traffic both ways was dictated by their standards and using only their expertise. Exclusive to the end.

At each city where we stopped, regional managers for Somule Gems arrived at the hotel with reports and suggestions on how to spend more of my money, along with small gifts meant to impress me and secure future positions. I often feigned fatigue and sent them away. Other groups visited, mostly the leaders of the NGOs I had supported with charity funds; they brought forward promising orphans eager for new lives. I was seeking a few apprentices, matched in pairs with Dolviet managers, to gain experience about Westend before they jumped back to Earth and to grow traffic along the supply lines and keep an eye on each other.

At one weigh station near the Ishim River, no larger than a German hamlet, initiates waited in a short line while their handlers bowed and grinned. The young people glanced left and leaned forward, eager to catch a glimpse of Rufus, the son of Cyrus the ketiwhelp killer.

I heard Kyros rabbe Sudl whisper in Arrivi to Rufus. "Why does Brianna bring more children to the savannah?"

"She is weak and needs to see adoration in their eyes."

By the time we had passed through the Muslim states and entered the exchange station for a six-day train ride, our company had grown to twelve and included three boys and six girls. Once all the cases had been stowed, and the young people had been assigned sleeping berths in a car linked just ahead of my private car, the warriors and I fell into a simple routine.

Rufus and Kyros deigned to take meals with me. They waited for my arrival in the bright dining car and ate the entrées that I had ordered and paid for. The anxious waiter asked in over-cheerful French about the topaz amulets. "They are in mourning for a family member," I said. He bowed awkwardly with no follow-up question before he left.

Rufus picked at his meal and asked in Arrivi, "Why do you collect these children? Do you even know their names?"

"There's plenty of time to start lessons and build loyalties."

Kyros rabbe Sudl wiped his mouth with a big napkin. "Oh sure, I know their names. The oldest are Leah and Bernice. After that—"

I held out a hand. "Nu delaya."

Kyros swallowed more wine and sat back, ready for the post-prandial tribal chant. Rufus prevailed upon him to forego the loud and heavy cadence, so instead Kyros told a meandering story of genealogy and famous battles. Since he was Southeast Arrivi, I recognized none of the tribesmen he lauded. I enjoyed the timbre of his speech and his wicked sense of exaggeration. After such and such impossible battle against the Borabean, 301 lay dead. But only one was Arrivi, and he had died of heatstroke.

We entered China through Xinjiang province and traversed the high Takli Makan Desert overnight. In the morning, the train stood for several hours in Dunhuang, changing personnel from Russian to Chinese and taking on supplies. I watched from the window while porters in tunics and baggy pants loaded goods from a cart. They stopped suddenly, and the noise subsided, so I craned my neck to glimpse the source of the interruption. Some Blackshirts were hustling a group of peasant families, tied together with ropes and shuffling in obvious fear, across the tracks and down the causeway toward a holding area. Laborers returned to their work with measured gestures, careful not to attract unwanted attention, and the way closed behind the new arrivals.

I told myself that this repression was not my problem; I was just passing through.

Presently, a detachment of Russian soldiers wearing blue uniforms with red tooling took up positions outside our VIP car at the end of the train. The officer entered with authority and tucked his hat under one arm. Rufus stood squarely in the aisle with his knees bent and a hand on his knife hilt. The officer stopped.

After a moment, he looked past Rufus's shoulder to me. "You are Brianna Miller of Arim?" he asked in English. "We are assigned."

"I have security already, as you can see."

"These, uh, warriors are included in our detail. The train now enters a province with some, uh, social unrest. Daniel Chin is concerned that your group experiences no, uh, in-con-ven-nience." His hesitant words and rounded accent made me think his English was newly learned, perhaps his third language.

"Nu delaya," I said, and Rufus relaxed his posture. Kyros placed a big hand on the officer's shoulder from behind and led him to a seat several paces from me.

"What do you propose?" I asked.

"We will take the adjacent car and establish a presence around your group."

"The adjacent car is for the students."

"They may have to move forward."

"How many in your squad?"

"Twelve."

"I cannot provide for twelve. Six only."

"We brought provisions, and you will be glad for twelve before we reach Beijing. I am Captain Chandliss, and you may direct any questions to me."

"Captain Chandliss, I assume you are Lithuanian by birth, and your real name has two 'z's and three 'k's."

He only smirked.

"Are the soldiers from your same province?" I asked.

"Most of them."

"Why not provide a Han Chinese detachment to manage our security?"

"My orders were brief," he said as he twisted to see where Kyros had stationed himself. "I gathered that your Dolviet escort would resent Blackshirts as security."

I grinned. At least he had the sense to acknowledge what anyone could see. "And what else did Daniel Chin say in conversation?"

The captain didn't react to the mention of Daniel Chin's name. "Orders from Paris didn't mention a bevy of students. You do have accommodations for them on the shuttle and the Company yacht?"

"My arrangements are made," I said tolerantly. "Thank you for your interest. The students will remain where they are, and you will take the next car. Since you have twelve men and provisions, I expect that the students will remain as safe as I am safe."

Captain Chandliss watched me for a moment. "Well. The train leaves in twenty minutes, so I'll excuse myself to put all in good order." He stood and nodded, unable to break military training. "Ah, how may I address these warriors?"

"Rufus, the son of Cyrus the ketlwhelp killer," I said with a hand gesture. "And behind you is Kyros rabbe Sudl of Southeast Arrivi."

He nodded to each warrior. "Ma'am," he said and left.

Kyros looked at Rufus and mouthed "ma'am" with humor. Rufus covered his mouth with one hand to hide his response.

Later, I was called into the student car, I assumed due to the presence of soldiers. But the issue was trivial; something about a stolen item and whom to punish. The boys waited in a silent row, cynical and without gestures. The oldest girl Bernice was in tears, as were two eight-year-olds. I sighed, regretting my decision to include them in my travel plans.

Leah approached with submissive gestures. "These ones need daily lessons to keep their minds off homesickness. They need a common goal."

I immediately thought of an old method Hakulupe Le had used in the Somule schools to bind students as a group, a method she had learned in prison, in fact. I spoke to the group. "Not all of you will board the shuttle to engage in space travel. I have accommodations for only seven, including the boys, so I must choose who is most worthy. To make this choice, we will devise a test. You will each share your history with the others, and at track's end in three days' time, you will each write the biographies of all the others, including the boys. After reading those papers, I will decide who remains with the clutch and who will return to their province. That is all."

Leah quickly spoke. "May we have writing paper?"

"I will ask Captain Chandliss."

"May we take our meals in the dining car?"

"What difference does that make?"

"Please."

"Captain Chandliss manages your safety now. I'll ask him."

"Thank you, Rularim. Thanks again." Leah knew when to flatter.

"I am not Rularim. I'm Brianna Miller."

"We all thank you."

"Yes, well. No more complaining and no crying." I left before she could make another request.

Less than an hour later, Captain Chandliss came into my car. Kyros stopped him at the door but let him pass after a tense moment. "The students want their meals in the dining car. I have no authority for this."

"Negotiate with the porters," I instructed, "so the group can take a meal after the other diners have left, twice a day. Ask for a set menu with bland dishes because they have to board the shuttle soon. No sweets from the dessert tray but maybe rice pudding for each."

His posture emphasized his disbelief. "Do you understand the expense?"

"Rufus will pay from the treasure of Kyle Rula."

The disbelieving look on the captain's face wandered to the warrior who was seated at a laptop with his back to us. Rufus turned slowly to fix me with a level stare. He opened the pouch at his belt and extracted a single uncut emerald as big as my thumb knuckle and placed it next to me. The gem was opaque with a sandpaper texture. Without glancing at the captain, Rufus turned back to the computer screen.

I saw the eyes of Captain Chandliss grow large at the sight of the gem. "Have it assayed at the next stop," I said. "Then pay the porters for their trouble and distribute the remainder among your soldiers."

The captain stood tall and looked at each of us, perhaps taking a moment to assess the opportunity. "My detachment will bear the current expense. I will have the gem appraised in Beijing where its value is far greater. I will subtract a commission for our service with the students and return the remainder to Rufus before your party boards the shuttle. We will take eight percent."

"Four percent," I said.

"Six percent."

"Four point five percent, and no gratuity."

"Done." The captain scooped up the gem and turned on his heel. He left hurriedly, passing through the door that Kyros was holding open, just as though he needed to escape before I changed my mind.

Kyros said, "Much is learned about a man when he resists temptation."

I turned to Rufus. "How many more of those do you carry?"

"That was the last one," he lied.

The train was sidetracked for several hours due to a military conflict ahead. We heard the cannon's report and saw flashes at ground level just before the many booms. I strolled alongside the tracks while the big engine idled and blew steam like an impatient racehorse. Near the tracks, porters and cooks negotiated in loud voices, using big gestures with the local farmers who had arrived in ramshackle trucks with wilting produce and live chickens in cages.

I joined Captain Chandliss where he stood near the front of the train to glimpse the distant billowing smoke. "A valuable talent, your fluency with languages." He said nothing, so I continued. "I have seen less talented men in Company offices. How did you draw military duty?"

"My province has no crony system among the Blackshirts."

The cannons stationed ahead near the tracks fired in rapid succession. Our heads turned toward the flashes and muted sounds even though we knew nothing could be learned from the display. "Will the tracks even be there for us to coast through?" I asked.

"If the retreat comes this way, we may see a hard time. The Chinese shuttle will leave soon without your party."

"There are many shuttles."

"But your accommodations are—"

"We travel differently compared to, uh, some adventurers."

"For this stretch of track, you travel the same as the poor. Everybody stays onboard tonight. Your warriors were issued side arms."

"And one for me?"

"No, ma'am."

"I'm a good shot. You may be glad I'm at your back."

"What example does that set for your students?"

I looked at him. "The best example. That I can defend myself."

"That the situation is so desperate, we armed the women?"

"Desperate?"

"Just, um, just keep everyone quiet."

In the morning the train moved again but in a stop-start motion that made me feel nauseated. The warriors watched the melee out the window as we passed a damaged village with many corpses, including those of livestock. "Get away from the windows," I told Kyros. "It's not our problem."

"Chikiocahi cylay," Rufus said.

I knew that Mekucoo phrase. On Somule streets the slang version was chi cylay, meaning stay alert. Trust Rufus to revert to formal Mekucoo in a crisis. I sighed and rubbed my right temple with the fingers of my left hand. I looked up when I smelled hot tea. One of the orphans, the ten-year-old with coppery hair, placed a tray next to me with a tea service and a dish of apricot treats.

"I have brought your tea," she said with eyes averted.

"What is your name?

"I am Evgenia, and I have brought your tea."

"You are no longer a servant, Evgenia. Don't cast yourself as less than others."

"Yes, Rularim."

"I am not Rularim," I said sternly. "Now go back to your place. No favor is gained by your act."

After she left, Kyros asked in Arrivi, "Why do you dash her hopes?"

"Nobody was generous with me at that age."

As Kyros reached for a soft treat, Rufus said, "Sheeks-Cylom evicted Karlyhi from the bush clinic because of you."

Kyros carried the food back to his place by the door. "Dacupitte visited Southeast Arrivi during the vaccine task because of you."

Rufus nodded in agreement. "Kyle Rula accepted the gualarep Brian on the flats of Arim because of you."

With food in his mouth, Kyros added, "Marcy first broke with Rabbenu Ely because of you, because of that beating in the yard of the bush clinic. Everybody knows this."

"Marcy broke with Ely?"

"Marcy is set aside now," Rufus said. "Ely keeps a Putuki woman in the governor's mansion, a daughter of one of his cronies. Barely more than a child."

"Oh, I have another one," Kyros said, enjoying the game. "Karlyhi broke down doors at the Bryant sweatshops because of you. Ah, and another. The convent was located on the savannah because of you."

"I never served there," I claimed, perhaps too snidely.

Near the Chinese city of Datong, the train glided through a rail yard attached to an industrial area that had been trashed by cannon fire. Some cleanup was in progress, mostly by squads of prisoners managed by Blackshirts. Groups of displaced families were corralled on one side, dirty and exhausted. More were being marched into the yard in a tight gaggle, jostled by soldiers in tan uniforms, apparently ready for transfer to the Blackshirts.

As the train waited near this new group, I saw a young man break through the crowd and sprint toward the linked cars. He was shot in the back before seven paces were achieved. The other prisoners barely reacted. Standing next to me at the train railing, Captain Chandliss tensed and balled his fists.

"Do you know them?" I asked.

"All the groups are the same, future conscripts for your world."

"There are no conscripts on the savannah."

"A paradise then?"

"A free land."

He chuckled bitterly. "Freedom is an illusion offered to keep us working."

"Your soldiers are not free?"

"Free to follow orders. Free to kill on command."

Hours later, the train was at the edge of the rail yard, finally, waiting for signals to exit the loading area and steam ahead. Rufus and Kyros stood with me at the back railing of the car while Rufus smoked a kari root stem. Captain Chandliss was on the tracks with two soldiers, awaiting the signal for final boarding.

Not seven paces distant, a group of families were being managed by a squad of soldiers in tan uniforms, perhaps waiting for orders to move into the yard. One man among the prisoners stood in an effort to disarm a soldier who had started to beat him with a switch. Two enforcers joined the fray after another prisoner stood to defend his compatriot. Soon, both prisoners were on the ground, but the soldiers continued to lay the switches on the women who cowered, two of them carrying children.

"Netta, om?" I said to Rufus.

"Three for two," he said, meaning we would most likely sacrifice three among our group to save two prisoners from the beatings.

One soldier in tan grabbed the bigger child from the arms of her mother and began switching her legs to raise welts. I sprang forward without thinking; I knew what that beating felt like. Rufus and Kyros followed, and I heard Captain Chandliss curse and shout orders to his men. We acted swiftly, more from experience than strategy. I held the girl and moved toward the mother while Rufus and Kyros pressured the soldiers in tan, who backed away, probably from the surprise.

"Blackshirts are coming," Chandliss shouted.

"They cannot reach us in time," Rufus said.

"They have sharpshooters." Bullets whizzed past my ears and struck the ground and the prisoners. Two of our soldiers fell. "Get back on board!"

I dropped the girl next to her mother, but the woman pushed back with strength. "Take her, save her." The girl fairly leapt into my arms while Kyros and the captain shouldered the fallen soldiers. The train whistle blew, signaling the all clear to leave the yard. We sprinted to the car railing with bullets flying all around. I heard the projectiles pelt the train's side and ping off the railing's metal edge. The train lurched as soon as we were onboard, and the barrage of rifle fire stopped.

Bernice appeared at my side and took the girl from my arms, covering her with a shawl. As we steamed away from the scene, I saw the mother stand and wave with both hands before a bullet struck her temple, and she fell as a dead weight. Blackshirts arrived to walk among them, and all the prisoners in that group were shot again at close range. One Blackshirt, a thin Han Chinese with authority, aimed his pistol at the train's end as we sped away, but he didn't fire. I saw him standing among the bodies with his pistol raised above one shoulder, backlit by sudden cannon fire from across the yard.

Inside the car, four soldiers from our escort waited at the windows, weapons poised to address any further assault. The soldier whom Kyros had helped onboard lay dead, with seven bullets in his back. Kyros checked a rip in his own shirt where blood trickled. "A flesh wound," he said. "His body was my cover." The other soldier, whom Captain Chandliss had carried fireman style, had also been riddled with rifle fire.

"Blackshirts targeted you," I said, "but not me or Rufus?"

The captain showed me a cynical face. "I'll have to ship the bodies back to their families. We'll take twelve percent of the emerald's value. And don't leave the train again."

Before I could argue, Bernice spoke from where she and Leah managed the rescued prisoner. "Brianna, you need to see this."

I approached to where they held the girl and saw her exposed back and legs. In addition to fresh welts, there were cigarette burns, some healed and some still raw. On her lower back, the Chinese letters for "whore" had been cut into her skin, maybe by a straight razor.

"The soldiers will see this," I said.

"But the shame," Bernice said.

"They will look, each of them."

Bernice and Leah parted, holding the girl, who turned away with her filthy hair hiding her face. The soldiers of Captain Chandliss's detachment stepped forward and peered at the sight. One soldier blanched, and one gagged before they hung their heads and silently returned to the windows. At least there was some decency left in that group.

"What else do you think she endured?" I asked the captain.

"Take the bodies," he told his men, who then shouldered their weapons and carried their compatriots out through the student car.

"Let's find her some clothes and food," I said to Bernice. I followed them into the student car where three students were quarrelling with raised voices, undeterred by the passing traffic of the dead defenders.

"What business is it of yours?" Evgenia demanded of the accuser. Apparently some trinket had been stolen, and the thief had been called out.

"Stop this," I said. "You two, come with me." The thief and the accuser followed me back into the private car. They jostled one another as they stood sullenly awaiting some new punishment. All they had known, all their lives, was punishment.

"You are Rosalyn," I said to the accuser in English. She shot me a flinty look as only a ten-year-old can reveal her emotions. "Tell me, how many brass buttons are on the coat of Captain Chandliss?"

Rosalyn squinted with suspicion. "Six on the front and four on each sleeve."

"How many barrettes in Bernice's hair today?"

"Two barrettes and four hairpins."

I chuckled softly. "You will be our quartermaster. Sit over there until Captain Chandliss returns." She probably didn't know what a quartermaster was. She made a sour face at the thief and sat in a chair in the far corner of the car.

I spoke to the second girl in Russian since she had not responded to any of my English comments. She didn't look up, so I tried French. "You are Camille, isn't that so?"

The twelve-year-old's face opened with surprise and question. These may have been the first words she'd understood from anyone on the train. "Sit here by me," I said. I took out pen and paper and placed them in front of her. "Write the names of the other girls," I said in French. She looked at me for a long moment before complying.

"Rosalyn," I said, "ask Leah to come here, and return with her." While she was gone, I encouraged Camille who sat small and warm next to me. "Circle the names of the girls you like." She made no gesture, so I added, "Circle the name of the girl you dislike the most." To my surprise, she chose Evgenia, the would-be servant, rather than Rosalyn.

When Rosalyn and Leah entered, I allowed them to wait while I wrote in French on the page I shared with Camille. "How is the patient?" I asked Leah. "Did you learn her name?"

"She was hungry," the sixteen-year-old said. "She may sleep now. Her language is unknown to us."

"We will call her Cleo for now, a strong name for a traveler. All of you together will be known as the clutch of Cleo Datong, for the place where we rescued her."

"Clutch?"

I continued without acknowledging the question. "How many in the clutch have English?"

"All of them."

"Camille has no English," I said.

Rosalyn smirked. "She's pretending. She's a liar and a thief."

"Leah, how are they progressing with the biographies I requested?"

Leah shrugged and stepped back a fraction. "So many interruptions."

"They can practice during meals in the dining room," I said. "You will also give them some math exercises to complete. The older girls can help the younger ones. The boys will work separately. And all the girls will begin to teach Cleo some English words."

"That's a lot," Leah said.

"Then you should begin right now."

"I don't know what math to—"

"Kyros can print out some pages," I interrupted. "I'll look over the completed work later. That is all." Leah and Rosalyn turned to leave together just as Rufus and Kyros returned. The area was crowded, and the men shuffled sideways out of courtesy.

"Rosalyn," I said. "Wait over there."

Leah left, and Rufus sat at the laptop. "Rufus, can Kyros sit there? I want him to print some math exercises for the girls."

The warriors exchanged looks but quickly traded places. "You just love giving orders, don't you?" Rufus said as Kyros booted the EAM. "Captain Chandliss is mansa bitter."

"I didn't kill his men. So Rufus, tell me, where is your pouch?" His hand went to his belt where the pouch usually rested. He glanced around to find it, and Camille, seated next to me, giggled.

"Give it back to him," I said in French.

She left her seat and, in an obvious strut before Rosalyn and Kyros, approached the warrior. I had written a request while we had been fooling around with the paper and names, just to test her skills. She had accomplished the task before the men were seated.

Rufus snatched the pouch from Camille's hand and emptied the contents into his palm, a king's ransom of uncut emeralds. "Two are missing," he said.

"Camille," I said. She ran her fingers through a pocket at her shoulder, dropped the missing pieces into his hand, and then returned to a seat next to me. Kyros watched with his mouth open. "A trained pickpocket among us? She'll need to be broken of that."

"Not at all," I said. "A talent more valuable than language skills."

THREE

BEIJING WAS COLD AND SMOGGY, AND CROWDED. RUFUS DIS-
played curt gestures as he looked at the city in which legions of
Chinese workers, defined as the enemy, resided. "These ones have
so much wealth, but I saw no sharing with the tribes we passed.
Only enforcement."

"The Chinese have wormhole travel. They serve where a profit
can be made."

"It's like a thorn tree branch," Kyros said. Rufus nodded as
though he understood.

"I don't take your meaning," I said.

"Many tribes live here, and many tribes live on Dolvia. The
branch has a fat knob on each end with a brittle arm between,"
said Kyros.

I met Kyros's look. "There's plenty of fiber in that arm, not easily
broken."

Captain Chandliss was overseeing the off-loading of body bags for his dead soldiers. He saw me on the platform and approached. "We'll escort you to the shuttle platform, and stand guard until you leave. I'll get the gem appraised there."

"Your time is not needed," I said as the clutch passed in pairs, oldest with youngest, and Rosalyn with Camille. "My managers from Somule Gems will arrive in a moment. As you predicted, the shuttle has already left. Another is scheduled for the day after tomorrow." I handed him a business card. "In the meantime, you can find us here."

He glanced at the address. "The corporate offices?"

"Cheaper than a hotel and more secure."

"You ruined my squad, you know," the captain said. "Half the men want to rejoin the insurrection."

I showed him a wide grin. "Will you be going home?"

"There's nothing there."

"I would invite you to travel with us," I said lightly, "but I know that your real boss is Daniel Chin. I can provide a recommendation, though, if needed."

He brushed his fingers along the bill of his hat. "Ma'am."

A young executive from Somule Gems approached hurriedly, sent to meet us at the train. Several porters followed, all wearing ornate patches on the breast pockets of powder-blue coats. They shaped a perimeter around the clutch of Cleo while Rufus and Kyros stood with the initiate boys. We filled the platform with bustle, so I grabbed Camille's arm and held her close to my coat. "I want no trouble today," I said in French.

She gave me a sly smile.

An idea came to me in the middle of making arrangements, so I stepped back to Captain Chandliss, holding Camille at my side. "Captain, if your squad is breaking up . . . I may have work for a couple of soldiers, the youngest ones."

He stared with his mouth agape, and Camille giggled.

"I intend market penetration for Somule Gems," I said grudgingly, "into the provinces we just passed through. I'll need a couple of managers with local language skills."

He didn't even blink before guessing my intent. "You recruit the people you know hate the Company so their loyalties will transfer to you."

"I am a simple businesswoman," I said quietly. "I see an opportunity for profit in the chaos, that is all. We can discuss this further when you visit tomorrow."

Our traveling group and baggage exited the terminal and entered two waiting buses to travel through the crowds of Beijing where anticipation of wormhole travel channeled executives from many societies. On the streets near the corporate offices of Somule Gems, I saw Middle Eastern sheiks and African delegations, and Asians from all parts of the Pacific Rim. A few women in business suits mingled with the groups, but far fewer wives and daughters. Wormhole assignments were for young and sturdy technicians whose skills were needed at track's end.

We had a large suite high in the corporate towers that housed Somule Gems. The shared rooms were filled with giggling girls and purveyors and tailors who outfitted each traveler with fashionable clothes. I had ordered loose and lightweight pants and jackets for traveling, along with sturdy boots for each girl. The display of goods and the attempts to get measurements for fittings was turning into a trial, however. The warriors had deserted me, it seemed, after the three boys had chosen jackets they liked. And the hired help stood by the window with their mouths open.

An hour earlier, the younger girls had been crying and hugging each other after their inoculation shots. Now their spirits were near manic. Earlier, I had spent four hours with Somule Gems executives in this most important branch office to reinforce good work and direct promotions, the glad-handling ambassador event.

I suppressed a yawn. I was watching Camille closely, but the distractions were many. "Camille," I said, "go sit with Cleo in the other room." The injured girl we had picked up was still too damaged to share in group activities, so each girl in the clutch took turns sitting with her. Camille looked at me with a wounded expression, but Evgenia giggled and made a face. Her teasing gestures made my decisions for the day much easier.

I saw Kyros signal from the anteroom and went to him. In the adjacent room, Captain Chandliss offered his hand for Rufus to shake. The warrior hesitated a full ten seconds before accepting the Softcheeks gesture. Rufus saw me watching. "Netta, om," he said. The two warriors walked into the kitchen area, I thought to smoke karl root stems near the ventilation hood.

"Ma'am," Captain Chandliss said. "We were just—"

I held up a hand. "No need for explanations. You settled the debt for the emerald."

"What did he mean when he said 'netta, om'? You said the same before when you picked up Cleo."

"It's a phrase in Arrivi that has many uses. As a question, it can mean 'What's going on here? Advise me.' From Rufus just now, it meant you and he are square in your dealings."

"I wanted you to meet the soldiers who have been released from military detail due to a . . . an incident on the tracks a few days ago." He gestured to four soldiers dressed in fatigues standing in a line by the suite door. "These are—"

"You brought four men. I said I have possible positions for two men."

"You may choose, of course," the captain said crisply. "It's just that, um, you mentioned an interest in language skills. These two speak and write Farsi, and he is fluent in Russian. They all know Arabic. And this soldier," he said, indicating a short man weighing no more than 145 pounds who stood by the door as if ready to escape at the first loud noise, "Mikhail speaks and writes Hebrew."

The captain's cynical eyes followed me, and I knew he would report my response to interested parties in Paris. Daniel Chin was always hedging his bets. "It's too bad, Captain Chandliss, that your loyalties are known. I feel we have each taken the measure of the other, and we could manage the long distance talk. Are you returning to Paris?"

"As it turns out, I will know space travel. I am attached, along with two others, to a courier traveling on the same yacht as your party, unless you have more delays."

"A courier?"

"Mr. Steven Swanweil is returning to Cicero with contracts for—"

He stopped short when I laughed, drawing fresh air into my lungs and fresh energy. It felt so good that I indulged in a second peal of laughter, even showing my teeth. The men only waited. Kyros showed his face at the kitchen doorway. I gestured simply, indicating that I was fine.

"I take it you know Mr. Swanweil," Captain Chandliss added dryly.

I suppressed a final chuckle. "I accept all four of these men." I spoke directly to them. "You understand, I intend to place you on ground duty in the Chinese provinces, to build a marketing network from scratch. This is a long-term assignment and not an easy adventure with guns blazing."

They only stared. The eyes of the biggest one skirted left to the captain's face.

"Kyros, do you have a moment?" I called.

Kyros came up, sucking his teeth and wiping his fingers on his trousers.

"Take these four to Human Resources on the eighteenth floor so they can fill out applications for apprentice training. Inoculation is not necessary; they're staying in China."

Kyros went to the door, and the boys from the clutch of Cleo followed.

"Our clutch should remain here. I have some decisions to announce."

The boys were immediately tense, aware that I had promised that some initiates would not board the shuttle. "Go in with the girls," I said and turned to Captain Chandliss, unconcerned about their hesitation.

"Wormhole travel takes ten days," I said to the captain. "Then a longer wait for the shuttle service at Stargate Junction in Westend. I'm certain we'll have time to tell more lies over a bottle of Kiam gin. Thank you for your service, today and earlier."

He placed his soldier's hat over his hair before brushing the hat's bill with two fingers. "Ma'am." Captain Chandliss was alone when he left.

The high spirits among the clutch of Cleo died quickly. When I entered the shared room again and dismissed the hired helpers, the girls sat or stood, holding their new garments. Rufus stood with the three boys. "Leah, ask Camille and Cleo to come in here. We should experience the next few moments as a clutch."

I looked around at their anxious faces. "There's no easy way to make these announcements, so I'll just get started." I turned to the oldest boy. "Ahmed, you're out."

His eyebrows wrinkled, and he emitted two short sighs.

I spoke softly. "However, I have duty for you, if you want. You may join the four soldiers who will develop a market for Somule Gems in the local provinces."

"But I learned Arrivi," he complained. "I understand the warriors when they whisper."

"And you can use those skills," I said, with a hand on his shoulder. "You can translate Westend messages for the managers, and transcribe their answers."

He hung his head. "What did I do wrong?"

"It's your age, mostly," I said gently. "These others are cut off from their roots, and I can hold their loyalty. But when you get home-sick, you think about a brother and horses and a girl with ribbons in her hair."

"You got that from the biography that I wrote."

I touched his arm briefly. "Wait here a short time. When Kyros returns, he'll take you down to meet the others. I value your hard work, and I look forward to receiving good reports about how you grow within this duty."

He nodded sadly and left to wait by the suite door.

I looked at the other boys in the clutch. "You will both travel through the wormhole to Dolvia." One made a stiff gesture of victory with a closed fist, and the other nodded several times.

Rufus watched me with hard eyes. "You just love to give orders, don't you?"

The girls stood in a group, tall and anxious, even Cleo. "We all got new clothes and inoculation shots," Bernice said quickly. She tended to give away her best move in the first volley, trying to do good for the others. Leah was a better leader.

"Evgenia, you're out," I said.

On her face I saw only spite.

"However, I want to send you," I added, feeling regret, "to a posi-tion in Paris with a good friend of mine who has daughters about your age. If you'll wait for a moment, we can boot the laptop for a trunk call."

She said nothing, but stepped back.

"Camille, come here," I said in English.

"Nnoooo!" Camille cried and scurried to hide behind the older girls. "No, I want to go with you." So she did understand English. Camille crossed to the traveling trunk and stepped inside, scrunching down to include herself in the luggage.

"Camille, you will travel through the wormhole," I said. "All the remaining girls will make the trip." There was a wild cheer that caught me by surprise. The girls jumped up and down and congratulated each other while Evgenia stood alone on the side.

"Bernice, bring Camille here." Soon the child stood before me, sobbing and hiccupping. I wiped a tear from her hot cheek. "Here is a lesson for you today. You must return the items, all of them."

She wiped a finger across her runny nose and reached into her pocket. She extended a handful of small items to me. "Return each to the original owner, all of them. Later, you and I will go down to the mall for some ice cream." She sniffled and nodded before she hesitantly approached each girl to offer an item she had lifted from their possessions. The girls took the treasures without forgiveness.

I stepped over to Evgenia and led her into my own room where a laptop was ready on the dresser for my close work. "Why does Camille get to go, and I have to stay?" Evgenia asked with a blotchy face. "What's so special about her?"

"Sit on the bed," I said as I engaged the call. Soon the image of Petra Mitterand came onscreen. Her hair was piled high, and she wore diamond earrings. "Did I interrupt a dinner party?" I asked.

"There was no going out while we waited for your call, so I invited everybody here."

"A celebration that I left Paris, then?"

"Yeah, sure. The cat's away, so the mice can play."

I only grinned. "After today we can use the EAMs, or extra atmosphere modems, to chat. There's a lag time, and the cost is breathtaking, so use it sparingly."

"Your man from Somule Gems installed the contraption today. Am I being monitored by the Chinese now?"

"Be circumspect," I smiled. "And don't mix the two servers. Laptop to EAM … that's a mistake they love to exploit. Is Heather there?"

Petra leaned back and signaled somebody offscreen. "She wants Heather," she said before turning back to me. "Who's that with you? I'm told you already have a clutch of young fanatics loyal only to you."

"How's your father?"

Petra's smile vanished, and her eyes went vacant. "He lingers."

Heather's face loomed behind her, so Petra scooted to share the camera's view. "Are you calling from Beijing?" Heather asked. "I thought you were offworld already."

"You remember I promised to send personnel your way. This is Evgenia who knows French and English and some Arrivi. She can translate our EAM messages sometimes."

"You're sending her to Paris?" Heather asked. It was obvious they had both indulged in champagne before the call.

"I'm sending her to you with the next courier," I said. "She'll arrive within three days."

"Oh. Welcome, Evgenia. We'll meet you at the airport." She turned to Petra. "Such a thrill, to fly into Paris. I wonder if she knows what a priv—"

"We're still on the call," Petra said.

"Oh, sorry." Heather slid off the chair and stood to greet somebody behind them.

Petra faced the camera with a sad smile. "I wondered why you didn't just fly into Beijing. Why the roundabout? To scoop up orphans for your new empire?"

"When I rule the galaxy, I'll say that I remember you. Go tend to your guests."

"Be sure to call me from Stargate Junction so I can practice with this new, um, thing."

"EAM, for extra—"

"I know," she interrupted. "Anyway, I may have news later about the blood sample."

When the call ended, my bedroom was filled with the blue-yellow light from the screen. I closed the laptop and turned to Evgenia, blinking my eyes several times. "Tomorrow you will meet the courier and go to the airport with her. Air travel can be grand fun so don't feel that you've been cheated. The others will visit an unforgiving desert overrun by snakes."

Evgenia said nothing.

"Go pack your things, then." She left without looking back.

I had little heartstone for Evgenia. I had learned over the years how to push back on the sudden grab of empathy that had laid me low with friends on Dolvia. Managing the future of the orphans was about managing Somule Gems and the future of the convent residents. I must trust that my choices worked for the good of all.

I had not carved out time for lessons as I had wanted; most efforts at providing structure had been pushed off on Leah and

Bernice. Rosalyn had spent time with a soldier under the command of Captain Chandliss for instruction on how to organize a soldier's rucksack. To her good character, I saw her in discussion with Leah to set rules for the contents of the matching rucksacks I had ordered for the clutch. I was pleased with my choices there.

I did take Camille with me for an excursion into the building's retail mall. My purpose was to impress upon her all the worldly goods available to a woman of position, so many that larceny was unneeded. Camille stood with wide eyes before the many display windows. When a woman passed with her purse open on her arm, we both noticed the poor choice.

She didn't miss the gesture when a shopper passed a small envelope to me that I slipped into my jacket pocket. Camille's eyes twinkled when she realized our outing had a purpose beyond the object lesson.

The package was for Cleo. I had bought counterfeit travel papers; an expensive undertaking and dangerous because payment left a paper trail. Chinese coins were the best choice, but the exchange rate was exorbitant and called attention to our traveling group. I knew about a certain pair of rare manuscripts, though, that had recently passed through the insurgent regions. The chain of custody was suspect, but the paper quality was real and the text nearly indecipherable, a sure sign of authenticity.

I needed a special stamp for Cleo, similar to the ones each member of the clutch carried, so I had the one from Evgenia's papers removed and correctly inserted into the forged identity papers for Cleo. There was little danger that inspectors would examine the passport of a child beyond inoculation affidavits, but I wanted all routes of suspicion closed. I paid with a certain companion rare manuscript, smaller and of poor quality, but validating the more decorative pair.

FOUR

A COMPANY SHUTTLE TOOK US TO AN ORBITING JUMPING OFF station where we waited half a day to board the wormhole conveyance, a Chinese-decorated yacht with windows in observation rooms only but with a spacious and well-lit promenade.

Across the way, I saw the clutch of Cleo and the curious looks from fellow travelers, maybe because of their clothes of similar cut and their identical rucksacks like French schoolgirls carried. More whispering started, due to their ages, I thought; a gaggle of children, mostly girls, where only executives and technicians could afford the fare. On one side stood the boys, Saed and Ankos, somewhat apart but watchful. Bernice was seated in the center holding Cleo, whom we had determined was a smallish eight years of age and who cringed at the sight of each passing man in uniform. Fourteen-year-old Claire minded Dominic and Camille, fast friends, who stared with open curiosity. Leah and Rosalyn the quartermaster were minding the left flank and were turned inward as though the display of their backsides closed access to the group.

I yawned, unable to resist opening my mouth wide. I was exhausted from waiting and riding, from sleeping in strange beds and waking in strange cities. And I was experiencing swimming dreams. How was that possible? I had not been troubled with them since I had left Dolvia's embrace. I awoke sometimes in the middle of the night, clammy and shivering. I dreamed of luxuriating in the billabong while rain pelted the water's surface. I flicked my marbled tail and glided into the flood current, celebrating the rush of murky, oxygenated water over my tough hide. I allowed the current to carry me from the flats, past the shattered butte and facing plateau and down onto the wide savannah where my prey nested. Hoards of transient birds fished the shallow sea that would be desert again within nine weeks. Schooling kariom drifted by while I waited in lily pad shade for the light steps of flamingos or herons.

I shrugged off the dream, assuming that my memory was stirring during an anxious time. I was taking the malaria prophylactic mefloquine to build resistance to Dolvia's diseases. I had been warned the regimen brought dreams of blood and violence.

I stood unfocused in the cool corridor while an overhead blower muted my hearing. Beside me, Rufus stiffened. I looked up to see piercing focus in his face. I followed his gaze across the way and saw Steve Swanweil standing with a briefcase in hand and easily sharing chikiocahi, or chi, with Captain Chandliss and two of his soldiers dressed in business suits.

I made a soft clucking noise. Rufus controlled his expression. "He may cross to greet me. This will be allowed." Rufus squinted. His eyes never left Steve Swanweil's face.

Swanweil had been a resident of Cylay on Dolvia since the time of the Bryant sweatshops. He had journeyed through the wormhole at least twice before that I knew of and was no doubt carrying Daniel Chin's instructions to Company officers concerning how to leverage the upstart securities exchange on Cicero.

Captain Chandliss looked at us and casually raised his hand to the bill of his hat, except he was no longer dressed in uniform and wore no hat. He made a furtive gesture to cover the absentminded salute. Kyros chuckled.

The call was made for boarding. Mr. Swanweil checked his pocket for the ticket and glanced around. He saw me and crossed without hesitation with the two guards trailing behind. Rufus and Kyros rabbe Sudl stepped shoulder to shoulder in front of me to block his way. "Hey, what is this?" Swanweil complained. "I'm a friend. I have a message from Daniel Chin."

He was no friend and carried no message, but I tapped Rufus's shoulder. The warriors parted, leaving barely enough room for Steve Swanweil to reach between them and shake my hand. He glanced up at Kyros's stern face, avoiding Rufus's stare.

"Very impressive," Swanweil claimed grudgingly.

"What is your message?" I asked.

Swanweil pursed his lips. "Daniel Chin wishes you a pleasant trip. And did you receive the special stamp he supplied?" Swanweil could have learned that much while loitering in Mr. Chin's office lobby.

"We travel at our own expense," I said, "due to business concerns on Dolvia."

"We saw the news of Kyle Rula's death," Swanweil said. "You will manage the treasure now, isn't that correct?"

I indicated the amulet on Kyros rabbe Sudl's arm. "These warriors and I are in mourning. The disposition of Kyle Rula's estate is for another day."

"I understand," Swanweil said. "Still, a unique opportunity, traveling together and all. Perhaps you can join me for dinner before we reach Westend."

"Perhaps, in the company of these warriors."

He looked again at Kyros only. "If you insist."

Over the next days, I slept a great deal and took meals in my cabin. My little public time was spent with lessons for the clutch and to manage expectations. "On Dolvia, you will be quartered together, including the boys, until you can tolerate the climate. You can spend the time on language lessons and learning more about the canon of old stories. These stories speak to ideal behavior and respect for the land. Meanwhile, I will travel to the village of Kyros rabbe Sudl to honor his good service. I will see you again a few days later.

"Each of your acts," I added, "when we disembark is a public act. Nothing is hidden or private. Dolvia sees all, and she whispers into my ear every morning at sunrise. I will know before morning tea about any misbehavior or theft."

We were through the wormhole and traveling at turbo speed toward Stargate Junction when I sat down with Mr. Swanweil in an open teahouse on the promenade. At my shoulders and without expression stood Rufus and Kyros rabbe Sudl. Mr. Swanweil's second, a Han Chinese man named Wan Su, placed snuff against his gums. His almond eyes drew into narrow slits. I assumed he was a smoker who suffered from nicotine withdrawal.

Near the entrance, Captain Chandliss stood sullen and vague with two others.

Swanweil's English was shoddy. His French was shoddy. "I'm not clear on your reasons for undertaking this journey," he began in French to exclude my companions. "Kyle Rula is gone; the period of mourning is past."

"Do you apologize," I returned in English, "for returning to your hometown, Mr. Swanweil? Call it a sentimental journey."

"With escort."

"These are my kinsmen. It's only correct that I should travel in their company."

"No such escort was present when you arrived in Paris."

"I traveled then as the ward of Dr. Pierre Mitterand, a colleague of my mentor Dr. Greensboro."

"You mean Mrs. Shaw, don't you?" he said. "The bush pioneer. Do you hear from her at all?" His questions were not even subtle.

"We both know she's excavating the Uburu lost city. Why do you ask?"

"I'm just curious," he said. "Tell me, this Cicero husband of hers, Mike Shaw, does she write about him?"

"Mr. Swanweil, I am a Parisian businesswoman just returning to Dolvia after a twelve-year absence. How could I hope to supply you with more information concerning Brigadier General Shaw's whereabouts than you can gain from your Consortium sources?"

He blinked. Wan Su blinked. "Perhaps your kinsmen have something to add."

"They have been traveling for weeks. Their information will be stale."

Mr. Swanweil looked at Kyros rabbe Sudl but again avoided Rufus's burning gaze. "Have you seen Mike Shaw?"

Kyros stared blankly and shrugged.

I bit my lip. "Anything else?"

His look darkened, and his smirk slid to the right. "Hartley banned the use of conscripts on the savannah, you know. He pushed the Bryant cartel off Dolvia entirely and allows no trading rights for them on the transport."

"What's that to me?"

"And now Hartley wants the Company to use Westend labor for asteroid mining," Swanweil added. "The general is making enemies left and right. Arrivi burn his effigy and the blue tams that peace-keepers wear."

"You mean, Putuki agitators," I said barely above a whisper, "bolstered by the Bryants and the Gora clans."

"So . . . you do follow Dolviet politics?"

"There's nothing new in what you say. General Hartley must balance pressures from many factions. And we all want to end the conscript trade."

Swanweil glanced at Wan Su who seemed adrift in his buzz from stimulants. Swanweil leaned forward and mock whispered, "Asteroid mining is a Company business. They will go to great lengths to maintain those rights."

I leaned forward so that we were nose-to-nose. "They don't own the asteroid belt."

"Only Company smelting ships have the capacity."

"I'm confident the Consortium can find uses for nickel and iron in Westend."

Wan Su looked at me finally and blinked several times, like that was a new concept to him. Men were so simple.

We disembarked at Stargate Junction and were met at customs by Jesse Hartley. What a surprise! As a teenager, I had spent time with her family on the Consortium transport orbiting Dolvia. Jesse was a young lady now, plump and rosy like her mother Billie. She gave me a quick hug, causing Rufus and Kyros to draw back with surprise.

She ignored the warriors. She knew something of native protocol. "Welcome to Westend," Jesse said with music in her voice. "My father invites you to dinner tonight."

From where he stood a few feet away, Steve Swanweil looked up sharply. He joined us and extended his hand to Jesse. "May I present myself? Steve Swanweil. I remember you from some time ago when I consulted with your father on the Dolvia Bryant crisis."

"Yes, of course," Jesse said and shook hands.

"How is your father?"

"He is well but busy," Jesse said flatly. "If you carry official communiqués, his office is down the corridor that way."

"Yes, well. Give General Hartley my regards. Steven Swanweil."

"I shall remember that," she said with ice. We turned away, and the warriors closed the access behind us. "Stargate Junction is such a pit," Jesse whispered. "Anybody can approach you here."

The customs holding area bustled with activity. We stopped at a security desk where clerks in mandarin-style business suits checked our tickets and added fees for services provided on this side of the wormhole. Jesse displayed her badge with the panda logo.

Rufus spied the bright emblem and stared into her face.

"This is a Company duty port," she shrugged. "Temporary badges are issued for visiting Consortium officers and their families."

Our luggage was tagged for storage and rooms assigned. Leah and Bernice managed the clutch with little instruction from me. "I'll visit after you get settled," I said.

Jesse turned to the customs official with a sweet smile. "These three Dolviets are guests of the general." The clerk reached for another form that Jesse needed to sign, a declaration of indemnity.

At the end of the corridor while we waited for yet another clearance check, the warriors stepped back, patient and silent. Jesse glanced at the amulet on Kyros's arm and continued in her cheerful way, "Our condolences on Kyle Rula's death. My father was distraught when he received the news of her suicide."

"Your words are more properly directed to Rufus."

She blushed and whispered, "He makes me nervous."

I whispered back, "He makes most people nervous."

"He seems to shimmer."

"You can see his aura?"

Her brow wrinkled. "Aura? Ah, no. Rufus has integrity or . . . moral fiber."

"No tongues of flame or presence of his ancestors?"

"No, that's silly."

We entered a darkly paneled office. The military officers looked up but nodded slightly to Jesse and said nothing. We passed into another office where several older women in business suits quietly spoke into low-fic headsets and studied comtech screens. One approached Jesse. "You father is waiting. Just go in."

"Thank you, Mildred," Jesse said and led us through a third tall door.

We entered a business office with wood tooling and plush furnishings. Two military attachés stood near the desk while General Hartley signed some papers. He made a slight hand signal, and Jesse stopped while he finished with the matter at hand. The general returned the stiff folders and thanked the junior officers. They saluted and looked Rufus and Kyros up and down as they exited by a different door.

General Hartley came around the desk. He was a big man and older now; the uniform's cut was generous at his waist. His brushed-back hair revealed streaks of steel gray. He showed an open palm at elbow height to Rufus. "Hiki, Rufus. Melinga."

"Melinga, General Hartley. May I present the one Kyros rabbe Sudl of Southeast Arrivi?"

"Kyros rabbe Sudl, welcome," the general said. "Would you take some refreshments?" He gestured toward a lunch buffet laid out on the side. Rufus saw the delight on Kyros's face and followed him to the sideboard.

General Hartley turned to Jesse and me. He smelled of eucalyptus and lemon. "Hiki Brianna Miller of Arim." He had handled the situation with aplomb, greeting the warriors first but allowing the women to speak within our function. "The shuttle is delayed until six watches from now," he confided. "For once I am pleased with Consortium inefficiency."

"How kind. I hope we're not a burden to Billie."

General Hartley's face clouded.

"I should have said," Jesse explained quietly. "My mother passed away some months ago. It was cancer."

I felt a rush of affection. This man had always affected me thus. "I am so sorry; I did not know. Perhaps I should ask at this point, how is Carl faring?"

"Fine," he returned with a forced smile. "Carl is a consultant at a Borabean silicide development site, and one of the Junction Boys. Heather migrated—"

"She knows, Father," Jesse interrupted. "They are friends in Paris."

"I have packages for you from her. Ah . . . in my luggage."

"Well," the general added with diplomatic stiffness.

"Shall we join the warriors?" Jesse gestured that we should walk left.

So the general's son worked for the Company now. Somehow that made sense to me. "The Junction Boys?"

"Several officers' sons and scholarship boys," Jesse said, "mostly Putuki, were trained at Stargate Junction, like a second college degree. Five of them work as a sort of think tank, advising the securities exchange on Cicero. They are called the Junction Boys, including Carl and Patrick Osborn. You remember Patrick, surely."

I nodded. I had stayed at his parents' house for a short time as a teenager serving Mrs. Shaw. That was before I had lived with Jesse on the transport.

Soon General Hartley was deep in conversation with Rufus. They sat near the buffet table with elbows on knees and heads together. Kyros was still picking food from among the buffet dishes. Jesse offered to accompany me to their suite so I could nap. "Your body clock must be in a spin."

The Hartley's suite had a large receiving room banked by bedroom doors and a long dining area with a kitchen behind. "General Hartley has done well."

"This is rented, reserved for an officer of high rank. We actually live on the transport that orbits Dolvia. My mother lived her whole life on one transport or another. She disembarked only four times that I know of. She was an adventurer's daughter and then an officer's wife."

The warriors were set to bunk together in a bedroom on the right, next to General Hartley. I was assigned the guest room next to Jesse's bedroom on the left.

"Also, I have something for you," Jesse said. "A gift from Haku-lupe Le." On the bed in my room she set out a package wrapped in brown paper and tied with string, denoting at first glance that it had been hand-delivered by some traveling savannah resident. "I will leave you to enjoy her news in private."

"There's no need unless you have pressing duties."

Curiosity glistened in Jesse's eyes. From the package I drew a hand-stitched linen burka, sky-blue with a lighter blue underside. Jesse caught her breath. "So beautiful."

"Try it on," I encouraged. She stepped before the mirror and pulled the lightweight cloth over her head, revealing her hand under the generous folds to pull the facial panel even at her chin. She looked my way and giggled, preening before the mirror.

The thoughtful package included two Arrivi long skirts and a pair of sandals. A second smaller package contained peridot jewelry plus a sizable section of natural netta and three small canisters of the paste that Dolviets used as insect repellent. With these gifts, Hakulupe Le had extended the life expectancy of the clutch of Cleo Datong from two turns of Nettom to beyond two rainy seasons.

Jesse sat on the bed, still wearing the body veil, and held up the peridot earbobs to admire. "Hakulupe Le is a good friend?"

"A cousin through my mother."

"I never knew."

"Publicly, she has no family. Among Arrivi the station of goulep is disgraceful."

"But you have family?"

"I am mixed blood," I said with a forced smile, "sometimes called creole by Softcheeks. My mixed parentage does not carry the same stigma that it did when the rabbenu's wife was young."

"I met Marcy," Jesse said. "The wife of Rabbenu Ely? She delivered this package to the transport."

"Marcy did? So generous. Did she travel officially?"

Jesse nodded, removing the burka. "With two warriors, like you now travel. She asked that I supply acclimation pills. I can get some now while we are thinking about it." She left and soon returned with a full prescription bottle.

"I won't need all these."

"For you and the students."

We grinned together. The savannah tested all who disembarked.

We repacked the gifts, and Jesse invited me to help in the kitchen. Basically, we made dinner for the men. I assembled five place settings at one end of the long table in the dining area.

The capon was just coming out of the oven when General Hartley arrived with the warriors and came to the kitchen doorway. "What are we having?"

"Capon tetrazzini with carrots and broccoli," Jesse said.

"I'm so glad I sent you to that Junction college. Otherwise dinner would be taro soup, kariom on salted patties, and chilled olives. We'll just wash up." The general led Rufus and Kyros to the bedrooms. Jesse saw me watching her father, so I flashed a quick smile. That familiar feeling crept over me, one I had often experienced in the Hartley's kitchen when I was a teenager and had helped Jesse's mother wash the dinner dishes.

For dinner, General Hartley sat at the table's head with the warriors seated on his right and Jesse and I on his left. Rufus asked casual questions during dinner to catch up with local events. "Frank Duerr is out of Dolviet politics," the general said. "He serves now as governor of the Two Forks province on Cicero. The Bryants are his ministers but control some Dolvia-based shipping contracts. Two Forks was my wife's domestic province, but life there can be hard. Young workers leave in droves for the transports."

"And where is the elusive Brigadier General Michael Peter Shaw?" I asked.

Kyros rabbe Sudl looked up from his plate briefly and slurped a noodle with his tongue. "That means he likes your cooking," I mock-whispered to Jesse. She only nodded to the big warrior.

"Mike Shaw is on Dolvia, we know that," Hartley said. "As to just where, well, he gets around pretty good."

"I thought he had a medical condition," I said.

"He's retired from the military," Hartley said, "but he wants the work."

"What work?"

"Oh," the general shrugged. "He talks to everybody."

"Except Steve Swanweil," I countered. Rufus and Kyros chuckled.

"Incidentally," Hartley picked at his food with a fork, "we are invited to dinner with Mr. Swanweil tomorrow. Just . . . uh—"

"You mean, he invited you to dinner, and you should bring me but not my warrior escort."

General Hartley glanced at Rufus. "Ah, yes." Rufus looked at me, but I only shrugged. Kyros went back to eating.

That night, I had swimming dreams, but not the tranquil images from my youth. Rather, I sidled through the shallows toward a young heifer trapped on the mucky bank. I clamped my strong jaws on her pulsating throat, tasting blood and water and mud, while younger gualareps nipped at her backside and flailing legs. The heifer's frightened eyes turned glassy. When her jaw went slack, we sang together and ripped open her stomach. I tore away pieces of muscle by catching the sinew in my front teeth and swirling my body around in the murky water. I swallowed my prize whole and went back for more, my jaws dripping with bloody lather.

I awoke with a start and wiped perspiration from my forehead. The effect of the malaria treatment, I told myself. I got up and pulled on a long robe. I opened the door cautiously and padded across the living area to the kitchen.

I grabbed some juice from the refrigerator and rinsed a glass. I turned suddenly and saw General Hartley leaning on the doorjamb in his bathrobe. He smelled of lemon and vanilla.

"Bad dreams?"

"Yeah. And you?"

He shrugged. "I don't sleep much anymore."

"I could offer comfort," I whispered, "as only I know how."

He glanced at the right-side bedroom doors, but I drew closer. "To give pleasure or to receive pleasure," I said in a teasing voice. "These are very different. To receive pleasure I would encourage you to put your big, capable hands on me." I brushed his hand with mine and toyed with his warm fingers. "To give pleasure, though, I would put my hands on you." I deserted my exploration of his fingers and brushed his flushed cheek lightly. "You can see how these are complementary actions."

He put his hands on my shoulders and set me aside at arms' length. "Down that corridor, I can have five women for nothing more than oblu twists."

I leaned against the counter.

"Where is the Brianna I remember?" the general asked. "The wide-eyed girl who braved transport life for the chance to jump back to Earth."

"That girl never had a chance."

"Perhaps she's just hiding."

"That's wishful thinking, I'm afraid." I made a motion to step past him and return to my place, but his hand was on the door-jamb blocking my exit.

"We know that you know Daniel Chin," he said.

"And we know that you know Daniel Chin."

General Hartley laughed shortly and lowered his hand. "Let's just hope that does not get us both hanged one day."

I pushed past him. I crossed toward my bedroom resolutely. "Brianna," he said behind me. I stopped but did not turn back. "If nobody said before, it is good that you have returned to Westend."

I controlled my face and showed him my profile only. "Thank you, General Hartley." I did not know his first name.

FIVE

IT WAS TOO EARLY THE NEXT DAY WHEN I WAS CALLED TO SETTLE
a dispute that had flared among the clutch of Cleo. I yawned with
a groggy head, thinking the trouble must be from Camille's light
fingers. In Jesse's front room I found Cleo clinging to Bernice, who
sat with the little girl on her lap. Bernice was plain and earnest, East
European with wide hips and soft arms. Her forehead was broad
and her chin pointed.

Cleo's features seemed more distinct, perhaps because I could
finally bear to look at her. More Tibetan than Chinese with small
eyes, Cleo had a round forehead and sparse black hair. Camille
stood next to them with her arms crossed. She was wearing a smirk
as though certain she would catch blame for the trouble. I sat with
them, wondering if tea was ready, and rubbed my left eye with the
heel of my hand. "Let's have it."

Camille spread the fingers of one hand. "She just fell down and
screamed. I didn't do nothing." She crossed her arms again and
stared left.

"Bernice?"

Bernice glanced at Camille as if angry the little girl had gotten her into trouble. "I wasn't there. They came back not ten minutes after they had decided to explore the promenade. I said to go as a clutch, but this pair returned without the others."

"Is everyone accounted for?"

Bernice nodded. I leaned forward to invade Cleo's sightline. The inscrutable Asian eyes were unfocused except for lingering fear. "Cleo, what is wrong?" I said in English.

"She has some Arrivi," Bernice whispered.

I reached to grasp the girl's wrist and was nearly flattened by the images I received. The point of view was close to the floor, like with Edwina's remote viewing images. Apparently, this was a fresh memory from when Cleo had screamed and fallen in the promenade. I saw a door close slowly, except inside was an exam room where a doctor held the shoulders of a wounded and dying conscript. Shaved head, vacant eyes, bloody arm. The doctor gently allowed the victim to lie back, limp and bony. I saw the spirit of the patient rise and float out before the snap of the security door. This blue apparition drifted hesitantly near the ceiling of the promenade, awakening hundreds of others. The view expanded, resembling a hoard of drifting jellyfish in community, bound together but not touching.

Cleo started breathing in labored gasps, echoing her corridor distress, and I released my grasp. I wondered how Bernice could tolerate the frequent contact while she comforted the girl. I glimpsed for just a moment Cleo's view of Bernice: cool and smooth with no disturbance in her aura. I had seen this before. Bernice had the mark of kant; she would not be reinforced by Dolvia. She would not prosper there. Cleo clung to her because there was no spiritual overload.

I looked at Camille, who was watching me with crossed arms and calculating eyes. I surmised she had touched Cleo in the corridor and had seen what I'd just seen. She wasn't sharing the news though. And Camille would probably resist touching Cleo again, ever again.

"Very interesting," I said. "Bernice, Cleo can stay exclusively with you for now. Continue with her language skills. All three of you will return here as soon as the watch changes. Now, go along so I can have breakfast."

I knew I would find Kyros rabbe Sudl in a café for breakfast, and Rufus would be with him. I dressed and left the dormitory. When I entered the promenade, I could not resist the urge to spy the corners of the ceiling to discern the blue souls of lost conscripts. Nothing, though.

I sat at a table with them and poured coffee from a pitcher. I added sweetener, a luxury available only at Stargate Junction, so why not indulge? "Can you see the souls of dead conscripts in the promenade?" I asked.

Kyros looked up with saucer eyes and actually stopped chewing. Rufus didn't move. "Cleo can see them," I added. "They hover near the ceiling."

Kyros glanced up, left then right.

"Many have reported seeing om while traveling," Rufus said without expression.

"Dolviet natives," I shrugged.

"Her family was—"

"Murdered," I interrupted. "Not conscript. Cleo's soul is shattered, with maybe an opening for a troubling spirit." Rufus met my look. "What do you see on Bernice?" I asked.

"She has the mark of kant," he said, "so Cleo finds her comforting."

I nodded. "You can help, Rufus. Cleo is like an empty vessel, and we should direct her attention to what Dolvia holds."

Rufus squinted with suspicion, so Kyros also narrowed his eyes.

"It's said that you have the aura of Cyrus the ketiwhelp killer," I said. "If Cleo can glimpse this aura, perhaps she will find hope for our destination."

"You just love to meddle with things, don't you?"

I shrugged again and raised the cup to my lips. "Of course, if you don't have this aura, then I only wasted a trip for coffee."

Kyros was grinning then and nudged Rufus at the elbow.

We strode through the promenade on our return to Jesse's suite. The warriors took positions at my shoulders as they had for many days. Kyros rabbe Sudl stopped when we passed the open entrance of a rented conference room. "Why do they talk?"

"What do you mean?"

"Tell secrets."

I glanced into the meeting where a Company executive using a slide show and pointer was telling an audience of mixed ethnic groups, all from Earth, about where to search out deposits of silicide. I drew in my breath sharply. An overhead screen displayed a graphic of a possible meteor path that had streaked over Urbyd centuries ago and dropped silicide fragments, more like dollops of honey, on Adydian land before the meteor had impacted the flats of Arim. The speaker was explaining how larger deposits from the fragmented meteor may be located in the ocean near Urbyd, the capital city of the Borabean clans.

I picked up a brochure and looked at both sides while a geologist spoke to offer conjecture about the behavior of meteors and the locations of deposits. He claimed that survey teams on Dolvia had had no access to the savannah controlled by Karl Wyley. Kyros also picked up a brochure, but the usher saw us lingering there. She snatched the brochure from Kyros and hustled us out of the entrance to close the wide doors.

I opened the brochure I held. It displayed graphics of the composition of silicide, explaining that the substance was a liquid in solid form just like mercury was a mineral in liquid form. The mined silicide that looked like crystals could be heated and spun into long strands for use in industry to facilitate long distance communications. Its ability to amplify light also increased and focused sound, or bits, in long distance messages.

"So many secrets," Kyros said.

"The properties of silicide are known," I told Kyros. "The only question is where to find it in quantity until their scientists develop methods to synthesize it."

Kyros frowned. I assumed the technical terms were difficult.

"The evidence is skimpy, I agree," I said. "Who might tell the men of the Company about the tunnels in the aquifer lined with crystalline silicide?"

"Joey Osborn," Rufus said.

"To take the mineral, they must drain the old water," Kyros said. "Sacred water."

In General Hartley's apartment, Jesse watched from the safety of the kitchen while Rufus sat to tolerate my experiment with Cleo. Camille yawned and sighed, then looked around at the many valuable objects set out for decoration that maybe would not be missed before we left for the transport. She saw me watching her and gave me a false grin.

Rufus sat on a turned-out chair with Kyros at his shoulder. Bernice led Cleo forward.

"What is needed?" Rufus asked.

I tried to contain the humor in my voice. "Allow Cleo to touch your wrist where the blood of Cyrus courses through your veins near the skin." Rufus extended his forearm and palm like a god on high. Bernice gestured by touching her own wrist, so Cleo reached to touch Rufus there.

Immediately, I smelled spent gunpowder and the coppery tang of fresh blood. A strong breeze seemed to trouble Rufus's hair, as if blowing it away from his shoulders, while red flashes of the battlefield coalesced into tongues of flame. Cyrus stood at his other shoulder, tangent to Kyros, recognizable by his many scars and cauliflower ears. Several figures hovered behind, maybe ancestors and sacrificed warriors.

Camille caught her breath. I was glad for that; she was participating in the vision.

I reached to pull Cleo's hand from his wrist. When I touched her, I also saw a woman with her auburn hair bound in a warrior's queue, standing with a son and two daughters. So Cleo was touched by om, able to view the aura of Cyrus and the future for Rufus. I would need to manage her education. Cleo looked at me, the expression on her face unchanging. There was no need for words. "Bernice, take her," I said.

Kyros rabbe Sudl was slack-jawed and wavering even as the girls were leaving. "Honor to Rufus, son of Cyrus the ketiwhelp killer and grandson to my ubermother Kyros."

"Honor to my cousin Rufus," I added.

He only stood and left the room. Kyros blinked twice and followed him out.

Jesse joined me with questions in her face. She, like Bernice, had discerned nothing.

For dinner that night, I wore the Arrivi skirt and sandals provided by Hakulupe Le and coiled my hair in the traditional fashion, even adding the peridot earbobs. I carried the sky-blue burka as a shawl. In the mirror, my skin appeared more olive and my eyes more green. I could have been Kyle Rula herself. The fanciful thought came to me that all was seen. Why else had Hakulupe Le provided the needed covering?

General Hartley approved of my outfit choice. He said nothing when I entered the living room, but his expression registered pleasure. He looked gallant in his dress uniform with the many medals and white gloves. Jesse was also pleased with my looks and said so more than once. The warriors sulked on the side. They had not been invited to dinner.

Before we left for Steve Swanweil's dinner party, General Hartley spread a map on the dining table. "Just a refresher for you," he said.

Rufus and Kyros Rabbe Sudl came closer, always ready to talk strategy. "The Borabean continue to pressure Uburu land."

General Hartley indicated a rosy and relatively flat country comprised mostly of sand dunes on the map. "The many clans of Borabean live along the ocean; their capital city is Urbyd. East are the Canyon of Buttes and Southeast Arrivi where Kyros's extended family lives. And this—" He indicated a thin stretch of gorge-filled mesas sandwiched between the Southeast Arrivi region and the rosy Borabean boundary. "This is Uburu land."

"So you're saying," I postulated, "Company executives count the Uburu mesas as a simple barrier, a passageway to the savannah?"

"You cannot argue with geography."

I only sighed. "When I was young, the savannah was the whole universe to me."

"The land is all any of us need," Rufus added.

Presently, General Hartley and I entered Swanweil's event. The rented room was large and impersonal with a dining area on one side that included hired waiters and catered food, just another in a long series of official events for the general. He introduced me to three Company executives and their Han Chinese wives who wore western-style cocktail dresses with platinum and diamond jewelry. They bowed and murmured their hellos.

Two Consortium officers in dress uniforms and white gloves, each with his stiff hat tucked under one arm, saluted the general curtly. I looked for Captain Chandliss but didn't find him there.

The call came that dinner was served, and the guests moved into the dining area just as Tuang Cho joined the group in a huff. A highly placed Company official, now fifteen years a Westend resident, his current position I could not name. He whispered some news into Swanweil's ear. Steve only nodded and led him to us for introductions.

At dinner, Steve Swanweil tried to be charming, and in fact was. "Everybody knows the purpose of the new Arrivi armistice is to keep the Mekucoo in, the Borabean out, and the Siibabean down. We of the Consortium do not view the cease-fire in the same way as the tribes. The time of warriors is past. They can no longer be allowed to gain tribal honor through extreme behavior."

"You mean like the Borabean," General Hartley said, "who send their sons and daughters on a children's crusade. Brianna, unarmed Gora children as young as eight were seen to enter the battlefield carrying their own death shrouds in their packs."

"The kahnates will always fight." Swanweil said. "Landless Cylahi are jealous of erriv-raising Arrivi, who hate the Putuki bazaari because they trade in arms and gasoline. The Mekucoo are raised to fight. They have no other occupation."

"You inflame the Borabean Goras," Hartley insisted, "against a people they barely know and then push against docile Uburu families simply because they're in the way."

"I have done none of these things." Swanweil said. "I am a Cicero businessman. The Uburu look to Dacupitte for leadership, and all he does is get their women pregnant."

Wan Su spoke in a crisp English accent. "To survive, the savannah tribes must have a stable internal structure of governance and control of the militia. At least the savannah's welfare ministers are academy graduates."

"So are the insurrectionists," I said.

The Chinese gentleman smiled falsely.

"It's ironic when you look at it," Swanweil added. "Rabbenu Ely came to power, all those seasons ago, by opposing Company mining interests. Now he makes backroom deals with the same corporations."

"Karl Wyley won't allow silicide mining on the savannah," Hartley said. He saw the question in my eyes. I had long known Company executives called their greatest enemy by his anglicized name, but I had not thought General Hartley would refer to Karlyhi thus. It was unseemly.

"Karl Wyley maintains the soldiers' payroll and the widows' pensions," the general explained, misreading my look. "The people will follow him."

"As long as Wyley wins the skirmishes," Swanweil added. "And what happens after Rabbenu Ely bleeds the coffers dry? What of Karl Wyley's popularity then?"

Wan Su chuckled. "Besides, he was seen on the videotape."

"What videotape?" I asked.

"Joey Osborn is dead," General Hartley said. "For some time, he was suspected of profiteering. He was caught red-handed with charity shipments meant for displaced Uburu." The general shrugged. "Things were done."

"They cut off his ears," Swanweil added with a hint of glee, "and slashed him all over with belt knives. They left him for the insects on the desert and recorded the whole messy business."

I glanced at General Hartley, not willing to reveal that such actions were traditional ritual punishment for respected tribal enemies.

Swanweil continued in a self-satisfied way. "Wyley's on the tape. Not him exactly, they all wore hoods. But his leg scar is obvious. So that's it. The only respected voice on the savannah was Kyle Rula. A true meydani, not a souk who spends the day in a six-by-six bazaar stall. And now she's gone. By her own hand, gone."

"Perhaps Brianna Miller intends to take her place," Wan Su postulated.

I smiled sweetly. "Nobody can replace Rularim."

When we arrived back at General Hartley's apartment, it was late. The others had gone to bed. "I should have told you about Joey Osborn before we went to dinner. You know Karen divorced him."

"Arrivi don't divorce."

"It was quite a scandal," he nodded. "Karen once asked Marcy if she wanted to do the same, divorce Rabbenu Ely. But Marcy did not have the courage."

"And Joey's children, Patrick and Kelly?"

"Patrick is fairly bitter, more due to his father's execution than the divorce. Kelly lives with her mother Karen and is being trained to teach at the clinic school."

"The clinic school? Truly? My memories of that place are ... well."

General Hartley drew closer. He smelled of eucalyptus and lemon. How did he accomplish that after the long day? "Brianna," he whispered. "About last night—"

My arms ached to reach out for him. "My role has changed," I said with conviction. "My gestures are more than my own. I cannot." His shoulders drooped with regret.

"Good night, General Hartley." I retreated to my room and gently banged my head against the wall.

One more arrangement was needed before we left Stargate Junction. I decided to purchase some conscripts and approached Steve Swanweil whom I knew could broker a transaction. "A dirty business," he said behind an expensive handkerchief. "But I can assure you that they are clean of parasites and bugs. Very big on cleanliness, these Chinese. Are you in the market for miners to dig for silicide?"

"Five girls who have lost family, ages six through fourteen."

His eyes glistened, and he seemed to shimmer in the bright lights of the promenade café where we sat. "Well, that's different," he said, pleased with himself for securing this private meeting. "The managers will be suspicious about your motive. Maybe to expose to the press or make some trouble."

"Just younger girls, then. They will soon forget . . . this place. And I'll sign a confidentiality agreement."

"Paperwork?" He waved a finger in a tight gesture. "That will only raise a red flag. No paperwork. Leave this to me. I can—"

"We will select the girls. You will bring some out for inspection."

"We?"

"I will make the selection, I mean," I corrected. "But I'm seeking companions for the clutch I have already found, so I'll bring along a few of them."

Swanweil took a moment to cross his legs the other way. "This selection, as you call it. Are you trying to make a public incident to inflame gossip on Stargate Junction?"

I placed a single uncut emerald from Rufus's stash on the table before I stood. "I'm certain you can manage a quiet venue. I don't need to know the details."

"What rate would you consider?"

"For girls too young to work and without family to keep them in line? They have no value here. Managers put them down like unwanted puppies."

"If you want five and want to choose, then they have value."

"I will pay half the price the managers suggest."

He smiled knowingly. "A place to start, at least."

Later, I led Cleo and Rosalyn as we followed Swanweil down a long corridor. He turned at the door of a low-end brothel well out of the sight of on-duty Blackshirts. "A brothel? Really?" I asked.

"Where can conscript women be seen in this section?"

We walked through the over-decorated receiving room to a blank kitchen where several bald children in conscript clothes greedily ate soup with bread, some seated and some standing. Each was focused on the meal and displayed little communion with the others.

I had already instructed Cleo. "Bernice will need a task to fill her time while you are on another part of the savannah," I said in Arrivi. "The ones you choose today will be in Bernice's charge when you are not. Do you understand?" She only nodded.

Rosalyn asked, "What will happen to the girls who are not chosen?"

"As quartermaster of the clutch," I said, "all your life, you will decide who benefits and who is left in her current condition. Unless, of course, you don't want the rank of quartermaster."

Rosalyn frowned but looked to me for direction. I indicated that they should move among the conscripts. I kept my barriers firmly in place and was even glad Swanweil was there so I had reason to show no weakness. "Do you have family?" I asked him.

"Three daughters." I just stared, so he added, "They live with their mother's extended family on Cicero. I'm a good provider."

"You have daughters, and you can tolerate this?"

He squinted suddenly. "You said you would make no trouble. I'm helping here."

Rosalyn returned to me with a limp and sad Cleo, her head hanging so the straight hair obscured her face. Rosalyn's eyes sought mine. "Draw out the ones who will leave with us," I instructed. Rosalyn sighed shortly and returned to touch the heads of five girls ages six to eight. They stood immediately and gathered with no jubilation or even hope.

Swanweil held out his hand. I opened a small pouch. "I have native peridot, one gem for each girl." I placed five into his palm.

Swanweil kept his hand out. "And two more for my silence. Call it a broker's fee."

I chose one more, larger and a darker blue. "If I hear rumors of any sort, then I cannot guarantee your safety." I dropped the gem into his hand, which he quickly jammed into his pants pocket.

"Reputation is everything," he said to conclude our deal.

Leah waited for us in the corridor and took charge of the group. "Get them settled and set them to learning Arrivi," I instructed. "Don't share your clothes but use what I have provided. They're not members of the clutch, only tangent."

"I understand." She led them away like goslings following a waddling goose.

The shuttle ride was uneventful, but when the warriors and I entered midship of the aging transport, my first encounter was with Patrick Osborn. Now age twenty-two or more, Patrick wore round-rimmed glasses and combed his rich auburn hair straight back from his low forehead. Patrick eyed Kyros rabbe Sudl. Rufus stood on the side while the clutch of Cleo passed with the many pieces of luggage.

"Patrick Osborn, you remember me?" I asked with melody in my voice. "I stayed at your parents' house in Somule when—"

"My parents left Somule seasons ago," Patrick said. "They were divorced."

"I am sorry. I did not know," I lied.

Patrick bowed slightly as the Company men passed, then shot me a hateful look. "You and General Hartley know everything about me. Dolviets are just ants under your microscope."

"I don't take your meaning."

"Surveillance cameras," he said expansively. "A Consortium camera was dedicated in our Somule house. We were watched for many seasons, playing in the yard, going to school. What can you learn from me now?"

"Patrick, I never . . . I mean, I was watched along with you. Just the same as you."

"The tribes murdered my father," he retorted "They want nothing to do with me."

"You prefer transport duty?"

He stuck his chin out, considering my face. "Where is the Dolviet treasure held in my name? What council seat waits for me?"

"Patrick, it does not have to be—"

He bit out the words. "Profiteer they called my father. Collaborator. But consider his options. Karl Wyley closed Somule and pushed us out. In Cylay they destroyed my aunt's enterprises. What choice did we have, huh?

"Like they ever did the Bryants a good turn," he continued. "Ha! No, I can stay here along with Carl Hartley, the general's son. We're accepted at the highest level as the Junction Boys. I owe the tribes nothing."

"Patrick, I can see you're angry, but—"

"Leave me alone! I don't need your pity! None of them. I don't need nothing from them!" Patrick stomped away, his back arched. I looked at Kyros rabbe Sudl, who sadly shook his head.

Late that night, or so it seemed to me, the shuttle to Cylay on Dolvia was accepting passengers. Our luggage for the clutch of Cleo was stamped again and hauled down the gangway. Steve Swanweil passed by, accompanied by Wang Cho and two others. They would disembark in Cylay on the savannah and travel by helicopter to Urbyd. My plan was to wait for the next shuttle and to disembark with Rufus and Kyros in Urbyd, followed by a chopper flight to Cylay. I lingered with the clutch mostly to avoid another encounter with Swanweil, but he was busy acting as host to the Chinese executives and was unconcerned with me.

I turned to Leah. "Hakulupe Le and some others will meet you at the launchpad. The first days are the most difficult. Take the acclimation pills and start with the paste in your hairlines."

"We know. You said already."

"Fine, then. I'm certain all will go smoothly. I'll catch up with you soon." I smiled at each girl and boy as they passed me to enter the gangway to the shuttle.

Captain Chandliss and his two followers were also boarding. He stopped near me. "You aren't taking this shuttle?"

"I will linger here with the warriors. There's another shuttle soon."

"In ten days. You can afford the—"

"I prefer to think of this time as an opportunity to reinforce the long-distance relationships for Somule Gems."

"With General Hartley?"

"Jesse Hartley and I were childhood friends," I said evenly. "But one principle I learned early is to keep channels of communication open. One day you may need to reach me with a message, but my movements will be guarded by others." I saw his brow wrinkle as I removed a peridot earbob tangled in my hair. "Present this to the warriors, and you will be allowed to join me. We should keep a channel open, you see."

He accepted the semi-precious gem encased in stiff wire in his open palm, glancing around as he considered my move. He then drew from his pants pocket a thick chain with a charm attached. "This chain held my lockbox key when I served in the local police."

I held up the chain and noted the attached charm. "Saint George?" I guessed.

"Saint Christopher, the patron saint of travelers."

"I can remove the charm."

"No, it's all one piece and unique on Dolvia, I would think."

"I wish you good fortune in your adventures, along with your companions."

His hand lifted to touch the bill of his hat, but he caught himself this time. "Ma'am," he said and turned toward the gangway. I returned to the company of Rufus and Kyros.

We spent the idle time over the following days with transport surveillance images, which the general discussed at length with Rufus, agreeing through discussion what to expect and what to resist. I communicated often with Sarah at the savannah convent, mostly about the clutch of Cleo and how they should be assigned after acclimation. I wanted to keep them together, but she said the two boys had requested to work with Kyros rabbe Sudl when he arrived. She said that Saed and Ankos found the classroom stifling and the lessons remedial. I argued that the boys would adjust and must learn to follow her instructions without complaint. However, since I was stepping out of the project of growing managers from the clutch of Cleo, I relented and allowed Sarah to make the decisions.

I contacted Petra Mitterand in Paris as I had promised. She showed me a bitter smirk. "The blood of Rufus is not special," she said over the trunk call with an eight-second lag time for send and receive. "Heather claims you knew that the whole time; that your last act on Earth was to snooker us."

"I didn't know," I said honestly. "I took a sample of Rufus's blood on impulse after you and I had agreed to visit Pierre. How is your father?"

"He refuses to blame you for anything," Petra said. "He says I must reinforce our agreements and hold on tight. He regrets ever walking away from you."

"His condition colors his reasoning," I said after the lag time. "And did the student Evgenia arrive safely?"

"Heather takes her bitterness out on the girl," Petra's image said. "Evgenia's now a servant to Heather's daughters. In a month, she'll be their mortal enemy."

I sighed. "We sow the seeds. . . . Heather was always a fair-weather friend, sniffing around for points on a new venture. What work has she ever accomplished?"

"I suspect she's been approached to share any secrets."

"Her father and sister here in Westend are stellar friends. I don't get the disconnect."

"Well, for Rufus's blood—" Petra said. "The lab is running additional tests. They may combine it with the stem cells from Kyle Le's blood and see if the colony of HeLa cells is strengthened. I'll keep you posted."

"I'll be out of touch awhile. Send any news to Sarah at the savannah convent. You have the codes."

"I wish you an easy disembarkment."

"All my best to Pierre."

In the quiet hours, mostly when bad dreams woke me suddenly, I inspected the extra contents of the package I had received in the Beijing mall. I compared the sketches of a land survey to a brochure picked up from a midship seminar. The brochure gave away no secrets, of course, but displayed the Company mindset, the assumption that Arrivi land held more silicide.

My purchased survey indicated the terminus of the meteoroid as the flats of Arim, that the meteoroid became a bolide, meaning it exploded in the air before impact, sending debris from the hard casing of the head in all directions. The casing material was maybe a weighty compressed mineral called tektite. The survey postulated that silicide had dribbled in liquid form before the explosion, so the search for silicide on the savannah could be confined to the path of the debris stream. The conjecture could not be verified until a sizeable "nose piece" of tektite was found. I had an idea of where to look for this nose piece and who could find it for me.

Before the shuttle was scheduled to depart, Jesse and I enjoyed long afternoon chats and excursions into the midship mall to support the local commerce there. I dined mostly with the warriors and enjoyed hearing the many chants of warrior exploits from Kyros rabbe Sudl when we relaxed over a bottle of Kiam gin. For shared meals with the general, I devoted my attention to Jesse and barely glanced at him. I needed no trouble in that direction. I did learn his first name, however; it was Eugene, or Gene as an officer called him in Ops one day.

I slept a great deal, as did Kyros, before we met for computer sessions to learn the Borabean language. Rufus was a quick study and had had some contact with the Borabean previously, but Kyros had little talent in the area of language skills.

SIX

THE CONSORTIUM SHUTTLE SETTLED ON THE LAUNCHPAD SITU-
ated just outside the Borabean capital city Urbyd. The name trans-
lates as "visited by Bydquii," their ancient ocean god. Several Islamic
men, wormhole travelers wearing kaffiyehs and lightweight gala-
bias, left their seats and filed out. They were the same executives
who had attended the midship seminars on where to find silicide
on the dunes. One glanced darkly over his shoulder at Rufus in his
western suit, and the challenge between them was palpable.

I stood and reached for my pack but stopped when Kyros rabbe
Sudl cleared his throat and glanced at the Arrivi burka I carried as
a shawl. I pulled it over my head and business suit, covered from
head to calves, and stepped back so the men could lead.

We entered the customs area of an air-conditioned terminal.
In this arena, Kyros rabbe Sudl was an Arrivi businessman traveling with a woman of his tribe plus a Mekucoo bodyguard. When
we entered the long promenade, the glare from the big windows

hurt my eyes. Comtech screens blared Company-sanctioned news delivered by China-doll announcers. I was dreading my first steps outside, having traveled all this time in Company comfort.

A Consortium officer approached, and I felt there was something about his mustache.

It was Milo Sector, now a militia colonel. He was older but still trim with a strong jaw and showy lip hair. His face was deeply tanned and care-worn. "Milo Sector?" I asked in English, but then bit my lip. It would take some effort for me to function within the mute woman's role.

He signified on Rufus with the open palm gesture. "Hiki Rufus, son of Cyrus," he said in Arrivi. "Melinga."

Rufus nodded.

"Kyros rabbe Sudl," Colonel Sector said. Kyros shook his hand, proud of his newly learned western gestures. "We should go," Milo added without acknowledging me.

"But my luggage," I spoke out.

Colonel Sector and Rufus glanced down the corridor in opposite directions. Colonel Sector took my arm. "My officers will bring the cases," he whispered sternly in English. "And no more talking."

We hustled out the sliding door where we were greeted by a shimmering wall of desert heat. I reflexively drew in my breath. "You have acclimation pills," Colonel Sector whispered as though angry. "Take one now."

"I am fine. I just—" He did not allow me to finish; instead, he led us across the asphalt parking lot. Blue heat radiated above the tar. Hotel airbuses, idling and giving off exhaust fumes, waited to shuttle VIPs into the city. We passed behind a low hangar while I panted, making my facial panel bow in and out.

"Not much farther," Colonel Sector whispered and hustled me left, never releasing my arm. We reached an eight-passenger helicopter with slowly rotating blades. As we crossed the landing pad to the open hatch, Milo Sector made a circling gesture in the air. By the time we had scrambled aboard, the Arrivi pilot had powered up and was lifting off.

Colonel Sector slammed the lightweight door. The overhead blower forced chilled air into my lungs. Rufus and Kyros rabbe Sudl pulled off their suit coats and ties. Their white shirts were soaked with sweat. I was honestly surprised because I had not conquered my own discomfort enough to consider theirs.

Colonel Sector ducked his head into the pilot area and asked staccato questions. Then he relaxed and sat next to me. "If you want to take that off," he said in English, "I can help you with the safety strap."

I pulled the burka over my head and exposed moist hair clinging to my forehead and neck. The pilot glanced back with a frown. Arrivi women wore veils almost constantly and would surely hesitate before uncovering on Borabean land. Given his sensibilities, I might as well have exposed my naked bosom to the seated men. I respectfully gathered the draped material as a shawl and placed it on my shoulders. Kyros rabbe Sudl stared at the pilot, a gesture that natives call the evil eye, until the man turned back to his station.

"The first few minutes outdoors are the most difficult," Colonel Sector assured me.

"I am surprised to find you still doing helicopter duty," I said.

"I saw your name on the roster and assigned myself the detail," he grinned under the mustache, "so I can face my wife later."

"Your wife?"

"Hakulupe Le waits in Somule with our two daughters."

I grinned. "I have been away a long time."

Kyros moved to the copilot's seat. He glanced back sheepishly before stripping off his soiled shirt and donning the sleeveless Arrivi tunic. He pulled an inadequate curtain from behind the pilot's shoulder before changing into the Arrivi pantaloons.

Rufus stared out the hatch window. "You will want to see this." He moved aside so I could glimps our aerial view of the streets.

The Borabean city was limestone and terra-cotta with gleaming religious buildings. A clustered business district showed a few seven-story warehouses with more under construction. The street grid on our southern view ended abruptly, replaced by a morass of broad and brightly decorated family tents and livestock stations, some of them crowded with sigpywa imported from across the ocean. Sigpywa were centipedes of a sort, four feet high and six to ten feet long. They had skeletal plates over a soft and oily body, feathery feet, and a pincer mouth. Sigpywa tolerated the harsh climate and could survive longer than a camel on the desert. But they were worms; there was no getting around that.

Borabean also had horses, introduced to their culture by Han Chinese Company men decades ago. Horses impacted their culture more than sigpywa. Horses were for glory; sigpywa were for transport.

We overflew cooling silos, low and wide, laid out in a uniform warehouse section where silicide waited for offworld transport. And beyond them were the long buildings and chimneys of three smelting furnaces. Rows of operating lights along high catwalks between the buildings resembled holiday fairy lights. Blue flames belched from tall and narrow stacks like corporate oriflammes. The metallic-tasting air invaded even our fast-moving conveyance.

We briefly skirted the roiling green and white ocean before the pilot banked left and flew inland. I met Colonel Sector's knowing look. "The Company has succeeded here, huh?"

"Borabean clans have schools and roads and hospitals," Milo shrugged. "An extensive military. Abydian families are paid a yearly dividend like a tax return."

"And when the silicide runs out?" I asked.

"Their kids will be educated," Milo said.

Rufus had taken a turn in the copilot's seat and now wore a tunic and dungarees from a Mekucoo militia clutch. He took the seat between us and adjusted his sheathed belt knife. His arm amulet rested on tanned skin just below a wicked battle scar.

I leaned toward Colonel Sector. "The young men will leave for transport duty. Families will have no future, just like on Cicero."

Milo shrugged again. "A boom economy is difficult to argue against."

"You're right, of course. Arrivi would do less?"

"The tribes don't need Softcheeks," Rufus claimed. I looked up, surprised that he spoke.

Colonel Sector was sanguine. "This chopper is Softcheeks technology. And you just spent the last full season, Rufus, cradled by

Chinese technology, going and coming. In what way are you independent?"

"Mekucoo need only the land."

The chopper blades provided a comforting swoop-swoop-swoop noise as we settled in for the long ride. We overflew Uburu land, high mesas with terraced crops and clustered adobe villages under slate roofs. Occasional fields looked torched or lay fallow. Some roofs were caved in where gardens were overrun by feral goats. Torturous footpaths once lovingly maintained by family groups had been bombed or washed out, leaving survivors stranded on green mesa tops.

"Since we're out this way," Milo said, "I thought we could accommodate one more passenger." The helicopter passed between the mesa walls where sharp-edged aretes poked out from tamarind and gum tree clusters. The pilot caused the chopper to hover before he set it down in a narrow Uburu gorge with a trickling brook. He kept the engine idling high as he and Colonel Sector peered out, searching the bush for waiting personnel. After several tense moments, the pilot pointed, his gesture too quick and jubilant.

Colonel Sector pulled back the lightweight hatch. I glimpsed the movement of three men in the bush. A big soldier with camouflage greasepaint on his face and arms, wearing a sleeveless T-shirt instead of his uniform's shirt, ran from cover without a weapon or heavy gear to scramble into the compartment. The chopper left the ground and deserted the isolated gorge in a flash, resuming its pre-arranged flight path with barely a hiccup.

The fieldman sat back on his heels and grinned at me. "Brigadier General Michael Peter Shaw," I said in English. "How thoughtful of you to drop by."

"Hiki, Brianna Miller of Arim. It is good to find you within Dol-via's embrace."

"He's retired from active duty," Sector said. "He consults now."

"Milo, how is your family?" he asked the mustachioed man.

"Hakulupe Le has several messages."

"Yeah, yeah. There's time now, plenty of time."

Mike was older, of course, but trim and alive like he had never been during his desk duty as Director of Natural Disasters Control under the Consortium mandate. His medical condition had melted away the paunch and added deep grooves to his face. Mike took his turn in the copilot's seat, not bothering to pull the small curtain. He grabbed a canteen and dirty towel from under the cushion and methodically removed the paint from his face and arms. He had always been a methodical man. Within my memory, his wife had complained of it often.

He wiped mud from his boots and pulled on a pilot's shirt with insignia. He winked at me—I must have been staring—and grabbed a padded helmet with visor and plastic low-fic. Mike traded places with the pilot, who stowed his headgear and changed into an offi-cer's uniform similar to Milo Sector's, appearing to all the world as part of our escort.

When the transformation was complete, Colonel Sector whis-pered to me in his confidential way, "You're one of us now. You know too much to travel alone."

"An in-sur-rec-tion-ist," Kyros added. He and the pilot chuck-led. Rufus said nothing.

Pilot Mike Shaw set the chopper down in the vehicle mainte-nance yard of the Cylay garrison. I pulled the burka over my head and business suit and allowed Kyros to help me step down. I held the billowing folds against my sides and turned back when the chopper powered up. Mike Shaw's face was hidden behind the pilot's helmet. He saluted and lifted off for destinations unknown. Watching through the gauzy facial panel, I wondered which of us was flying under false colors.

A captain approached Colonel Sector with a manila envelope. He pulled out what must have been surveillance photos; I glimpsed them by craning my neck. Milo handed them back with brief instructions before he joined us. "Duty calls," he shrugged. "Your luggage will be sent along. And I will see you again in Somule, I am sure."

"Thank you for greeting us."

"Hakulupe Le sends her best. You want to go out through there."

We hurried past the airplane hangar to the yard's edge and were quickly passed through the guard gate to enter a torrid and wasted oppressive slum. The stench of animal and human offal made me gag. I took short gasps to capture the required oxygen from the hot and foul air. An ECCAV waited in the muddy alleyway. Our freshly uniformed pilot–escort carried a karkar and took the front seat next to the driver.

Kyros, Rufus, and I climbed into the back seat where the floor rug was missing and the seats were patched. Taped windows were partly rolled down, so my hope for air-conditioning was dashed. I struggled with the burka but finally pushed it out like a tent. Within its privacy, I swallowed the acrid acclimation pill, not even caring what Rufus thought.

The city of Cylay was nothing like Urbyd, the Borabean capital. In the section we traversed, nothing was new. In the past, the Dolviet poor had been the Cylahi tribe who accepted their lot and some unfortunate Putuki who were sometimes helped by clan members.

But this. Wrinkled and toothless men in shorts only with shoulder-slung karkars leaned against tumbledown shacks. Women crouched under the veil at open cooking fires in the doorways of abandoned businesses and spoke to each passerby, begging for alms. Pot-bellied children, many with rust-colored hair, stared at nothing. On a street corner, a woman lifted her voluminous skirts and urinated into the gutter without care of who could see. I considered a petition for a new jump back number.

"These are not Arrivi," Rufus said in harsh tones, using English. "Many displaced Uburu. Warriors serve in the militia, but the women have no skills and no family."

"Are you making a speech?"

Kyros chuckled. "Dolvia's embrace has made him chatty."

Rufus scowled before he took a kari root cigarette from inside his tunic and lit it with a utility match. I was grateful when the aromatic smoke masked the stench from the street. My nostrils disregarded the pervasive latrine smell, free to take in olive oil cooking odors, the desert breeze, and the scent of drying urine on heated adobe.

I stared at passing bazaar stalls of rotting wood. The few straight walls and whole roofs were corrugated zinc and sheet iron, lending a metallic flavor to the dry air rushing through the open ECCAV windows. It was the time of siesta in Cylay, so black plastic was secured over the market goods with rocks and old tires. Along the alleyways stood shacks constructed with flattened cigarette cartons. Pigs rooted in open sewers where old women struggled to wash a few garments. Insects buzzed the tear ducts of staring children, too many toddlers with telltale rust-colored hair.

"So many redheads."

"The first sons of Dacupitte are fathers now," Kyros said.

"Some fathers," I complained. "They live in army barracks and take meals at the cafeteria. These children don't know them."

"Dacupitte was raised with Kecouroo," Rufus said. "He barely knew Hamish Nordhagen."

"He was raised with tradition, as were you."

Rufus blew smoke from his nostrils and stared out the window.

I was being disagreeable; I knew that. My heartbeat was elevated, and I saw vibrant colors, the pill's effect. I would not sleep for several hours, but I could breathe.

We passed an academy and adjacent goulep convent, both constructed of red Arrivi brick and swept clean daily. A small crowd of veiled women with children, some of a dark Siibabean complexion, extended their arms through the locked gate and begged a passing resident who was hurrying to some overdue task. She only shook her head and stepped away.

"These ones are too many," Rufus said. "The sacrifice too great."

The driver pulled the ECCAV onto a laterite road, bumpy and noisy from the crenellation. We entered a wide plaza with a center non-working fountain. To the right was a high and gleaming wall of rabbenu limestone, biscuit-colored with rosy veins, a variety of limestone found only on rabbenu land. The deserted sidewalk led to an ornate wrought iron gate with a gold-embossed family crest that sported baroque swirls. As we sped by, I saw interior working fountains plus the high columns of a limestone mansion that mimicked some Earth architectural conceit. Uniformed guards with karkars stood sentinel in the late afternoon sun, their siesta not allowed. "Why don't the women beg here?"

"Soldiers force them away," Kyros said.

"Soldiers who are their family?"

"Rabbenu Ely's guards are mostly Putuki," Kyros said darkly. "Family members of the bazaari he favors."

We passed the plaza location where Kyle Rula had committed immolation. A funeral shrine with delicate orchid branches and sputtering candles were clustered there.

"At least Kyle Rula is remembered," I whispered. On this subject Rufus was mute.

We pulled up at a hotel. The entrance had been defaced by embedded bullets from a long spray of karkar fire. Windows were open, denoting no electricity for air-conditioning.

The lobby contained aging and musky settees and a threadbare rug. EAM stations for guests were marked with "out of order" signs. I wondered if there would be running water even. The Putuki man behind the counter saw the warriors' arm amulets and leveled his gaze on Rufus. I was invisible to him under my burka.

Kyros spoke in Arrivi, "A reservation waits for this visiting meydani." The clerk did not move but kept his gaze on Rufus only. Then it came to me; Rufus was the Mekucoo son of Kyle Rula who had recently inflamed the tribes with her public self-execution.

I pulled off the burka, eyes averted, and folded it carefully. All present gasped and stared at my Softcheeks business suit. I held out an open hand to Kyros rabbe Sudl to receive the three passports and stepped up to the counter. He and Rufus took up bodyguard positions, facing out on each side of me. "Brianna Miller of Arim," I said in a loud voice, using English. "I require accommodations for some days for myself and these men in my employ. A reservation has been made, perhaps by the Consortium General Hartley, on my behalf. You have it there, don't you?"

The desk clerk sputtered and looked down, rifling through some papers. I slowly faced out with my haughtiest look, staring down the curious tribespeople. He found the needed forms and room key.

"And a separate room for these bodyguards."

He reluctantly provided a second key.

I indicated our waiting pilot/escort. "This man will accept delivery of my luggage," I continued in English harshly, "so nothing is stolen. Please send fresh towels to the room, also a hay-gee-am. You have an hay-gee-am available for guests, I assume?"

The clerk nodded with his mouth hanging open. We had no need of the HGEAM, or holographic extra-atmosphere modem, but its use was a privilege I demanded. "And have dinner for four sent to my room within sixty minutes, with a bucket of ice. A full bucket of ice."

With my back arched, I walked in long strides past the staring tribal workers toward the elevator. Behind me, Kyros cleared his throat. He made a slight gesture indicating the staircase. We three moved in that direction. I had to assume the elevators were not working. No matter, our rooms were on the second floor.

The Putuki maids got a workout that day. They held palms high in Arrivi style and carried water for my bath since the faucets did not work. They turned down the bed and opened the windows to the balcony. They set out orchids in shallow bowls on the table and bed stand.

Once refreshed from the scented water, I wore the Arrivi skirt and paneled tunic that Hakulupe Le had provided and coiled my hair at my neck. When I joined them, stepping around the luggage pieces, the pilot's face registered pleasure. "Kyle Rula arises from the flames," he said in Arrivi to Kyros.

"Rularim has not forgotten Arrivi words," I returned.

He stood tall, surprise and pride replacing the pleasure on his face.

The meal was delivered, and the warriors joined me on the balcony. The Putuki maids withdrew. I wondered how it was their tribe included unbending men and such ingratiating women. I sipped the cold drink and began to feel whole again. All the traveling and being passed from one competing faction to the next had worn on me.

"I apologize for my harsh words earlier, Rufus. It has been a long trip."

"You are Dacupitte's woman," Rufus shrugged slightly. "You may say whatever you wish."

"I am not Dacupitte's woman."

"It is seen."

"That's a convenient vision from a season of om," I repeated. We had taken meals together twice a day through our travels, yet Rufus and I were not close.

By the time we had finished the Arrivi repast, murmuring was heard in the hallway. Kyros rabbe Sudl signaled the pilot to quiet the crowd and looked at me with question.

"Unless it is Karima Le or Hakulupe Le," I said, "ask them to come back tomorrow." Rufus and Kyros rose to carry out my instructions. "Kyros, why don't you take the hay-gee-am to your room?" I added. "Place a call to Jesse Hartley and access the library files if you care to."

We both knew how the petitioning tribesmen would view that action. Kyros showed an open palm at elbow height. "May you prosper from Dolvia's embrace."

I could return only what was demanded by honor. "The reputations of your ancestors are enlarged by the goodly acts of Kyros rabbe Sudl."

The hotel corridor traffic was being diverted to Kyros's room where the tribesmen were most likely staring with wonder at the floating heads the HGEAM produced. Putuki maids approached the quiet balcony but waited. I signaled that they should come forward. "The orchids are beautiful," one offered in Arrivi as she stacked dishes on a tray. "Do you have a suitor?"

I had assumed the flowers had been provided by the hotel. I looked at the dish to find a note from the sender, but none was there. Perhaps they had been delivered by way of a conceit Dacupitte had picked up from General Shaw, a form of claiming territory.

"Do you wear a burka?" I asked one Putuki servant who was staring.

"When I go out on the streets."

"Would you consider a trade?" I showed a finely decorated tan linen burka I had brought.

Her face lit up, but then she frowned. "I could never afford—"

"A trade for your everyday burka, so I can step outside without drawing attention."

"Truly?" She could not believe her good fortune. She returned shortly carrying a simple length of black cloth with an unsteadily sewn facial panel.

"Part of the trade is the secret," I said. "Tell nobody that I left." We swapped burkas, and she bowed several times.

The tattered burka was like a cloak of invisibility. On the Cylay streets, I was a slight and hesitant shadow with no fear for my security even from beggars. I walked to the plaza expecting to find a teeming bazaar after the siesta hour had passed. The place was deserted except for two couples, a young soldier with his veiled girlfriend and a Putuki man in a business suit with his painted, and most likely paid, escort.

I strolled past the mansion's gate and cautiously peered into the yard. Two guards were standing at their posts, nothing more. The outer wall extended for two city blocks, and I traversed the white sidewalk thinking what a comical figure I presented, a shadow without substance.

I turned the corner and ambled up a narrower street lined with high acacias. Within a few steps, the limestone wall became red brick topped with barbed wire. Shriveled razor grass lined its base. Presently, I came to a narrow gate where I lingered, embarrassed by my fascination with Rabbenu Ely's home.

Set back from the street, the building's bay windows were illuminated by desk lamps spilling amber light onto the dry lawn. At the base of a well-tended mida tree, as if constructed with its back to the picturesque home, stood a rounded hut built in Mekucoo fashion. I took it for a guards' latrine but then saw wisps of smoke hovering under the thatch. What could its purpose be? While I was staring, a woman dressed Arrivi but without a burka carried a bucket of water toward the dwelling, her steps crunching the closely chopped savannah grass.

"Marcy?" I whispered. She did not turn.

"Marcy," I called out. "It's me, Brianna." I pulled off the concealing burka. "Brianna Miller of Arim!"

She set down the bucket and approached the gate hesitantly. Tears stood in her eyes. She looked up the street, undid the bar of the lock, and pushed open the gate.

"I have just disembarked," I said. "I'm having a look around."

She put a finger to her lips and locked the gate. She led me into the hut while still carrying the bucket. A simple cooking fire burned on one side, and a pallet was laid out on the ground. Gourds and a grinding stone were stowed along the wall. Marcy lived here.

We sat cross-legged on straw mats as she lit a tallow. In the flickering light, I realized my suspicions were true. Marcy's soulful eyes were both bloodshot and yellow, resembling broken egg embryos. She was suffering from hepatitis, a curable disease. It was curable, I wanted to shout. But not perhaps in her advanced state.

"I know what you think," she said in Arrivi. "The set-aside wife, why don't I leave?" She shrugged. "Who would mind Ely's diet, huh? Who would see that his pillowcase was freshly scented, huh? Who would trim his kari root and bring orchids to freshen his room?"

She offered steaming tea in a chipped mug. "You did not know Ely when he was young," she said just above a whisper. "His reputation grew while he was a teacher and accepting Lucy's kids into his classroom." She leaned forward. "Which was Karima Le's backyard."

She sat straight-backed, full of dignity, with square shoulders and her legs folded under her. "Ely wanted to end the fighting and build for the future. It was correct that my husband should be rabbenu. He stopped uranium mining and returned the sufferstone to the ground. He secured property deeds and the system of welfare ministers. The acts of Ely were right and good for the times. A man of his time, entitled to enjoy the trappings of his station."

She glanced into my tea mug; a guest must not go thirsty.

"Rabbenu Ely saw that for this larger Borabean struggle," she continued, "with their offworld partners. . . . He saw that a larger treasury was needed. The Arrivi council approved tithe collection and grain storage. They approved the securities exchange where they now amass their paper fortunes. Welfare ministers, many of them gouleps, were sent out. Ely cleaned house of petty graft and the abuse of women. No woman has been flogged in the time of Ely."

She nodded, proud of this accomplishment.

Her listing of brave deeds was not for me, not really for me. It may have slipped Marcy's mind that I was once beaten by the hand of Rabbenu Ely in front of tribal leaders. "This struggle has changed many," she added. "Did you know Borabean children carry their own death shrouds in their packs onto the battlefield?"

"I heard that," I barely whispered.

She looked up, blinking back tears, tortured by her personal demons. "When so many have died, life becomes cheap. Ely is no longer with the people. He is no longer for the people." She met my gaze and confided, "Ely tells himself that he acts in the name of the people who cannot act for themselves. Do you know a Mekucoo who cannot act for herself?"

She smiled sadly. Her attempt at humor pressed my heartstone. "Many here," she gestured, perhaps indicating Cylay, "have no education, no family, and no ties to the land."

"You grew up without these ties," I said. "Have you done so badly?"

For a long moment, Marcy looked into my face. Perhaps she remembered the day she had mouthed those same words to me. Tears spilled onto her cheeks. I set down gently the mug and stood. I held a palm high to signify on her. "Our ancestors' reputations are greatly enlarged by the goodly acts of rabbenu's wife Marcy."

She quickly wiped her cheeks and rose to stand tall. We left the hut together. I looked up and caught my breath. Dolvia's two moons were hovering together, so close I felt I could almost touch them. It was as though Nettom and Nettki had dropped by to commune with us. For the first time I felt acknowledged, that I was home.

"I can get some medicine," I said.

"It is no matter now. I was only waiting."

"Waiting for what?"

"For the return of Brianna Miller, the new Rularim."

"Ha!" I said. "Put your faith in Hakulupe Le or in Kat."

"Lupe is the wife of a barracks officer, and Kat belongs to the land. You are the one, the daughter of Klistina Le of Arim and Kyle Rula's beloved Brian Miller."

"I always suspected that."

"Kyle Le was good with secrets."

I pulled the black burka over my head.

"I can call the soldiers to escort you back," she said.

"It is not necessary." I looked up through the facial panel and indicated the moons. "I have Dolvia's embrace."

Marcy accompanied me to the gate and loitered there while I walked away.

When I returned to the hotel, I saw Rufus standing by the entrance, his belt knife prominent. Just as a test, I walked past him and turned back. He had not noticed me even though he ached forward to find me. Wearing the burka, I was invisible to my cousin and traveling companion. "It's alright, Rufus," I whispered in English. "I'm here now."

He looked at me sharply but then sighed.

"Were you just composing your explanation to Dacupitte regarding my disappearance?" I asked with humor.

He grabbed my upper arm and led me into the lobby. "Enough of Cylay," he instructed in succinct Mekucoo. "We leave at first light."

I pulled away. Even under the veil, I was my own woman.

In the men's lounge off the lobby, a comtech broadcasted Company-sanctioned news. I heard the female commentator's voice and caught a glimpse of Rabbenu Ely's image on the screen. I went to the doorway but hung back there. Only three men sat in the room, and two were reading, yet I could not bring myself to enter where I was not welcome.

The large and colorful screen flashed an image of Rabbenu Ely, heavier and perhaps darker in complexion than I remembered, sitting at a platform table with his Putuki ministers behind him. A Borabean official sitting at his side mirrored his posture. They each signed copies of the armistice, after which they stood and exchanged documents while shaking hands. Tuang Cho stood between them with his arms held out graciously at his sides. The ground-born politicians turned to the camera and continued shaking hands.

My heart pulled down in my chest. I thought about General Hartley's map and the argument of geography. I walked toward the staircase, wondering why my heart grieved only while in the company of my Arrivi cousins.

Rufus watched me drag my shadowy self up the stairs, and then he left.

SEVEN

WE EXITED THE HOTEL AT FIRST LIGHT TO BOARD THE TRAIN. IN Paris at that time of day, the city was quiet and dozing with only produce deliveries stirring in the streets. On Arrivi family farms, the men and women and their children were well into the day's work.

I wore the sky-blue Arrivi skirt and burka, and my luggage was brought along by hotel porters. Arrivi businessmen who sought a moment of Kyros Rabbe Sudl's time—he was a wormhole traveler and HGEAM user, after all—had also purchased tickets for this ride. Several silent Mekucoo warriors were on hand. Curious souk women on their way to open shop in the local bazaar detoured from their route to follow us down the street.

While we waited in the train terminal, a veiled homeless woman, stinking of olive oil and body odor, sidled up to me. "Tell your fortune?" she asked, exposing a dirty, bony hand from under the folds of her burka. "I have second sight. I can see your future."

The warriors reached to grab her arms and pull her away. "Three in ten are meant to die," she called out as they hustled her toward the door. "Three in ten are married to life. Three in ten love life but embrace death and thereby tip the balance." The warriors forced her outside and returned to their places.

I glimpsed a young girl, an academy student traveling alone under the veil, sitting patiently in her train seat near the common car window and holding an old volume away from her gauzy facial panel to read the print. My heart contracted. Her whole life was ahead of her, and already she was compromised by studies not of her culture.

We boarded the private car, and right away Kyros rabbe Sudl sat near the entrance and began hearing a string of petitions from Arrivi. Under the veil and seated at the car's distant end, I waved away the Putuki steward and stared out the window much like the young student had. This car had bench seats and windows that passengers could adjust. We felt the jerk and rolling start. I glimpsed the Mekucoo warriors who had formed a perimeter for our promenade. They were leaving the terminal, headed in various directions.

The train cleared the station and left Cylay behind, steaming along tracks constructed on an earthen levee with frequent viaducts to ensure year-round travel, even during the heaviest rains. And there was the savannah; rolling dunes and red sandstone outcroppings with hearty oleastra and acacia still showing lush green. I saw endless sky the same color as my burka. I was, finally, within Dolvia's embrace.

From under the veil, I searched my pack and grabbed a clothbound blank book in which I had intended to record my impressions while traveling. The first page held a list of needs; most had been met. A few questions were scribbled next. Will we be allowed to disembark? Will I survive without netta? What about Pete?

There were four used pages and nothing more. I was no writer.

The train lurched, jolting me from my reverie. I grabbed the armrests as we came to a halt there on the open savannah. Immediately, the compartment door was flung open, and Rufus showed his face. "You will come." Kyros quickly stowed the petition papers and left. Rufus made an impatient beckoning gesture. I followed him to the door and peered out at the sunlit plain.

The savannah was empty in all directions except for a rusty lorry sputtering and spewing exhaust fumes. Rufus and Kyros stood on the sandy trackside, ready to help me step down. "We don't need these elaborate precautions," I complained from under the veil. "We have safe conduct with the armistice that Ely signed."

"The Borabean word for safe is target," Kyros said.

"You don't expect me to walk cross-country?"

"Arrivi women make their living standing upright," Rufus said.

"But my luggage, my—"

"You will come."

I sighed. "May I get a few personal items?"

He and Kyros each gazed out at the horizon. This female request would be tolerated.

In the train compartment, I quickly swallowed an acclimation pill and grabbed my pack. At the compartment door, Kyros reached to guide my veiled steps as I set foot onto Dolvia's savannah. The train whistle blew. The line of boxcars and passenger cars immediately lurched forward, and all comfort steamed away. I removed and folded the burka.

Rufus rode in the back of the lorry next to a fuel-filled industrial drum. I was crowded into the middle front seat between Kyros and a Cylahi driver who wore a severed human finger dangling on a beaded necklace. We headed toward Southeast Arrivi and Kyros rabbe Sudl's home, bouncing along for hours without the benefit of roads.

We stopped three times for the driver to fill the radiator and allow the engine to cool. Once the lorry would not restart, so he jiggled the wires under the dash and tried again. Nothing, just a grinding noise. He fashioned some tinfoil around a foreign-made cigarette for a makeshift fuse, which actually worked. The engine roared, and the exhaust pipe spewed black fumes, so we piled in and resumed our journey. I was surprised at how quickly I had come to consider the old lorry as a lifesaver.

During the siesta hour, Kyros and I languished under a rickety lean-to and drank murky tea. Rufus and the driver preferred to stand in the blazing sun near the lorry. Each rubbed aloe grease on his arms and chest. Rufus added some grease to his straight black hair, causing it to gleam in the sunlight.

I asked Kyros about the driver's finger trophy. "It's Siibabean and ... aging. He claims the prize makes him invisible in battle. Some woman told him that as his prowess disappeared into her."

We approached Southeast Arrivi just as the overheated air shimmered as high as the clouds, lending every vista a gauzy bluish effect. We bypassed lush rice paddies tended by unveiled Arrivi women with their long hair braided down their backs and their skirts tied up into pantaloons. "Rice crops have been plentiful?" I asked Kyros after I had again gotten under the burka.

"Don't care for rice myself," he said. "The women grow fat and lazy from it."

Isolated from association with other families, Southeast Arrivi were inwardly focused. Ritual must be satisfied with the return of Kyros Rabbe Sudl. A communal fire was set in the dusty yard, and we gathered in a circle with the men on the right and the veiled women on the left. I was allowed to stand with those in leadership along with my escort. The elders bowed to me, and I removed my burka within the community, being a wormhole traveler and sister of Arim. Rufus disapproved; there was no need to look his way to know that.

One rabbenu offered me a tattered pad on which were marked several pages of slashes with a tally number at the bottom. "What is this?" I asked Kyros.

"The census. He has believed it's part of ritual since the time you visited with Dacupitte and Sheeks-Cylom."

"You mean from the vaccine task? That was fifteen years ago."

"You must thank him," Rufus whispered in English.

I bowed and tapped the pad, holding it high like a war trophy. The people cheered; the women indulged in loud and long clucking. We sat near the leader's place for a communal meal. While we accepted the rice dishes with gracious bows, I asked Rufus, "This rabbenu does not read. There's no academy here?"

"They live too close to Gora land. Warriors cannot guarantee the safety of convent ministers to serve as teachers."

"Says who?"

"By Dacupitte's word."

"We can fix that right now." I stood and entered the firelight.

Rufus quickly followed, unhappy with my abrupt move. He grabbed my arm. "You would counter the word of Dacupitte?"

I pulled away from him. "You cannot have it both ways, Rufus. Either I am Dacupitte's woman, or I am not. Which is it?"

His jaw worked in a way that told me he was grinding his teeth. His gaze went past the waiting residents as his eyes sought the horizon. "You are Dacupitte's woman."

I gestured that Kyros rabbe Sudl should come forward for the ritual blessing. Rufus stood with feet wide apart and hand on his belt knife while I slowly strutted around the center fire with Kyros. The jubilant people raised a loud cheer, with clucking from under the many burkas. We stopped near Rufus. "This one you know as Kyros rabbe Sudl," I pronounced loudly in Arrivi, "has greatly served Arrivi while we traveled among Softcheeks tribes. In many lands with many important leaders, the reputations of your ancestors were greatly enlarged by the goodly acts of Kyros rabbe Sudl."

The people cheered and chanted while slapping their legs. There was loud and rhythmic clucking. They were ready for celebration and dancing. I held up a hand, and they grew quiet. "As part of Kyros rabbe Sudl's reward for his great service, an endowment is made from the treasure of Kyle Rula." Some audibly drew in their breath. Kyros stared at me. "An academy will be established here in, uh . . . in a location to be named later."

The people cheered. Dancing broke out. The rabbenu graciously bowed to me.

I held up a hand again, and they fell silent. Well, with some murmuring. "We know from experience the academy works best when managed by village mothers. We need an administrator who—"

A large woman immediately came forward. Kyros spoke harshly to her and pushed her shoulder, but she pushed him back. She pulled off her burka and dropped it to the ground, defiantly standing at his side. She was his equal.

"Who is this?" I asked.

Kyros hung his head. "Bibi Le, my wife."

In all his stories of his genealogy that had filled our idle evenings while traveling, Kyros had not mentioned this woman. I thought my idea was fit punishment. I led her forward. "This one Bibi Le will keep the count and manage the funds," I called out in Arrivi.

The people stood and cheered. I stepped back with Rufus and watched as the tribespeople came to Kyros and Bibi Le with bows and backslaps. During the commotion, a couple of young girls, too young to tolerate the veil, stood at Bibi Le's side. Kyros led two slightly older boys to Rufus for the warrior's greeting. Bibi Le had given Kyros four children. I later learned the boys' names were Kristos and Karry.

Rufus removed his arm amulet and stripped away the binding cord. He handed the glassy topaz to Kristos, the older boy. Kyros removed his amulet and handed the smaller stone to Karry. The warriors' time of mourning had passed. Rufus saw me watching and nodded grudgingly.

Two more youths approached with ingratiating gestures. I eventually recognized them as Saed and Ankos from the clutch of Cleo, already tan and barefoot, wearing uniforms from the clutch of Murd.

"Melinga, Rularim," Ankos said.

I excused his poor protocol and shook their hands western style. "Kyros will take you underwing now. You can help with the construction of the classroom building."

"Thank you," Saed said. "Thanks for this opportunity."

"This is only training," I said sternly. "You will return to Earth as managers for Somule Gems. Set that goal in your mind."

"Yes, Rularim," Ankos said. I was worried about his chances of success.

After much dancing and storytelling, we were led into a long adobe building that served as a dormitory. I was assigned the last cot, the most private. I showed the open palm gesture to the unveiled rabbenu's wife who watched me with humor. Before we settled in, another woman started an animated conversation with her in Arrivi. What made them assume I did not understand their words? She wanted me to heal her daughter who had leg sores. Rabbenu's wife said I was too tired to provide miracles. I sighed and approached them.

"I'm no healer," I explained in Arrivi. "What does she have?"

"She is lazy," rabbenu's wife said.

Behind her burka, the worried mother averted her eyes in shame. "Will you come?"

"I can promise nothing."

"Please, just come."

We walked through the now quiet village to a small family home. I ducked under the red tile overhang and entered the adobe doorway. On the left, a young girl languished on a pallet under a lovingly decorated Arrivi burka spread over her like a sheet. She had clear olive skin and richly braided hair resting on her shoulder. Her shiny eyes had healthy whites, and her tongue was pink.

"May I?" I asked in Arrivi and pulled back the veil. She was plump with swollen arms, perhaps from attempted native curatives. Her stomach was not distended, and her internal organs were not swollen.

Her mother guiltily moved the veil to reveal her leg sores: five red ulcers each about the size of a coin. I had no answers. Surely this ailment was not the pox, which would have spread to her face and arms; maybe it was impetigo or syphilis. Or her condition could be anthrax from working with goats. "Do you have these…," I tapped my lower abdomen, "down here?"

The girl shook her head no. It was most likely an indigenous disease and contagious.

"Do others suffer?"

"Young girls who labor in the rice fields," rabbenu's wife said. "But the others complete their daily chores," she added for the girl's benefit.

"Sheeks-Cylom should see this," I said. "Can she travel to the clinic?"

"Too lazy," the elder's wife repeated.

"You feel fatigued?" I asked the girl. "And dizzy?" A shameful tear rolled down the side of her face as she nodded. "Probably some memory loss as well. She must see a doctor."

"You can arrange this?" the mother asked. "You can reach Sheeks-Cylom?"

"Perhaps. We can talk again tomorrow."

That night, I had tortured dreams about blood and violent sex. I woke in a cold sweat and immediately became tangled in the mosquito netting over my cot. As I wiped the salty moisture from my brow, a dream image faded from my grasp as quickly as I realized its presence. Something about the gualarep Edwina . . . swimming with Edwina. . . .

I lay back and drifted off without strife.

Early the next morning, I sat with Bibi Le and rabbenu's wife. Our breakfast meeting at a woman's fire near rabbenu's hut—three unveiled women seated cross-legged on the ground—drew a small crowd of staring children and young veiled matrons.

"Convent teachers will arrive soon," I said. "There must be a classroom building provided, and the teachers' needs met. Children of all ages must be encouraged to attend daily from first light until the siesta hour."

Bibi Le stared and nodded, but I was uncertain how much she understood. They were a backward group. I gave Bibi Le the clothbound book I had carried through the wormhole. "You must mark the calendar day and make a slash for each child. The count is yours to make." The principle was the same in each village. Tribal children tolerated classroom hours only when truancy brought family shame.

I made the mistake of using the English word truancy during our talk. "True-and-see?" Bibi Le asked, eager to show she understood the Softcheeks language.

Before I could answer, a transport helicopter entered the village air space and set down near the livestock pen. Southeast Arrivi gathered in a curious circle, probably wondering why so many visitors had arrived all of a sudden. Veiled women whispered and clucked disapprovingly as six Siibabean warriors in tan uniforms and jack boots stepped down and faced them off with blank stares. In truth, Siibabean were supremely healthy and more-than-handsome, tall, and muscled with shimmering black skin and perfect teeth. They were traditional blood enemies, though, from before the Gora clan of Borabean had occupied that exalted position. The Arrivi women were not titillated.

The chopper pilot stepped down and removed his headgear, wearing tan shorts with sandals and no shirt. He reached back to place the helmet on the seat. Pilot privileges were a source of high honor. He was not as tall as his escort and was chocolate-colored with many scars. I heard excited whispers about his obvious leg scar. Karlyhi often added paint to the ugly mark to increase its display.

One mother explained to a veiled girl that it was Karlyhi, he who had herded feral erriv with the gualarep Ralph in the days of Captain Michael Peter Shaw. My throat constricted because I remembered the beating Karlyhi had once given me in the clinic yard. The mother added that Karlyhi was maybe a match of honor for southeast Arrivi.

"He is Cylahi by birth," the woman's daughter objected. "Why should I accept Cylahi?"

Smart girl.

The village rabbenu and Kyros rabbe Sudl stepped forward to greet Karlyhi. Rufus spoke to the Siibabean in their language to diffuse any insult. Kyros brought Karlyhi to me where I stood in the women's group with Bibi Le, beside the rabbenu's wife and the sick girl's veiled mother.

"Hiki, Brianna Miller of Arim," Karlyhi pronounced while showing his palm.

"Hiki, Karlyhi," I said matching his gesture. The elder's wife grinned. I was a constant source of entertainment for her.

"You will come," Karlyhi said indicating the helicopter.

I sighed. "Does every man on the savannah have the right to order me around?"

Karlyhi's dark and implacable face did not change as he considered that. "You may walk, if you prefer."

Rabbenu's wife chuckled. She piqued my sense of competition. "There is one here who must go to the hospital," I said. "You will take her in the chopper and stop at the clinic."

"No room."

"Your praetorian guard can walk back."

He frowned slightly, probably wondering what prae-to-ri-an meant.

I turned to the wide-eyed mother and added, "Bring her."

She just stared. In her experience, women did not talk back to warriors or give orders. I began to regret my generous gesture.

Rabbenu's wife shortly hissed, and the mother hustled away.

Karlyhi and I stared each other down the whole time we waited. Kyros kicked at the sandy yard with one foot, uncertain what was needed for hospitality. Finally, Rufus left for a moment and returned with my pack, handing it to me with a hard stare. The standoff was broken. I donned my burka, and we moved to the chopper.

The Siibabean frowned when they learned that four among them would have to walk back to quarters. They frowned again when three veiled Arrivi took their seats. Rufus joined us in the cramped space and signaled his honorable goodbye, the son of Cyrus the ketiwhelp killer, so the Siibabean felt no loss of face. The chopper lifted off. I looked back to see Kyros facing the bewildered warriors. The women's group dispersed. These visitors were not the same, not to be welcomed the same. The Siibabean turned on their heels and marched out of the village in their signature tight formation and quickstep.

After twenty minutes or so, the helicopter landed on the open savannah. I stepped down and stared through the facial panel in all directions. A sloping rise led to the back side of the Canyon of Buttes. Narrow wadis provided a rigorous passageway offworlders would not discern.

The sick girl made the first gestures of stepping down. "Nu delaya," I called out in Arrivi. "You will ride to the clinic where Sheeks-Cylom will look at your sores."

She looked to her mother for reassurance from under her veil before she settled back into her seat while the remaining Siibabean stepped down. Two helicopter rides, all over the region. It was a big day for her.

Karlyhi's men joined him while he removed his headgear. Another pilot scrambled into the seat. Rufus gave the pilot brief instructions and stepped away as the chopper lifted off. Finally, Rufus and I stood on the sandy dune with only Karlyhi and his captains.

"The Canyon of Buttes?" I asked Karlyhi. "Isn't that sacrilegious?"

He frowned and walked away, probably wondering what sac-ri-le-gious meant. I stowed the burka in my pack and tied up my skirt as pantaloons. We climbed the treacherous wadi walls for more than forty minutes. Although we labored in the shade and with a rushing breeze, the exertion was extreme. Once again, I wondered how difficult it would be to secure a jump back number.

We reached the ridge that overlooked the canyon's interior. Below us, narrow columns of buttes stood in timeless communion, mostly in shadows, while mist swirled at the base of some, indicating the presence of heated netta water. We skidded down the grade and entered a large camp populated mostly by Siibabean with established huts for clustered family areas. I started to pull the veil from my pack.

"Nu delaya," Rufus said. "These are interlopers on Arrivi land. You will not hide."

"Once it was a crime to reveal the canyon's location to Siibabean," I whispered.

"This is a new season."

Several young gualareps were gathered by the stream, my first view of Ralph's progeny since my return. They were similar to oversized monitor lizards, with bowed legs and long snouts and marbled hides. As a teenager, I had spent time on the savannah with one of the original three imported from Cicero. My favorite gualarep, Edwina, had enjoyed swimming in old water pools.

Gualareps were the direct progeny of either Ralph or Brian, all in their first decade, and the males were not ready to breed. It was said they could find each other by scent from three kilometers away. This was a clutch of female reps, perhaps littermates, probably attached to different scout groups and able to throw their thoughts. Softcheeks called the gift remote viewing. Using this method, Karlyhi's forces learned about distant troop movements without the help of technical systems, thus side-stepping Company spies.

The big reptiles waited in an uneven row. We skirted their position when we entered the compound. They scurried back as if spooked. "What is wrong with them?" I asked Rufus.

"I've never seen that before."

Karlyhi lived in a large open tent under maybe twenty-four supporting poles, sporting Siibabean and Cylahi designs. Warriors gathered near the entrance as I approached with Rufus, who kept closer to me than any time before in our journey, his hand on the showy belt knife. That made me uneasy.

Karlyhi stood with his captains and just stared. The others matched his blank expression.

"Look, it has been a long day," I complained. "Perhaps some tea and access to a hay-gee-am." The Siibabean shuffled their feet. "I need to tag Sheeks-Cylom at the clinic with a report on the girl's symptoms."

Karlyhi smirked. "Sheeks-Cylom is at the Uburu digs."

"Then your chopper is headed to the wrong place."

Rufus looked at Karlyhi, who shrugged. "The son of Cyrus," Karlyhi said, "directed them to Sheeks-Cylom's location. And we don't send email from here. That only invites Company spying."

Karlyhi turned and went inside.

While we were following, Rufus whispered, "It's good to get your facts straight."

We entered a large area under the tent where Karlyhi probably held discussions with his captains. A map similar to General Hartley's was stretched between the poles behind the table. When we approached, the gathered Siibabean warriors stopped talking before they slowly filed out, each showing a cynical face. Rufus and

I joined Karlyhi at the rough-hewn table where olives were set out in a wooden bowl.

We had been childhood friends, we three. Well, maybe not friends. We were each a product of Hakulupe Le's academy. But now, all this time later, what was there to say? "So, what about Joey Osborn?" I asked, referring to the videotaped execution.

"I don't need permission to rob the desert of that one," Karlyhi said.

Rufus chuckled, showing his teeth.

"We must all work within the group," I said.

"And you see that?" Rufus asked, emphasizing the word see.

It was Karlyhi's turn to laugh. He pushed back his chair. "Come sit here," he said, indicating his lap, "and tell me about it."

"Don't you have enough women?"

"Not Dacupitte's woman."

"Only you two see me that way."

"I see a Company whore," Karlyhi said. "The daughter of a Company whore." This felt the same as when we had been students in Sheeks-Cylom's clinic yard.

"Then why do you ask me to perform a favor?"

"Isn't that your function?"

"I inherited the treasure of Kyle Rula. What do I need from you?"

"To learn where the treasure resides perhaps," Karlyhi said, winking at Rufus.

"Satisfy yourself on another," I said.

Karlyhi shrugged. "On many others."

We began the report then, using English. I told them about the dinner with Steve Swanweil and what was on General Hartley's mind, as well as my encounter with Patrick Osborn. I didn't mention the offworld interest in silicide or my need to find a replacement for Somule Gems management since among warriors strategy was not my area.

"What is troubling the gualareps?" Rufus asked later.

"The cohort has been jumpy for days," Karlyhi said. "Nobody has the answer. Perhaps they grow bored with the lull in the fighting."

"I need to journey to the fortress," I said.

"You sent the chopper away," Karlyhi returned in his biting manner.

"Just the same."

For some time, a woman had been watching us from a respectful distance. She was a person of some importance I felt, at least in the camp. Karlyhi signaled that she should come forward. Two Siibabean entered with her. "Meet Omiibuk," Karlyhi said in Arrivi.

Her looks would have brought considerable repeat business to my Paris club: clever and, frankly, sensual. She embodied the best Siibabean qualities—lean and dark with perfect teeth. Several tight braids rested on her shoulders, and her uniform sported a Softcheeks-purchased sheathed belt knife.

"Brianna Miller of Arim," he told the woman in Arrivi. "My childhood sweetheart."

Karlyhi and Rufus grinned. Omiibuk was the favorite, I surmised.

"I put you under Omiibuk's protection," Karlyhi said to me, still grinning. "She will guide you to the fortress."

"She will murder me from jealousy," I complained in English. Omiibuk's gaze never left my face.

Karlyhi shrugged. "Then she won't be allowed to return here."

"That will be a comfort to me at my funeral pyre."

Karlyhi and Rufus laughed, showing their teeth. This was great sport.

"Your lesser mistresses," I claimed in Arrivi that she understood, "will murder her to gain her place and kill me to silence the witness."

Karlyhi indicated the tribesmen. "These are her brothers."

Omiibuk spoke a long stream of Siibabean words angrily. My language skills were rusty, but her concern was something about how they could even know I was Brianna. I could be a Company plant, a witch, or even—

"When entering the savannah—" I spoke out in Arrivi, hoping my accent did not rob the words of their meaning. She fell silent. "When entering the savannah," I said in a calmer voice, "look over your shoulder often, for that will be your view during your triumphant return."

The Siibabean brothers laughed, and Omiibuk smirked grudgingly. My words were a Siibabean saying from when they had struggled against Mekucoo and Arrivi, from the time of Cyrus. The surprise counted for more than the weighty sentiment.

Rufus's gaze was clear. It could have been approval; one never knew with him.

"At the fortress of Arim, there's a certain medallion," I added, "given to Kyle Rula by the holy woman Oriika. It will be yours, Omiibuk, if I arrive there without incident."

"The treasure is at the convent," Rufus corrected in English.

"Who moved it there?"

"Who can get past the gualareps?" We both knew only Karlyhi commanded the reptiles' loyalty. "It's good to get your facts straight," Rufus repeated. The approval had vanished.

Omiibuk focused on the matter at hand. "I could kill you and take the medallion and more," she claimed in Siibabean.

"But then you cannot wear it with honor," I returned in Arrivi. "It was Oriika's."

Her eyes went into slits, as did her brothers' eyes. I took that for tribal greed. They wanted the gold but also the honor. What began as a taunt from Karlyhi had been turned on its ear. Omiibuk was now something more than a favorite mistress. She would travel with Arrivi leaders, maybe even retain status when abandoned by Karlyhi as the favorite. I was more than the prodigal sister of Arim, heiress of the flats, the fortress, and the treasure of Kyle Rula. I knew when to proffer gifts from the largesse.

Karlyhi showed me that implacable face. "Now do you feel safe?"

"Now I feel properly escorted."

EIGHT

THE CROSS-COUNTRY WALK TOOK MORE THAN TWO DAYS. WERE it not for this Softcheeks trailing behind, Omiibuk and her brothers would have taken up the Siibabean quick march. They stopped often and carried a quantity of water, all the while spying on me with disdain.

I constantly wore the burka.

The savannah had benefitted from a long season of abundant netta, so I had difficulty imagining the expanse as a desert. Acacias were verdant, and tamarinds bloomed, and succulents sent out networks of roots. Oleastra was everywhere, so laden with fruit that a native could survive for a season by foraging only.

We crossed a road; that was something. Two lanes of crenellated laterite stretched out north and south with no apparent reason and no traffic. Singing above were high tension wires strung between rickety transformer towers shaped like rich Putuki women, or so the brothers of Omiibuk claimed. They were named Siize and Siiloba.

Rufus was at home on the savannah; it was written all over him. He carried the karkar and his ammunition pack with ease and wore only the Mekucoo leather leggings. His too-white skin was slathered with aloe paste, and his straight hair was bound in a warrior's tail. His task to return the manager of Somule Gems was nearly complete, so his thoughts turned to duty and the companionship of warriors.

We passed a woman walking at a steady pace, her tent-like burka gritty, and a gualarep lumbering alongside. Maybe it was Sarah or Lupe, or even Kecouroo. I strained to see her face through my facial panel. But no, she was a person unknown to me. This minister only nodded our way and glanced at her gualarep as if sharing something. I felt jealous of her sure-footed gait and her far gaze to the horizon, a life I could have embraced except for my travels.

We stopped at the savannah convent, the original one constructed over a pool of cavern water, made of red brick with arched doorways and windows. A shoulder-high stonewall encircled a yard that held manicured rows of oleastra bushes. Refusing entreaty to bathe and take some refreshment, Rufus lingered with Omiibuk and her brothers outside the gate. In the view of the brothers, being a devout Lutheran was most likely contagious.

My visit was to last only through the siesta hour, so the unveiled residents, largely Putuki women dressed Arrivi, came forward with murmured greetings. "Melinga to the sister of Arim," they said. "Melinga."

I had met the turnkey Sarah as a released sweatshop worker some time ago during a journey I once undertook to the Canyon of Buttes. While living in Paris, I had conducted business with her through the Somule Gems contracts. A competent manager, self-deprecating to the extreme, Sarah oversaw the stores of gum arabic collected by residents and barrels of olive oil being aged in the convent's cellars. Today she was calm and calming, her liquid gaze fathomless.

"Except in Cylay, the burka is not worn within convent walls," she said.

I pulled off the veil, revealing my hair matted against moist skin. "These women cannot all be rejected by their families," I said, indicating the crowd of residents.

"Most are students or forced off family farms by the fighting. They grow oleastra for the export of its very fine oil to Paris." She led me to the sanctuary with the others trailing behind, passing under a lintel where the words chiseled in the stonework read "Hagia Sophia." Sarah turned to the students, towering over them by inches. "Please, a moment's peace for Brianna."

As they reluctantly stepped back, we two entered a high and clean room with many rows of wooden benches. In front was an altar with a crucifix and the embossed English words "Do This in Remembrance of Me." The students gathered at the open arched windows, staring and blocking the breeze. Sarah and I went to the first row of benches and sat quietly until a young girl carried in tea in two mugs with lids.

"Melinga," I whispered. She showed me an open palm and left. After a couple of sips of the bitter tea, I asked Sarah, "Do you pray to Dolvia or to Jesus?"

"To God the Father."

I tried to control the cynicism in my voice. "And does he answer?"

Sarah looked around as if to indicate all that had been provided. "This convent," I countered, "was gained through the largesse of Kyle Rula and the suffering of gouleps."

Sarah nodded slightly. "And Brianna Miller who brought us out of bondage."

"You have not repeated that to anybody, I hope."

Sarah only sipped her tea. I glimpsed the blue scars on her wrists from when she had been bound at her sweatshop workstation thirteen years before. I imagined there were similar scars on her ankles, plus many more. I sighed and looked into the teacup. Christian principles of frugality and generosity had served these women whose men preferred a foreign fight under Karlyhi's command or profiteering through cronyism with Rabbenu Ely. Who was I to argue with the duality of Sarah's faith?

"Where are the gualareps?" I asked.

"You don't know? Edwina put a ban on remote viewing. She believes you have returned from the dead."

"What?"

"You were absent from her dreamscape, and now you have returned." She considered my nonplused look. "You have arisen. Kyle Rula sacrificed her life as a substitute so you could return."

"Well, did you reason with Edwina?"

"I don't spend much time arguing with gualareps." We chuckled together.

"Sarah," I said, "I have a task; I am not certain for which convent group. I promised Southeast Arrivi an academy. Some should go in advance and direct construction of a classroom building. Ask for the one Bibi Le."

She blinked twice. "It will be accomplished as you say."

"Go soon so my promise doesn't seem like, um, empty grand-standing."

"We can provide fresh clothes if you would like, plus water to bathe."

"Yes, I would very much like that."

While Rufus and the Siibabean waited stoically, I took an extra hour and visited a convent classroom where children of all tribes were surrounded by books and maps and EAM screens. I saw a big globe map of Earth but not one of Dolvia. Many giggling and eager children had rust-colored hair, descendants of Dacupitte, my sup-posed betrothed.

"What is America like? Tell us about America."

"America is clean with many varieties of weather and big parks. In America, the whole savannah would be a wildlife preserve."

"Then where do the people live?"

"In glass houses, just like in the photos."

"Did you set foot on the land of Miller?"

"Yes, I visited Mon-tan-na and Brian Miller's family. His parents have passed on, as it is said there. His sister is a grandmother."

"Are the children of Miller redheaded?"

"Red hair comes from Heather Osborn. But I also visited the land of Osborn and the land of Nordhagen."

"Do they preserve wildlife?" one freckled, Irish-looking girl asked.

"Mostly they have crops and raise livestock, the same as Dolvi-ets. In Ireland, they grow potatoes, a tuber like taro. In Scotland, they herd sheep."

"What is sheep?"

"A sheep is a short-legged and furry heifer that gives no milk."

"Sheep would die here."

"Yes, the land of Nordhagen is very cold. Also, the days are short."

"No wonder Dacupitte's father preferred to serve in Westend."

"You know Westend?"

"We have a map." I wondered at these schoolchildren who had never seen sheep but who accepted a star map as mundane.

The girls from the clutch of Cleo waited outside the doorway. They had grown rosy and healthy, already taller than I remembered, as if some playful god had stretched their bones without changing their girlish faces. I enjoyed hugs and chatter before taking Leah aside.

"How are they doing? Any surprises?"

"Cleo talks in Arrivi now, when she talks," Leah said brightly. "The conscript girls sleep separately but take lessons with us. How long can you stay?"

"My escort waits at the gate." I saw her face fall with disappointment. "I promised the clutch future work, not adoption. You must get close to Sarah and Hakulupe Le."

"I understand," Leah murmured.

"What do you think of our gualareps?"

"We're slated for lessons with them tomorrow. I'm certain it will be . . . exciting."

I chuckled. I had seen this hesitancy before. "Well, bonding with one is not needed since you'll jump back to Earth one day soon. Soon enough."

I spent several minutes with Camille asking about her unsavory habits. She only shrugged. "Women here have so little." I had to assume she meant nothing of value to steal.

I noted that Cleo was attached to Bernice and with a desperate stare at close events. I thought I would ask Sarah to separate them, but that could be for another visit. I walked with Sarah and the teachers out toward the stone wall. "There is little in place for class-rooms," I said to Sarah, "in the southeast village, I fear."

"It is no matter," Sarah said. "The first teaching task is to make adobe bricks and build straight walls, their introduction to the value of mathematics and new tribal chants."

Near us, the students and teachers giggled and whispered. Rufus stood with Omiibuk and her brothers outside the nearby gate. He glanced over his shoulder and frowned. The young women ducked behind the oleastra bushes and giggled again.

"Rufus could enjoy the privileges of Dacupitte if he wanted," Sarah said.

"The only one who will know Rufus that way," I said, "is the one who sees his aura."

"Do you see that?"

"We're cousins."

Her liquid gaze was pinned on me. "Do you?"

"I am mixed blood, not reinforced by his ancestors."

"Then what do you see?"

"Nothing. It just seemed like the right thing to say at the time."

"We don't shrug off these visions."

"Please, you have enlarged my reputation enough." I leaned forward and whispered, "After all, I am risen from the dead."

Sarah smiled. "At the sacrifice of Kyle Rula."

I got under the burka and was led to my Siibabean escort.

Omiibuk and I were not friends, but she respected my, well, my determination if not my stamina. On the third day, we skirted south of Somule and saw the hotel towers reflecting the morning sun; that is, looking over our shoulders as Siibabean were wont to do.

The late morning sun was beating down with insistent energy when we arrived at the flats of Arim. Lime green and salmon-colored geyscrites formed majestic cathedral walls. Old water gurgled through subterranean passages, creating springs with orange and lavender sediment, much of it heated and poisonous. Mineral pools reflected the sky in crystal clear detail.

I rested again, having reached the limits of my strength. Rufus sauntered ahead with Siize and Siiloba. Omiibuk lingered with me, preparing herself to receive the gold medallion prize. So I rose and adjusted the voluminous veil, preparing to walk the last stretch together. We came upon a boulder situated in the middle of the flats, once designated as a mercy seat for those with a message for Kyle Rula, except now a sculpture of the four sisters was erected there. Chiseled in rabbenu limestone, biscuit-colored with rosy veins throughout, the large artwork depicted a life-size statue of Karima Le walking behind with a sure-footed stride, her arms spread as though gathering the others under her protection. Katelupe Le, the renowned martyr featured in many tribal chants, walked on one side wearing a man's clothing and with a ketiwhelp easily pacing beside her. On the other side walked Kyle Rula carrying a large book, the veil draped over her arm trailing behind. And demurely seated in the foreground as though she impeded their progress was Klistina Le, gazing out with question and hunger.

"Do you know these women?" Omiibuk asked.

I indicated Klistina Le. "This one was my mother—although she died when I was six. Katelupe Le was already martyred in the Company prison. I was raised by Karima Le, the oldest."

"And the other is Rularim? Such a monument belongs in the Cylay plaza."

"It seems to draw some traffic here." Orchid branches had been lovingly laid at Kyle Rula's feet; also several bowl tallows burned there.

We walked around the towering artwork and found at Katelupe Le's feet a length of knotted rope and several glassy stones. "This one is the ideal," Omiibuk said. "Her name and Kecouroo's reside in Siibabean chants."

"Kecouroo?"

"A great enemy, the Mekucoo."

"A better ally."

We arrived at the fortress entrance before the siesta hour. A small and mean cave dug into the escarpment wall, the residence of Rularim was nondescript. Rufus joined us near the opening. "You have been inside?" I asked.

"My mother's house."

"I did not mean to imply—" I said. "I was just wondering. . . . Some tea perhaps?"

"You will bring the medallion now," Omiibuk said. I was still trying to figure how to tell her the reward was at the Somule convent because I had forgotten to ask for it.

Rufus watched me without expression. No help there.

Omiibuk's brothers stared left and signaled her, so we all strained to see a tall Mekucoo woman and a waddling gualarep crossing the flats. Still slender with closely chopped nappy hair, Kecouroo was dressed in a form-revealing one-piece leather garment with a gold and topaz jewelry. A necklace of a series of tektite stones bound with a leather strap was prominent on her bodice, and a finely tooled pouch rested on her hip. The male rep with her must have been Brian.

My experience with Brian was from when I lived on Cicero with Dr. Beecham and the Shaws, Mike Shaw being a colonel then. I had seen Brian once at the zoo and had shared dreams, intermittently, for less than six weeks before jumping back. His dreamscape did not extend into the wormhole.

Kecouroo stopped maybe twenty paces away, looked down at the gualarep and gave some signal. Brian waddled toward the fortress entrance. Kecouroo nodded to the Siibabean siblings and joined me where I waited under the veil with Rufus. Siize and Siiloba honored her with their silence.

"Have you entered the fortress?" she asked in Arrivi as I removed the burka and folded its draping material.

"We just now arrived."

"Putting it off, huh?"

I felt that Kecouroo could see right through me. "No, no. We were . . . I mean, I was—"

She glanced at the waiting escort. "I have brought the needed item."

"You brought the medallion?" I stared at her face. "But how could you know?"

"Brian said that you made a promise to this one," she said, indicating Omiibuk. "That is why we came."

"Brian has words?"

"Words are for the young. Brian has pictures."

"But I thought he only—"

"Enough of this," Omiibuk said in Arrivi. We had skirted the edge of her patience. "Where is my reward?"

Kecouroo drew a heavy gold chain from her pouch and extended it toward me, but I chose to step back a fraction. "She would more highly prize the gift from your hand," I said. "Trust me on this."

Kecouroo thought about it for a moment, her face blank with wonder, before she turned to the others. "Step forward, Omiibuk," she pronounced in Arrivi. "daughter of Sergio and future mother to Karlyhi's son."

Omiibuk liked the sound of that. And, of course, I should have guessed Kecouroo would know her family lineage. With great dignity, Omiibuk knelt before Kecouroo and bowed her head. "It's not necessary to kneel," Kecouroo objected, but Omiibuk did not move.

The brothers and Rufus waited.

Kecouroo looked over at me.

I only shrugged.

Kecouroo held up the long chain. "This medallion belonged to Oriika, holy woman to Arrivi, and was bequeathed to Kyle Rula during the wedding feast of Haku rabbe Murd and Karima Le. Kyle Rula treasured the medallion especially because it had been Oriika's." She placed the chain over the kneeling woman's head. "Let it be known the gold medallion is bequeathed by Brianna Miller of Arim to Omiibuk of Siibabean."

Omiibuk stood and inspected her prize, turning to her brothers who nodded proudly. "The name Kecouroo," Omiibuk claimed, "daughter of Cyrus, is long resident in Siibabean chants."

Kecouroo only nodded while the brothers signified on Rufus, who surprised me when he held a karkar over his head and called out, "Hai."

"Hai," each brother said. The siblings turned on their heels, their task complete, and marched away in the Siibabean quick-step. Omiibuk grasped the bouncing medallion. They would arrive at the Canyon of Buttes within two days.

"There's news you must know," Kecouroo immediately said to me.

"Please, some tea and a siesta?"

"Naturally, but first you must greet this one." We approached the fortress entrance where Brian waited. "Let him know that you remember him."

"Hello, Brian," I murmured and held out one hand. "Remember me? I am Brianna. Brianna Mil—"

"Ka," the big reptile said. I jerked back.

"Use pictures," Kecouroo said.

"Ah, I was never any good at this."

"Just remember the truth about Cicero and the zoo. He can pick it up."

I hated remote viewing. I had not used mental pictures for years and had never excelled at the discipline. Brian waited, his fleshy tongue flashing at casual intervals, so I sighed and closed my eyes. I remembered I had been upset that day on Cicero when I was eighteen. Mike Shaw had just told me the truth about how the gualarep Ralph was murdered. A Softcheeks doctor had shot Ralph, then skinned him and roasted a section of his flank at the butchering campsite. But that was another story. Dr. Mitterand had invited me that same day for an outing to the zoo. While he had been talking with some other visitors about the tribal conflict, I had wandered down the corridor and seen the caged gualarep. I had sat on the floor and sent him mental pictures once shared with Ralph, pictures of hunting flamingo in the billabong.

Suddenly, standing there with Kecouroo and Rufus, my mind filled with a rush of images. Brian was telling me the same story, only from his point of view. How he had languished in the rank stagnant water, his mind adrift. How he had watched a young girl with olive skin settle across from his cage and put her head between her knees. He had received images of clamping down on a flamingo while hundreds more took to wing in a barrage of pink and white.

"Ka!" Brian said. "Ka, ka, ka, ka." He sent pictures of his handlers moving him into the zoo clinic, then to a truck, then onto the shuttle. How he was cautioned, by way of my dream images, about the increase in gravity, followed by a sudden weightlessness. How this Arrivi girl whom he had seen only once in a zoo corridor had eased his fear.

Images of Kyle Rula. The packing crate was being dismantled, and his binding straps removed. On the flats, many stood in a curious circle. But he only saw Kyle Rula, who had been present in his dreams; the one Brianna had given him to see. I received images of Edna and Edwina and swimming and hunting and egg-tending. And finally, there was only Kyle Rula, who shared the savannah and answered his question of why Brianna had vanished from his dreamscape.

"Ka, ka, ka, ka," Brian said. I opened my eyes and looked around. No more than a few moments had passed, but Kecouroo and Rufus were grinning.

I sat cross-legged on the ground so Brian could sidle forward to inspect my arms and face with his large and wet tongue. He stepped across my lap, rubbing me so vigorously with his strong flanks that I was nearly flattened.

"Enough," I called out. "I'm glad to see you too." I struggled to get up and wiped his saliva from my chin. Kecouroo laughed, showing her teeth, and led us into the fortress of Arim.

A blue macaw was still resident there. At the sight of Brian, he flew to a high perch and called "braaadt" in a grating voice. "Guala-reps cannot be here. No reps in the house."

Brian made a short hissing noise.

"Braaadt," the bird complained.

There was an extended room with an eight-foot ceiling. The walls were lined with free-standing bookshelves, most of them stacked with spiral-bound transport library translations. Behind a long table was an enclosed breakfront filled with Earth-printed hardbound volumes with gold-embossed pages, most expensive.

On the side was a separate carved-out living area that included a stove and table for eating, also four cots farther back. Rufus searched through the rough-hewn kitchen cabinets for staples while Kecouroo stoked the stove fire. I wasn't needed for their domestic activities, so I looked over the library book titles, mostly out-of-date technical manuals and botany encyclopedias. I pulled one down and noticed a white crust on my hand; it was birdshit. The manuals were covered all over with poop. I replaced the volume and searched for something to wipe my hands.

I was truly tired. At the kitchen table sharing tea with my closest relatives, I sighed and struggled to sit up straight. "We can allow you to rest," Kecouroo said, "but first comes my news. Marcy has torched herself in the Cylay plaza." My heart pulled down in my chest. I had no defenses to manage this heartstone. I remembered we had stood together in Cylay in communion with Dolvia's two moons when she had claimed that she was only waiting.

"The offworld media waited by the gates of Ely's mansion," Kecouroo continued, "to cover the triumphant return of the governor after he signed the armistice. Marcy wore Cylahi paint with an old uniform from the clutch of Quentin, from long before Ely was made rabbenu. She must have kept the uniform from her teenage adventures. She sat cross-legged in the plaza, and people drew away. Gasoline has a distinct odor. The jour-na-lists were interested though. Footage recording Kyle Rula's act had provided a sizable fortune for one among them.

"Nobody tried to stop her," Kecouroo added. "A horrific thing to see. She screamed with the orange burst and drew flames into her lungs. Rolling dark smoke and charred bones, the smell of hot fuel and burning flesh. A painful way to die."

"You were there."

"Many were there."

"You knew about this, when and where it would happen."

"Many knew."

Poor Marcy, I thought. What did she have left? Why hold on? "There are other means of protest," I said.

"The, uh, jour-na-lists—" Kecouroo and Rufus wore identical disdainful smirks. "They understand nothing. They photograph public rituals, whatever has action and color. Life does not take place within these moments. What are they expecting to reveal?"

"It's the way of their culture."

"Just theater," Rufus said in his succinct manner. "Political theater."

"Offworlders know nothing about past events," Kecouroo said. "Kyle Rula chose to complete this act, then Marcy, so the Consortium leaders focus on Dolvia's justice. We must have home rule."

I was seized with a sudden fear that Kecouroo might attempt self-torching. "You are not going to . . . I mean, you would not—"

"We view the struggle as an Arrivi matter. Ely abuses rabbenu power."

"I greeted Marcy, you know," I said, "not four days ago when we first arrived in Cylay. She has this hut . . . had a hut behind the governor's house. She told me about Ely as a young man when he was a teacher."

"Cyrus spoke of him," Kecouroo said. "Ely had wanted to build a future."

My turn to smirk. "Some future when your wife lights herself on fire on the day of your highest honor. Nothing can be done? A free election between Pete and Ely perhaps."

Kecouroo blinked as she watched me. "You think of Dacupitte sometimes?"

"No, I just remember he was next after Ely in prophecy."

"You remember Pete?"

"I remember those were your words and Kyle Rula's words."

"So you want Pete to be raised up?" she asked.

Rufus was grinning, but I frowned at him. "All I want is a siesta."

"I will go then," Kecouroo agreed. "One more item though. The holy woman has a word for you."

"You mean Kat?"

"She says, the one who asked nothing for herself has been enlarged."

I shrugged. "The treasure should have gone to the wives of Lynus and Rufus."

"There is more. She says your gathered things cannot save you."

"That's certainly cheery."

"The one who asks nothing for herself is required to sacrifice all."

I watched Rufus's face. "Then the treasure should not have been entrusted to me."

"You question Kyle Rula's last request?" Kecouroo asked.

"She questions everything," Rufus claimed.

Kecouroo stood preparing to leave. "Rufus must accompany you to the Somule convent, and then he is free to rejoin his clutch." She gave Rufus a kindly look. "And Cara asks that you spend a moment with him."

"Cara?" I asked. He had been a great Mekucoo leader, second only to Cyrus. I was surprised that he was still living.

"Cara is blind now and wasted," Kecouroo said. "but his mind is sharp. I believe he wants to know what women are like in Pear-ass."

"Paris," I corrected.

"Pair-ass," she said.

"Close enough. Oh, I just remembered. Two students from the clutch of Cleo may be assigned to you, at your village. Cleo and Camille. I hope you can find the time to guide them and let them know Edwina."

Kecouroo nodded. "The holy woman shared an image about you; I think I understand it now." Her hand went to the tektite stones in her necklace, fingering them idly. "Kat saw you seated with many arms, moving goods from one pocket to another, then moving the same items again."

I shrugged. "She only saw the operations of Somule Gems. I have greeted many managers in the past weeks."

Kecouroo dropped her hand to her side. "I'm certain you're right." They left then, taking Brian out with them. I wandered to the first cot for a long and delicious nap.

NINE

IT FELT ODD TO BE ALONE IN THE FORTRESS OF ARIM. I HAD returned to Dolvia's embrace, and I hoped the fortress would be my new residence. I brushed my hair and brewed tea before lighting a tallow and carrying it into the library. The blue macaw flew to the polished tabletop and sort of skidded to a stop. He tucked back his wings and tail feathers and strolled parallel to my inquisitive steps. Spiralbound books were grouped in overlapping science sections, mostly technical manuals. I also found books on civil law, philosophy, and botany, medical encyclopedias, and some aging Company whitepapers concerning Dolvia's mineral wealth and tribal structures.

I opened the breakfront, which was not locked. Valuables were stored there to protect them from humidity and bird droppings. The top shelves were lined with Softcheeks' Great Works: the Bible and Koran were shelved alongside Aristotle, Plato, Confucius, Augustine, Marcus Aurelius, Goethe, Kant, and Camus. It seemed that

Kyle Rula had investigated their philosophers to know the Soft-cheeks' minds.

One shelf down I found early ledgers that Kyle Rula had maintained, mostly to record wages. A Cylahi woman named Kura had constructed Cylahi gold jewelry as pieceworks, six acacia bracelets with gems, delivered the week of the Feast of Oria, paid in full. Sarah was the accountant of the treasure now, or at least that part traded through Somule Gems. Kecouroo held the mineral wealth, and apparently Hakulupe Le, or Vera, at the Somule convent managed the domestic largesse for grants and payouts against tithes.

The middle shelves held the module lesson books used in the convent schools. There were books on math, Arrivi grammar, business and accounting, logic, agriculture, the geography of Earth, and the history of Earth. I found illustrated stories of Oria and the adventures of Ohero and Ohunt.

The macaw flew to a perch over my head while I was investigating further. A desktop folded down to reveal narrow drawers for storing writing utensils and important papers. A long shelf held twenty-one hardbound and numbered journals, the kind that fits into a skirt pocket. These were Kyle Rula's personal works.

"Just read one," the macaw taunted. "Read just one."

He glided down to the desktop and walked gingerly up my arm. He put his forehead against my cheek, demanding affection. "It must be awful lonely here."

"Read just one," he repeated in brash tones.

A time-honored Earth tradition when seeking guidance was to drop a Bible onto the table and take instruction from the first sentence on the open page. So I looked away and pulled down the memoir volume my hand first touched. Kyle Rula's small handwriting was open and regular. There were occasional drawings of birds and what I assumed were maps of geysers and sketched footpaths through the flats of Arim. I allowed the journal to drop onto the desktop where it fell open to a center page. A quote set apart from the other paragraphs read, "Only from wrong answers can the truth emerge." The noted author was Francis Bacon, an Englishman.

"Read just one," the macaw taunted.

"Don't you have family or reason to nest on the savannah?"

"Braaadt, Murmurey bird. Murmurey above."

Great, I was in conversation with a parrot. I thumbed through the journal pages, a random collection of quotes and daily thoughts with infrequent essays on issues that troubled Kyle Rula. "A writer is somebody for whom writing is more difficult than for other people." That sentiment was from Thomas Mann, a German novelist who once lived in America.

With some poking around, I discovered that her early journals contained mostly copied quotations while the middle ones were filled with her observations. The final volumes held Kyle Rula's reasoned pearls of wisdom.

"All things fade into the storied past, and then the old men die."

"Women must closely guard the spirit in our faces. How I long for the veil."

"Do not burn up your time seeking the gifts of Dolvia. Rather, praise Her with each breath to reveal your task."

I pulled down another volume and fanned the pages. My eye fell on my name, a passage written circa our journey of cleansing to the Canyon of Buttes. "What word for Brianna who poses questions from a pure heart, so like her father? Let your wheels move only along old ruts."

My wheels? What possible meaning?

I replaced the volume brusquely and closed the breakfront. The macaw flew to his high perch, displaced by my abrupt gestures. What did tribal men know that we did not know? Which warrior had read Marcus Aurelius? Who had torched himself in the plaza?

My actions caused a rattling in one of the drawers, so I opened it to find loose beads of silicide and peridot, perhaps from a broken necklace. There were larger crystals of silicide, two that fit snugly in the palm of one hand. Perhaps I would test the legend of their power and see if they gathered light on the desert and amplified remote viewing. I held the two bits in my fist and went outside to breathe the cool evening air.

Nettom, the male moon, hovered behind the distant butte. Nettki, the lazy female moon, had not yet risen. Brian waited there as if guarding the entrance. Rufus was absent, perhaps gone to visit Cara. But I thought not. Mekucoo land was a three-day walk from the fortress.

"Well, Brian, let's take a stroll. From where did Kyle Rula view the sunset?"

He sidled off to the left, and I followed him up a winding path to the knoll's ridge. We gained the summit and stood overlooking the basin and the flats. Below us among the gurgling streams and crystal-clear ponds, acacia trees stood in tall clusters. To the left were two squat factory buildings used mostly to manufacture furniture and some storehouses. There was a depository for harvested gum arabic, and a business office where piecework was delivered for payment. The EAMs Brianna used to chat with Sarah were there maybe.

The monumental, shattered butte and facing plateau, half a day's walk from our position, were black against the night sky, backlit by Nettom. I experienced a rich calming sensation of acceptance and strength. Wait a minute; I knew that feeling.

"Edwina? Are you here?"

She came out of the shadows. "Ka, ka, ka, ka."

I sat cross-legged on the ground. She raised her sizable head and regarded me, flicking her fleshy and forked tongue at casual intervals. "What game are you playing, huh? Fearful of ghosts, are you? Of the one who has replaced Kyle Rula?"

She fingered me with her tongue, my arms and face. "Ka," she said, and nuzzled her marbled nose under my chin.

"Yes, Edwina, it's me," I said. "I went a long distance away, to another star."

Go again? she asked.

"No, I shall never leave Dolvia again. Am I forgiven?"

Later; forgiven later.

"That's good enough for me. Look what I found in the fortress. Do you know these pieces? Are they from a necklace of Kyle Rula?" She fingered the silicide bits with her fleshy tongue before slurping twice, but I received no message or image of truth.

I stood and brushed down my long skirt. "It's so beautiful here. I had forgotten."

Without warning, I was struck with a flood of images: swimming and basking and racing across the desert and egg-tending; static views of Kyle Rula and Kecouroo and Karlyhi and Pete and

Hakulupe Le and Mike Shaw; welfare ministers traveling the savannah and Siibabean warriors spying on troops. The rush was not organized but had a certain rhythm, a cadence. I realized it was all the gualarep community singing with mental pictures, celebrating within remote viewing, and I was included. I surmised that Edwina had lifted the ban she had imposed because of her uncertainty toward the arisen Brianna. Gualareps could relax and share together again, no longer expending energy to exclude a counterfeit Rularim.

Then came more kinetic pictures. Hakulupe Le, sitting at a small desk with a lamp, glanced up over her reading glasses and smiled. I saw Mike Shaw turn away from some engine tinkering, then just grin and shrug. I saw Karlyhi, seated with his captains in the Butte Canyon tent, suddenly jolt and stretch his neck to cover.

And I saw Kecouroo seated among Mekucoo in Somule, watching a tribal dance. She calmly looked across the center fire and met Dacupitte's gaze as though they shared a secret.

I looked at the silicide bits in my palm, but light had not gathered there. I sighed and looked again out over the vista, standing with two gualareps, wondering why I sought mystery and secrets to treasure. And then I saw the shape of Dolvia, stretched out under the reflected light of the risen moon; she moaned softly and turned her golden shoulder as if disturbed during a peaceful slumber.

The following morning, I rooted through some trunks stored in the fortress seeking fresh clothes. I discovered a thick pile of decorated veils, all richly stitched and weighted on the ends for easy wear. Facial panels were variously open or with lace sewn to cover the nose and mouth only or with the lightest gossamer mesh.

I didn't know Kyle Rula's intent for the burkas, perhaps stored for an offworld market. But they were mine now, and I had an idea for the treasure's best use. I thought of Pierre Mitterand's words that his situation should serve as a warning to me. The accumulation of wealth was no security against his wasting disease. My new wealth was not a place where I should sit and judge or sit and watch passing events managed by others. These burkas from Kyle Rula were the first of many resources I would expend to raise my profile and the volume of my voice so I could implement my plans, all to secure a greater future for others, for the gouleps who were my sisters and the women of the savannah.

I was brewing tea when Rufus entered. "You will come," he said.

"Where to now?"

"They wait for you at the Somule convent."

"They have waited this long, so another hour won't hurt. Sit down, have some tea. Tell me about the Borabean struggle."

Rufus thought about it, as he always did. He sat as if ready to spring into action while I served him Arrivi style. The blue macaw flew to a high perch.

"Does Lynus serve on Borabean land?" I asked. Lynus was Rufus' older brother.

"Lynus and some others."

"And what do the Borabean want from us?"

"Control of Uburu land, or so they say."

"But you think there's more?"

"They fight a holy war. They won't be content until their grudge abates."

"And what grudge is that?"

"That we follow Dolvia."

"What?"

"According to Borabean ways," Rufus said, "there's a redeemer whom we must accept as our redeemer, like the Lutherans say."

"Their redeemer isn't Jesus Christ?"

"Alousha."

"Has Lynus accepted Alousha?"

"Lynus has married among them. I met Alaise. She seems . . . fine."

"Does Kecouroo think she's fine?"

"Kecouroo would have preferred Dulcinea, the Uburu woman."

I smiled slightly. "And have you met Dulcinea?"

"The warriors who pass through Uburu land—each in his turn pursues her."

"So she is a great beauty. And who has succeeded? Karlyhi perhaps?"

"Dulcinea won't look upon Karlyhi's face. She fears Omiibuk's wrath, I think."

"Who does she favor?"

Rufus shrugged. "Dacupitle."

"Naturally. And do they have children?"

"The one Dulcinea is, uh, she is untouched. Unwilling to give herself without . . . you know." Rufus looked away.

My mouth turned down; an itch crept across my back. I needed to address certain assumptions. "How many wives do you think it is correct that Dacupitte should have?"

"Dulcinea knows the prophecy that you are Dacupitte's woman."

"Perhaps Dulcinea makes an excuse to hold the warriors' interest."

"Holding their interest is not a problem for her."

"I would like to meet this woman."

"She never leaves Uburu land. She cares for an aging father."

"I like her more every moment," I grinned. "And now you can rejoin the men. Will you enter Borabean land?"

"Lynus and I look Borabean due to our father's birth. We can walk among them."

"Rufus, I ask these questions for good reason." I fiddled with my tea mug. "I wish to enter Borabean land, perhaps traveling with your group."

"You would be a great prize for them to capture and demand ransom."

"Then I should travel with a high profile, as an ambassador perhaps."

"Borabean women don't sit in council."

"Nor do Arrivi women. Will you bring it up with the others?"

He looked away. "You should speak to General Shaw."

"I thought to discuss this tribal matter with you first. Is Mike Shaw nearby?"

"At the Uburu ruins with Sheeks-Cylom."

I nodded three times. "I shall travel to Somule and the convent, then to the ruins to greet my mentor, Mrs. Shaw. But I want to enter Borabean land. Will you talk to the men?"

"I will speak with Karlyhi."

"Good. That is good."

Under the burka and carrying a small pack, I walked with Rufus toward Somule. Two Arrivi men waited by the road: Orin rabbe Murd and his oldest son Hakki, who were sharing dried kariom on a salted patty. They had no weapons though. It was strange to be aware of karkars only by their absence. I held my palm high in the traditional greeting.

"Hiki, Brianna," Orin said. "Melinga. You remember Hakki rabbe Murd from when you were children under my mother's care?"

"Melinga, Hakki rabbe Murd." He was big and stout like his father and grandfather, with deeply cut laugh lines on his tan face.

"Many erriv are hard about here," Orin added. "We thought you might walk this road, and so we waited."

"How thoughtful. How is your mother?"

"Karima Le waits with the others in Somule," Orin said. "You know my father has robbed the desert of one."

"He lives on in your faces," I pronounced in formal Arrivi. "The flats of Arim are safe resting adjacent to the land of Murd."

He bowed slightly. "Melinga, Brianna Miller of Arim. And Rufus, you know that Cara waits for your visit."

"Yes, I heard. Melinga."

"Melinga, Rufus."

Somule was very different from Cylay; it was an agrarian and artisan community within Karlyhi's rebel stronghold. A covered wooden walkway led from shop to shop, perhaps to keep clients dry during the rainy season. A native bazaar was conducted under the stretched canvas of many individual booths crowded onto another walkway. Under burkas, souks managed the sidewalk banking and the barter for kitchen staples from their clean and orderly stalls. All the women wore burkas, even Cylahi and Mekucoo. Some burkas were only blank material with facial panels, while some had patterns denoting the wearer's family or occupation.

The railhead and electricity relay station were intact. The hotels were operational, even the lobby Chinese restaurant. I saw no tribal beggars except Cylahi, who had always been poor. Militia officers with karkars easily shared chi with academy students, all dressed alike. We went to the convent where many waited to greet us, but the one I saw was Vera standing by the gate. My throat constricted. She had been a teenage friend. Vera limped toward us and gave me a big hug. She was slight and bony under the burka.

"A hug?" I asked.

"You taught us, from when we took lessons on the transport." She smiled at my blank look. "Did you think I would forget?" I forced a smile. "Come in, come in," she said. "Oh, Rufus, Cara wants—"

"Yeah, yeah, yeah," he muttered and went to join the men.

Vera and I crossed the wide yard and set foot on the wooden verandah that banked the entrances to many classrooms with open windows. My traveling trunks were stacked there, wrongly delivered to the school instead of the fortress. Our footsteps sounded on the platform as we peeked in on each class. In one classroom, Hakulupe Le guided a large student group, her reading glasses perched on her nose before those lambent green eyes. The homilies lettered on the blackboard behind her were these:

Praise is nothing. Does the peridot lose its beauty from a lack of praise?

A thing worth doing is worth doing right.

A fool and his money are soon parted.

All Dolvia's gifts reside in the present hour; get right with Her.

The young people saw us on the exterior platform, straining for a better view, and started whispering together. Hakulupe Le turned irritably, then saw us. "Go on, then." Her students rushed into the yard, as well as those from the other classrooms. Many crowded around Vera and me, whispering melinga and touching my burka.

Hakulupe Le came to the door. "You don't need to wear that on the grounds." Vera and I pulled off our veils. Two older girls received them from our hands and folded them lovingly. Hakulupe Le came forward and gave me a hug. "You will stay for a short time?"

"For a couple days, then I must journey to Uburu land."

"We were hoping you would take up classroom duties."

"I cannot. But you should hold smaller sessions."

Vera interceded. "The students all want to be taught by Lupe's own hand."

"And Kecouroo?"

"They left this morning. They could no longer wait for your arrival."

I blinked. "They?"

"Kecouroo and Dacuplite."

I only smirked as Vera glanced around shyly.

"The students have prepared something for you," Lupe added. "It is here."

Students of many ages stood in rows in the dry yard, boys and girls mixed together and all wearing white-shirted school uniforms. They began moving about and slapping their legs, and loud clucking was heard from the back. They broke into a rhythmic tribal dance there in the heat of the day, bringing their knees high and stomping in unison while moving their extended elbows with the beat, chanting together.

> Brianna's mother was Klistina Le
> Mated to Gaucho as Dolvia would have it
> Brianna's teachers were Hakulupe Le
> And Kecouroo who labors at the bush clinic
> Also Dr. Beecham and the hay-gee-am
>
> Brianna visited the stars with Sheeks-Cylom and Mike
> Then onto Earth and the land of Nordhagen
> From Paris she's fetched by Kyros and Rufus
> She returns to us as though arisen and despite
> Dacupitte's promise to get even her pregnant

They broke into a more aggressive dance. Hakulupe Le and Vera could not stop laughing. "And they learned this at academy?" I asked. "Remind me to cut your funding."

Vera was finally able to catch her breath. "This way."

We descended from the verandah to the sandy yard where two young girls ran to Hakulupe Le. "These are my daughters, Millicent and Anna." Millie was the oldest, maybe ten years, with straight dark hair and fair skin, much like Milo Sector's. Anna clung to her mother's skirt, so I knelt before her, easily adjusting my pack. "Hello. I am your cousin, twice removed." Anna sank deeper into the skirt folds.

"They believe you are arisen," Vera offered.

I stood and met the look of humor in Lupe's green-green eyes. "You correct that story in the classroom, right?"

She shrugged innocently.

We walked around the building's side where a covered cart waited in the acacia shade. Two erriv heifers with mane braids of Murd shook their heads and flicked their tails in the growing heat and dust. We could still hear the front yard celebration because students began another irreverent chant. In the cart's rear, ensconced on many decorated cushions, as though on flying carpets, Karima Le waited under a stretched canvas cover. She was more than stout, with her thinning gray hair pulled back in a tight bun. Her all-knowing eyes had dark circles.

I showed her the open palm gesture. "Hiki, Karima Le of Arim. It is an honor to see the spirit in your face." She struggled to lean forward, apparently unable to stand. She reached out, and I stepped into her hug. So many hugs that day.

"Brianna, you have returned at last," she said with honey and gravel in her voice. "Let me see your face. Kyle Le so often claimed she could see Brian Miller in your face." She smiled down at me. "So thin. A meal at the house will do you good, you and Vera."

"We'll come by soon," I said, suddenly happy. "I saw the sculpture on the flats. The artist made an excellent likeness of you."

"They could have waited a decent time to erect such a thing."

"Still, an honor. Oh, and we saw Orin and Hakki rabbe Murd on the road."

Tears stood in her eyes. "It is no matter," she whispered, and her voice seemed coarser. "I was only waiting here to greet Brianna. Is there anything you need?"

"Only your continued good opinion."

"Remember me to Pete." She sat back against the soft pile.

Two unveiled women came forward showing open palms. I greeted each; they seemed so sad. Then they led the heifers and cart away. Karima Le shortly waved from under the canvas cover. Near the gate, the helpers donned their burkas. In the wagon's back, Karima Le did the same, lending honor to Karlyhi's law.

I turned toward my friends. Humor had gone out of the eyes of Lupe and Vera. Why suddenly so sad? "What?"

"Nothing," Lupe said. "Come, I can show you our new library."

Much later, we walked to the officers' barracks in Somule. We had tea on the verandah at Colonel Sector's residence. "I brought gifts." I unrolled my pack and gave Hakulupe Le and Vera each a burka from the fortress cache.

"But, this is not—" Vera began.

"There are many at the fortress. The macaw will despoil them."

Hakulupe Le felt the fabric on hers. "So beautiful, but rightfully yours."

"My gathered goods cannot save me."

Colonel Sector came up from the yard, followed by one other. "Hiki, Brianna," he said. "You remember Captain Manenowski?"

"I remember a Lieutenant Manenowski."

The small man with a pencil-thin mustache leaned over and placed a kiss on Vera's cheek. "We'll just wash up for dinner," Milo added, brushing his much showier dark mustache with two fingers. They entered the house together.

"Vera, all this time. . . . You didn't tell me!"

"I did not know what you would think. I mean, my feelings were—"

"You're too sensitive. I am so pleased for you."

"Oh, thank you, Brianna." She leaned over for another warm hug.

"And now, Hakulupe Le," I said, "if there are no more surprises, perhaps we can discuss something new. I was thinking the academy should offer additional studies, university level. Your best students, from several seasons back even, could undertake specific disciplines."

"What exactly?"

"Well, the library at the fortress. Books could be grouped and annotated and translated where necessary. Also, Kyle Rula left some writings that should be added to canon. We should develop advanced courses in the basics, of course: conservation, medicine, engineering, and civil law. We can solicit more teachers from Cicero or from General Hartley's forces."

"And where would we hold this college?"

"Not here?"

"At Beecham Place perhaps," Lupe said.

"Where's that?"

"The evac hospital established by Dr. Abercrombie when you were a student, Brianna. It was renamed after Dr. Beecham's death. A sizable academy operates there."

"Beecham Place," I repeated. "I like it. So, there will be enough students?"

"Mostly tribal women. The men leave to fight."

"Yes, well, that will have to change."

"Perhaps," Vera whispered wickedly, "you can take up the question with Dacupitte when you see him?" Lupe grinned at Vera, also delighted at the possibility.

After the evening meal, I stepped out on the verandah and talked with Milo Sector while he smoked a kari root cigarette. "I need to visit Uburu land," I said.

He pulled out a map from some stacked papers, spread the folds on a table, and secured them with a couple of tallows. I stared at the detail, substantially greater than on General Hartley's map. "Our Uburu allies hold the high ground," he said, "but the area is a tactical nightmare. Moving equipment and especially monitoring Borabean maneuvers, these are most arduous."

"Arduous?" I teased. "Arduous. And on which of these mesas lives Dulcinea?"

Milo grinned, his mustache moving to show his teeth. "She is lovely." He pointed to a place not far from the Iamida River. "Here, in her father's village."

"Then I will go there after my visit with Sheeks-Cylom."

"I can pilot you to the digs tomorrow, if you like."

"My personal pilot?"

"I must travel there for meetings with Generals Shaw and Hartley." He saw my incredulous look. "You did not know he had disembarked?"

I only shook my head no.

"I wondered why you linger here," he said.

I needed to cover my reaction. "The students call you Milo-pilo, their favorite."

"They're good kids, most of them."

"And they make good soldiers?"

"With extra training."

"Uh, huh. I want to view your training grounds if you don't mind."

"We can work it into your travels here."

"Great," I said, "but first, the current morass of Sheeks-Cylom."

Milo grinned again. He knew I had a long and rocky history with Dr. Greensboro, who was Mrs. Mike Shaw and Sheeks-Cylom.

In the morning, I attended the academy's Lutheran church services with the others, it being Sunday. I wore a Western dress with a wide-brimmed hat and white gloves. Hakulupe Le and Vera wore traditional Arrivi skirts and, while indoors, carried their new burkas as shawls. Seated in the pews were many married women, plus a tight contingency of older academy students, female and male. Lupe and Vera sat with their Consortium husbands. The children were in Sunday school. The Softcheeks minister was dry and uninspiring, but the tribeswomen were patient. This church was a refuge, so they ascribed to its rituals. When communion was served, I allowed the plates to pass by, uncertain of my spiritual acceptance.

Karen Osborn, the divorcee, led the choir's hymns by Handel. Her eighteen-year-old daughter Kelly, wearing black-rimmed glasses and with her auburn hair pulled back from her low forehead, stood in the front row and sang off-key loudly.

When we all filed out later, the minister offered to baptize me and confirm me in the faith. I said I would give it some thought, just as Kelly came up in a rush. "May I travel with you?" she asked without preamble. "I have been reading some. I want to research tribal folklore to find my roots."

"Just go outside."

"But this is important. I know my mother was not a sister of Arim, but—"

"No, I mean to find your roots," I said. I led her down the church steps into the bright morning sunlight where several people waited. Colonel Sector stood with Rufus and some others, ready to pilot us to another section of the savannah. "This is a living culture. To know it, you need only go outside."

Kelly drew in her breath sharply. I followed her gaze to the men's group where something shimmered near Rufus. That felt very strange, so I considered the glimmering for a moment and gestured to Lupe's daughter Millie. I gave her my prayer book, the only thing I carried. "Give this to Rufus." Millie stared with wide eyes. "You know which one is Rufus?"

She nodded and crossed the yard. She shyly handed the book to him and pointed back at us. When Rufus looked up with question, Kelly took a step back, and I participated in her vision due to my proximity. I saw Rufus's hair lift as if blowing in the wind, and tongues of flame stretch out behind him. The battlefield and ancestors of Cyrus were resident in his aura. Rufus shortly thanked Millie and turned back to the men. The disturbance in his aura vanished just as Millie shrugged and walked away.

I only chuckled. Kelly was for Rufus; Kelly only. "You may travel with me for now, Kelly," I said, "with your mother's permission."

TEN

LATER THAT AFTERNOON, CAPTAIN MANENOWSKI SERVED AS THE pilot, and Colonel Sector sat next to me. Kelly and I wore identical sky-blue burkas. She had protested that the honor was too great, not worthy of the colors of a sister of Arim. I insisted she must carry out my instructions if she wanted to be my travel companion.

During the flight, I watched Kelly and Rufus, hoping to glimpse a confirmation of Rufus's warrior image at close quarters, but she avoided his look, and he ignored her as he did all women. The helicopter touched down on Mekucoo land. Rufus jumped down from the copilot's seat and sauntered off to keep his oft-solicited appointment with Cara.

We skirted the Iamida River, which lingered in Uburu land, a sluggish meandering streak of mud with wide banks and blanched mida trees in clumps. We flew over the digs site, a denuded and terraced mound within a narrow valley, more lush with tamarind and mida trees and thick underbrush. The Softcheeks camp was situated on high ground under a twisted thorn tree. Several canvas tents were clustered in the shade, and two sizable pole huts constructed in Mekucoo style.

"How did she get permission for this encampment?" I asked.

"Sheeks-Cylom found the pox cure," Colonel Sector said. "The vaccine saved thousands."

"I had jumped back by then."

"How can you jump back to a place you have never been?" Kelly asked.

"It's just a figure of speech." I adjusted the facial panel so I could stare out the hatch window.

Milo looked past my shoulder at the encampment. "This will no doubt become a university site one day," he added dryly.

Mrs. Shaw in a tan skirt and jacket met us at the landing pad. Martina, who still served Sheeks-Cylom, wore an Arrivi gown. I held an open palm high and said hiki. "You remember Kelly Osborn."

Under the sky-blue chador, Kelly showed her empty palm. "Hiki, Sheeks-Cylom."

"We don't wear those here," Mrs. Shaw said.

"This site serves as home to offworlders," I said, "to whom Kelly and I have not been presented."

"What game are you playing?"

"I mean only to honor Sheeks-Cylom with my deference."

"Brianna, there's no pretension here."

"I am glad to see you also."

Mrs. Shaw saw Colonel Sector's grin and made a sour face before leading us to a long table near the tents. General Hartley and the offworld scientists sat there with open bottles of beer, easily sharing chi. They stood at our approach, so Mrs. Shaw introduced us. Kelly and I held one hand high and repeated each man's name in turn. They were trim and strong-jawed, these Softcheeks adventurers, and two had gray streaks in their hair.

We also greeted General Hartley holding our palms high. He was commonly called Hamilcar by warriors, but this was not a military situation. Fewer than ten days ago, I had been his guest at Stargate Junction. I suddenly felt embarrassed by the unresolved tension.

"Hiki, General Hartley," I said in my turn. "We were not told you had disembarked." I came to understand Kyle Rula's longing for the burka. I could not otherwise have tolerated this encounter.

"If you booted the EAM occasionally," Mrs. Shaw returned bitingly.

"Drinking beer in the middle of the day?" I asked him.

"You must not drink the local water," Hartley said in a hoarse voice. "Beer is the best substitute, even warm."

General Shaw came up with two others and the gualarep Edna. She waited outside the circle of scientists. "If you will excuse me for a moment," I said.

Edna's hide was a rich, rich dappled green, even across her long scar. With my back turned to the group, I removed the burka and sat cross-legged on the ground. Edna fingered me with her tongue and stepped across my lap, rubbing me strongly with her flanks.

"Fine, she removes the veil for the gualarep," I heard Mrs. Shaw call out.

Saw Edwina? came the question.

"She will forgive me later. What about you?"

Left no word, she told me.

"That was thoughtless," I sighed. "My heartstone then was more than I could bear. I sent the one Brian to you."

Softcheeks, she claimed with humor.

"My three objections, you mean? Perhaps I do think like them now."

Sheeks-Cylom forgiven?

"Yes, well. I must find a way to make the peace."

Fun-ding, she suggested.

"She needs funding?"

"Ka, ka, ka, ka, ka," Edna articulated. I only chuckled.

The officers stood together in a tight circle of camaraderie, discussing their concerns regarding the troop deployment. While Mrs. Shaw and the scientists returned to their excavation duties, Martina showed Kelly and me the sun-warmed tent we were to share. "The men sleep in the buildings?" I asked.

"Everybody sleeps in tents. The buildings are for specimens."

"Naturally. How many students are here?" Question took residence in Martina's eyes. The scar over one eyelid brightened when her forehead wrinkled. "So, you no longer teach?"

"I miss teaching."

"Yes, well. We shall have to look into that."

Later, I wandered alone down to the pole huts, thinking to have a look. The closest structure had a rough-hewn window with the broad wooden sash painted tropical blue. That seemed strange, but then the reason came to me. Kyle Rula's ban on the use of the color blue did not extend into Uburu land. Just inside the window was an EAM situated under a desk lamp. In the shadows behind it, mosquito netting was draped in beige loops to cover some dug-up treasure. While I was loitering there, Dr. Greensboro came in and sat at the EAM. With reading glasses she stared at the screen and entered her notes using the keyboard. A dark and nappy-haired Uburu child, the daughter of an excavation laborer, came to her side. She took the toddler onto her lap. The plump big-eyed girl snuggled closer and sucked her thumb while Dr. Greensboro again stared at the screen. Sheeks-Cylom planted a casual kiss in the girl's unkempt hair.

It was the same the universe over. A woman's status within a cohesive community was gauged by how children responded to her. Memories washed over me of my days at the bush clinic and the hours of English lessons. A truth resided here that Dr. Greensboro and I must ever embrace. I had selected to leave Dolvia and know the Softcheeks world. She had remained and served the tribes during difficult times. Sheeks-Cylom had gained honor.

Our company gathered again at sunset. Legions of offworlders were eager to know Mike Shaw's whereabouts, but he sat relaxed at the rough table as though he were attending a family barbeque. Kelly and I approached the table with the open hand gesture before removing our burkas. Mrs. Shaw rolled her eyes. General Mike Shaw heaved a grateful sigh of relief. Here was one tirade of righteous indignation he need not endure later that night.

The scientists were a delight. All spoke Arrivi with some Uburu phrases. They argued in English about era demarcations on the core samples pointing to the possible causes of the ancient social collapse. One scientist named Dr. Spinelli showed Kelly and me a topical line drawing of the flats region. "The Arim flats are not a collapsed volcano cone," he said, "as early Company surveys assumed. Rather, an ancient impact crater violated the mantle's integrity there. Fissures travel along a discernible baseline.

"And the savannah pools?" he added. "These were created by secondary spray. Debris was dispersed in a circular pattern. We suspect the meteoroid was a bolide." Pointing with this pipe stem, Dr. Spinelli indicated on his drawing the old water pool sites, including the grottos where the gualareps often swam. "At the bottom of each deep pool, one can expect to find ancient displaced debris."

I grinned at him, gladly sharing chi. His conclusions were similar to my own. He winked at Kelly from under his bushy eyebrows before lighting his pipe.

"Who has a copy of this map?" I asked.

"It's part of the grant papers, kept confidential," Mrs. Shaw said.

"A Consortium grant?" I asked, perhaps too quickly.

"We know how to keep a secret," she returned flatly.

I turned to Dr. Spinelli. "And where is the silicide, do you think?"

"In the ocean beyond Urbyd."

"Not under the savannah pools?"

General Shaw joined our talk from the head of the table. "Company fieldmen think they have found a debris stream of meteor deposits under the dunes of Madquii land."

Behind the smoke from his pipe, Dr. Spinelli nodded in agreement. "If it's too difficult to extract in quantity, the Company will lose interest and turn to a different profit center."

General Shaw waggled a finger. "But this changes the balance among the clans of the Borabean."

I saw General Hartley glance my way. "And so, General Hartley," I said lightly, "do monsters live hard about here?"

"They do now," he returned dryly.

"It's the cenzea," Mrs. Shaw claimed. "This area is seismically still active and gives off carbon monoxide that collects in certain depressions. Creatures eager to devour carrion from the ditches grow dizzy and cannot crawl out to catch some fresh air. Trapped by their greediness, they join the other dead.

"Also, the fissures occasionally rumble," she continued. "Warriors assumed some huge creature lived here, and so they fled."

"When it's only the air?" I asked.

"Dolvia's breath. You can actually see it on a misty morning."

"And the local water?"

"Brackish and sulfur-laden," Dr. Spinelli said.

"Will an eruption come?" I asked.

"Who can say?" he said. "The ground is hot in places but so are the flats of Arim."

"Are they perhaps connected?"

"We have not found the evidence," Mrs. Shaw said. "Tomorrow I can show you the underground site."

Our group broke up soon after that. Two crescent moons hovered in the night sky as if resting back-to-back like tipped saucers. Mike Shaw and his wife walked away together. I had called them the battling Shaws as a teenager and while serving Mrs. Shaw in Cylay. Now I came to admire their marriage. The rough edges had worn away, and they fitted together well.

Kelly and I were making our way to the tent when General Hartley caught my arm. "Please, just a few moments." Kelly walked on, and the others studiously ignored us. "You know what I want," he whispered, his heated breath near my ear.

"Do nothing," I instructed without meeting his look. "I will come to you." I joined Kelly in the tent where she busied herself laying out her few necessities. She watched me for a time but said nothing. I liked her for that.

It was deep night when I moved among the tents to approach the one occupied by General Hartley and where a tallow burned. He threw back the flap and waited inside. "Blow out the light," I whispered before joining him inside, where I caught the scent of eucalyptus and lemon.

He held me close and covered my face roughly with kisses. "I was afraid you would not come."

"Stop this. Are you a green lieutenant?" He dropped his hands and avoided my stare. "Am I a backroom romp you snatch between appointments?" I asked.

He sighed and stepped back, seemingly hurt by my reproach.

"Put the mattress on the ground," I instructed. "Take off your jacket and shoes and sit there." He complied using measured gestures and waited silently in the dark while I rested on my knees before him.

"The Consortium general. The man of action, always taking charge. Events exist only in their acting out, huh? Is that how you see the world?

"There are many worldviews, don't you know," I whispered. "In my world you have no power. I am the general, and you are my green trooper. You must dumbly submit to my demands. You must complete my instructions without complaint."

I made him sit on his hands while I drew near. I made him close his eyes and wait while I unplaited my hair and allowed its perfumed weight to fall against his face and arms. "Your arms are weak and unschooled," I told him in a stern whisper. "Your legs would buckle at the first volley. What good are you to me in your greenhorn condition?"

I made him lean back and say nothing and do nothing. I felt him tremble under my touch. I became the general's general.

We remained at the digs four days. Each morning we took up our various duties, and each night I slipped into General Hartley's tent.

On the first afternoon, Mrs. Shaw led me into a deep cavern in the mountain. The common room there had been carved by human hands and displayed many totem heads and statues of amalgam creatures. That was something. Carved dancing women with inscrutable smiles and generous, exposed bosoms lined the walls between niches for idols and raised platforms for sacrifice.

"The low tunnels lead to burial crypts," Mrs. Shaw explained.

"And the poisoned air?"

"This rock is not porous. Cenzea escapes along the cone's backside."

"Are there no traces of these people?"

"We found some remains. Reconstruction can be accomplished in the Cicero laboratory."

"How long have they been extinct?"

"Carbon dating says they vanished twelve hundred years ago."

"Well, concerning the present," I said as we left the cool interior, "I sent you a patient from Southeast Arrivi, a young worker with leg sores."

"Ah, yes, *Pfiesteria piscicida.*"

"Excuse me?"

"The Latin term for fish killer," Mrs. Shaw said matter-of-factly. "It's a microorganism naturally occurring all over the savannah, perhaps feeding on seasonal bird droppings. Pfiesteria can experience several life cycles in wet and dry conditions. It breeds in stagnant water and grossly multiplies there. In large concentrations, the colony emits a toxin that brings dizziness, memory loss, and skin lesions. Telltale signs include the leg sores you saw."

"What can be done?"

"The rice paddies are at risk," Mrs. Shaw said. "The organism may become dormant in dried rice, thus making the whole crop suspect. If it can survive the cooking fire, there's danger of ingestion and internal colonies. Their rice crop may not be fit for consumption."

"Pfies-ter-ri-a does not die with cooking?"

"The girl was lethargic and thoughtless. I took blood and stool samples. We can only wait for Cicero test results."

We walked back to camp where the mound-top air was heated and muggy in the late afternoon sun. "Your research grant is from Earth?" I asked. Sheeks-Cylom hesitated, gracing me with a hard stare. "I was just thinking. . . . We may establish colleges at the academy sites. Martina was a teacher before. We can send students here."

"Students?" Mrs. Shaw asked.

"For graduate study. You have four scientists here, so perhaps four students. Martina could structure the basics and maybe add a class for the Uburu children whose parents labor for the scientists."

Her eyebrows were raised. "And this college will be established with what funds?"

I blinked twice. "From the treasure of Kyle Rula. The excavation site will receive a portion as long as you welcome students."

"This is no place for women."

"You thrive here. Martina thrives here."

"There will be no burkas," she said with conviction.

"On academy grounds, veils are not worn. You know that."

She shrugged one shoulder. "I'll discuss this idea with the Soft-cheeks scientists. Their time may be too precious for lessons."

I only smirked. "You do that, Sheeks-Cylom."

In the camp, a group of children had gathered around Dr. Spinelli, who was photographing smaller specimens with an expensive camera that sported a rotating telephoto lens and high-powered flash. The nappy-haired kids touched his arm and begged to have their photos taken. "You have made friends," I said as we joined him.

"They don't care about this camera. They want the insty-print."

We returned to the long tables where Dr. Spinelli pulled from his rucksack a cheap throwaway camera. The children gathered in wiggling groups, calling his name and making big faces. We heard a distinct whirling noise, and the print rolled out the front.

The young people giggled and strained to watch the photo develop. The ninety-second lag time was excruciating for them.

When their images came into clear definition, they touched Dr. Spinelli's arm and carried away the prints to show their parents.

Colonel Sector and General Shaw joined us, coming up to prepare for dinner. One Uburu girl lingered, hoping Dr. Spinelli would take her photo also. He complied and handed her the print. Without even a thank you, she rushed off with the undeveloped treasure. The men laughed together. "Milo-pilo, you have competition as their favorite," Mrs. Shaw teased.

At dinner, General Hartley came in with the other men and avoided looking my way. I had insisted I would not return to his tent if he betrayed our secret with even a glance. He must obey me with each gesture.

After our meal, Dr. Spinelli took several real-camera shots of the offworld friends, plus Kelly and me, all smiling together in the gathering dusk. I didn't see the prints, of course. I was offered the opportunity to scroll through the digital images using the viewfinder, but I only shook my head.

Later in the deep night, after I had satisfied myself with General Hartley's further torture, I allowed him to speak, but only if he did not gush like a sophomoric schoolboy. "Am I allowed to offer a gift?" he asked.

"That depends," I claimed in a stern voice. "I'm not obligated to you in any way. As though you threw it into the grotto."

He produced a small box that held sizable diamond ear studs.

"I cannot wear these," I said. "They are offworld-made, so people will know where I got them." I felt him smile there in the dark and realized my voice was not stern.

For the second day of our time at the Uburu digs, Kelly and I sat in the gentle afternoon sun while the others completed their excavation and militia chores. I wondered if the scent of eucalyptus or vanilla lingered in my hair. Kelly stared out. "It's so different here with the offworlders. There's a certain tolerance. No tribal logic."

"Tradition is often strengthened from contact with other cultures," I hedged.

Kelly glanced at me. "My brother Patrick is angry."

"I spoke with Patrick on the transport."

"He wrote to me about it. He—"

"Karlyhi executed your father," I said. "There's no escaping that. Joey Osborn was found profiteering, and they had proof." Kelly looked away, but I knew that the truth was always best; speak out the hard truth and embrace it. "What does your mother say?"

"They had divorced already. That part hurt—the public divorce. Karen thinks my father's execution only . . . only proves she was right." Kelly sighed again. "My aunt is Carline Bryant, as you know. She wants me to attend college at New Shanghai on Cicero."

"That's your option, of course."

"What do you think I should do?" Kelly squinted at me from behind the black-rimmed glasses.

"What I think means nothing. You must seek Dolvia's reinforcement."

"But you are the new Rularim. Don't you have a word for me?"

I smiled slightly. "I inherited Kyle Rula's land because she had no daughters. Have you sought out the holy woman?"

"What holy woman?"

Kat had not revealed herself to Kelly. I thought that strange in light of my sure knowledge of Kelly's future. "You must remain faithful to Dolvia. She will supply your answers."

On the third night that I went to General Hartley, I was actually sleepy from burning the candle at both ends. I lay beside him and allowed his deep murmur to wash over me after I had insisted his conversation must be of a general nature. The general may speak generally. "Dolviet societies are insular and have few offworld allies," he said. "On Cicero, work in New Shanghai has centralized the local talent. The Company allows no women administrators, but they recruit ambitious Consortium men like my son."

"Like Carl?" I remembered Carl Hartley as brutal and arrogant. When we were all teenagers, he had abused a Cylahi student while I had crouched in the lunchroom kitchen. "Jesse is faithful to you," I said. "I was thinking to offer her a reason to jump back. Perhaps to manage Kyle Rula's wormhole accounts."

"Even as a sibling to Carl Hartley?" It rankled him, I could see, that his son had taken up Company work.

"Kelly is a sibling to Patrick," I shrugged. "Joey Osborn was a blood sibling to Pete. Carline and Pete are half-siblings."

"It is never a clean us-against-them, huh? Brianna, I need to know. Will you—"

"I must get back now," I interrupted. "And when we leave this place, no sniveling. Don't give me a reason to hate you."

On the fourth afternoon of our stay at the Uburu digs, I joined Mrs. Shaw as she sat at the EAM next to the mammoth specimens. "Would you like to inspect our animal skeletons and pottery frag ments?"

"Not at all. You Softcheeks are something."

"And you are a force of nature."

I knew where this was going, so I changed the subject. "You have no children, Sheeks-Cylom. Arrivi can provide a fertility potion."

"I take precautions. My lifestyle is not conducive to pregnancy."

"Always in control."

"What do you know about it?"

"I know that Dolvia blesses you. Dolvia's reward is fecundity."

"Where did you learn that word?"

"From Softcheeks. Where else?"

"Dolvia must especially love Dacupitte," she offered too casually. Mrs. Shaw was not above trying a cheap shot.

"General Shaw is a handsome man and would make sturdy babies."

"So would General Hartley. Do you have something to share?"

"General Hartley has offworld-born children. Dolvia blesses Sheeks-Cylom, not General Hartley."

"Have you made a special prayer? Well, you can just unmake it. Today!"

"Dolvia does not need my prompting. She has Her own ways."

"You have always been a thorn in my side, Brianna."

"I often thought about you as well, during my travels."

As I strolled out of the hut, she called after me, "Don't you call down the devil!"

That night I again instructed my greenhorn student who had come along in his schooling and provided physical surprises for me. I pulled away and sat up, fixing my hair. "Mrs. Shaw will soon have reason to return to Cicero. You must arrange it so she spends time with Jesse."

"Where will you be?"

"Far from you."

"Brianna, these last days have been—"

"Don't start."

"Please," he begged shamelessly.

I put a finger over his lips and lay down with him again.

The following afternoon, General Shaw gathered us together at the shaded table. General Hartley and Colonel Sector stood grimly at his shoulders. Mike folded and refolded a newly printed EAM note. "Karima Le has torched herself in Cylay's public square, the same as Kyle Rula and Marcy. Consortium comtechs have broadcast the event on Westend stations."

Kelly burst into tears. Martina wailed and retreated to her tent. The scientists waited in respectful silence. Mrs. Shaw sank into a seat there. "What are the people saying?"

"There's universal mourning. Warriors are reconsidering their actions."

"As well they should," Mrs. Shaw added.

"When Kyle Rula torched herself," Colonel Sector added, "that was a wake-up call. But she was the body politic and always suspect among the families. Marcy's act was like atonement, an apology for her husband's vices. But Karima Le, that's different. It's like your own mother destroyed herself."

"I saw her at the Somule academy," I said. "She had this cart rigged up and traveled with two helpers. She must have been on her way to the city, to the site of Kyle Rula's self-execution to do the same. I saw Orin that very morning on the road. He must have known his mother's mind, but he said nothing."

"Karima Le was crippled, you know," Mrs. Shaw said, "and had a full life."

"So it's alright with you that she's gone?" I countered. "This makes no difference, her gesture of protest?"

"No, I was only saying—"

"How many more?" I asked. "How many more Arrivi women plan to complete this . . . this useless act?"

"You tell us," General Shaw said.

I stopped short, realizing that my anger was misplaced here. "I met both women recently, but neither told me her plans." I had seen nothing in the auras of Marcy or Karima Le that had betrayed their intent. The silicide beads were useless, and I did not possess second sight.

"Who is next?" I whispered in a calmer voice. "Milo, Hakulupe Le does not have this in her mind. She's not considering—"

He showed me a worried face.

"Tell her I said she cannot," I insisted. "She's too good for this, too valuable. The academy teachers will burn themselves in groups to keep Lupe from robbing the desert of one." Milo stared at the ground. We all waited in silence there in the waning sunlight.

"I would like to rename the bush clinic," Mrs. Shaw announced. "There's a thriving village there now. Perhaps we'll call it the Karima Le of Murd and Arim Memorial Hospital and College. What do you think, Brianna?"

"Good and right," I said.

General Hartley and the Consortium soldiers were set to leave first, headed to Cylay to catch the shuttle for the transport. As the officers loaded equipment and rucksacks into the helicopters, General Hartley caught my arm. "Travel with me to the transport. I can protect you from all this."

I jerked away. "You would protect me from my destiny?"

"You left before, with Mitterand."

"I was an orphan then. And goulep."

"And what are you now?"

"Not your mistress." I turned abruptly and walked away.

The scientists were encamped at the digs, but Mrs. Shaw planned to travel to Somule with her husband and to implement her plans to rededicate the clinic, so Kelly and I caught a ride with them. While we endured the tense ride with the wind whipping through the open sides, Kelly pushed her glasses higher on her nose, holding her hair tight with one hand and staring out the hatch. I remembered when helicopter rides were the highlight of my season on the savannah.

We were in the Somule barracks yard and separating our packs from the pile removed from the chopper when General Mike Shaw joined me for a moment, his face hard with tension. "I hope you know what you're doing. General Hartley is—"

"Your wife told you?"

"What would Dacupitte think?"

"Pete can justify his own actions before he should question mine."

He made a furtive gesture with one hand. "The general's reputation—"

"You aren't worried for my reputation?" I asked in a sharp voice. "Tell me, General Shaw, did you ever think your marriage is the aberrant structure here?"

"What?"

"Which tribe values fidelity?" I asked. "What transport doesn't have a row of pleasure suites? What Cicero politician has not been tainted by some scandal?"

"Milo is faithful to Lupe. Even Manenowski with Vera."

"Three faithful men in Westend," I shrugged, "and two of them exhibit this behavior to hold your good opinion." It was painful to see his hard stare, but I had to make my stand. "Look, I have plans for new industry with the tribes. Don't . . . just don't spoil my actions with gossip."

The general snorted like he was trying to blow the dust from his nose. "We expected better from you, Brianna." He turned on his heel and deserted the work of the laboring soldiers, striding away with his shoulders hunched and his hands held firmly at his sides.

Kelly waited, holding my pack and hers, question obvious in her face. I took my pack from her gruffly. "Let's go." I worked my jaw to relieve the bad taste of almonds in my mouth. It was the same the universe over. Men could have women in groups any night of the week, but as soon as one risked himself, they closed ranks and placed blame. The woman was at fault for her scheming ways, trying to grasp security beyond her station. Men were so simple.

ELEVEN

THE KARIMA LE OF MURD AND ARIM MEMORIAL HOSPITAL AND
College was dubbed Mayschool by the resident students on the
very day of the dedication ceremony, just prior to the coming rainy
season. The college consisted of a clearing in the Mekucoo bush
above flood level that was once the site of a single building that
Sheeks-Cylom had called a clinic.

Kelly and her mother Karen, both wearing veils, accompanied
me for the day trip. I picked them up early, driving into Somule
using a rented ECCAV; Kelly was impressed with that. Our drive
was uneventful, speeding across the dry flats until we mounted the
grade leading to high ground. The winds picked up, and the rented
ECCAV was buffeted onto the shoulder of the road, only to careen
closer to the dry tamarinds that defined the tangled brush.

Finally, we turned off the exposed road into a protected area
where redbrick three-story buildings had wide arches in front of
clapboard dormitories, ready to receive convalescing patients.

Higher on the steep grade, clusters of round pole huts were constructed in Mekucoo style to provide student living quarters. The original clinic building had been torn down long ago, replaced with the college's Lutheran church. Most teachers were former gouleps after all, or trained by them.

On the academy grounds, the custom of veiling was honored for those who wished it. The absence of burkas was not punished by the local militia as it was in Somule and Cylay. I walked with Kelly and Karen past the whitewashed hospital dormitories where battle-wounded warriors limped and lingered in the yard. Missing a limb or bearing napalm burns, the warriors met our curiosity with flinty eyes and the set jaws of veterans.

"So many," I whispered.

Kelly squinted behind her black-rimmed glasses, her forehead wrinkled with concern. "These are few. Beecham Place takes the majority."

"At least the armistice has brought some relief."

Before we entered the church, I saw Rufus standing with one other warrior, so I stepped aside to catch his attention. I spoke to him about the treasure of Kyle Rula, ready to explain my plan for the silicide. He stared at the horizon as I made it through . . . well, about the second sentence.

"Your words are not a warrior's concern. Take them to Kecouroo."

What a delight Rufus was.

The dedication services were held in the church where the walls were white and the windows made of colored acrylic to depict scenes from the legends of Oria and Cyrus. Beside the altar, oversized drawings of Kyle Rula, Marcy, and Karima Le were displayed on separate stands. Candles were lit and sprigs of laurel or oleander rested at the base of each image. This was mostly an Arrivi event, not well attended by Mekucoo or Putuki. The loss of these women from immolation impacted Arrivi families only.

Leah and Rosalyn from the clutch of Cleo were present, taller and just budding as women. Dressed Arrivi with their hair grown out to coil at their necks, they murmured their melingas. I gifted them with burkas from the store at the fortress. Leah tried to refuse, but I could see the pleasure in their eyes. They were assigned to Haku-lupe Le and Vera, respectively, and followed the daily duties of each woman. The younger initiates, Cleo and Camille, were assigned to Kecouroo, and I would see them later in the day.

During the dedications, Orin rabbe Murd and his extended family were honored for their service, while many spoke of the former leadership of Haku rabbe Murd and the generosity of Karima Le. Promises were made that the Feast of Oria, more broadly attended, would include chants about this family and how they had bolstered the wealth of the stronghold of Karlyhi.

At the mention of his name, I looked around for Karlyhi but didn't see him or Omiibuk or her brothers Siize and Siiloba. I was puzzled by the absence. Perhaps they had withheld their presence so Orin could shine. Judging by the honor he received, I wondered whether perhaps he was being groomed to replace Ely as rabbenu on the correct day.

When the services ended, Hakulupe Le invited me along with Kelly and her mother to join a group of women in leadership. As we walked to a conference room in the hospital building, I caught

Lupe's arm. "Listen, don't travel to Cylay. No gasoline and matches for you."

"You count me as next?"

"Nobody is next," I said sternly. "Besides, the gouleps won't allow you. They will burn themselves in groups to prevent your sacrifice. Where is the benefit, huh?"

"Kyle Rula's act brought you home."

"You cannot lead by torching yourself. It's a flawed plan."

"I have business in Cylay," she shrugged. "We will establish a securities exchange in competition with the Junction Boys. You want control over the domestic market for gum arabic, don't you?"

"You have a plan?"

"You're not the only schemer on the savannah," she said with humor. "In Cylay, we will accomplish much for the academy system."

"But no gasoline and matches. Promise me."

"I have young children, a faithful husband, and a new enterprise," Lupe said. "Why would I remove myself now?"

At the tea, we all sat without veils, even Karen, and talked in small groups. Mrs. Shaw then announced her pregnancy, adding that General Shaw insisted she must endure her term on Cicero. He wanted her to have the baby at his family farmhouse, and I had to chuckle to myself. The general wanted to be certain the infant was not imbued by Dolvia with an ancestral spirit perhaps. They had quarreled about his choice, as always. "I have so much work here, and the scientists may soon find answers at the Uburu dig." Mrs. Shaw sat with Lupe and me for a moment. "All these years later," she said, staring me down. "How is it I fall pregnant now?"

I shrugged. "Dolvia blesses the Sheeks-Cylom."

Lupe only laughed, those green-green eyes twinkling. "Shall I tell a happy story?" she said. "Sarah from the savannah convent sent teachers to Southeast Arrivi to start the new convent school. It seems you gave Bibi Le a book for the truancy record. Bibi Le roused the children and young mothers each morning for several days, but then came the weekend. What does Bibi Le know about a five-day workweek? She has worked every day of her life. So she came to each doorstep and called out the children's names. True-and-see! True-and-see! Why weren't they in the classrooms? The local rabbenu's wife tried to reason with her, but Bibi Le was adamant. It was her duty, given to her by the arisen Rularim. True-and-see was her stubborn defense."

"So I created a monster?" I asked.

"The families started hiding their children on weekends," Lupe said. "Finally, they got the book from her and marked the idle days. Bibi Le does not read, you know. She sets down the daily record for the presence of macaws near the well or a heifer bearing twins, then a slash for each child. She knows which is absent because she knows them all."

I made a special effort to speak to Leah and Rosalyn from the clutch of Cleo. They seemed to blend with Arrivi tradition well enough. Lupe had good reports for Rosalyn and her interest in learning to manage the accounts for Somule Gems. Leah watched my gestures closely. "You're more relaxed here than while we were traveling," she ventured.

"I grew up with these women," I said.

"Mrs. Shaw was your mentor?"

"She taught me English," I said, "and she allowed me to travel to Cicero where she'll go now to have the baby."

"None from the clutch of Cleo is assigned to Mrs. Shaw," Rosalyn observed.

"I'm not that cruel."

Karen stayed with the women's group while Kelly and I traipsed up to Kecouroo's village, a couple of kilometers deeper into the bush. I watched Kelly while I followed her steps in a single-file fashion. She was too plump in a Softcheeks way, her hips round and her thighs solid. Her shoulders sloped, and her arms were short, not at all the physical type of the statuesque Mekucoo women. And those dark-rimmed glasses; surely Karen could have chosen a more appealing style? Kelly squinted in the sun and pushed them up on her nose, an unattractive gesture. Would she ever grow into a young lady whom Rufus might think to court?

The village was very like I remembered, with communal activities and circular pole huts and no men. I was confident there were no EAMs or online connections with the fortress or the convent.

Protocol must be satisfied first. We showed open palms to the aunts and cousins and admired their offered beadwork on suede. I promised to search out offworld markets for them. I greeted Camille and Cleo, who were dressed Arrivi but followed instructions from the village women. I gifted them veils from the store at the fortress even though they were too young to require covering. Cleo handled the volume of cloth with little understanding of my intent. Camille said she would store the burkas for later wear.

"How is Cleo doing now?" I asked.

"She's not chatty, and she misses Bernice, I think," Camille said. "She follows Kat everywhere."

Here was a new development. "Kat, the holy woman? You know Kat?"

"She showed us the grotto and swimming with Edwina."

I grinned showing my teeth. "You have been to the grotto?"

"Isn't that what you intended?"

I stood tall with a quick gesture. "Yes, of course. My instructions fulfilled." Camille only grinned with question in her eyes. Her eyes were brown; I hadn't noticed that before. Camille and Cleo went back to their chores.

Kelly and I entered Kecouroo's hut where two native girls lay in the back with feverish sweats. "Not the pox?"

"Too much contact with other peoples," Kecouroo offered in her succinct manner. "Sit here. We can smoke awhile."

Kelly stared wide-eyed from behind her glasses while Kecouroo and I shared a hand-rolled kari root cigarette. Kelly pretended to inhale in her turn, but she was really too young. Kecouroo seemed unkempt in this domestic setting, not the towering schoolteacher I remembered. The necklace of mismatched tektite stones held in place with a simple binding cord looked homemade, especially when compared to the fine tooling of her carrying pouch. "I came to discuss the future of the treasure of Kyle Rula," I said. "Since the treasure is rightfully the inheritance of Lynus and Rufus, I need your opinion."

"That which belongs to the sisters of Arim should be used by them. By you and Kelly."

"Just because Kyle Rula had no daughters," I countered. "Also, there's Kat."

"Who is Kat?" Kelly asked.

Kecouroo did not flinch at Kelly's ignorance of the tribal holy woman. "You must not trouble Rufus about this. You embarrass him. Shall I tell you why Mekucoo warriors own nothing?" The kari root had its effect on us. Relaxed and talkative as I had never seen her, Kecouroo spun a tale familiar to her tribe.

"Once the warriors dressed in the richest finery," she began, "and carried stretched leather shields decorated with beads and feathers. Bronze-headed weapons with gold ornaments were fashioned by Cylahi artisans. Our headdresses rivaled Siibabean for their gorgeous display. Two brothers, however, fell to quarreling over a robe of blue macaw feathers their father had left. Rightfully, the robe should have been destroyed at the old man's funeral pyre. The panels were too lush, and none could bring himself to add it to the flames.

"So they fought a duel," she continued, "Each brother arrived at the appointed site wearing his full regalia, and they exchanged blows from dawn to dusk. Tribesmen who had already gathered for the funeral remained to place bets. They treated the spectacle as a communal holiday. But there was no clear winner, and fights broke out over the distribution of the wagered goods. On the second day, additional duels were fought. Bad blood sprang up over the proper attire and who could enter the competition. Who had honor.

"Over ten days, recognizable factions arose," Kecouroo said. "Warriors borrowed kinsmen's armaments for each contest. Points were won for display as much as courage. Finally, a rule was made that all duels must take place simultaneously so each man wears only his own regalia. This, of course, was a battle, and also had no clear winner.

"So the factions met again in the field," she said, "each side wearing the colors provided by their women, strutting and baiting the other. In the late morning came the clash, an angry battle over the proper ownership of a blue-feathered robe. For hours they fought, and much blood was spilled. Brother against brother, father against son.

"Nettom had risen," she said in cadence, "by the time they had exhausted themselves. The holy woman went among them giving a word. What if Siibabean had descended on the villages in their absence? What if Siibabean came now? Could the warriors muster the strength for defense?"

It must have been the kari root aroma that made me yawn. I thought I saw the holy woman Kat leave the sick girl's bedside and join our group. In a shimmering sky-blue burka, she casually sat cross-legged at Kecouroo's shoulder and nodded to me.

"And so the law was made," Kecouroo finished. "A Mekucoo warrior owns nothing but his knife and shield and sometimes a karkar, only what the women are willing to provide for defense. The warriors must live for the company of ancestors and the honor of warriors, nothing more."

Kelly pushed her glasses up on her nose. She had not discerned Kat's arrival. "Where is the blue macaw robe now?"

"The holy woman buried it, along with the bronze and gold," Kecouroo said. "Nobody knows where."

"So we must not use blue feathers for decoration?" Kelly asked. "Is that why?"

"Perhaps."

I felt strangely sleepy. I stretched out before the fire and rested my head on the mat. I heard Kelly articulate her idea about how the stories related by tribal women should be compiled, perhaps as an elementary textbook, so schoolchildren could benefit from each oral tradition. "And Brianna wants Kyle Rula's diaries translated," Kelly added. "She wants college courses developed for the literary arts. Isn't that so, Brianna?"

My eyes rolled in my head. I could not think of a response. The last thing I remember was my regular breathing and Kat's chuckle from behind Kecouroo's shoulder.

I dreamed I was a gualarep in the waving grasses of Siibabean land. Thick-trunked hardwoods and graceful weeping willows banked the cloudless sky. I stalked a family of bushpigs and caught one piglet by the leg while the rest squealed and scattered. I placed a marbled foot over its hoary side, so I could taste the racing blood and sweet terror when my incisors penetrated its neck and skull.

I ripped at my meal and threw the ragged pieces back in my throat to swallow whole. Ketiwhelp came up yapping and nipping at my prize, attracted by the scent of blood. I jerked around and flicked my tail to slap them silly and retreated from the crushed grass while ketiwhelp, yearlings of the same litter, snatched the scraps of my kill. Concealed in the long prairie grass, I rushed their group. They yelped and scampered away. I tasted tail fur and stem from one, easy to identify after that day. Short-tail, I called her.

I awoke before dawn, still curled up in the middle of Kecouroo's hut. Somebody had covered me with a mat. I saw the backs of slumbering figures with pallets laid out in different positions. They must have stepped around me for the evening meal and while preparing to sleep. I knew I had been dreaming. What was it? Some vision sent by Kat? A nasty trick Kat had played, making me drowsy like that. I stretched and straightened my gown and quietly stepped outside.

Edwina waited there. "Ka, ka, ka, ka," she said.

"Swimming? You bet!" While we followed the trail to the waterfall and grotto, I was indifferent to the threat from hunting wildlife since no predator was more lethal than Edwina. I didn't notice the wildflowers that sought the patches of sun or the loops of vines heavy with new growth. I tried to conquer my irritation, focused on feelings of rejection from Kat and Kecouroo. I was a wormhole traveler and the manager of Somule Gems. I had ideas to share for industry and for a new enterprise that could one day make us all richer than an Abydian emir. But they had tricked me and not solicited my ideas while sharing favorite stories, content with what they had already secured. I didn't want to think poorly of the schoolteacher I had so admired as a student, but even her necklace of tektite stones seemed backward and trusting of old conceits.

I got my feet wet, then slipped into the chilly pool. "Edwina, is there tektite here? Black stone like Kecouroo wears. Is there tektite at the bottom of the grotto?"

Heavy, was her answer.

"A piece too heavy for you to bring up? Are there other pieces, smaller pieces, just to handle and see?"

Edwina flicked her tail to splash me. *Orders?* she asked.

"No, I'm not giving you an order. It's just that—"

Rufus hates orders.

I dove into the pool below the waterfall and swam using short sharp strokes that expressed more about my inner dialogue than my eagerness to reach the grotto. I had the means to bring Softcheeks technology to the savannah and methods to avoid the exploitation of workers by mining companies, but I had been afforded no opportunity to speak among the women of the Mekucoo.

We swam toward the waterfall. "I never gave Rufus orders. He just saw me with the students. And I want to ask you about Cleo too."

I grabbed Edwina's shoulder, and we dove deep under the waterfall through a narrow passage to the grotto. I came up with my lungs bursting for air. I must be out of shape; that effort didn't hurt when I was younger.

The grotto was smaller than I remembered. The water was cold and the spray sparse. The cave, when we reached it, had far less water volume and seemed dirty with spiders and blind albino amphibians. I wished I had not come today but rather had left the grotto in my memory as a young girl saw it, magical and mysterious.

Edwina left me in the shadows and dove deep, absent for more minutes than I wanted. I looked overhead at the vaulted ceiling and wondered how difficult it would be to get some heavy equipment secured above to haul up the silicide deposits in volume.

I felt bubbles tickle my legs and knew Edwina had returned. That was her favorite trick: to release a circle of bubbles while she lingered below. She breached the surface, glowing all pink and tan. I grabbed her shoulder, and we dove again, returning to the pool and waterfall. As I dragged myself out of the water and struggled with my sandals, Edwina dropped three sizable pieces of tektite on the bank.

"These were in the grotto?" I asked, reaching to touch them.

"Ka" she barked, and I drew back my hand.

"You win. They are yours, not mine. I get it."

She gingerly picked up each piece in her wide jaws and threw them into the back of her throat for easy carrying. We walked back to the village, seeking patches of sunlight to warm our bones. "Edwina, the water level is low."

Desert, she said.

"The savannah will know a new cycle as a desert? Do the women know?"

Know what?

"Um, nothing. Listen, is there another gualarep, maybe feral? I mean, maybe with no words?"

Brian, she said, in their special way.

"No, I mean a younger male, a wild gualarep."

What is wild?

"Not submitted. With no friends."

Edwina sidled to a patch of sunlight, and I joined her for an early morning hour spent there. "Come on, Edwina," I said while my skirt dried in the sunlight. "I have violent dreams, since before I entered the wormhole. You see the images too. Is there a wild male gifted with remote viewing? One that the ketiwhelps pester?"

Cyrus, came the answer.

"Not the spirit of Cyrus? An ancestor as gualarep?"

Cyrus the ketiwhelp killer, she informed me.

On our return to the village, I found a contingency of six warriors stoically waiting outside Kecouroo's hut. One Cylahi had gray in his grizzled beard that barely covered his chin and jawline. The others of mixed tribes were younger and apparently loyal to him.

From behind them, Edwina hissed. The warriors turned as a single body with karkars and knives poised. "Ka, ka, ka, ka, ka," she said as though that was great fun. She lumbered off, her tail swinging laterally with glee.

The men returned to their waiting. Rufus and Kecouroo emerged from the hut. "Who are these?" I asked. Rufus fixed me with that disdainful look before walking away. I did not care, reveling in my secret that I knew who would be his wife. Walking in Kyle Rula's place for this short time had taught me the quiet pleasure of holding tribal secrets, just as Mrs. Shaw's example had once taught me the value of righteous anger. I decided then and there that my ideas for developing the deposits of silicide could wait for a compatriot who actually liked me.

Rufus turned back and held his karkar over his head, calling "Hai!" to the waiting men.

Their leader called back, "Hai!" and Rufus sauntered off.

"These warriors are sent by Karlyhi," Kecouroo told me. "You will teach them now."

"Teach them what?"

"College."

"You misunderstand. College is . . . is, uh—"

She indicated the leader. "This one is Mark, Lucy's surviving kid and cousin to Marcy. He will know civil law from you."

"Which dialects do you read?" I asked, but he only stared. "Surely you read?" I looked at the other warriors in his cohort.

"Which ones attended academy?" None met my look.

"These are hamstrung," Kecouroo said.

I knew hamstrung. Vera had been hamstrung, her ankle tendons sliced to cripple her mobility, although the warriors were more likely wounded during battles with Siibabean. That would mean each had been crippled for more than twelve years. Siibabean had been our allies at least that long. So the youngest was a minimum age of twenty-six, too old to have tolerated academy training.

"No good for Uburu climbing," Kecouroo added. "Easily sighted on Madquii dunes."

I looked at the leader who stared ahead with a warrior's discipline. They were for college because they had been deselected from warrior duty. Karlyhi probably thought he was more clever by half to send warriors who could not serve in an ambush. "You know this means Siibabean have selected the college students," I said.

Smile lines showed on Mark's face. Tribal logic appealed to him.

I sent them to sit with Cara, the aged and blind Mekucoo leader. They were instructed to learn his tribal chants and carry on the oral tradition, a great honor. They bowed and hobbled off, each with his head and shoulders bobbing in a different direction dictated by his old wounds, a comical delegation. My instructions to the warriors were an interim measure. I was not so easily thwarted as Karlyhi's trick presumed.

I heard a child cry out and turned to see Cleo with Edwina near Kecouroo's hut. Camille rushed forward, along with Kecouroo and Kat. We found Cleo inspecting her hand as though it had been burned or bitten. Her eyebrows were drawn together in anguish, the first emotion I'd seen her display. The tektite stones Edwina had brought from the grotto were scattered on the ground.

"You didn't nip her, surely?" I asked Edwina.

Touched by om, was the answer.

Kat and I exchanged glances, but Kecouroo didn't react. I had always wondered how much she could communicate with Edwina. "Cleo, what happened?" I asked.

She rubbed her palm with the thumb of her other hand. Kecouroo knelt before her and picked up one piece of tektite. Cleo's eyes grew wide, and she drew back.

"This stone burns?" Kecouroo asked.

Cleo looked about, maybe wanting to escape. Kecouroo caught her arm to steady her.

Kat signaled me, and I gently drew Kecouroo's hand away. I helped her to stand. "This one is touched by om," I barely whispered. "She will remain in the village of Kecouroo and learn from the holy woman what Dolvia would have her know. Camille will stay as her helpmate."

Question and bitterness hovered in Kecouroo's eyes. She lowered her gaze and sighed. "Let it be so."

Just then, Kelly came out of the hut, yawning and pushing her glasses up on her nose. "What's wrong?" she asked. I glanced her way, and when I looked back, Kat was apparently gone. Edwina had also lumbered away, perhaps seeking sunlight to warm her blood.

"Honor to Kecouroo," I said quietly. "Daughter to Cyrus the keti-whelp killer, niece to Cara and friend to Kyle Rula. She who has guided the steps of Dacupitte, whose child I will bear." Tears stood in her eyes, but Kecouroo said nothing. Kelly just stared, looking from one face to another.

"Camille," I said, "take Cleo inside and put a salve on her hand. You are responsible for her now, you and Kat."

"Who is Kat?" Kelly asked. Kecouroo turned away to hide her bitter tears.

An hour later, Kelly and I were preparing to walk down to Mayschool where I would put another section of my plan into place. Kecouroo waited for the ritual goodbye, so we bowed and exchanged small gifts. I offered a burka from Rularim's store. Mekucoo sometimes wore veils while in Somule or Cylay, where Kecouroo seldom visited. Still, she seemed touched by the gift because Kyle Rula had been her good friend. She gave me three tektite chips, similar to the ones in her necklace. "Keep them close," was her encouragement.

Kelly set off down the trail, but at the last moment, I turned back. "Kelly is for Rufus," I said without preamble and saw Kecouroo's eyebrows go up with question. "Mark my words." I showed an open palm at elbow height and left, not even looking back. Her Mekucoo manner valued succinct certainty more.

At Mayschool, I caught up with Hakulupe Le. We stood in the catalpa tree's shade while I explained certain developments. "Cleo and Camille will remain in the village of Kecouroo for now. Ask Edwina about recent events there."

I described the delegation led by Mark, who by then sat with Cara. Lupe shook her head and lowered the liquid gaze of those green-green eyes. "The treasure is our duty now," I said. "And the holy woman has mentioned distribution since the treasure cannot save me. So . . . I have a few ideas, and I was wondering if I can count on your help with supporting new—"

"Whatever is needed, Brianna," Lupe said simply. "You know I want the academy to grow."

My ideas came out in a rush, perhaps not organized to a real plan. "We must make a beginning and rely on a mentoring system for these warriors. Match a promising senior male student with each man. Assign each an area of study, something they can accomplish in stages. Then have the students report back to you at intervals."

Lupe shrugged, hesitant and frowning. "They will learn only the warrior way."

"The warriors will learn the value of academy studies and tell others."

"And that is enough?"

"Some will fall away," I said, "so others must be found. Dolvia has used Siibabean to her purpose."

"Only male students?"

Somehow I felt pressure to take several steps toward implementing my plan, maybe because the puzzle piece I had long envisioned for Kecouroo had suddenly come into place, albeit without her help. "Select senior female students to be mentored by you and Kecouroo and Vera and Sarah and. . . . Well, the best teachers are absent by their own hands. That's why you must not torch yourself."

"And you?"

"I must meet Dulcinea the Uburu," I said quickly, "and learn more about Borabean. Kelly can remain with me for now. Later I can send her to Carline on Cicero. Oh, and send some students to Martina: four college-level candidates to shadow the Softcheeks scientists, as long as Martina promises to not turn them into servants. Have Vera parcel out the needed grant funding so each group is accepted by the mentors."

Lupe was measured with her words, her part of the discussion feeling positively cosmopolitan in comparison to the backward Mekucoo. "It's good you have returned to Dolvia's embrace, Brianna. It's good you follow Kat's word for you and distribute the treasure. I will undertake what you have instructed."

At least that part could be accomplished. My new enterprise gained root within a structure that was long established with women already trained in their functions. My ideas needed new blood though, and maybe managers less content with following a vision that spoke only to preserving what they already had.

TWELVE

 village and were greeted heartily in Arrivi. She was everything I had expected, with soft features and a gentle manner. She wore a loosely woven dress of bright and regular patterns under a sleeveless goatskin robe that hung to her knees. Her soft boots were made of decorated animal skins. She supplied similar garments for Kelly and me, claiming that the Uburu sarong and baktu were worn during the dry season, but the rains were approaching. "To guard against frost," she said of the warm garments.

"What is frost?" Kelly asked.

"You'll find out."

Here was the woman who held Pete's attention; Pete whom I had not yet greeted since my return to Dolvia. Her gaze twinkling with friendliness, she asked about A-me-ri-ca and wormhole travel. I made gifts of a burka that had been Rularim's and translated versions of The Iliad and The Odyssey by Homer. I was confident Dulcinea would appreciate the story of Helen. Or perhaps the example of Penelope, the wife of Odysseus, would interest her more.

A timber and earth hut was provided for our stay. While Kelly unpacked, Dulcinea took me to greet her father, a great honor. He was blind with milky eyes and a curved spine. He felt my face all over with his callused and big-knuckled hands and said in Uburu, "This one has character. She will know much trouble."

"All of us will have trouble, Father."

"She shall know more trouble than those who follow."

While we walked back for a meal with Kelly, Dulcinea asked, "You sometimes travel with the one Rufus?"

"My cousin and brother to Lynus."

"We know Lynus. I also met his wife, Alaise. She seems fine."

"Rufus said the same. Did he get that from you?"

"Rufus makes up his own mind."

I only laughed. "Truer words were never spoken."

We sat before a low table in the slate-roofed hut. The floor was covered with goatskins, and the walls hung with a woolen cloth. A fire burned in the open oven while Kelly served tea in Arrivi fashion. "I see you have learned our ways," I said to Dulcinea. "Are you as well versed in Abydian customs?"

"Abydian put earrings on insects and line their tombs with images of beetles." Seated with us, Kelly pushed her black-rimmed glasses up on her nose before turning to a fresh page in her notebook, ready to record exotic tales.

"Their history," Dulcinea continued, "does not harken back to immediate heroes such as Cyrus; rather, a never-ending march of fat kings. Their crony system is all."

"They should do well with Putuki," Kelly offered dryly.

Dulcinea shrugged. "One of a disparate culture cannot judge these things. Lynus married among the Madquii."

"Perhaps it was his one-fourth Borabean blood stirring in his veins," I said.

"Alaise is no beauty," Dulcinea confided. "She has a faint mustache."

Kelly covered her mouth to hide her smile.

"And this redeemer they follow, is he true?" I asked.

"There are several Borabean tribes," Dulcinea said. "We tend to think of them as one, just as they think of us as gehenna. Their desert tribes with no experience in sea trade are the religious fanatics."

"What is ge-hen-na?" Kelly asked.

"Barbarians. Foreign tribes who are . . . uh, not them."

"Gehenna," I repeated.

"The leaders of the Abydian clan overthrew the ruler who was a son to Cyrus's father, and imposed civil and religious law. Their muezzins, orators in the temple, inflame the people against the savannah tribes, perhaps to distract from the failure of their most recent five-year plan for commerce.

"They remember Cyrus," she continued, "as a monster who ate the beating hearts of his enemies. They portray Karl Wyley as a butcher who uses terror and silent death as primary weapons. Stories are told of how he takes prisoners out on the savannah and cuts them all over, then makes them undertake a death march in the sun."

I glanced at Kelly before I averted my eyes. Dulcinea stopped, perhaps realizing she had touched a sore spot. "Borabeans call Dacupitte morta chi," she added, interjecting a cheerful note in her voice. "It means death on the wind."

Kelly forced a smile and looked down at her notes.

"And their name for Rabbenu Ely?" I asked.

"Ely is not seen as a warrior, rather as a statesman. Our spies report that Ely meets with Tuang Cho and Wan Su from the mining Company that once had a refinery on the savannah."

"I saw this Wan Su before I disembarked," I said. "What's your take on him?"

"Take?"

"Sorry, I must shed Earth idiom. How do you see him within the group?"

"A butcher," she said with a downturned mouth. "He visits the desert emirs, and later, their temple rhetoric against Arrivi becomes louder."

"Is Wan Su his own man?" I asked.

"Is any Company man?" Dulcinea said dryly.

"I need to learn more Borabean words. Is there one here fluent and available?"

"Work with Alaise when she visits."

"That is good."

The following morning at sunrise, I pulled on the soft kid boots and the long lambswool vest. I placed a woolen shawl over my head and coiled hair. I joined Dulcinea while she milked the goats and gathered eggs from the fowl hut. The mesa air was crisp and wet, so unlike the savannah. The maize fields were fallow with ragged cornstalks grouped in unsteady triangular stacks. Grass crunched under our steps, dusted with an overnight frost.

Dulcinea pointed across the vista of mesas and savannah. The folds of her shawl resting on her hair-framed bright eyes and cheeks flecked with a healthy flush. I saw the attraction that caused our warriors to act the fools. She pointed again, and I followed her gesture. Through the mist between two snow-topped mesas, I glimpsed the vast plain that was my childhood home. In the distant horizon, barely a speck, stood the monumental butte on the land of Arim. "We are neighbors," Dulcinea whispered before she led me out of the biting wind.

We collected sugar beets from cold storage. "I'm sorry," she said, "for my blunder yesterday about Karl Wyley's methods. He carries out these vengeful acts?"

"Kelly's father died that way. He was profiteering."

"I didn't know."

"Don't think less of Kelly. She's for Rufus." Dulcinea stared into my face. "She does not know yet," I added, "but Dolvia has given the sign."

"Warriors do not speak of these things. We must talk more." Carrying our load, we approached her father's hut to prepare the morning meal. "Tell me about the one Kyle Rula," Dulcinea said. "We hear many stories, but which is true? Did she overfly the savannah on Murmurey wings?"

I shook my head no. "She could speak out your fate in seven words or less."

"She was blessed by Dolvia, as you say." We smiled together. I was glad I had traveled to Uburu land, glad that the tribes were allies. I hoped to spend many days with my new friend.

Standing outside the elder's hut with three others was Dacupitte, dressed in the militia uniform and jackboots and with a Mekucoo tunic pulled on for warmth. They stamped their feet and blew into their cupped hands. Pete's orange hair was twisted in thick dreadlocks and bound in a warrior's queue that hung to below his shoulder blades. He was stockier than I remembered. At age forty-two or more and the birth father of whole divisions of red-headed soldiers, he stood confident and relaxed among those who served him.

His face lit up when he saw Dulcinea. And then he saw me.

Dulcinea stopped, so I stopped and turned to her. "There can be no trouble between you and me," I assured her. "Dacupitte is my adoptive brother and no more."

"I feel no . . . need for him," she whispered.

My face broke into a big smile. Here was a woman like myself who needed no man to define her. I had not thought to meet one ever in the universe, and Dulcinea was my neighbor. Smiling and giggling, we approached Dacupitte.

"I cannot provide a meal for all these," Dulcinea said, indicating his men.

"We have rations. Is there an enclosure?"

"The communal building is down the way."

Pete nodded to his men, who shouldered their karkars and walked left. He turned back to me with suspicion. I pulled the shawl across my lower face and held a hand high in the Arrivi greeting. "Hiki, Dacupitte."

"Hiki, Brianna," he said. "It's good to see the spirit in your face."

"Melinga."

"We have much to discuss."

"Join us," Dulcinea said with humor in her voice, "while we prepare my father's first meal." My new friendship with her felt like a conspiracy. Because we were together, Dacupitte's woman and Pete's amour, neither were available to him. He could corral only one woman at a time. In the large one-room hut, Pete was made to sit near the fire in polite conversation with the blind elder while Dulcinea and I labored by the stove. I came to understand the value of her stately manner. Her father's status was a shield behind which Dulcinea maneuvered her own choices without damage to a warrior's pride.

Each of us waited for Dulcinea's guidance, for even the slightest gesture. We paid court to her while she acted as though adoration was only good manners. And yet this early morning event was warm and inclusive, and I wanted to stay forever.

Before the eggs were hard-boiled, Kelly joined us, yawning and carrying her steamed-up glasses in one hand. She saw Pete, and her eyes went to saucers. She put on the black-rimmed glasses and stared before turning to Dulcinea and me. We giggled again.

"Chi cylay," I told Kelly. Pete shot us a disapproving glance.

We sat at the table with the elder, and Dulcinea served. "I should serve here," Kelly objected.

Dulcinea placed a hand on her forearm. "On another day. This once, allow me the honor." Kelly was much flattered, and Dulcinea thus made another friend.

"Carry the village maize surplus down the mesa today," the elder said to Pete.

"As you wish. We brought mill-made clothes and binoculars for your militia."

The elder's milky eyes focused on nobody. "We are grateful for guidance from those trained in scouting."

"Our needs now are for wool blankets and goatskin coats."

"This cold snap is early," the elder shrugged. "There's plenty of time for discussion. Is General Shaw traveling with your group?"

"Not today."

While we sat over tea and superficial talk, a knock came at the door. Kelly answered it, and one of Pete's captains entered. Pete stood and signified on the elder. "We still have much to discuss," he told me.

"I am confident you will return," I said. "Incidentally, I have something of yours." I reached into my skirt pocket and produced the engagement bracelet that Rufus had offered in Pete's place. His face turned stone cold. "You must keep it."

"Not at all. You must offer it to the one your heart seeks."

"It is seen," he claimed in a louder voice.

"I don't see that." I emphasized the word "see."

Pete took one step forward and grabbed the bracelet, then left with his second man. We three burst into silly laughter behind the closed door.

When we left the hut an hour later, the frost had vanished in the strong sunlight. Dulcinea and I had decided to walk down the mesa side for a Southeast Arrivi visit. Kelly remained behind to learn Uburu cooking techniques from Dulcinea's aunt and to record their fireside chants in her notebooks. I looked forward to talking with Sarah from the savannah convent and to viewing the progress she and Bibi Le had made with the academy there. I also wanted to broach a new topic with my neighbor, one I had withheld from Kecouroo.

Our woolen clothes felt weighty and wrong. "I have an extra Arrivi skirt but no sandals for you, I'm afraid." We stopped and changed into lighter clothes, rolling the Uburu garments into slings. As we continued on the narrow path, I realized the disadvantage of the long skirts of the Arrivi gown. We stopped again, and I showed Dulcinea how to tie up the length into tight pantaloons. Finally able to maneuver in our tribal clothes, we picked our way along the steep grade.

Breathing hard, I pursued my education of Borabean ways. "What do you know of mining for silicide on Borabean dunes?"

"The deposits they found were paltry." Dulcinea seemed to experience less exertion than I did. I was not ready to tolerate long walks without discomfort. "Survey teams," she continued, "crisscross the dunes, but the desert does not display her treasures. Now they look to the ocean near Urbyd. Water is easier to see through than sand."

By mid-morning we had descended past the militia stations for Dacupitte's men and picked our way along the torturous paths just above the wooded valley floor. Once we reached a stream in the wide gorge, I looked up at the mesa, surprised that it was stubby and terraced.

We spent the night with another aunt to Dulcinea who received us with great ceremony. Her husband and oldest son were away fulfilling their militia duties. Her younger sons wore baktus only and kept sleek livestock in permanent wooden corrals nestled among the tamarinds and towering hardwood eucalyptus called mida.

The family lived in a two-level house made completely of wood. The thick overhead timbers seemed regal and excessively wealthy. Two daughters wore lovely sarongs and showed me the richly patterned lambswool they had learned to weave during the cold weeks. "The grandfather of these ones," Dulcinea explained, "was a master ship builder for the Abydian king. When Kyros returned to Arrivi land, he traveled with her wagons and settled here. Some mida trees were fallen from a windstorm. We seldom harvest them, but this dwelling benefits from his skill with struts and braces."

I allowed the sisters to inspect the workmanship on our Arrivi gowns and gifted them burkas once owned by Kyle Rula. They were greatly pleased to receive something so valuable, and from Rularim too.

I unrolled one veil and snapped the ends so it fluttered in the air. The older sister stepped under it and pulled the facial mesh straight. The second sister wanted the same ritual. While they giggled and preened, I sent the image to Edwina because I knew she liked mental pictures with color and light. Later, we were served a hearty meal using dishes of pewter and drinking mugs of thick glass. I thought this aunt was the richest woman I had ever met. She also deferred to Dulcinea in all matters of custom.

By late morning of the following day, Dulcinea and I had traversed the open desert approaching Southeast Arrivi. Dulcinea wanted to know more about the women of the savannah. "Warriors don't land their women in my presence," she said lightly. "Tell me about Sheeks-Cylom, the one who raised Karlyhi."

"She did not raise him exactly, not a nurturing personality."

"But she was his guardian."

"After his Cylahi mother was lost in the refugee camp, Karlyhi lived at the clinic. She gave him responsibility beyond his station because he was useful to her at the isolated camp."

"And this Sheeks-Cylom, you don't care for her?"

"She was my mentor and allowed me to travel offworld. But she is . . . unforgiving."

"So you and Karlyhi were raised together."

"We grew up in the same bush compound anyway."

"As a young girl, I was in a savannah refugee camp." She saw my look of disbelief. "I was only eight, but it was a difficult time for Uburu; the heat and insects, the strange food. I remember mostly the glowering and half-dressed warriors from tribes I did not know. Our women became secretive and hoarding. Warriors turned selfish, driven by fear. Our laws were useless to us there, and many were glad to walk back to our farms.

"That was where I first saw Dacupitte," she added. "He was viewed as a great leader, the strongest voice among many. We avoided Karlyhi, but Pete wanted dialogue with the elders. And General Shaw, everybody admired General Shaw."

"I lived with General Shaw and his wife a short time in Cylay," I said.

"Truly?"

"His wife is Sheeks-Cylom, you know."

"Now wait a minute. Sheeks-Cylom ran the bush clinic. She and General Shaw—"

I only nodded.

Dulcinea was silent a long time. "She has two mantels?"

"Actually, three," I grinned.

We stopped and pulled on our burkas against the heat. We increased our pace under the burning sun. "And among the tribes," Dulcinea asked, "whom do you admire?"

"Kecouroo."

"Ah, yes, the famous Kecouroo. My aunt, you know."

"What?"

"She visited for a time as a young woman and had a son by Moab who led during the gold mine conflict. But she too much missed her own people and left. That son is my uncle by marriage, Kenru."

"I never heard about this. She never spoke of children."

"It broke her spirit to leave him, but that's the law, or was in those days."

"And does she ever see him?"

"Surely, more than twice a year that I know."

"Time is truly a loop," I said in Arrivi, shaking my head.

"I don't know those words."

"It's an old saying," I said. "We are often through events before we know their meaning in our lives."

"Time is a loop," she repeated.

"And this is a good mercy seat," I added.

While the sun hung low in the sky, its pink and amber light struck our eyes and made westward travel difficult. We rested under some oleastra bushes and talked until Dulcinea stopped in midsentence and caught her breath. Edwina came up at our left, waiting some feet away and holding high that regal head. Her marbled flanks were golden with flecks of blood red. "There is no danger," I reassured Dulcinea. I walked to Edwina and sat cross-legged on the ground while she fingered me with her tongue. "Will you meet my new friend?"

No pictures, she said.

"Perhaps Dulcinea is willing to learn."

Pete's girl.

"Only in Pete's mind."

"Ka, ka, ka, ka, ka," she articulated.

Dulcinea wanted to be gracious but could not keep herself from drawing back with each near contact. I had seen this before. There was no communication between Vera and Edwina, for example, and Mrs. Shaw was limited in this area. While Dulcinea gathered fuel for our evening fire, Edwina took her leave. "You must not dislike Dulcinea for her reserve."

No swimming.

"That is true. Swimming could have won her over. Maybe another time."

"Ka, ka, ka, ka, ka," she said and sidled off into the gathering night. She sent a single image of the woodland Uburu sisters enjoying their burka gifts. I was forgiven; hard feelings between me and Edwina had vanished.

We built a sizeable fire that night and unrolled two pallets for sleeping. The stand of acacias we had selected for camp included a natural spring with a round head where the fresh water was cold and sweet. Dolvia's two moons were in quarter phase, nestled above the horizon like spoons in a drawer. By the fire, Dulcinea parceled out rations of cornmeal and goat meat. "I suppose your lizard friend waits in the shadows nearby."

"What makes you think that?"

"You built a big fire for warmth where caution demands a more protected camp."

I pulled from my skirt pocket the silicide beads I had found in the fortress and had to sort them from the tektite stones Kecouroo had provided. I showed Dulcinea the silicide. "Do you recognize these?"

She only glanced into my palm. "From the Abydian clan?"

"From the savannah. Do you find silicide on Uburu land?"

She shrugged. "Along some creek beds but not in mesa rock. It gathers light?"

"Yes and has positive and negative electrical charges, but that's too technical. Maybe Dolviets can manage the resource and build the industry here rather than have our mineral wealth extracted by others for profit."

"Have you taken the idea to the warriors? To Rufus or Dacupitte?"

I sighed and tugged at my earlobe. "Why involve the men? Which among them can keep a secret?"

Dulcinea spoke haltingly in the gathering night. "Have you shared these ideas with Kecouroo or the women who run the Arrivi academy?"

"They too much love tradition," I said bitterly. "Even if we can find the silicide, and even if we can dig a quantity from the ground, even then we need secure storage where Borabeans cannot simply take it."

"Not on Mekucoo land or with Silbabean?"

My back itched, and I squirmed to scratch between my shoulder blades. "Well, my view is . . . just my opinion, of course. Storage should be near the largest deposits, not just ours, but Borabean deposits also, so we can trade with them."

"More than storage, you want to establish a refinery? And what does General Hartley say?"

I stopped short, staring at her features underlit by the campfire. What did she know about General Hartley? Dulcinea measured her words. "When the warriors said you wanted to visit, I wondered if you had some kernel to dislodge about Dacupitte, but I didn't know, so I asked Kenru. He asked Colonel Sector who said you were the mistress of—"

"I'm not his mistress!" I stood suddenly and started to pace before the fire. "This is my deal with my funds and my connections." I made a quick gesture for emphasis. "Women have learned to manage resources, and they have the academy now. But I'm talking about something more, about commerce and leverage. We can use the silicide to build a real future with a seat at the table, not just with the Consortium, but with offworlders too."

"With Daniel Chin?"

I stopped and waited three beats. "Where does that come from?"

"You think we cannot see your intent from your actions?"

"I was being discreet. What slip-up?"

"You want to visit Borabean land for what purpose?"

"Most of the silicide is on Arrivi land. I mean, I suspect it is." I was pacing again. "You think Borabeans won't invade once they deplete their deposits?"

"How do you know it's on Arrivi land? On the flats?"

"Under the flats, mostly."

"But how do you know?"

"I saw the land surveys. The grottos and the tunnels where the gualareps swim are full of silicide, which may be the source of their gift for sharing thoughts."

Her brow wrinkled with disbelief. "Because the water has silicide, like netta water?"

"I have no proof," I said, working off the excess energy by pacing. "I have only my hunch and some connections for testing samples. If those tests turn out as I think they will, then we have a true treasure here. Arrivi can develop the resource through all its phases to reach the end market, to make and store the superconductors."

"Superconductors?"

"They are long strands of silicide used to focus light and send messages, bundles of messages, without extra noise."

"That is technical," Dulcinea said slowly, her manner so different from mine. "You will need the general's help to import the large equipment."

"I know how channels work for shipping and tariffs. I know who to contact for special orders." Now I was pacing and nodding. "I have this knowledge separate from the warriors and the officers."

She brushed her chin slowly with one hand, thinking it through. "You must be patient with me, Brianna. I only speak out the questions many have voiced. What if the silicide runs out? The quantity for this whole region is from a single meteor rock, I was told."

I turned my back while I paced. "It may run out. Before that though, the Company may just steal it. Then where will we be?"

Dulcinea watched me pace around the fire. "Are you asking my opinion," she said, "or inviting me to join a new enterprise?"

"The other women are content with what they have now. Are you content?"

She turned her head left and right, watching me move about. "Just so I understand," she said, "you want to mine silicide on the flats of Arim to store somewhere private in the Uburu mesas. You want to import Softcheeks technology to start a new industry and maybe trade with Borabean for their reserves as well. Don't Borabean already have refinery furnaces in their capital city?"

I sat heavily in my seat before the fire. "So what if they do?"

"So we will need to be keep your designs under wraps," she postulated quietly, "until we know what we're about. We can store some weight of silicide in a wadi I know next to the gullies that hold cenzea. Then the Company men will rob the desert of some when they try to grab our wealth."

I just stared.

"Have you thought of a name for this new enterprise?" she asked.

"Something neutral that carries no insult to traders."

She pursed her lips and ran two fingers along the side of her jaw. "We need a name that implies strength, I think, and energy. Not a made up word like tektite or a derivative word like silicide. Rather, a word of power that speaks to our vision of what the tribes can achieve. What do you think of the name StrikeStone?" She looked over at my staring face.

I held out my hand. "Let's shake on it."

It was late the third morning when we approached Southeast Arrivi village from under the veil. I felt sad that our mercy seat was ending and wanted additional long and delicious days spent making plans for industry. "I have wanted to ask," Dulcinea shyly said, "but I have no courage. I should ask now while we're alone. This prophecy about you and Pete, do you hold with it?"

"Pete has many children."

"But no wife."

"I nominate you."

Dulcinea waited a long moment, perhaps mustering her courage. "Uburu needs are different from those of Mekucoo. I want a husband who stays at home, who works the fields, and who is always there when I need him. These militiamen are enamored with karkars and helicopters and . . . how to say, being at advantage. None is husband material."

"Especially a handsome man in leadership?"

"Especially Pete," she agreed.

"There are good men who work savannah farms," I said. "Orin rabbe Murd and his son Hakki. There's Kyros rabbe Sudl. There's—"

"I have often thought," she said. "Soldiers are, I mean no offense . . . they're second tier. Offworlders or landless younger brothers. Or feckless." We grinned together. "A good man does not volunteer. He waits to defend his own fields."

"Mekucoo are raised as warriors," I said. "Cylahl have no land and weak family structures. Putuki are merchants. Arrivi farms pass to the oldest brother now, so those born later become his employees. Only women are married to the land."

"And so it is with us," Dulcinea said. "One day hot-eyed men will no longer loiter at my father's house. I want to choose the one who stays because it's in him to stay."

"That's not Pete."

We walked arm-in-arm then, sisters under the veil, and came to the adobe village of Bibi Le where I had promised a new academy upon the return of Kyros rabbe Sudl from wormhole travel. The buildings were strangely deserted, and the foundation for the new school was empty with tools and materials strewn everywhere. Beyond the livestock pens, a loud explosion was heard.

"What was that?" Dulcinea asked.

We pulled off our slings and burkas and allowed them to fall to the ground. I raced toward the noise but stopped short when a second detonation caused the rice field embankments to spray into the air and release their water. Veiled Arrivi women, Bibi Le first among them, stood in groups wailing and clucking and pointing. Facing them with shouldered karkars stood a line of Consortium soldiers from Colonel Sector's division, blocking access to the fields. Village men, some glowering and some resigned, were restrained by ropes tied at their elbows.

Four helicopters waited on the side. Colonel Sector and his men concentrated on their work by the plungers. Kyros rabbe Sudl, his face grim, stood talking with them.

The signal came that the laboring soldiers were clear of the planted explosives. Colonel Sector detonated another charge. A pop-pop-pop indicated the charges were active before a mound of earth rose with a booming noise and spraying dirt. The remaining rice fields were flattened, and water flowed into a wide delta. Colonel Sector put a sympathetic hand on Kyros's shoulder.

I saw Mrs. Shaw near the storage silos wearing her doctor's coat over the tan skirt and blouse, her pregnancy burden just beginning to show. She carried a wide-brimmed hat and gloves in hand and spoke shortly to Karlyhi. She made an imperious gesture circling one finger in the air. I knew what she was saying even before I'd rushed to Karlyhi.

"What are you doing?" I demanded. "What does she want?"

Karlyhi's face was grim. "The rice is tainted."

"Who says? Sheeks-Cylom? Since when is her order the law?"

Mrs. Shaw didn't show surprise at my arrival at the end of her event. "Brianna, I know this is hard, but it must be done. The pfsteria infestation."

I was shouting, unable to control my rage. "On your word? Just destroy the people's livelihood and fly off in your chopper. That's your solution?"

"I am sorry. This storage must be destroyed."

Colonel Sector and Kyros rabbe Sudl joined us. "Kyros, you agreed to this?" I demanded. "You let them just . . . just—"

"General Shaw said years ago," Colonel Sector added, "rice farming would come to no good."

How I hated him in that moment. Southeast Arrivi had taken up the cash crop under Softcheeks encouragement. They had molded their lives in trust of a better method. Then the haughty Softcheeks had returned to detonate the fields and call it a day.

"What about the people?" I demanded. "What will the people do now?"

Colonel Sector looked at Kyros and avoided meeting my eye. "A grant will stake them for a new erriv herd."

"A research doctor named Ingram will monitor their recovery from ingestion," Mrs. Shaw added, staring at the ground. "Regular testing."

"Lab rats," I sneered. "You have turned them into lab rats. And now you want to publish a white paper on the progressive stages of sickness."

"I don't have to listen to this." Mrs. Shaw stomped toward the helicopter.

I scrambled after her. "You will listen! You and your research goals and your good intentions!"

Behind us Colonel Sector signaled his men to mount the helicopters. He shook Kyros's hand and nodded to Karlyhi. The Consortium soldiers released the village men, who stood in a stunned group. The soldiers quickly loaded their equipment while the choppers powered up.

But I saw only Mrs. Shaw. "You think you are goddamned god on high," I sputtered. "Pushing around these aborigines. You think you can waltz in here and—"

She turned, finally, and faced me. "It had to be done!"

Colonel Sector helped her climb into the chopper and joined her, taking the opposite seat. Her protruding stomach was more obvious when she was seated. I stood at the hatch, shouting over the engine noise. "Maybe what you did here was needed, and maybe it was correct." I leaned in facing her, my nose inches from hers. "But it cannot be made right!"

I slammed the heavy door and backed away from the blades' disturbance. Two choppers lifted off. Karlyhi's Siibabean guard waited near the other two. I was trembling with rage. Tears streamed down my face as I watched Sheeks-Cylom exit the scene of her latest good deed.

"So, that's the Sheeks-Cylom," Dulcinea ventured ironically from behind me. She put an arm around my shoulders and quickly dabbed my face with her sleeve, removing the tear streaks. She walked with me to where Karlyhi and Kyros waited by the silos. Karlyhi nodded to Dulcinea. "May I present the one Kyros rabbe Sudl?"

"Hiki, Dulcinea," the big man said. "Our village is sorry for this trouble on the day of your visit."

"You're sorry?" I asked in that same demanding tone. "So sorry? They did this to you! They made you take up rice farming and change your way of life. Now they want to put you on the dole and make you dependent on them for . . . for bread!"

"He only meant—" Karlyhi began.

"And you! General Shaw's native puppet. He taught you trucks and helicopters, so you let him just . . . just destroy the land."

Karlyhi looked directly into my eyes. "The rice makes workers lazy."

"So you intend to destroy it?"

"I was thinking that we could sell it to Borabean."

There was a short silence before Kyros chuckled. Dulcinea glanced at each of their faces and smiled shyly.

I took a deep breath. "You would need to go through a third party."

Karlyhi's implacable face betrayed nothing. "We can offer them a good price and use the funds to stake the village. Not all benefit must come through the treasure of Kyle Rula."

"That is good," I said, collecting myself. "I must find my burka." I turned on my heel and strolled left past the staring villagers.

Karlyhi spoke to Dulcinea behind me. "Brianna can be a terror once she gets mad."

I was sitting near the livestock pen still shaken from the emotional outburst when Dulcinea joined me; she just plopped down on the sawhorse next to me as though we were siblings. "You have been traveling constantly since your return to Dolvia? Maybe you need rest and solitude."

"Is that what they told you?"

"Karlyhi said you must come." She saw my pained look and added, "He offered us a ride in one of the helicopters, much easier than climbing the mesa side."

"Don't tell him our plans," I said peevishly, "for the StrikeStone venture, or any of the men. Certainly not Sheeks-Cylom."

"Just us tribal girls," she whispered. "Two whom you brought to the savannah wait to greet you, the boys from the clutch of Cleo Datong."

"I remember. They wanted to live with Kyros because they knew him already." I stood and allowed my new friend to lead me back to the others.

PART TWO

Reverence to water, fire, air, and stone
The purest being fire that consumes
To release the spirit and reshape the fuel
Spent in this world but made new
Companion to ancestors, desert reborn

THIRTEEN

from Kelly Osborn

SHE DIDN'T HAVE TO BE LIKE THAT, BRIANNA MILLER. RULARIM arisen. Ha! She was a tyrant. Always with, "Kelly, do this," or "Kelly, bring me that." She treated me like I was her servant. No, her slave.

So, I'm not the prettiest thing on the block. Boohoo. I have none of the gifts of Dolvia because I'm mixed blood. My father was Joey Osborn, son to Heather the colonial savior by her first husband Carl. Spiritual gifts are reserved for full-blooded Arrivi only, like Kyle Rula who had second sight and Kat who serves as the holy woman.

That doesn't mean I have no value. Brianna always preached that a woman's voice must gain volume. A place where her ideas carried weight. Except she never listened to me.

It's true that I am not blessed by Dolvia like Dr. Greensboro. She has no native blood, but she established the bush clinic and became known as the Sheeks-Cylom. Her actions were amplified by forces she did not know, and she served as the agent of the season of cylay even without a spiritual gift. So being a know-it-all means nothing. Anybody can be a know-it-all.

The house in Somule is my family home. Brianna Miller treated it like a, a backdrop to showcase her generosity with the tribes.

After Mayschool had been dedicated, Brianna chose Somule instead of the nearby fortress of Arim, which she claimed was too lonely with just the blue macaw for company. In my house, we slept for days and spent hours in front of the EAM while Brianna made more plans for her new venture called StrikeStone. She cautioned Karen and me to keep the plans for silicide exploration a secret. She wanted secrets to hold over the warriors like Kyle Rula had.

Many people visited, but different groups from those who had gathered around Sheeks-Cylom or who had petitioned Kyle Rula in her day. This was our house, and we had authority here, Karen and me, but Brianna turned the living room into a conference room and the kitchen into a communications center. She sat with Putuki businessmen and Uburu militia leaders and groups of souks from the local bazaar.

I was in service, barely noticed by Brianna or her guests. Some days I served tea three times in the afternoon while Brianna listened and laughed and told stories about the Softcheeks world. She seldom told the same story or asked the same questions either. I noticed that. Brianna was segmented, flashing the part of herself the guest expected to see and changing with a simple turn to show a different face to others.

She ordered the Mekucoo tribesmen, for example, to train Edwina with a net, to teach her how to push a heavy rock into the net for some reason. Then Brianna ordered from Cylay a pulley system and sent Mark and the other college warriors to Kecouroo's village with the contraption. Later it was said that, with Edwina's help, they hauled up a sizeable piece of tektite, more than just the chips that Mekucoo women treasure. Brianna called it a nose piece and ordered that nobody touch it. The nose piece was stored at Mayschool in the enclosure by the men's building that had served before as the shrine to Hamilcar and the floating heads. The weighty meteor fragment waited, I guess, for Brianna to puzzle out how she could turn a profit without selling the secret.

I accompanied Brianna when she visited the local shops where she lingered overlong, using smiles and big gestures, and bought the many retail goods. One Putuki businessman named Simon Sumuki opened an EAM café in Somule with a comtech mounted overhead and two cramped rows of individual screens where patrons paid by the minute to read email and explore news sites from the transport. In the back was a large screen with many consoles where the village kids, mostly boys, played online games with unusual big weapons and some with tunnels and magic potions to capture and hide. Simon was an oily guy with a deformed hand, a birth defect. Brianna treated him better than she treated me.

She befriended the Putuki souks and talked about channels for the delivery of goods and how the Company-sanctioned news on the comtech carried no truth and what the young people were buying with their oblus. We carried home bright packages, or I did, and Brianna put the trinkets on display so that the front room was filled with throw pillows and knickknacks and wall hangings. The kitchen was soon supplied with every appliance a cook may want.

Brianna cared little for these; she was more interested in supporting the local economy and to appear to be supporting the souks.

"It's best to keep a channel of communication open, Kelly," she
confided.

She had a comtech delivered and positioned on the kitchen
counter so that, during any meal, she could turn from the EAM to
watch the Consortium-sanctioned news. Mostly I kept the volume
turned down, but the flashing pictures captured my attention more
than once, and twenty minutes would pass before I could tear myself
away.

Soon souks and barefoot kids and older matrons began reporting
to Brianna about tribal events and what each hiccup could mean.
The kids loitered on the back porch, peering through the screen
door to watch the comtech with an Asian announcer delivering
news from Cicero or Stargate Junction. The kids cared little for
the content of these programs, only the wonders of the comtech of
which there were four in Somule.

All Arrivi visited, in fact, except Dacupitte and Rabbenu Ely.

We saw Dacupitte on the street one day. I was carrying packages and scurrying after Brianna's footsteps on the raised wooden
walkway. I bumped into her, in fact, when Brianna stopped short
at the sight of Pete with two Mekucoo warriors, lean and brown,
standing across the way. Pete was taller, less lean, and with orange
dreadlocks streaming down his back—the display that Brianna
used to comb out for him when she was under the care of Mrs. Shaw.

They saw each other and just stood there, unwilling to cross the
distance between them. They were like opposing magnetic fields,
each with a broad reputation but unable to enter the public space

of the other. Brianna had Dolviet blood at least, whereas Pete was Scots-Irish. Her mother was Klistina Le, the forgotten sister of Arim, a Company whore, an unmarried woman, an orphan of no estate except the inheritance of the treasure of Kyle Rula.

Dacupitte nodded slightly and turned to walk into the shadow of the alley, followed by his seconds. Brianna glanced impatiently at me with the packages. "If you want to get something done in this world," she bit out between clenched teeth, "don't look to Rufus for help."

"Rufus?" I asked, but I wasn't heard. Why did she mention Rufus?

Her eyes were hard, and her mouth turned both up and down in a smirk. "My betrothed seeks only the good opinion of warriors. What does he know about women or love or fidelity?"

I blinked, uncertain whether she expected an answer. "But, um, he has legions of children," I whispered. "He must know something about women."

Her smirk grew hard. "He knows nothing about the pleasures of sex, I'd wager. He did each of them doggie style." I suppressed my chuckle. Brianna walked on, and I followed. She was never boring; I admit that part.

I was waiting later at the native bazaar for her to complete the next purchase, and I overheard two Cylahi, dirty and ragged, seated behind the line of booths there. One was composing a new ballad for his turn at an evening campfire.

> Dacupitte can have any
> Woman except the two he covets
> Dulcinea is afraid of
> The other called his beloved

They snickered together before they glanced around, unaware of me.

Brianna seemed arbitrary in her business dealings and found no work for the Arrivi with rust-colored hair, those who were said to be the sons, and now grandsons, of Pete. Perhaps she trusted the word she received from Kat or in communication with Edwina. But I will say here, without prejudice, that I saw in her a confidence that bordered on arrogance as she elevated some who lived in Somule and neglected others.

Brianna talked via EAM with a woman named Petra Mitterand who resided on Earth. A trunk call to Earth cost a deep shaft of Cylahi gold, I was betting. Still, they giggled with gossip and talked about hem lengths and hat styles in Paris. Petra claimed that the blood of Rufus had been added to the previous sample from Kyle Rula. The magic had happened, and the colony of stem cells was strengthened for new growth and use in developing vaccines. They seemed jubilant about the news. The patent and medical applications would grow their wealth well beyond the reach of the treasure of Kyle Rula, or so was the claim.

Brianna saw me watching while they talked. When the trunk call ended, she seemed to deflate, no longer pumped up by her contact with this foreign souk. Brianna sighed and chewed the crust of an Arrivi patty. "Tell me about your notebooks of compiled tribal chants," she said out of the blue. "How many do you have now?"

I was unsure if I wanted her poking her nose into my writing efforts.

"I can find a publisher," she added, "to print a chapbook for the local market, not too expensive." I stepped back two inches, silent in my resistance. Brianna placed a hand on my shoulder and left the kitchen as though all was decided.

Brianna called for the clutch of Cleo to visit for an outing to the fortress and the flats of Arim. She told the old stories from tribal canon and distributed hand-stitched burkas, stepping into the mantel of Kyle Rula without effort. Surely others could see how she played a role, or several roles, and each directed at the person in the room? She spent extra time with Camille and Cleo, their round faces and eyes full of adoration, before she sent them to serve next to Dulcinea the Uburu, a place of honor that others coveted.

Brianna argued with Hakulupe Le over that assignment, the one time I saw them exchange heated words. Bernice was cleaning up the tea service in the front room. Rosalyn and Leah were in the kitchen, entranced by the comtech with its blaring news, so I stepped to the screen door leading to the back verandah, eavesdropping on my betters.

The way it ran was that Cleo had secretly visited the Mayschool shrine where the meteor rock was resting and had touched it, both acts being forbidden. Cleo was found later, dazed and wandering and speaking in a strange language. Brianna said the event proved that Cleo was touched by om, and Brianna wanted to separate Cleo from Kecouroo, who looked backwards too much in Brianna's eyes.

"Cleo must learn from Kat," Hakulupe Le insisted that day in the garden, her green-green eyes flashing. "Kat resides in Kecouroo's village, and that doesn't change for your convenience."

"Cleo must be mentored by Dulcinea, along with Kat. I have a need—"

Anger flashed in Lupe's eyes. "Your needs are not greater than Dolvia's needs."

Brianna blew air from her nostrils, a frustrated sigh. "Perhaps Dulcinea's future is only tangent to Arrivi prophecy. We live in a larger world now."

I leaned forward to hear their words on the breeze, in competition with the volume of the comtech where the two girls whispered with giggles. "Look, there's Captain Chandliss," Leah said suddenly, pointing at the comtech. A human interest news story was airing about Softcheeks technicians who had found work on Dolvia.

Leah rushed to the doorway. "Hurry, Brianna. It's Captain Chandliss on the news!"

Brianna and Hakulupe Le entered in a rush, bringing the savannah heat and odor from their warm braids with them. They stood tensely to view what remained of the story. A scuba diver, apparently Captain Chandliss, waved to the camera, pulled on his mask, and fell over the side of a bobbing boat into the deep surf beyond the bay of Urbyd.

Leah showed a bright face. She was smart and funny but generous in the way of a leader. "He said he found the silicide. He said it was over the shelf."

"What does that mean?" Lupe asked.

"He said con-ti-nen-tal shelf," Rosalyn said. She was more watchful and seemed to count the number of everything—four of these and fifteen of those. Good with detail was how Brianna had described Rosalyn's talents. "Where the water is suddenly much deeper," she added.

Brianna looked at Hakulupe Le with glistening eyes. "Silicide in deep water is more difficult to capture, maybe slowing operations for months." Lupe only nodded, but I knew Brianna saw an advantage if Borabean and the Company had difficulty reaching the mother lode of silicide.

"I'm glad Captain Chandliss found work on Dolvia," she told the girls, showing them a different face. "He was the diver, right?"

"And his two soldiers on the boat with him," Rosalyn nodded. The girls were grinning, even Bernice. His success was their success. They turned immediately to the EAM to search out the print version of the story and share the news with the others of their clutch living at the savannah convent.

Brianna sat with the girls. With big gestures, she told the story about when she had served Mrs. Shaw, who had taken a sample of Kyle Rula's blood during a brief visit to the hotel in Cylay. I suppose Brianna was trying to say that any event on any day could lead to bigger developments, just like the blood sample had led to the pox cure and more wealth than the treasure of Kyle Rula. Or maybe she just liked the sound of her own voice.

I was left to stand next to Bernice, just turned fifteen and the oldest of the clutch after Leah, and whom Brianna seldom noticed. Bernice was said to have the mark of kant, meaning she was not reinforced by Dolvia, so Brianna reneged on her plans to promote Bernice into a management position and even separated her from Cleo when she could. Bernice's only duty was training five former conscripts who were bought by Brianna to serve Cleo's gift. "The conscript girls are doing fine," Bernice reported. "Sarah has given them Arrivi names so they feel more at home."

"Like Tina Tektite." Rosalyn named one conscript and giggled with Leah.

"I quite forgot," Brianna said. "How are they getting on?"

"The tektite clutch understand nothing," Leah complained. "Not fresh air or freedom or that they can say no to Bernice." Leah and Rosalyn exchanged glances, sharing a private joke.

Bernice shrugged. "Before at Stargate Junction, they knew only work and hunger and watching others die. They are grateful. Every day."

"Well," Brianna said, pleased with herself, even though her contribution had cost her little. "Don't teach them too much about saying no."

Later, I asked Bernice about the attitudes of the clutch of Cleo. She was white and soft, the body type of Softcheeks called Eastern European and with a plain face. "Each morning at sunrise," Bernice recited, "Dolvia whispers into the ear of Brianna Miller. Until I can hear that refrain, I must trust her words for me."

I only blinked, wondering where that fanciful story had gotten its start.

Everybody was leaving Somule. Brianna had the nose piece of meteor rock shaped into a tallow bowl filled with wax and a taper, like that ruse would fool anybody sensitive to the presence of tektite. Cleo and Camille were ready to visit Dulcinea; they were only waiting for Kat.

Hakulupe Le prepared to leave for Cylay, packing her few goods with silent and measured gestures. I was helping Lupe with the linens. "Why does Brianna show a different face to each person?" I asked. "Isn't that dishonest, to segment her efforts?"

Hakulupe Le stopped her constant activity, lowering her hands slowly. "What is your real question?"

I sighed and gathered my courage. "Am I like Bernice? Do I have the mark of kant? Why am I pushed aside while these offworlders are coddled?"

"You asked three questions," Lupe said, "one for each of the three planes of Softcheeks. You are more like Brianna than you know."

"That's no answer."

"Be patient," Lupe said. "Brianna will have a task for you soon enough." She turned me toward her, a sure sign that a lesson was coming. "Kyle Rula in her time was a hermit and secretive. Mrs. Shaw focuses on her own goals and is mostly unconcerned with commerce. Only Brianna Miller can turn Dolviet goods into enterprises on many planets. Each woman had a role to play, just like you will have a role to play. Soon enough."

I could add to that stellar group Hakulupe Le's name. Her birth in the Company prison had sparked Kyle Rula's call to resistance to the Company refinery. In another season of om. Then the Sheeks-Cylom had leaned on Lupe's strength to run the bush clinic. These days Brianna delegated to Lupe the duties of distributing the treasure, unconcerned with monthly reports or managing the consequences, like what Mark and the men of the college did with their gathered knowledge. Brianna had arranged for the publication of a chapbook of the compiled chants from Cara, for example, thus depressing Mark's income from when he was solicited to tell the stories by savannah campfires. Brianna just decided matters, leaving Hakulupe Le to implement her instructions while Brianna turned to decide something unrelated, and the consequences be damned.

After the Somule house was quiet again, Dr. Spinelli visited. He was to greet Dr. Ingram, a Softcheeks who was set to study a mite infestation in Southeast Arrivi families after the tainted rice crop had been destroyed. Two days before the shuttle carrying this colleague was due, Dr. Spinelli arrived on our doorstep for a visit. That evening, he had a long talk with Brianna, sitting on the back verandah in rocking chairs and drinking beer from bottles.

Today Dr. Spinelli sat in the kitchen with me while he used the EAM and smoked his pipe. He smoked a pipe like Dr. Beecham. I had asked Brianna once if Dr. Spinelli was related to Hank Beecham or from the same Softcheeks college where people smoked pipes. Brianna only shook her head and went back to the task I had interrupted.

Dr. Spinelli glanced at the muted comtech when a new segment began but easily turned back to his research on the EAM, just as though he had heard that bit of news already. The only news segments that held his attention were the field reports from John Milan, a Softcheeks journalist stationed in Cylay. Dr. Spinelli sent me several glances under the bushy eyebrows while I cut vegetables for the evening meal.

"This is your house, isn't it?" he asked causally.

"My father's house that my mother now owns, along with some other property."

"And does Brianna pay you a salary?"

"For what?"

"For guesting in your house, and your service here."

"She's my mentor, like Mrs. Shaw was her mentor at the clinic. Brianna has filled our house with all these." I indicated the EAM and the comtech.

"She provides no income for you?"

"Karen and I participate in the treasure of Kyle Rula. Helicopter rides on the savannah and lodging in Mayschool and Cylay."

"Who manages the accounts and distributes the funds?"

"Hakulupe Le and Vera, along with Sarah from the savannah convent."

"And do they report to Karlyhi?"

"About what?"

"About how the funds are used. To ensure no graft or waste."

He seemed unconcerned, but his questions troubled a sore spot I had been nursing. "Women manage money separately from the men," I said, "so the community grows."

"And this growth is dictated by Brianna?"

"She's the new Rularim. Dolvia whispers in her ear each morning at sunrise."

The bush of his eyebrows drew together when he frowned. "And you never thought to follow the money? Where it comes from, where it goes?"

I moved to the sink to wash the cut vegetables. "Why are you stirring up trouble?"

"A man would ask these questions of economics."

"Only to find his place; only to seek opportunity for graft." I didn't like the tone that had crept into my voice.

His voice was calm. "And you don't seek opportunity?"

"My task will come soon enough, or so Hakulupe Le has said."

Dr. Spinelli's questions started me on a road of dissatisfaction, or maybe pushed me along a road I already traveled. My back itched, and I remembered the faces of Bernice and the warriors with rust-colored hair for whom Brianna had no use. Was I the same? Was I trusting a structure that had no use for me?

Dr. Spinelli brought Dr. Ingram to the house the next day, fresh from the shuttle landing, sweating and high from the acclimation pill. He was bald and maybe wall-eyed behind the thick glasses. He ate with his mouth open. Brianna played the host with him, much as Mrs. Shaw would have, but she had trouble hiding her poor opinion. Dr. Ingram would need to look to Mrs. Shaw and the profit center attached to her research with the Softcheeks grants. Brianna Miller found no use for him, and this time we were in agreement.

Brianna sat down with me that same afternoon, setting a new task like she had with so many women and girls before me. The talk about the publication of my chapbooks was just to soften me up, offering the carrot before the stick so to speak. "Kelly, you will travel to Cylay in the company of Hakulupe Le and your mother Karen," she instructed. "You will speak with Softcheeks journalists."

I took off my black-rimmed glasses and hung my head in shame. I could commune with Softcheeks because I was mixed heritage and my parents had divorced before my father was caught profiteering. No Arrivi woman of honor would have drawn this assignment.

"You can stay at the Consortium barracks," she said. "Colonel Sector will provide security. Rufus will be there, uh, sometimes." She waited a moment and added, "This work falls to you because of your language skills and your interest in compiling tribal chants. You will meet with John Milan who writes for the Consortium news."

"But who will serve here?"

"We'll close the house for a time. I have enjoyed our rest. We accomplished much in this new season, wouldn't you say?" She patted my arm. "A good mercy seat."

I forced a brief smile.

"I will visit the Uburu digs," she continued, "and Dulcinea, where you can join us later." She presented a wide smile showing her teeth, the face she thought I wanted to see. "Always keep in mind that a secure place waits for you among the tribes. You have honor in Kecouroo's village."

In the village of the backward leader Brianna had tried to undercut. "When do I leave?"

"Today, when Colonel Sector returns to Cylay with his family."

"What must I do?"

"The way journalists define events for the Westend audience is unfortunate. Help John Milan find a better narrative." John Milan was viewed as the most balanced among the offworlders. He had reported Dolviet events since the exile of my aunt Carline Bryant seasons ago.

"How long must I remain there?" I asked.

Brianna was over-cheerful, her method of offering sugar to flavor the vinegar. "Later you can travel to Cicero and visit your aunt Carline Bryant. Not all tribal girls earn offworld travel, and to New Shanghai no less."

"When is it my turn for death by fire in the Cylay plaza?"

"Never," Brianna said, her brow wrinkling for a moment. "You will live into old age, much to the delight of your numerous grandchildren. Tribal children." I was secretly glad I was not required to enter the governor's plaza in Cylay drenched in gasoline. I knew I could not complete that deed.

It was late when we gathered by the helicopter in the barracks yard. Most Arrivi traveling to Cylay needed to cross the heated desert by train or beg a ride with militia lorries. Only those in leadership were honored with chopper rides, part of the largesse that Dr. Spinelli had questioned. Nettom was sinking into Nettki's domain. My mother and I waited in the yellow moonlight dotted with military lights, carrying small packs that included our burkas. My mother was added to our trip so I had decent companionship in Cylay, and she beamed under the attention. Riding in the command chopper was a great thrill for her.

Colonel Sector and Hakulupe Le were already aboard cradling their sleepy children. Vera was also seated and wearing the shoulder strap. I showed my mother how to work the safety strap. We lifted off, and Captain Manenowski piloted us over the night desert.

The Cylay barracks were quiet in the blue night when our chopper landed forty minutes later. Uniformed Consortium soldiers helped us to step down. They saluted Colonel Sector smartly and reported while he stroked his big mustache with his forefinger and thumb. Leah and Rosalyn waited in the yard, even this late at night. They showed Karen and me where to walk and claimed that our supplies would be delivered, all very formal and structured. Hakulupe Le had a residence with her husband in the married men's barracks, and Captain Manenowski and Vera lived nearby. Karen and I were shown to a sparsely furnished apartment in the same building.

"We can improve these rooms tomorrow," Lupe said to Karen, her green-green eyes flashing in the tallow light.

She left after receiving bows and melingas from my mother, and Karen set out her many new consumer items purchased by Brianna, talking all the while. I sat on the musky cot and tried to ignore her prattle. "This Cylay trip will give me a chance to learn more English words," Karen said. "You will explain the terms I don't understand, huh, Kelly? I can write them down, or we can discuss them."

"Yes, Mother."

"Loosen your hair, and I can brush it for you. You too much neglect personal care."

"Not now, Mother. Maybe later."

She came to me, full of authority and enthusiasm. "Always you shrug off the immediate. This late in the day is not good for writing." She removed the binding cord and unplaited my long braid. "You must ready yourself for the interview. You represent the tribes to Westend now." She began stroking the length of my hair with a stiff brush.

"Brianna has greatly honored us with her attention," Karen continued with each stroke. "You must learn to be properly grateful. You serve in leadership now. Not equal with Hakulupe Le, of course, because of her long service at the academy."

I shrugged her off and put my glasses under the pillow. I turned my back and lay on top of the covers, unwilling to struggle with her. Karen instructed me pointedly. "We must do our part, and no shirking, do you hear me? Whatever they ask. Duty above all."

I hated that word, duty. Where were fun and adventure and romance? Where were my spiritual gifts and my place in tribal canon? Not journalists and exiled aunts on Cicero and more of the same. Duty would rob me of my best years.

John Milan came to us at the barracks apartment. As an investigative reporter, he wanted to greet the people within the community. Karen and I had been resident in Cylay for only two days, but we didn't correct him. When Colonel Sector brought him to our doorway, John Milan carried two cameras and wore a khaki vest with pockets stuffed with photography stuff. Karen wore the burka gifted to her by Brianna and greeted him in Arrivi fashion. I was brought forward, draped in my sky-blue veil that I so often wore. "May I present one who has traveled with Brianna Miller," Colonel Sector said, "and who is compiling tribal chants for publication. Kelly Osborn, granddaughter to Dacupitte's mother, Heather Osborn."

I held one hand high in the traditional greeting, "Hiki, John Milan," I said in English. "You honor our poor household with your presence."

He nodded curtly. "Hiki, Kelly Osborn. Melinga." Colonel Sector took his leave while John Milan was made to sit and was served tea and fruit. I sat opposite him under the veil but refused the refreshments. While he was holding up a light meter and focusing his camera, John Milan asked, "Can we dispense with the burkas?"

"Must we begin with photographs?"

He gestured to the window over the stove. "The natural light."

"My mother must be covered in your presence," I explained, "being full-blooded Arrivi. I am of mixed heritage though and can therefore commune with offworlders."

He set out his cameras on the table. "As the widow of Joey Osborn, your mother requires no covering. Protocol has been met for this meeting."

Karen whispered under her breath, "Pro-to-col."

"You will not photograph the spirit in my mother's face for all Westend to view. Also, I am under no obligation to show my face for the offworld media."

"Please," he said.

"You may photograph us as we are now. Anything more will be decided later."

He shot a few frames, mostly of my mother at the stove. He asked her to turn slightly so that the light fell on her facial panel. Working a different angle, he encouraged me to hold up the chapbook of tribal chants that I hoped to emulate with my research. It was all staged and without honor. I think John Milan felt the tension. He bowed to our resistance and set the cameras aside. "You don't mind if I use an audio recorder?" He placed one on the table.

"Netta, om?" Karen said. I explained in Arrivi that John Milan would record our voices and transcribe the words later for his article. Karen nodded, and John Milan immediately reached to switch on the recorder. It came to me that he understood Arrivi. I must use a different dialect for privacy. Karen knew some Uburu; I would try that.

"I just want to get some background information, if you don't mind," he began. "This burka you're wearing . . . it's similar to the one Kyle Rula wore at the time of her suicide. What is the significance of this color?"

"Death by fire," I corrected. "Not suicide. Death by fire in protest against Rabbenu Ely's rule. Kyle Rula completed a deliberate act, not one of despair."

His eyes skirted left, then right. "We can get to that in a minute. First, just to clear up this . . . people have asked." He smiled to be friendly. I began to understand Kecouroo's suspicion of journalists.

"The tradition of the sky-blue burka," I said, "dates back to the time of Brian Miller, when Kyle Rula was younger than I am now. She made similar veils for her sisters so they could be covered as Dolvia covers herself."

"Those would be the sisters of Arim who are immortalized in the sculpture on the flats," he said, mostly for the recorder. "In what way is Brianna related to Kyle Rula?"

I heard Karen muttering and knew she repeated his word im-mor-ta-lized. "As you well know," I said, "Brianna inherited the flats and the treasure of Kyle Rula after her death by fire that was in protest against—"

"Yes, yes." John Milan referred to his notes. "But Kyle Rula and Brianna Miller are not blood relations? Brianna Miller is not a sister of Arim?"

"There are no more sisters of Arim, only women of the savannah. Brianna could inherit because Kyle Rula had no daughters to receive deeds to the land."

"What about Karima Le's daughters?"

"What about them?" I asked. "Brianna Miller is a daughter to Klistina Le, the youngest sister who had no other children, and therefore Brianna was first in line to inherit."

"And what about Kyle Rula's sons?"

"They were raised Mekucoo like their father, Cyrus the ketiwhelp killer. Within that tradition, the men own nothing."

"So Brianna Miller became the second Rularim?"

"She inherited the flats. The title of arisen Rularim was won by way of Brianna's generosity in supporting the many academies on the savannah." It felt odd indeed to defend Brianna's act to outsiders.

"And what is your connection? Why do you wear the same veil?"

"Brianna has chosen to honor me thus. She is not required by law."

"But what's the connection?"

"Her father, Brian Miller, loved my grandmother, Heather Osborn."

"And did they have children?"

"No."

"Not Dacupitte?"

"Dacupitte is the son of Heather Osborn by another man."

"By Hamish Nordhagen," John Milan said. "A Company officer at the time."

"That is correct." I was fully glad for the burka's covering. His questions probed close to the heart, to the few remaining tribal secrets we harbored.

"That makes Dacupitte your cousin," John Milan added.

"Arrivi do not reckon these connections as you do. We are more concerned with ancestral spirits and who is blessed by Dolvia."

"Are you blessed?"

"If I was blessed, I would not be in Cylay. I would not have drawn this duty."

After John Milan set appointments for additional interviews and left, I spoke with Hakulupe Le. As the days passed, our evening habit was to sit at her dinner table and discuss what John Milan might solicit next. Millie was often there, also eight-year-old Anna, and Michael Peter who was still in diapers. Captain Manenowski and Vera and their daughter Marsha sometimes joined us but not that first night. Only Karen was there.

"John Milan wants me to remove the burka."

"How do you feel about that?"

"I will do what you instruct."

"Your aunt Carline Bryant is well-known on Cicero," Lupe explained. "Her husband's cartel has a business venture on Stargate Junction. And besides, you appear genuine in front of the camera."

"Genuine?"

"Forthright," she said.

"You mean not pretty, not sexy. Nothing to excite John Milan's … thoughts?"

"You always call him by both his names," Milo Sector observed from across the table. His black mustache, wet from sipping tea, showed some gray. "Why not simply John?"

I looked away.

"Do what you think is best," Lupe said. "Undertake nothing that makes you feel uncomfortable."

John Milan and I met twice more; once for a walking tour of Cylay's shantytown and once in front of the shrine to Kyle Rula. Both workdays were draining. I established that for interview sections in front of the cameras I would remove the burka, but I would wear it for travel and always in my mother's veiled company.

He readily agreed, so my coppery hair and black-rimmed glasses became familiar images to the Consortium audience while John Milan's news byline was running the exposé about Dolvia's troubles.

In the cramped alleyways, viewing the desperate condition of so many families, I was made aware of why Hakulupe Le and Vera lived in the married officers' quarters and how Karen and I were honored with an apartment there. A filthy stream trickled through the muddy pathway. Unmanaged pigs rooted among shelters made of discarded packing materials treated with an odious preservative. The toxic metallic odor felt nauseating in the noonday sun. Cooking was achieved over open fires that burned the dried dung of erriv that the women gathered from the livestock pens. Children, too many with rust-colored hair, were ragged and unwashed. The women were vacant-eyed and starved, and the few men aged or crippled from battle wounds.

We were accompanied by a camcorder operator plus a . . . what to call him? A traffic director, I guess. The Softcheeks smeared a cream under their noses to block the offal smell. I saw them swallow acclimation pills. The traffic director began telling the tribespeople to go here and stand there and don't move. He called them the unblessed ones.

"What does that mean, the unblessed ones?" I asked.

"You said that if you were blessed, you would not be in Cylay," John Milan explained. "These ones live here. Ergo, they are unblessed."

"Er-go?" I repeated. John Milan and his friends exchanged wry glances. It came to me suddenly that they talked about us over dinner the same as we discussed them. I must be more careful with my words for description.

The staging was set, and the natural light was deemed to be good, so I removed my burka. Curiosity lit the eyes of one boy who looked to be age eight or perhaps ten and stunted from malnutrition. John Milan encouraged me to speak to the staring children and gather certain ones, mostly big-eyed girls with the darkest skin, into my arms. He centered himself directly in front of the camcorder and gave his pithy impressions of Rabbenu Ely and Dacupitte. I was told to not look into the camera but rather to look at him as though we were having a conversation while I answered his broadly worded questions about political pressures and how these people suffered because Karl Wyley had displaced them while he was consolidating his power.

Another time they assembled the same equipment before the plaza shrine to Kyle Rula, a short obelisk made of Rabbenu limestone with a carved alcove and a badly executed likeness of the first Rularim. The candles and orchid sprigs were fresh, placed there by many Arrivi and daily tended by convent residents. A seven-story municipal building was under construction across the plaza from the governor's house. The only other new businesses were a couple of EAM cafés frequented by offworlders and tribal boys who liked the multiplayer video games.

John Milan encouraged me to wear the burka for this session because that was more reverential. He wanted me to place an orchid sprig near the candles and stand as if in prayer. I tried to explain we did not pray to ancestors, only to Dolvia, but he said the posture was good for the cameras.

Back at the apartment, John Milan requested a certain kind of interview where I would shed a tear at the mention of Kyle Rula's name, you know, because she was my hero. I struggled with that and claimed Karlyhi was my hero, and everybody's hero. I wanted to talk more about the self-executions and the reasons for them. John Milan claimed he understood the reasons, and Consortium viewers understood them. Why dwell on morbid events?

"I thought journalists sought morbid events." I knew immediately those words were harmful. I needed to censor myself more closely.

John Milan smiled slightly, letting it pass. "If you cooperate, I can get you invited along as an interpreter during our visit with Rabbenu Ely."

"Co-op-per-ate," Karen whispered so she would remember.

"You mean to the governor's house?" I asked. He nodded, and behind his shoulder Karen nodded eagerly. Few Arrivi had seen the inside of rabbenu's Cylay mansion. I sighed and did as he instructed, but I hated myself and hated Brianna for assigning this task to me.

For our visit to the governor's house a couple of days later, John Milan did something that told me all I needed to know about his motives. I chose a different burka to wear for the occasion, not willing to compete with Brianna should she dress traditionally. The ECCAV waited next to the barracks' yard with the driver and camcorder operator seated in the front. The doors stood open, hinged upward like a Murmurey fledgling exercising its wings.

John Milan waited there on the side, dressed in a business suit for the occasion. Karen and I came down, both covered by our burkas, when he stopped us. "I could not secure two extra security passes into the event. I tried everything."

My mother's shoulders drooped with disappointment, and I saw John Milan smirk. He had guessed that Karen was more disappointed at not touring the rooms than she regretted not being present to protect my virtue. All pretext of graciousness vanished because we had each seen through the other's mask.

The ECCAV arrived at the wrought iron gates. A Putuki guard barely glanced at the media passes John Milan displayed and waved us through, just waved us into the yard like it was normal. We joined the other ECCAVs on the circular drive and stopped in our turn at the entrance. John Milan greeted the other journalists waiting there, especially one Regan Villines, a stringy-looking woman who was no longer young, her face weathered and tan.

"Did you get the interview with Karl Wyley?" Regan asked under her breath.

"I will know from Sector this afternoon." They slapped a high five, a Softcheeks gesture that young warriors liked to imitate.

The governor's house was truly splendid inside with cool rabbenu limestone walls and tall windows. I put on my glasses and stared through the facial panel. Rows of mammoth lights hung from the ceiling, like clustered geyserite formations shot through with light, and all exactly the same, called chan-del-liers. The furniture was odd, however, with curved spindly legs on narrow tables that held little weight.

We strained to view the activity behind the closed doors, designated French because of their narrowness and many panes. I was shoved aside. "Just stay behind the camera," John Milan whispered abruptly. And that was the deal. His tribal exposé was nearly complete, and his next assignment may be secured that day. John Milan no longer needed this tribal girl's input.

We were not related after all.

The French doors finally opened, and we were ushered in by uniformed Putuki soldiers wearing polished laced-up boots and karkars slung over their shoulders. We entered a high-ceiling conference room with rows of folding chairs. John Milan sat with Regan Villines while his camcorder operator and traffic director claimed a prime spot for their equipment. I drew my hand out from under the veil and touched the fuzzy wallpaper. John Milan came to me impatiently, guiding me by the elbow to a seat next to him without presenting me to Regan Villines.

I was the only veiled woman in the company, and the chants I had compiled from Kecouroo and the others were unpublished. Besides, my research was filled with traditional chants, other peoples' words. And under John Milan's tutelage, I was now compliant in mouthing Softcheeks words. That was the day I decided to begin a new work, a geste perhaps; heroic poems of my own composition peppered with my opinions.

"They have been in conference for three hours," Regan whispered to John Milan. "What announcement do you expect?"

"This is for the cameras," he sneered. "We'll learn nothing here."

I turned my head at that duplicity. We had just spent days capturing managed images for his cameras, but he spoke against others who did the same.

The door opened, and three Putuki ministers entered, followed by two Consortium officers, one of them Colonel Sector. They stood in a row while Rabbenu Ely and Dacupitte in a tan militia uniform stepped up on the speaker stage. Pete was followed by Brianna Miller, who wore a sky-blue burka as a shawl, and a man I didn't know who was wearing an Uburu militia uniform.

Rabbenu Ely stepped before the bundled microphones, looking rotund and gray in a dark business suit and wire-rimmed glasses. "Thank you for waiting. If we can get started." The members of the media corps quieted and took their seats.

"We are here today," Ely began, "to announce a strategic alliance negotiated by our good friend Dacupitte. As rabbenu, I speak for all the tribes and lead the Putuki. Dacupitte represents the Mekucoo and Siibabean. Brianna Miller, as you all know, is Arrivi and today holds proxy for the Cylahi. And Kenru is from the Uburu tribe that holds the mesas. Each of these groups has received Consortium financial assistance based on the number of warriors serving in the militia and their proximity to the recent fighting. With the retreat of the Borabean forces, a new balance is struck. As rabbenu intended when I signed the armistice, a strategic alliance is now in place."

"For which Ely gets a usury rate of twelve percent," John Milan whispered to Regan.

He had followed the money, aware of who prospered and who paid for that prosperity. I decided, now that I saw the patterns, that I would watch Brianna's acts and ferret out similar structures with her businesses.

"Trade contracts," Ely continued from the podium, "are renegotiated with investment opportunities for all parties through specific Consortium cartels."

"Some things never change," John Milan claimed cynically to Regan. He looked at me with stony features in the hard light. I thought I saw his lip curl. "Your aunt Carline Bryant is the worst of them. She uses forced labor and now wants the gum arabic trade."

I only blinked. I knew nothing of this. I had not seen Carline since childhood.

After the announcements, there was a short reception. I was invisible under the burka, even as a curiosity, but I saw everything. Dacupitte towered over the others, easily sharing chi. I could not take my eyes off him. Then he shook hands with some tardy guests with razor-cut hair who wore business suits with Mandarin collars. I knew them, my brother Patrick Osborn and Carl Hartley, the general's son.

Dacupitte led them to where Brianna stood with Kenru. She stiffened visibly but shook Carl's hand, and Patrick's hand. Then she looked around as if searching the crowd.

I came forward. "Patrick?" He turned, and the look on his face was . . . I don't know. "Patrick, it's me, Kelly. Don't you know me?"

He moved to stand squarely between me and Carl before he taking my elbow and guiding me away from the others. "What are you doing here?"

"Karen and I are in Cylay for a time."

We fell silent when Brianna passed with Dacupitte. We saw her exit into another room where Rabbenu Ely's ministers greeted them. Then the door closed against our prying eyes, and Patrick turned back to me. "We're staying at the barracks near Colonel Sector," I said. "You should visit."

"Why are you dressed like that?"

"I took part in a media exposé. Karen and I were photographed with our burkas."

"Eyes of Oriika! What possessed you?"

I drew in my breath sharply. "I was invited. I was duty bound."

"Duty? What do you know of duty?"

"What?"

Patrick glanced around quickly. "Come along. I can get you out of here."

"I don't want to leave. I was invited."

"What were you thinking?" he demanded, but without waiting for an answer. "Look, just go to the door and wait for me."

"But why?"

"Just do it."

I stepped away as Carl Hartley joined Patrick. "Who was that?" Carl asked.

"Nobody," my brother said; I was certain he said that.

Patrick spoke to John Milan who shrugged, I guess claiming he was not concerned with how I was escorted home. So Patrick stepped back to me. "I can get you out through the kitchen." He guided me to another door, his hand firmly grasping my arm above the elbow. The tension pulled the facial panel from my eyes.

I pulled away. "What is wrong with you?" I asked. "What's going on here?"

He only grabbed me again, tighter this time, and hurried through the bustling rooms. We entered an interior garden with colonnades on both sides. Patrick led me toward a gate as though he knew his way around the governor's house. He had been here before, and he had the run of the place.

Across the way, I glimpsed Kenru, who stood facing the garden from the other colonnade path, standing like a guard. Behind him, Dacupitte watched while Brianna and Rabbenu Ely exchanged harsh words. I knew the tone well enough, but I could not make out what they said. We passed Kenru, and Ely's words drifted to us. "What you need is another beating!"

Patrick seemed to increase his sense of hurry, drawing me away from the scene. I looked back and saw Ely raise a hand to strike Brianna. Dacupitte caught his arm in midair and quickly turned him around, the Mekucoo belt knife firmly at his throat. Two ministers rushed forward, and Pete pushed Ely into them. He and Kenru took up defensive positions in front of Brianna, but nothing more happened; nothing that I could see through the burka's facial panel.

Meanwhile, Patrick spoke to give orders to the gate guard. I was led outside and hustled into a waiting taxi. Patrick threw some bills into the front seat. "Take her back to the Consortium barracks," he told the driver.

"Tell Karen to start packing," he instructed me. "You're leaving Cylay."

"But why?" I asked through the window as the taxi pulled away. I looked behind to see Patrick sharing chi with the Putuki gate guards.

We were a few blocks distant when I spoke to the Cylahi driver. "Go back to the convent academy, please."

"But I was told the barracks."

"I have money if it costs extra." I knew it was a shorter drive to return to the plaza where a convent was located next to the governor's house, but rates varied considerably in Cylay. I left the taxi in front of the convent gate where filthy and weary women begged for alms. I gave them the extra money I had promised the driver and grabbed the bell cord. With tears, the women murmured their thanks.

A goulep came across the convent yard to the gate. "Nu delaya," she said to the crowd.

I was allowed to enter and adjusted my burka. "Hakulupe Le, please."

More desperate women pressed against the wrought iron with outstretched hands. "Pity," one said. "Have pity on me." Two convent residents came across the narrow yard carrying baskets and handed patties through the bars to the beggars while I was led to the schoolyard.

I entered an administrator's office where Rosalyn sat with Vera staring at an EAM screen. Leah chatted with Hakulupe Le while they stood at the window with sunlight behind them. During my time in Cylay I had greeted them only twice. These of the clutch of Cleo served here while I was pushed off on two-faced journalists.

Lupe came to me. I pulled off the burka and stood with lowered eyes, resisting my tears. Lupe removed her glasses and said to the waiting resident, "Teaching is so unfair. I keep getting older, but the students remain the same age. Some like Kelly here are thoughtful enough to visit as adults." I waited, fairly trembling with my news. She dismissed the silent girl and fixed me with those lambent green eyes. "What is it?"

"Patrick was at the governor's house. He was . . . he was angry. Then Ely tried to strike Brianna. Pete and Kenru—"

"We can just have some tea," Lupe suggested in a calming voice. "Tell me everything as it happened."

We talked for more than an hour, around and around about what the events could mean and how much I had hated the John Milan task. How Dr. Spinelli asked questions I had not considered but should consider. We talked about Patrick's attitude and how he had bristled at the mention of our mother. I cried more than once; I don't know.

I remember one comment though. Lupe said, "Ely has always hated Brianna for what she is. It's good that Pete finally stood up for her."

"You mean he hates her because of the treasure?"

"That too," Lupe said. "As a young man, Ely had pursued Brianna's mother, Klistina Le. But she was enamored with the blond and handsome Brian Miller." Lupe smiled, trying to cheer me up I think. "Then Klistina Le ventured offworld, a bad time for her. When she returned without honor, she still spurned Ely, who later married Marcy. So Ely hates Brianna, the daughter of the woman he could not have."

"But that was before, in the time of Brian Miller."

"Youthful pains are the ones most regretted."

"You should add that to the school blackboard as a homily."

"Perhaps I will. Let's get you home or back to the barracks anyhow."

"Why does Patrick hate me and hate Karen?"

Hakulupe Le sank back down into the seat. "He's angry about how his father died. Patrick thinks working with the Junction Boys is a better life than in Somule maybe."

"Is it better?"

She raised her eyebrows. "I don't know. But you'll soon find out, huh, when you travel to Cicero. I have never traveled offworld. I'm certain you'll like it as much as Brianna did and return with many stories to tell."

I knew Lupe was chatting me up to strengthen my spine. My experiences were nothing like what Brianna Miller knew. I was unblessed.

FOURTEEN

I HAD NO TASTE FOR TRAVEL. BRIANNA MAY HAVE ENJOYED OFF-world adventure and no doubt missed the variety. I struggled moment to moment with the fear of botched connections, of disappointing others who waited, of the staring faces in waiting areas, and nobody for companionship. I carried the burka as a shawl because wearing it would have brought more attention and would have been hypocritical, we decided, since the spirit in my face had been broadcast on comtechs across Westend in the exposé by John Milan.

I felt small and soiled, like a bloodless and bony corpse. Except I sometimes felt bloated and pulsating, filling the chamber with my putrefying self. My arm ached where I had been inoculated so I would not carry Arrivi diseases to Cicero. I longed for the savannah, the distant horizon; I missed Kecouroo's kindliness and Haku-lupe Le's probing instruction. I even pined for my mother Karen. They were the fabric of my life, how I structured the day.

Finally, I reached Cicero, which was cool and sunny. The gravity was different and brought on nausea. Carline Bryant waited at the disembarking place while officials checked my case and inoculation papers. Her short hair was coifed back into an upsweep style that failed to mitigate her heavy features and the cruel line across her lip. She saw me and gestured I should come forward. I was quickly passed through customs, and I suspected she had paid a bribe. I did not know Aunt Carline really, a sister to my dead father Joey Osborn. After the divorce, Patrick had chosen to live with her, but I had remained with Karen. I don't remember that the choice was ever put to me; Karen must have insisted.

At any rate, Carline placed a hand on each shoulder and carefully removed the shawl. "Fine," she said as she glanced over my features. "Just fine. We'll cut the hair and find different glasses for you. And we'll put you on a diet, of course. No more fried kariom on salted patties for you." I just stared while she turned with instructions to the porters and then waddled up the walkway. Carline weighed nearly ninety kilos, and I would have to go without?

Carline lived in New Shanghai where her husband had a business, or several businesses, along with his brothers. The city's location spread through five granite fingers extending into the ocean, not that I was allowed to visit the bustling city with its gleaming high rises of eccentric design and blocks of condominium buildings separated by empty parking lots. The business languages were English and Chinese. The building and street names had little resonance with local customs or local heroes but rather reached back to some Chinese philosopher or western inventor—Edison Avenue and Mao Tse-Tung Park—or so Carline explained during the taxi ride to her home.

All the people on the streets used cellphones for business or to contact family or friends. These sleek devises also displayed photos and videos and games to play, very modern. They were for local use, meaning for Cicero, but could connect to an EAM using the recharging stand. Carline offered me a cellphone, already charged and with essential numbers added. "So you can't get lost," she said. I mostly played board games on it later when I was bored.

Carline lived in a gated compound with layers of security. The wall was not made of rabbenu limestone, but rather many stacked oversized stones of different shapes, and was topped with coils of razor wire resting within rows of diagonal bars. We left the taxi on the street and servants carried my small pack and Carline's many purchases across a wide yard to the largest house. A chopper landing strip was in the middle of the drive although I never saw it being used. Several two-story houses of similar design were gathered there, for the brothers and their families I suspected.

I wondered at the fortress mentality but remembered that their buildings in Cylay had been stormed in another season by angry tribespeople whose loved ones had known abuse in the Bryant sweatshops. I later learned that the buildings of their Two Forks munitions factory were even more strapped with security checks.

I was given a small room on the second floor that looked out on the garage without a view of the interior yard. Before Carline left to "make callbacks," she introduced me to a Putuki maid named Lula who would wash my clothes and bring afternoon tea.

Our first struggle was about my hair. Aunt Carline wanted it short enough to show the nape of my neck, but I screamed and flailed my arms, making a scene in the New Shanghai boutique. I felt like a chastised child and cried openly. We compromised, finally, on something more than shoulder length called a blunt cut. A Putuki woman swept my shorn coppery tresses into a dirty pile on the floor. She whispered, "It grows back with time." I felt heartstone for her, my first awareness of suffering on Cicero other than my own.

Many Putuki and some Cylahi had migrated to Cicero seeking work. The labor rates were so out of balance that workers could send a sizable portion of their wages to their families on the savannah, a life-saving duty. Putuki were the preferred domestic servants for Cicero women of status, but never the haughty bazaari men, only the women. Cylahi men who had migrated did manual labor, mostly construction and roadbuilding. Cylahi were deemed a discipline problem because so many were rootless and publicly intoxicated.

Carline chose wire-rimmed glasses to replace my black ones, very like the style Rabbenu Ely always wore, except they made my face look fat. In patronizing tones, Carline complimented my hazel eyes. Cicero clothing styles—dubbed western though I never learned west of what—were acceptable to me although the trousers chafed my thighs. When I mentioned it, Carline said the rash would heal once I lost some weight.

Food at Carline's table was dry and stringy, mostly Cicero-grown vegetables and soups. There were starchy dishes I wasn't allowed to taste. Carline's table conversation was mostly about my duty and how I must be diligent and complete each task without complaint. She sounded like Karen. How I longed for the Arrivi patty with dried kariom, dipped in olive oil, and served with fried Uburu corn chips.

Carline explained I should take some training while I visited; what did I prefer? I had nothing to say, so she decided for me. "Any tribal woman must have experience as a nurse. You will volunteer at the hospital and take classes in nursing." Her husband scowled at me from over his soup, and it was done. That exchange was typical of Carline's half-hearted efforts to serve my needs while I was a guest.

I spent many long days at the New Shanghai hospital and took instruction from an intern there named Dr. Richardson. He was lazy and a thief serving his morphine habit. His behavior meant nothing because they had no serious patient influx, just infant croup and women who wanted him to feel their uncovered abdomens. And he was cruel to the Putuki women who did cleanup and maintenance, judging them and acting dissatisfied with their work that was exemplary.

I had no friends there and few tasks. Hardhands assumed I was not able to read or take instruction since I was tribal, even though I read the library medical books for diversion and fooled around on the EAM.

I sat frozen, stilted and captured. I did no writing but read some fiction and Chinese philosophers in translation. The improbable stories seemed constructed in comparison to my experience on the savannah. One writer, Confucius, spoke about duty to the state and the state's duty to the individual. If the state neglected its duty, what was the person's best response? "Naturally, different people should get different answers," Confucius responded.

That was no help.

One American named Edith Hamilton wrote, "All men would be tyrants if they could." That was memorable.

I was called into the maternity ward where three women were heavily laboring and one was in breach. I reached out to help but heard a hiss because my hands were bare. I was made to wear a cotton pullover and plastic gloves before I could do prep and cleanup in the emergency. I was invited into the ward on occasion after that, mostly for mundane tasks like shaving a woman with labor pains.

The nurses had pro-ce-dures for everything and added rules upon rules. It was explained to me that one man's healthy kidney in New Shanghai was removed because he was mixed up with a different patient. So all the hospital patients wore wristbands with their names and blood types printed real big. That was a regulation, not a procedure though.

It was like a dance where nurses knew how the other would act, and most obvious when something went wrong and other pro-ce-dures were needed to calm a patient, monitor falling blood pressure, or if a baby was in breach.

Just the same. I was allowed to work with the new mothers for their comfort until the pains were close together. And I would bring the bathed newborns to them for the first suckling. That put a smile on my face.

One day I was loitering in Aunt Carline's backyard. It was cooler but with no hint of rain on the horizon. Brown leaves on the high branches of the cottonwoods rattled in unison. Sean Bryant came to my side, silent and not curious. He was present at home very little, a short and slight man of Irish descent with bowed legs. Sean was older, a son of those in the original wave of indentured colonists.

Passion had gone out of their marriage, if it had ever existed, and only shared business interests remained.

"Do you miss the savannah?" he asked, mostly to cover an awkward moment.

"The hills here get regular rain," I said to be neutral. "My desert is all about succulents, oleastra, and vining hyacinth."

"In Two Forks near the factory," Sean said, "we have creosote and agave, and fewer ocotillo than the area south of there. We have no acacia except those we have planted." Acacia produced a cash crop for the Bryants, or would one day. Within a decade they would harvest gum arabic and trade the commodity in competition with Sarah at the savannah convent.

Sean Bryant stared off for a while, then added, "I remember the vining hyacinth. A bell flower that lasted just a few hours before insects left it ruined." Another pause. "What else?"

"Cicero has one moon. So lonely."

He looked up, amused I suppose. "Earth has one moon, larger though." Then he went inside. Sean Bryant did not speak to my comfort or his hospitality; we just happened to be in the same place for a moment. I did not know the cactus varieties he mentioned. I seldom left the compound except for work at the hospital or in the company of Carline on some errand.

I hated my life.

My brother Patrick visited twice, mostly interested that I was decently dressed and losing the baby fat. I was age eighteen, not a baby. And he was no specimen himself, with a low hairline and soft, bumpy upper arms. Patrick had a big rump. He sat with Carline and talked about transport duty and the freshly imported goods in the promenade shops there. She slipped brandy into his tea. Carline liked men, meaning she had no time for women, even relatives, except as an audience for her endless tales about how the men courted her. I had heard that she was an astute businesswoman, but I suspected the business part was accomplished in relative privacy by Sean Bryant and his brothers. Carline just took the credit in public situations.

She spoke against specific people on Dolvia: Karlyhi and the long-dead Kyle Rula. "Rularim was too good for us in her own mind, always keeping secrets," she said with a curled lip. Mostly, though, she hated the tribes as a group. It was pre-ju-dice. Someone at the dinner table had called her prejudiced.

"So it's finally in place, this law of impunity?" she asked Patrick.

"General Hartley was no help at all," he said, "but Company executives lobbied the Consortium directly. What happened to my father won't go unpunished again."

"You can take a lesson here, Kelly," Carline said. I looked up sharply from my plate, surprised she thought to include me in the talk. "Karlyhi's high-handed methods will no longer be tolerated by Colonel Sector and the Consortium. Now we have an avenue of redress."

"I don't know what that means."

"Hardhand personnel," Carl said in a similar tone to hers, "are no longer victims of tribal logic. Soldiers have impunity for their actions, and disputes can be settled only in a Consortium tribunal. No more ritual deaths on the savannah."

"A tribunal?" I asked. "Like the trial of Kyle Rula?"

Carline waved a hand. "That was in a different season of om."

"You should be glad," Patrick said. "Justice for our father's death. Impunity means no other Hardhands will suffer."

"Im-pu-ni-ty," I whispered under my breath.

"You were kept out of events," Carline added, "for your own good. Dolviets weren't loyal to Carl in the time of the colonists, or to my brother Joey."

I held out a hand. "Brianna said the tribes had evidence of—"

"Ha! Did you see this evidence?" Carline demanded. "Were the facts brought before a judge? No, Karlyhi just decided Joey was selling information and killed him. Karlyhi murdered your father. How does that rest with your need to return to the tribes?"

I sat back, surprised at her vehemence. Aunt Carline wanted me to join her sense of outrage, except she was so often angry that I didn't know which was real and which was an effect of the brandy.

Later, I looked up the word impunity in the library at the hospital. It meant freedom from unpleasant consequences. Consortium soldiers who were mostly from Cicero, called Hardhands, could act without fear of punishment from the tribes. Bryant employees could indulge themselves on tribal women without fear of Karlyhi breaking down doors. Impunity: must be from the French language on Earth. Brianna Miller had claimed that one can hide much meaning in a few French words.

Then Patrick visited again and brought with him Carl Hartley, long-limbed and square-shouldered. He wore his hair razor-cut at the neck but hanging over his brow to resemble an actor in the movies

Carline watched into the early morning hours. She much preferred handsome men, and I firmly believe it never crossed her mind that their reservation toward her stemmed from her more-than-plump looks. She was loud and crass and overbearing and . . . well. . . .

Carline had no trouble parading me out and explaining to me, in the most patronizing tones, how she and Carl Hartley had similar names. Carl and Patrick knew the story. I knew the story. She knew she had repeated it more than once, but by then she'd had a couple of sherry drinks, so repetition did not matter.

"It was all my mother, don't you know," she began. "Heather knew three men in her lifetime, but it was Carl Osborn who first brought her to Westend. Then after we were exiled to the slave quarters off-world, me and Joey. . . ." She emphasized the word slave. "After that, after my father was murdered by conscripts where me and Joey had been made into slaves. After I witnessed my own father's murder at the hands of a mob. . . . Then Heather took up with Hamish Nordhagen and gave birth to Da-cu-pit-te. You know him as Pete. But Heather didn't raise Pete, didn't complete any of her motherly duties. No, instead she lived at the fortress of Arim and married Brian Miller."

Carline gave a short laugh, very unattractive. "Ha, ha. It's all so twisted. Me and Joey were put with Karima Le, Kyle Le's sister, and made to sit through long days in the humid courtroom for that famous trial. You think I don't remember? You think I was too young? I remember everything. Pete was hidden with Kecou-roo. They hid Heather's shame, so she was free to go onto her next man, to Brian Miller.

"After Heather died," Carline continued, "Brian took up with a native girl, a sister of Arim who had been a common whore on the transport, and he didn't marry her. Klistina Le was sister to Kyle Le and mother to Brianna Miller, who became a common whore on Earth.

"These same tribespeople said Joey's business activities were immoral," Carline insisted. "Joey was faithful to your mother, Kelly, even though he had plenty of opportunity. The tribes justified killing him for being 'immoral' when they cannot even get it straight for themselves who was whose father. Heather was my mother, but I'm telling you straight; the way she died? Just chickens coming home to roost; just roosting chickens."

I assumed the roosting chickens phrase was from Earth. Carline used Earth sayings all the time. She winked at me like it was a great joke when she used the colorful images, like she had stolen and repurposed them.

"And Heather was the colonial savior," Carline continued. "Can you believe it? A savior whom Billie Hartley named her children after: Carl and Heather. At least Jesse wasn't saddled with that same legacy. How is Jesse anyhow, Carl?"

Like she really cared how Jesse was, or any woman.

Later, I saw the two friends together on the porch, holding their postprandial drinks. "Let's go to the casino," Carl said. "Maybe there's some action tonight."

"I hate it there."

Carl crowded Patrick and grabbed his wrist, guiding Patrick's hand to his own abdomen. "We could stay in and play." When

Patrick pulled away, Carl sneered at him. "Then help me find some other amusement. That's what you're good at, isn't it, distracting me with morsels?"

"Carl, do we. . . . Does it have to be—"

"You choose," Carl said. "Them or you. I can just as easily stay in tonight."

Patrick and Carl Hartley left then. They were headed for the casino and later the cock fights in another part of the city. They had access to a whole world that excluded me, though I was no longer curious.

Carline emphasized that I must be more presentable by their standards. "Kelly's really too old for the coming-out, don't you know," she had said. "But we shall see. Maybe next season." I was future marriage material only; marriage to a man who would also leave me sitting at home while he spent the evening enjoying masculine pursuits. Why had Brianna Miller sent me here? What was her purpose? What was I expected to accomplish more than my own unhappiness?

Steve Swanweil came to dinner, and that time Carline's brothers and their wives attended. Another man was there named Frank Duerr, the governor of the Two Forks province, who was sometimes featured on the local comtech news. I was certain I had seen him interviewed on the comtech news. But Swanweil was the interesting dinner guest. He seemed to shimmer; his oily hair and tailored suit gave tracers of himself, like he was standing behind an empty acrylic vase distorting my view of him. How did he achieve that?

And Carline left him alone with her barbed comments. He smoked kari root cigarettes and talked business with the men, mostly about exchange rates and expected shipments. "The tribes are furious about Hartley backing the law of impunity. They demonstrate in Cylay and burn posters of the general's face marked with red slashes. Putuki get in front of the cameras and shake their fists. 'Death to Hamilcar,' they chant. 'Death to the sor'shum.' That's their word for the Consortium: sor'shum." Swanweil looked at me, and flames seemed to shoot from his eyes. I blinked, and he looked away and the image vanished, so I shrugged it off.

Swanweil stood on the back porch after the meal, talking with the Bryants brothers, who were carbon copies of Sean Bryant. I spied on them from the lighted interior. They discussed gum arabic trade on their upstart securities exchange and how the licenses and treasure of Kyle Rula must be dismantled. "Brianna has separate licenses now under Mitterand's name," Swanweil said, "and she's importing smelting equipment, along with instruments used for geology. She thinks she's so clever to have them delivered in pieces at different locations, like we cannot figure that out. Some essential pieces never make it through customs."

From the bar, Carline called my name, and I nearly jumped out of my skin.

I did talk to Patrick again while he was packing to travel with Carl. "Why do you stay near him?" I asked. "Carl laughs at you and makes you do stuff."

"What do you know about it, Kelly?"

"But you're one of the Junction Boys," I said. "You can work for a salary."

"At some clerk's desk in Two Forks?" he asked bitterly as he pressed the last of his essentials into a square case. "Or I should collect taxes from Cylahi, I suppose? Walk between villages with a gualarep at my side."

"None would follow you."

Patrick slapped me roundly. I stepped back in surprise, pressing a cooling palm against my cheek. There was no regret in his red-rimmed eyes.

"At least I don't volunteer to empty bedpans like you," he spat out as he snapped the catches closed. "Is it true that you shave the pregnant women, um, down there?"

"I was helping. Part of duty."

"What do you know about it?" Patrick pushed past me and left carrying his case.

I rushed into the bathroom with a tight chest and turned on the faucet to cover the sounds of my sobs. I had been proud that the nurses had begun to trust me and assign regular tasks. To prepare a new mother for the pain of birthing. Sure, the work was messy. It was the maternity ward after all.

I hated my life.

So one day I was hustled into the waiting ECCAV and made to accompany Aunt Carline on an errand she had devised. She was to be interviewed at a comtech station in New Shanghai, her opinion solicited on the state of affairs on Dolvia. I was sick of her opinions, so it seemed odd to me that she was to speak to them out in a public arena.

I sat in the waiting area, bored and dispirited. A young Cicero woman hurried out and looked around tensely. She grabbed me by the arm so that I was made to stand. She looked me up and down. "This will have to do."

I was escorted to the audience section of the studio and directed to sit in the second row there. Others filed in, people who had been waiting in a different room than me. The upshot was, the news broadcast intended for the following day's morning show was a contest between Carline Bryant and Sheeks-Cylom, known on Cicero as the wife of the general or Mrs. Shaw. She was raising her twin boys here and doing research on some old bones she had found at the digs on Uburu land.

Brianna and I had visited Mrs. Shaw at the digs. That was where I had first met Dr. Spinelli. On Cicero, Mrs. Shaw was viewed as a radical with an imbalanced view in favor of the savannah tribes. She had Softcheeks credentials and knew all the players in the Arrivi struggle, so her imbalanced view made for good comtech talk show segments.

Mrs. Shaw engaged with Carline at the host's prompting and argued each point. "Since the armistice," the host said into the camera lens, "there has been a shift in the balance of power on the Arrivi savannah. There's evidence of an alliance between the Uburu forces led by Kenru and specific Borabean clans, especially the Madquii. Mrs. Shaw, what in your opinion is the impetus of this new development?"

"Im-pe-tus," I whispered. I would have to search for that word in the dictionary.

"The Uburu are an invaded and displaced people," Mrs. Shaw said. She was dressed western and with each hair in place. To me, she seemed wiry and self-assured. "The Uburu have no holy war. Rather, they want peace and to plant crops for the next season. Assurances of safety in their mesa homeland are essential."

"Uburu are opportunistic," Carline countered. "They flood the savannah as refugees with each political hiccup, are more dependent on the dole than even the Cylahi tribe. Uburu should be taxed and their land managed by people who can provide better cultivation methods."

Mrs. Shaw spoke in whole tones, playing to the camera. "If you mean coffee cultivation, that cash crop brings the very dependency you claim to deplore."

"So you view this alliance as a positive development?" the host asked Mrs. Shaw.

"Borabean are a collection of tribes, the same as Arrivi," she said. "The grievous acts of the Gora clan should not shadow the neighboring Madquii families, who have no sympathy for ambush and massacre. We must look more closely at the structure within the Borabean leadership."

"Divide and conquer, you mean," Carline spat out. "Mekucoo warriors want to promote Aegiv as a puppet and manage Madquii commerce against the peoples' will."

"Anaxagoras is not a duly elected leader," Mrs. Shaw said. "Rather a usurper like Khalif Ananke himself. Who is violating the people's will here?"

"Anaxagoras made the coalition!" Carline claimed. I didn't know any of the leaders they were discussing. How did these wives living on Cicero learn so much about Borabean politics?

"Anaxagoras rules the Goras clan by force of arms," Mrs. Shaw countered. "And has violated the very treaties he signed."

"Arrivi broke the agreement with their military strikes into Gora territory."

"Arrivi don't butcher children and torch the land."

"Karl Wyley doesn't honor his word!" Aunt Carline said with a red face. "He killed my brother for no reason at all."

"Joey Osborn was profiteering," Mrs. Shaw said evenly. "There was evidence."

"Ha! We have the order of impunity now." Carline sat back with a smug look. "Never again can Karl Wyley torture and kill a businessman without consequence."

"The order of impunity is illegal," Mrs. Shaw countered. "The tribes will not follow it, even Gora. The residents of the savannah are subject to tribal law, everyone."

"Safety must be guaranteed," Carline said, pointing an index finger. "How else can a Hardhand businessman consider investment in Dolviet industry?"

"Arrivi are not seeking outside investment."

"You want to push us out so you can have free access to the silicide."

"Ladies," the anchorman said, "we are getting somewhat offtrack here. Unfortunate as it was, Joey Osborn's death is long past. Perhaps we can focus on current events. If you would allow me to guide our discussion, we can wind this up." He looked up to a booth situated over the heads of the audience. "Are we still taping? Good, good.

"Now, Mrs. Bryant," he continued, "in your opinion, what is the greatest need among the savannah tribes you call Arrivi?"

"Education and the restoration of the family structure. Children grow without knowing their fathers, without guidance to understand the events around them."

"And Mrs. Shaw, your assessment?"

"On this point we agree," she said with a sly smile. "Liberal education, and not indoctrination of ideology, will shape the future."

"In-doc-tri-na-tion," I whispered.

Later, Carline was talking with the show's producer, flirting openly while he stood reserved and indifferent. I took a deep breath and stepped to Mrs. Shaw's side. "Sheeks-Cylom," I said, embarrassed to use the tribal name to gain traction. "It's me, Kelly. You remember? I visited the Uburu digs with Brianna one time."

"Kelly, of course I remember. You look so different, taller I think. How is your mother?"

"Fine, just fine. I received a letter from her yesterday. She says—"

"Kelly, allow me to introduce Jesse Hartley, the general's daughter."

"Jesse?" She was in her twenties, big-boned and with dark hair. She had a porcelain complexion, nearly transparent, and she hugged me. "Kelly Osborn, Patrick's sister. So good to meet you at last."

"It's good to meet you." Tears stood in my eyes, and I felt overwhelmed by loneliness. Nobody had spoken kindly to me since my farewell to Hakulupe Le in Cylay.

"We're going to dinner," Jesse said. "Can you join us?"

"I would love to but . . . I'm here to visit my aunt Carline Bryant."

"I can take care of that right now." Jesse walked resolutely to where Carline talked with two men from the studio crew and lightly touched her arm. They spoke cordially for a few minutes, and Jesse returned. "All set. Let's go."

"But . . . what did you say to her?"

"Only that the general," Jesse said in low tones, "gladly accepts her kind invitation to dinner, and could I borrow you for a few hours? An acceptable trade-off in her estimation."

"General Shaw for me?"

"General Hartley will visit next week. General Shaw is retired from Consortium service now, retired but not out of work. Nobody knows his whereabouts, not even his wife and twins." Jesse gave Mrs. Shaw an exaggerated wink. "So tell me, what is your website address? I can add you to my circle of friends."

"Website?"

Jesse glanced at Mrs. Shaw before she smiled, very diplomatic. "We'll make one together. We can use a template and quick as one-two-three, we're done. You can add photos and chants and a blog about your travels and—"

The following weeks were a swirl of activity. The debutante ceremony for that season was approaching, and with General Hartley's personal invitation, I was to be presented along with twenty-two other young women. He had sat, smiling and nodding, through a tedious meal his daughter had arranged so I could spend an afternoon with her and Mrs. Shaw. I felt embarrassed for him, and for myself, when Aunt Carline poured her third drink. Carline didn't mention the law of impunity though, or the demonstrations in Cylay.

General Hartley suggested that night that I should travel to Stargate Junction and come out as a debutante. I would be by far the oldest, he cautioned gently with a hand on my wrist. I remembered Carline claiming more than once that I should wait another season! Clearly, she had never intended to make the effort.

Over time I had heard so many stories about the debutante ball. Heather Osborn had danced with Hamish Nordhagen at a similar dress ball. General Hartley, then a young lieutenant, had met Jesse's mother Billie at the same transport event and courted her for more than a season before they married. After the Company had lost the fight for the uranium refinery, after their wormhole supply lines had contracted, after the Consortium of Westend Planets had taken over the transport administration, the debutante ball became one of the few rituals Hardhands retained as part of the Westend protocol.

I was unsure of my role in the charade, so inconstant. I spoke to Mrs. Shaw. "People fight and die on the savannah," I said. "Women scrape together a meal for their children. While they suffer, I should wear western clothes and dance with Hardhand officers?"

"We must grab each opportunity to live large," Mrs. Shaw said. "Privacy does not serve here, Kelly."

That sounded familiar.

I chewed on that for a several days; privacy does not serve. The concept was similar to a question I had long entertained about what to exclude from my writing. Which gesture was instructive, and which was private? In company, however, I chose to follow the example of Jesse Hartley and her father, the general. He showed to each faction the face that was expected, just like Brianna Miller, to guide the talks and to keep his place. His voice had volume.

Aunt Carline could play queen bee all she wanted, but her gaming arena was small, crimped by her lack of generosity and her preference for young men. Her voice did not carry the volume of General Hartley's words. I began to understand the usefulness of politics and Brianna's special concerns. All this time while I had been feeling rejected, I was being groomed so that my voice would be heard.

And I was allowed to move about more freely. I suspected Jesse had spoken to Carline. I visited Mrs. Shaw, who mostly labored with research at her place outside of Two Forks, with Martina acting as her Putuki nanny to manage the twins and many visitors. I visited Dr. Spinelli, who had arrived for a residency at the New Shanghai hospital doing research on his potshard finds. He was always bright and gracious with his bushy eyebrows and ever-present pipe.

My best experience during those weeks was with Jesse Hartley. Mrs. Shaw was patient but brusque, not a confidante. Jesse, by contrast, wanted to spend time together swapping clothes and sitting on the bed with gossip and giggles. We made a personal website for me, and I was added to her friends, who were mostly daughters of Consortium military living on the transport or at Stargate Junction. They talked about the soldiers passing through and clothes and music.

It was all kind of silly. It produced nothing.

Jesse had a playfulness that felt unseemly next to Carline's hard judgments. Jesse recounted wicked stories about Brianna as a young ab-o-ri-gi-ne who had stayed with Jesse's family and studied in transport classes. She talked about Billie Hartley and how she missed her mother and how she felt estranged from Carl.

Estranged was a good word. I felt estranged from Patrick.

Mrs. Shaw joined us without ceremony one afternoon and added to our storytelling. "Brianna was mentored by many. She was General Hartley's unofficial advisor when he was a transport colonel after Karlyhi closed Somule to outsiders. Then Dr. Beecham was a solace to Brianna after our evacuation from Dolvia. And Dr. Mitterand, but I don't know that you could call his role mentoring. His acts were several rungs down from being a mentor."

Jesse ducked her head and blinked. Mrs. Shaw reached to finger the fabric of my burka, set aside there. I saw the scar on her forearm that I knew was gained when Pete had sliced the skin and sucked the poison from a spider bite during the time of the vaccine task.

"Prior to any of them, of course," she continued, "Brianna learned from my husband General Shaw, from when he was a colonel. During the Uburu refugee crisis, Brianna was sent to Cylay to stay with me and avoid Karlyhi, who was just coming into his own then. My husband provided her with her first taste of Westend politics and who was who. Brianna's personality was shaped by General Shaw, not by Pierre Mitterand or any of the others."

She pulled the folds of the burka to her and refolded it carefully. In my experience, Mrs. Shaw and Brianna Miller were constantly at each other's throats, a deeper and more mean-spirited competition than mine with Aunt Carline. It was a question of control, I had assumed. So why should Mrs. Shaw be prideful about General Shaw and how he had helped Brianna as a young person?

"It's too bad women don't get medals or ribbons like the Consortium officers," Jesse said when we were alone. "Mrs. Shaw would have a whole chest full of medals. The bush clinic, the vaccine task, raising Edna and Edwina, mentoring for you and Karlyhi."

"Brianna would have too many to count as well," I said, entering the game. "In service to General Shaw, bringing the gualarep Brian to the savannah, managing Somule Gems in Paris, calling forth the clutch of Cleo, mining for silicide."

"And your aunt Carline would have just as many," Jesse said. "Present at the trial where Brian Miller argued for Kyle Le."

"Maybe, but all her ribbons would be black. Ran a sweatshop in Cylay, allowed the abuse of Arrivi children, traded in armaments, wants to monopolize the trade in gum arabic."

Jesse chuckled. "We should draw some ribbons and present them to the women. Except maybe not. Too colorful and hard to coordinate with any ensemble for the comtech appearances."

"The men don't mind the clashing colors," I added. "But the women would look ... wrong." We laughed together again.

FIFTEEN

BEFORE THE DEBUTANTE CEREMONY WAS THE FEAST OF ORIA. I
needed to travel to Dolvia before I could journey to Stargate Junction. I had been absent a full season, which felt more like an eternity. I had missed the rains, and the savannah was a desert again.

I resigned my position at the New Shanghai hospital. They won't miss me. I was sorry I hadn't spent more time with Dr. Spinelli. I had twice visited his lab where he inspected markings on old pottery fragments using a big lamp with a mounted magnifier. His notes and diagrams were entered in a notebook using longhand. I had thought I was the only person who preferred to write with a pen.

Dr. Richardson's activities in the hospital had escalated to loudly accusing the Hardhand and Putuki staff of stealing the morphine he had consumed. I even saw him greet Carl and Patrick one day to hand off a package in exchange for an envelope. I considered reporting Dr. Richardson but left it alone. A clean exit was all that I sought.

Mrs. Shaw planned to leave the twins with Martina and to also attend the Dolviet feast, and Jesse invited herself into our company. "All these years and I have never disembarked," Jesse claimed during one of our long and private talks. "Now I will visit two Westend planets. My father grows more conservative each season, so I should get this done before he sends me to a convent." The convent reference escaped me. We had Lutheran convents on Dolvia where academy trained welfare ministers lived, a station of high honor and secure income.

"On Earth," Mrs. Shaw later explained, "a convent is separated from the world. Jesse only meant that to protect her, the general might choose to send her far from the fighting."

"And would she go?"

"It is just a saying," Mrs. Shaw said irritably. "Jesse makes her own decisions."

Then there was Aunt Carline. I wore a western dress to dinner and tried to include only those gestures she wanted me to display, elbows off the table and all, but her resentment was palpable. "So, you have made friends at last here in New Shanghai," she said after a drink of sherry. "And now you will journey to Stargate Junction. You are finally presentable as an Osborn, not a barefoot sister of Arim who gleans the savannah for gum arabic."

I was town-raised in Somule and had no experience of gleaning the savannah like Arrivi women who lived on family farms, but I said nothing.

"And don't think I cannot see through Brianna's intent with the conscripts," she added.

I looked up. "What intent?"

"Just polishing her image," Carline said. "Not truly generous; all for appearance sake."

Carline was one to talk about appearances. In truth, I had changed under her tutelage. I was much improved, trimmer and with my hair contained. I was mostly reconciled to how the glasses shaped my face. Also I could bathe, suture, and bandage a wound in record time, or at least the plastic dummy resident in the hospital library.

"I'm so grateful for your interest, Aunt Carline," I said evenly. "And for the expense you endured on my behalf. I apologize if I was too much trouble."

"Trouble you were," she said quickly, "but the goal was accomplished in spite of your behavior. Patrick will be pleased."

I doubted that. It was typical, though, that she should reference off the men, the goal measured by his acceptance, not by something we agreed between us. I was glad to be free of my apprenticeship at New Shanghai and didn't even bother to seek out Sean Bryant for the honorable goodbye. I left the cellphone on my dresser at Carline's house.

At the last minute, Mrs. Shaw bowed out of our trip. It seemed one of the twins had the croup, and she felt she couldn't travel. Jesse's face fell, and she claimed she didn't have to go, just an impulse to see the savannah. "But you can come with me," I said. "We'll stay at Somule, and I'll rent an ECCAV to drive to the feast on the flats."

"Actually, it's held at Mayschool this year, Kelly," Mrs. Shaw corrected.

Jesse looked at me with pleading eyes. "I know Mayschool," I said. "I practically grew up there."

"You can meet Hakulupe Le at Cylay," Mrs. Shaw said, "and travel with the military chopper, just so there's no discomfort."

"Are you sure?" Jesse asked.

"I'll contact Lupe and set the permissions," I said cheerfully. "No worries."

Jesse was pleased. "Let's go, then. We'll talk all day, and I so want to see the geysers and hot springs on the flats I've heard so much about." And so we set out on our adventure.

My big lesson of culture shock after we disembarked the shuttle at Cylay was tied to Jesse Hartley. Dolvia's gravity affected her greatly, and the blistering heat. Colonel Sector drove us to the barracks in his open jeep; that was a thrill. Hakulupe Le left her duties training the clutch of Cleo and joined us for refreshments of tea and corn chips. Karen was there; I was glad they had thought to include my mother. We talked about recent events, about my looks and how I was so thin.

"How goes your writing?" Lupe asked warmly. "I look forward to the published chapbook, all the new English words to learn." I did not have the courage to say I had done no writing for a whole cycle, so much wasted time.

The tribeswomen accepted Jesse without the need for Arrivi burkas, like she had always lived among us. Jesse asked many questions about our customs, only safe topics. She hugged each person; Jesse was big on hugs. Acclimation pills had made her silly and fearful. Hakulupe Le told me later, "Jesse has always lived on the transport, Kelly. Artificial gravity is, well, artificial."

On the afternoon of the second day, when Jesse felt less dizzy, she and Karen and I accepted a chopper ride to Mayschool. We took a detour and overflew the flats with its geysers and bubbling pools and clumps of tall acacia trees, then past the shattered butte and facing plateau. The pupils of Jesse's eyes were dilated from the acclimation pill, and she just stared and stared. "So vast," she kept repeating. "The savannah is so vast."

Mark and two other Cylahi with college unloaded the chopper. Mark limped noticeably; another in his group had a face scar and only one eye. Karen barked orders at them. Jesse shrank from contact. I signified on Mark with one hand held high.

"Melinga," I said, but Mark only nodded.

Jesse needed to stop often as we walked the final distance up the knoll to Kecouroo's village where we were to be quartered during the feast. We rested at one point, Jesse gasping and wheezing. She turned to me with saucer eyes and pointed at the bush near some clumps of ferns and shriveled razor grass. I glimpsed the marbled side of a gualarep, who sidled away. Karen giggled and turned away to conceal her laughter at this offworlder, so ungracious.

"Don't be alarmed," I said to Jesse. "Edna and Edwina prefer Kecouroo's village and swimming in the grotto nearby. There's no danger."

"They are tame but free?"

"Yes, free to roam the whole region, even Uburu land."

Jesse did not ask to stop again while we conquered the final leg to the Mekucoo village where Kecouroo waited for us in the yard.

"The sure knowledge of our ancestors is enlarged by the spirit of Kelly Osborn," Kecouroo said with an open hand gesture.

"I have missed my place at Kecouroo's side," I said. "I am glad for this opportunity to share the Feast of Oria together. May I present Jesse Hartley, daughter to the general."

"We know the general called Hamilcar and are pleased he entrusts us with this visit from his beloved family member."

Jesse had that silly grin from the acclimation pills. "The name Kecouroo is known throughout Westend. I am honored to be included for the feast."

Later, in fact many times through the following weeks, Jesse and I talked about this greeting. Her disbelief was that Kecouroo held status even though she wore no shoes, with her toughened hands and the brief leather garment, and lived in a hut without running water or a privy. She balked at the sight of domestic fowl roaming free in the village, the casual acceptance of sickness, and the presence of men mutilated by warrior service.

And the weapons, Jesse was surprised at their presence. Every man and young boy carried an automatic slung over his shoulder. The empty hut we entered was stocked with two karkars leaning against the pole wall. A young girl, no more than age twelve, delivered boxes of ammunition and checked the gauges, trained to match weapons and consumables.

Karen quickly took charge of our hut, arranging who slept where and when meals were ready. Karen was too much like Aunt Carline, not in the area of men, but dictating how I dressed, what I ate, and correcting my words.

On the third day, Jesse and I took the opportunity for a day trip onto the savannah. We wore our western clothes again, but with Arrivi sandals good for walking the distance down to Mayschool. She was attracted to an EAM café there, all neon trim and polished surfaces, and looked around with disappointment when she realized the cramped stations were mostly unused, just students playing video games. "Do doctors and staff have a separate café?" I had not been in the hospital or most buildings of the school, so I couldn't say.

Then I drove an ECCAV I had borrowed from Colonel Sector's forces, and we carried a meal that Karen had thoughtfully packed. I voiced the desire to visit the flats and the fortress of Arim, but that was deemed too far. The winds over the high bluff buffeted the ECCAV. I struggled with the steering wheel, hiding my concern behind a smile in Jesse's direction. Perhaps this was too much car for me. We soon descended toward the basin though, and the winds were less there. Jesse and I stopped some distance down from Mekucoo land and spread our picnic to overlook on the expansive veld.

Jesse wheezed like an asthmatic and squinted in the sunlight from under her wide-brimmed hat. She dabbed her throat with a scented handkerchief and surveyed the far horizon. The desert's charm eluded her. We sat in the thorn tree's sparse shade over dried kariom on salted patties, a real treat. A sudden breeze kicked up, ruffling our dresses and troubling our big hats, and covering the picnic spread with gritty dust. If Edna had spied us, she would have seen tourists in offworld clothes with no understanding that one must give oneself to the savannah, freely entering Dolvia's embrace, in order to survive here.

"All this time," Jesse said. "Dolvia is nothing like I had imagined. I guess I was being romantic. Idealized images of each village and each person, taken from the general's stories. The scientists from the Uburu digs spoke so highly of Dolvia and what they had accomplished here."

"Dr. Spinelli easily shares chi with Arrivi."

"You see, there it is. I assumed friends were connected by proximity, like on the transport. But it's more a good opinion during long absences. How do you tolerate the loneliness?"

"I don't feel lonely here. I felt lonely on Cicero with Aunt Carline."

"But each village is so distant, Kelly. And there's no . . . no—"

"No promenade?" I asked. "No catalogue to order goods from Earth? No convenient market to select groceries for the evening's meal?"

"No bath, no closet, no soft bed." We smiled together.

"We gather for the feast," I said. "You will like the feast."

While we were driving back, tunanin swirled across the veld and approached our ECCAV. "What's that whirlwind?" Jesse asked. I slowed the vehicle while we watched the small funnel's erratic dance. "Ancestors surveying the land before the rains," I said, "called tunanin. Perhaps we are being spied on again, huh? Like when Edna was on the trail."

After we had driven to higher ground, I stopped the ECCAV for a rest. The dried kariom had made Jesse unsettled, and she needed to empty her stomach. I felt heartstone for her, so uncomfortable. Before we began again, Jesse pointed to people crossing the savannah below. "What's that?"

Their showy headdresses of black Murmurey feathers were easily recognizable. "Siibabean warriors in quick march. They must be coming for the feast."

"So handsome but not all the same. Who's the other?"

I knew who he was, and my throat felt tight. "Rufus, the son of Cyrus the ketiwhelp killer, travels with them."

"I know Rufus."

"You do!"

"He took classes on the transport at the same time as Brianna," Jesse said. "Of course, I was a little girl then. Rufus also visited the general on Stargate Junction, coming and going, when he journeyed to bring Brianna back from Paris. He stayed with us several days."

"Rufus on the transport?"

"I'm sure you knew."

"I did know in an idealized form, I suppose."

Jesse laughed and punched my arm lightly, maybe feeling better.

Hakulupe Le and her three children were waiting when we returned the ECCAV to the Mayschool barracks. "We can sit with you during the communal fire, if you don't mind."

"Hiki, Millie," I said. "Hiki, Anna." Michael Peter was walking but not talking yet. Anna held his hand. We took a short detour to the catalpa tree that had been part of Mrs. Shaw first clinic on the site. "Edna grabbed two stones from Sheeks-Cylom's hand one day," Lupe said with humor. "One was her and one was me, she explained, asking Edna which of us could leave. It was like a test of Edna's loyalty. Edna scurried up the tree to embed them in a branch there." Lupe chuckled to herself. "This was when Edna was a yearling and could climb trees."

We looked up at the lush tree with its twisted branches and broad leaves. "So the talismans," Lupe said, "one granite and one sandstone, are still there. Tribespeople sometimes visit and bury similar tokens that speak of their friendship over the years."

Jesse turned to me. "I want us to be friends like Hakulupe Le and Mrs. Shaw. Do you think we could—"

I was deeply touched. Jesse was older than me and far more experienced. "Of course, what a great idea."

We searched around, and each selected a stone. Millie volunteered to climb the tree and bury the pieces in the cleft that held several offerings. We applauded when she showed her beaming face from between the leaves and shouted that she was done. Jesse and I hugged while Millie scrambled down. Jesse hugged Hakulupe Le and then Millie and then Anna. She was big on hugs.

The Siibabean brothers Siize and Siiloba waited in the yard, serving as Karlyhi's guards for this day. Jesse was very taken with their looks. I didn't see Rufus who had arrived with them, I was certain. Karen was near the church building above the catalpa tree and gestured that we should hurry. Feast time was near.

The feast was poorly attended that season. The tribal women had little to celebrate and less to share because a warrior's duty was elsewhere. The bazaar tables displayed trade goods, fewer during this season of netta. Textiles and feather-laced Mekucoo leather, olive oil in decorated cans, plus handmade furniture. Savannah fresh produce was scarce, just black olives and dried kariom on salted patties.

Dried cumin, an herb highly prized for seasoning, was purchased only at the premium price of three oblu, but Cylay soft breads were available and Uburu treats, goat curd, and various maize products. Thin and salted corn chips, fried in oleastra oil and served hot, were a favorite and cost only a kam. This snack was replacing the Arrivi patty as a staple.

At sunset, we gathered before the communal fire for chants and dancing. Kecouroo was near Cara's place, and Rufus was seated next to them, filling a seat reserved for Dacupitte who was serving with Kenru on Uburu land. Orin Rabbe Murd and his three sons dominated the Arrivi section. I sat with my mother in the Arrivi women's group, setting aside our veils for this celebration. We tasted roasted lemur flank with dripping juices and maize on cobs that were pulled from the fire and dipped in oleastra oil.

Colonel Sector and Hakulupe Le, also their two daughters and young son, sat with Jesse Hartley, cordial and helpful with the general's daughter. The many girls in the clutch of Cleo listened to Brianna Miller and hung on her every word, she to whom Dolvia whispered each morning at sunrise. I looked away, glad that Brianna had others to order around.

Karlyhi and Omiibuk were nearly surrounded by Siibabean who were attending for the first time. I caught whispers about General Shaw on Siibabean land, how he'd dropped out of Dolviet politics, and how he was seeking a passage through the dense forest. What was on the other side?

The feast highlight that season was the chanted story of Aensilus the Madquii who got separated from his group during a skirmish on the dunes. He had wandered the savannah, dazed from a head wound. He had rested under a leafless oleastra bush and woke when a short-tailed ketiwhelp licked sweat and blood from his face. The chant told how the female ketiwhelp led him over the dunes into Southeast Arrivi land, telling him to follow the butterflies. Aensilus had resisted, weakened by his wound, and sat in the burning sun resigned to his fate. The yelping short-tailed ketiwhelp nipped at his ankles, forcing him to stand and stumble deeper into Arrivi grazing land.

Aensilus spent two days without water or food. He awoke late one morning to see Nettki hovering on the horizon. Butterflies danced before his view; he thought it was a dream. How could they tolerate the heat? Yellow ones with black-tipped wings fluttered near his matted tear ducts and chapped lips, and danced on the cool morning breeze along a path to the right. Without hope, Aensilus had followed them, sometimes glimpsing their clutch, sometimes wandering without direction. They led him to a depression in a red sandstone outcropping. They waited in the sun, yellow and black wings crinkled by the unrelenting heat, dipping below the rocks and fluttering out as if asking why he hesitated. Aensilus reached down and felt cool water. There was a pool of old water under the stones, life-saving water.

The short-tailed ketiwhelp returned later, bringing Kecouroo who bathed Aensilus' wounds and dragged him on a trapezoid stretcher to Uburu lines where his blisters and abrasions were treated. Aensilus asked her about the ketiwhelp; had the fox sought out Kecouroo and led her to the pool? Or was Kecouroo led by the butterflies?

"What ketiwhelp?" Kecouroo claimed she had stumbled onto his dehydrated self while traveling to Uburu allies along a well-known desert trail.

"Short-tail did not show herself?

Or the butterfly clutch?" he asked.

"I need no companion on the land,

And desert insects hide at noonday,"

She said, ready to be done with this tale.

Or so it was chanted. The words had rhyme and meter in Arrivi, but they didn't translate well. Too many voices in a single stanza was my assessment, not one of Mark's composition. Aensilus was returned by the Uburu militia to his father Aegiv as a gesture of goodwill. He was not present at the Feast of Oria to reinforce the chant's details, and Kecouroo only shrugged when I asked her. Was she holding a secret or just didn't know?

Brianna Miller pestered Kecouroo for more details. "This savannah pool with the butterflies," she asked. "Is it close to Uburu mesas? Does Dulcinea know about this pool?"

"The water rests along a known trail to Uburu land," was Kecouroo's answer.

"Can you take me there?" Brianna insisted. "What is it called, this butterfly pool?" Kecouroo only blinked and gave few details.

Jesse came to my side with bright eyes. "Brianna has offered me a position with Somule Gems," she claimed. "I will jump back to Earth and meet Petra Mitterand, the doctor's daughter."

I struggled to manufacture joy in my heart. "A valuable opportunity," I said. "Paris will be a step up from Mayschool."

Jesse's brow wrinkled. "I have enjoyed our time here. I know I'm a disappointment to you. And to Kecouroo."

"I want us to remember this time as . . . as good," I said. "Growing together before you jump back."

Her face was too active. "And we still have the junction ball to attend. It'll be great. You'll see." Jesse seemed scattered, really waiting to go home. "Oh! And Bernice will serve on the transport near my father," she added. "His staff will train her. You know Bernice, right?"

"One of the clutch of Cleo," I said.

I looked over at Brianna Miller where she was deep in conversation with Hakulupe Le, probably giving orders to build spheres of influence for the StrikeStone venture and to manage the fates of warriors and savannah women with her business enterprises.

I sighed, and my heart pulled down in my chest. "Always remember, Jesse, your spirit and mine are planted together in the catalpa tree at Mayschool. We are bound, just like Sheeks-Cylom is bound to Hakulupe Le."

Jesse followed my gaze to watch the women laugh together. "I hope we grow as close as Brianna and Lupe," she said.

I was glad when the Feast of Oria ended. I had viewed our festival through Jesse's eyes. The homegrown produce laid out on dusty tables, the handicrafts and hand-powered farming implements, the unpenned domestic fowl and pigs. I saw matrons with bad teeth, pot-bellied children with no supervision, scarred and battle-weary warriors. My extended family was . . . not appealing to my new friend.

Early in the misty morning, we stopped for the ritual farewell with Kecouroo. "Kelly Osborn has many choices ahead," Kecouroo said for ritual. "Some already decided, but others rest only in your hands."

"I will try to bring honor to the tribes and the name of Kecouroo."

We hurried down the knoll to enter the waiting chopper with Colonel Sector and his family. Once the big machine was in the air, the rhythmic swoop-swoop-swoop of the blades settled me somewhat. I saw Rufus standing in a clearing on the knoll, just standing there with Edna at his side where he knew we could spy them, his karkar and ammo belt resting on one shoulder. Like he knew.

SIXTEEN

MY MOTHER KAREN TRAVELED WITH JESSE AND ME, DRESSED TRA-
ditionally with the Arrivi burka. The spirit in my face was known,
and I was to be presented at the coming-out. It would have been
hypocritical, we decided again, for me to wear the veil now. People
stared at Karen but hid their judging looks. We could hear them
whispering behind us, so rude.

The comments acted on Jesse Hartley's nerves. "So rude," she
kept saying.

Offworld travel was a marvel to Karen. She would tap my shoulder and whisper and then giggle. Except that she was covered from
head to knees, her own ungracious reactions were more rude than
any. For myself, I quickly learned to withhold my gestures and keep
my face still, not from fear of what they might be thinking; rather,
a correct posture within the close quarters. Everybody kept themselves within themselves. After several days, however, I found it
tiring to hold my spirit anchored against my backbone. I thought

of Rufus enjoying the first rays of sun and stretching his spirit out over his domain.

Bernice Datong occupied a shuttle seat next to us. After we docked on the orbiting transport, she was greeted by managers of Somule Gems, the first among the clutch of Cleo to be assigned. Staff members for General Hartley were slated to introduce Bernice to accounting for wormhole traffic in gum arabic and oleastra oil. Bernice waved goodbye before she followed them to her new duties. No hug for her, I guessed.

Anyhow, many days later we arrived at Stargate Junction, a mammoth space station shaped like a cylinder with nine decks and many docking bays. Two rings were attached by many spokes, and solar panels paddled along inside the rings. For protection maybe. A visitor leaving the shuttle must pass through security checks and customs before greeting waiting hosts. I felt lightheaded from the artificial gravity, and the air had a metallic chemical taste. Some said the air was oxygen-rich, but I don't know. It tasted bad.

Hardhand Blackshirts and men of the Company gathered there, more than I had seen together. They mingled freely with visiting Cicero officials and with Consortium officers. There were even a few Abydian, one named Aristides chief among them.

General Hartley was in session, as they referred to his work, but his first civilian secretary Mildred, an older woman in a tailored business suit, waited to greet Jesse. "Mildred, may I present Kelly Osborn, sister to Patrick Osborn, and her mother Karen." Patrick was one of the Junction Boys, so highlighting that connection made sense in this arena.

"Hiki," I said, holding one palm high. "Melinga."

"Melinga to you," Mildred returned.

Karen and I were assigned adjacent rooms along a blank hallway. The keys had sequential even numbers, 214 and 216. "Se-quen-tial," Karen whispered so she would remember. Odd numbers were for rooms across the hall, an interesting system.

It seemed strange to be quartered in these blank rooms instead of with Jesse and the general. I felt the snub and wondered if I would be sleeping elsewhere if Karen had remained on Dolvia. Jesse left to tell her father about how she was invited to jump back. I closed the door against the hallway noise and felt an immediate release, alone for once. My spirit soared to the ceiling and around the walls, hovering somewhere, wondering what this place was. Where was the long vista across the veld?

I stretched out on top of the covers and placed an arm across my eyes, trying to shut out the sensory stimulus so that my spirit could rest. I had images of swimming; my eyes just above water level, and the rushing current along my hide. I drifted in the shallows for a time and sped toward kariom prey with one flick of my muscled tail.

And that was my first episode of seeing om, as it was said. This phenomenon had been reported twice before, General Hartley told me much later: once with Brian Miller while he visited the transport and separately when my grandmother Heather Osborn danced with Hamish Nordhagen at a transport debutante ball. My experience was the first reported episode for someone at Stargate Junction, though, some distance from Dolvia. Swimming images disturbed my sleep most nights; violent sequences of taking down a young erriv and devouring it by ripping at the flesh with my strong jaws and swallowing the pieces whole. I sometimes woke thrashing and in a cold sweat.

Many theories were put forth, but Jesse's argument of culture shock was, well, sane. "Too much oxygen," the general postulated, referring to the air content on Stargate Junction. "It goes to the head."

It was decided I should try to react little to what I saw, as well as I could manage, and to share the images only when I disembarked again. We placed a trunk call to Colonel Sector who made a special trip to an Uburu mesa with the HGEAM in tow so I could reach out to Brianna Miller with my concerns. My image hovered in the light like General Hartley's when he had earned the name Hamilcar. All this was accomplished through a network of friends to reassure my questioning heart. It escaped me for some time how careful and giving they were, Arrivi and Hardhands. I only felt I was being a bother.

"I had swimming dreams while I traveled with Rufus," Brianna said when we contacted her by way of HGEAM. Her image hovered in the light of a cycling cube. "I miss them now."

"Should I seek to know someone here?" I asked her likeness in a blue light.

Two beats, and she answered my hovering likeness on Dolvia. "Only those who present themselves to your line of sight."

"Brianna, who is that with you?" I asked. A young woman in a traditional gown and braided hair stood smiling at Brianna's shoulder. The gown in a similar wash of blue light made her likeness seem to fade in and out.

"What do you see?" Brianna asked.

"Who is that with you?" I asked again.

"May I present Kat, the holy woman?"

"Hiki, Kat," I said, still wondering.

"Hiki, Kelly with the auburn hair," Kat said. "Melinga."

Our connection was interrupted, and hard blue light flooded the operations room where Karen and I sat with Jesse, along with the general and his technicians.

"It's best not to boot again," the general said. His tone was sad with deep longing. I knew something of the source of his regret. I remembered the whispering I had heard during our visit to the Uburu digs seasons ago. But Brianna had chosen duty on the savannah over other opportunities. "We cannot risk exposing her location to prying eyes," the general added.

"What did you see?" Jesse asked.

"Brianna and the holy woman Kat."

"Two people?"

"The same as you."

"I saw only Brianna," Jesse said.

Karen touched my shoulder. She explained in Arrivi, which both Jesse and the general understood, "Kat is covered by Dolvia. Only those who are embraced know her."

"This means nothing," I said to Jesse, careful to make light of these questions in the presence of others. "Part of my culture shock."

"I am confident that's the case," Jesse said.

"Too much oxygen," the general repeated. We left the room while the officers saluted General Hartley smartly. I still jumped when they snapped-to like that.

My small concerns were a side irritation for the general, who was focused on the aftermath of a mining explosion in the asteroid belt that orbited a planet I had not heard of, a gas giant with many moons and more asteroids rich in nickel. It seemed that workers had been killed in the blast near their quarters, but questions circulated when only enforcers returned to the Junction for burn treatment and to await reassignment. Why so few surviving conscripts?

More than that, new workers were available from lands called Striiduc, a seafaring group that lived beyond the Borabean! Even with my recent planet hopping, on Dolvia the Borabean dunes had represented the edge of the world to me. I shook my head to learn that whole societies hugged the shores of the ocean and sought favor with the Chinese Company for trade and labor.

Jesse greeted two men who were Striiduc named Otieno and . . . I didn't catch the other strange-sounding name, even though both spoke English. They were rough and tanned with lined faces, no doubt weathered by the sea. They wore loose trousers tucked into laced-up boots and sashes instead of belts. Their vests were embroidered with cheerful designs that depicted daily work like cooking and fishing from sailboats. Their manner was similar to Borabean but different. These Striiduc clans knew about using explosives and mining nickel, experienced men who had mined copper, the most difficult ore to process, in a remote region of their own land.

Otieno had two friends from another nation on Dolvia called Cochin. They were portly and jovial and bald on the tops of their heads. They wore wide coats and ruffled lace at the neck and cuffs. One officer joked that the Cochin ambassadors looked like Benjamin Franklin, whoever that was. I heard whispers that they had cities and roads and diesel-powered vehicles for each family in Cochin. Their merchants had metal ships, not the wood ships of the Striiduc, and sold armaments to any buyer. I saw how the Cochin guests of Otieno greeted the Borabean and Company men daily. I whispered to Jesse. "If no conscripts survived asteroid mining, why does Otieno want the work? Isn't it dangerous?"

"Conscripts receive little training and have a language barrier," Jesse said, no doubt information she'd gleaned from dinner at the general's table. "These ones believe they will prosper using their own techniques, with their own bosses. It's like work for a subcontractor."

"But it's Company work. Nobody prospers under the Company."

Jesse shrugged in her sanguine way. "The general tried to say that. They must be allowed to pursue open trade where they can."

I saw General Hartley patiently answer repeated questions from the reporter Regan Villines about conscript labor. She wanted to know why the Consortium didn't move to outlaw the slavery. "This is a Company matter," he articulated clearly. "Please direct your questions about working conditions for conscripts to Company executives."

Anyhow, my ability to objectively report events at Stargate Junction was compromised, so I here offer only the images, more or less in sequence, I think. Within the swirl of events, images from om overlaid my sense of what the gestures could mean.

Dr. Spinelli was there with his pipe and his good manners, sharing chi with Regan Villines and John Milan. John Milan spoke to me only twice at Stargate Junction, both times for a greeting. I think he was involved with Regan Villines. When he was drinking alcohol, he seemed overtired and moody. The travelers had a game going of drawing maps from memory. John Milan sketched features of the expansive savannah on his table napkin, the caldera created by a meteor impact millennia ago. Then Regan Villines drew the street grid of Urbyd and named the streets in sequence. When asked for a diagram of Cylay streets, she laughed, claiming that morass of alleyways had no predesigned grid.

"All the more reason we need a map," Dr. Spinelli quipped. To draw into focus the eternal face of Dolvia was more valuable than the fleeting dreams I knew.

But the images, sudden unwanted visions I didn't understand. I saw my brother Patrick talking at Karen. She was veiled and standing in the Junction concourse. His voice was low, but his face was red. Knives came out of his mouth and slashed her down, long red marks across her blue burka. She was not harmed in a corporeal sense, of course, only in the spirit.

I saw General Hartley at dinner one night talking with his son. Carl and Patrick advised the Company on Westend's uneven currency rates and on how to gain advantage at the Cicero securities exchange, that is, when Carl wasn't indulging his other tastes.

Anyhow, Dr. Spinelli was seated next to me and droned on about the Uburu potshard finds. He was focused on ancient latrine debris, the charred epicarps of wild olestra from before the collapse of the volcano's cone. His delineations made me feel tired, my limbs weighted with impatience with the finely worded definitions. Who cared about 800-year-old latrine detritus? What importance when so many lives were at risk?

Across the table, Carl spoke intimately with General Hartley, openly seeking his approval, charming and seeming to shimmer in a disjointed way. The general leaned forward to hear his son's words, except his heart was absent, a blank place in the left quadrant of his chest. Perhaps Brianna owned his heart. But no guessing should be reported here, only the images.

The general discussed the order of impunity, which was the buzzword for this event. Carl claimed he could now travel on Dolvia with more freedom because he was covered by this law; he was safe from punishment by the tribes.

The general took a broader view. "The tribes don't acknowledge the new order," Hartley told his son. "Besides, enforcement is at best uneven. Karl Wyley would be punished by Cicero law should he commit a crime there, so it follows that any resident of the savannah should feel the bite of tribal logic." The general had publicly endorsed the order of impunity, angering the tribes and causing demonstrators to target him, but in private seemed to question the law's value.

Later, I saw Steve Swanweil standing with two men of the Company, along with the Cochin traders and Striiduc sailors. The shimmering effect I had noticed while on Cicero was exaggerated. Swanweil fairly pulsated with fading outlines of himself in motion, like watching him through rippling water. I decided his spirit was agitated from contact with his Company allies. I resolved to watch in whose company he became most agitated.

Karen had wanted Patrick to be my escort for when my name was announced and I walked down the long staircase. That would have been a proud moment for her. But I did not want Patrick, and he was most resistant. "I only came for this trip because Carl invited me," he claimed. We were estranged siblings.

General Hartley broke into our tense moment. "I can escort Kelly for the coming-out moment. The dancing later is the high-light of the season."

Karen nearly swooned with gratitude, a high honor indeed.

"There's no need—" I started, but the general touched my arm.

"I have escorted a good number of our debutantes," he said. "Why do you withhold this honor from me?"

I agreed then, bound by duty to accept the formal Arrivi phrase. I knew it was diplomacy and to please Jesse. The general needed to make a good showing for the aborigine girl mixed among the Hardhand and Company debutantes. I actually felt sorry for him, especially since I had heard that influenza had broken out among the conscripts, perhaps brought to their quarters by survivors of asteroid mining. He had several cases isolated in the Junction clinic and was petitioning for a quantity of vaccine to be sent through the wormhole. Since the lag time was several weeks, the general was looking to the societies in the Consortium of Planets for a stan-dard version of vaccine.

General Hartley had several items on his plate, as it was said.

The night of the ball, I felt loneliest while I waited at the top of the stairs with the debutantes. We were a segregated group: the slight and demure Company women, traditionally dressed in layers of kimonos and with their Han Chinese escorts, stood opposite western-dressed Hardhands in ball gowns and peridot jewelry, mostly daughters of crew officers and cartel CEOs. What could all this mean? The constant travel had worn on me, along with the vigilance and strangeness. My sleep in a blank room was … troubled. I wanted a secure place: a vegetable garden and long vista across the savannah. I wanted a husband's step on the threshold each night and a child's suckling. The tasting of many cultures had unraveled me rather than strengthening me for some future task.

General Hartley was late joining me. Many others descended the staircase while I loitered at the top, watching their heads as they mingled on the dance floor. I saw Jesse wearing the loveliest yellow gown, tailored to hug her form, with long white gloves. Her dark hair was pulled back to show the porcelain complexion, and she appeared mature among the eager young debutantes in ribbons and ruffles. She spoke to John Milan standing with a young reporter who had just arrived through the wormhole.

Aristides in his flowing galabia and textured kaffiyeh waited on the sidelines, flanked by members of his entourage. Steve Swanweil joined them. Even from a distance, I saw Swanweil's aura shimmer in a most aggravated sense. Swanweil was thinking this Borabean would make his future, the turncoat. I must remember to tell Brianna.

"Kelly, are you ready now?" General Hartley said behind me. I turned and saw his spirit for just a moment. He was adept at hiding his true heart, or the absence of heart. Weary and seeking rest but held calmly in place from discipline and long service, he expected nothing. Hope had left the general, and only service remained.

"May I say again how grateful I feel for this service?" I said.

"Not at all. Our Arrivi guests enliven the routine of cafeteria meals and duty shifts. What could be more pleasant?"

We waited for our names to be announced. The herald called out, "General Eugene Hartley proudly presents Kelly Osborn of the sisters of Arim on Dolvia." His words were not exactly correct but permissible. We slowly walked down the stairs arm in arm and shook hands with the waiting dignitaries who were glad to gain a moment with the general. My presence was su-per-flu-ous, meaning I didn't have to stay at the general's side.

I broke away from their business talk and joined Karen who waited under the burka, beaming with pride. Jesse brought John Milan forward. "Kelly, how you have changed," John Milan said. "Except for your veiled escort, I would not have known you."

"Hiki, John Milan," I said, keeping my arms close to my sides. "Melinga."

"And may I present John's new protégé Hershel Henry from Earth," Jesse said. She seemed to think that was an item of great humor.

"Melinga," I said, resisting the urge to hold my hand high with my palm upward.

"Hello," Hershel Henry said while staring at Karen's burka.

Dr. Spinelli joined us carrying the ever-present pipe. "I am instructed to ask you to dance," he said to me.

"We are all bound by duty," I returned and stepped onto the dance floor with him. Over the next forty minutes, I danced with each of the attending Consortium officers, also their duty. Even General Hartley found time for a couple of turns with me on the floor.

It was fun; I had not expected any of this to be fun.

During one swirling polka, Jesse passed in the arms of the new reporter, Henry somebody, and I glimpsed a shower of golden flecks over his shoulder, him only within the company. Later while I stood by the refreshment table and received a glass of punch from John Milan, I noticed Jesse talking with her brother Carl, and she was showered with silver flecks. I wanted to close my eyes to shut out the images, to retreat to my room so my agitated spirit would return to me. I wondered if my aura shimmered like Swanweil's.

But then . . . Jesse stepped with the general into the bar. Karen pleaded the late hour and retired for the night. Aristides and his people had also left. Carl and Patrick stood with Swanweil, deep in conversation with the Striiduc sailors. My coming-out party was ending, and what had I learned? I went to the bar entrance and saw Jesse and the general talking with that Henry somebody. The silver flecks over her shoulder mingled with the golden flecks that troubled Henry only. Well, that was interesting. Perhaps Jesse would not spend so many seasons serving with Somule Gems in Paris after all.

She signaled that I should join them. My step was light and my smile genuine. I was happy for Jesse. Henry seemed a bright and well-proportioned man with that Softcheeks ability to share chi. He had danced with me; I may have stepped on his foot. All in all, it was a lovely evening's entertainment, well worth the trip to Stargate Junction.

It was decided that Karen would return to Dolvia on the next day's shuttle to Cylay. I would linger a few days while Jesse made ready for wormhole travel and then return to Dolvia by way of the shuttle to Urbyd. From there, I could travel with the diplomatic courier to Cylay in the company of Dr. Spinelli, who was return-ing to the Uburu digs for the season.

At the shuttle loading bay, many guests from the debutante ball waited, including Carl and Patrick, who studiously ignored us. Carl spoke again to Aristides and seemed to attach their baggage to the Borabean entourage. Patrick glanced back at us, a bloodred cutting look of displeasure.

I hugged Karen, feeling the party's afterglow perhaps. "Thanks so much, Mother, for making this possible. And for your presence here."

"Your place is secure," Karen said. "And you must begin again with your writing."

"I will, I promise. Whenever I get a minute." Her eyes were insis-tent through the mesh of the veil. "Make writing part of your daily routine, every day for two hours."

"When Jesse has jumped back, perhaps, to fill the loneliness of her absence."

"If to fill loneliness, so be it, but you will write." She was only asserting her authority as a parent amid the others. I must not strive against her repeated instructions and ruin a pleasant moment. "Yes, Mother," I said, feeling magnanimous. "Melinga."

I moved into the spare bedroom in the general's quarters. Jesse and I packed and repacked her luggage for the jumping back. We sat on her bed with gossip and giggles. I asked what she thought of Henry.

"Hershel Henry," she corrected. "He likes himself too much, so arrogant."

I only smiled, content to keep my secret until a better time. "I enjoyed your father's generosity," I said to fill the awkward moment. "He seems weighed down by this flu outbreak though. Have you heard if the conscript patients are better?"

"They found a vaccine, sent by Dr. Richardson from New Shanghai. More can be made there for storage and—" She turned when she heard my chuckle. "You know Dr. Richardson?"

"Don't trust him. And tell the general: don't trust Richardson," I said. "He'll cut corners and skim the profit to feed his addiction." Jesse nodded with a questioning look but seemed to shrug it off. What meaning could the flu outbreak have, huh, when she arrived in Paris?

"The flu seems to be passing," she said to be positive. "The conscripts who died were already weak from the mining ships. It's a dirty business."

"Why does the Consortium allow conscript labor?"

She shrugged. "From before when wormhole traffic was Company traffic only. We had no leverage to block them. Contracts are not so easy to break, you know, and for a good long time the labor force was needed, conscripts and colonists. Now the Consortium societies offer their workers, but on different terms."

"The sailors from Striiduc," I guessed. "Did they win the contract for asteroid mining?"

"They are called smogens, or men who go adventuring. And those who follow are called a gefolge. It's like a clutch, I guess."

"You have little reason to learn their language. Better to focus on French words."

She rolled her eyes. "But tell me, do you know what gum arabic is?"

"It's sap from the acacia tree that Arrivi use for gluing furniture. Kyle Rula kept some at the fortress of Arim. The resin can be dried and used much later without loss."

"And now a commodity on the new stock exchange," Jesse said, "traded for munitions. Apparently, sizable stores of the resin are kept at the convents because Kyle Rula had it harvested through the welfare minister system. Compact packages and tolerant of wide temperature changes, quickly restored to its original elasticity with water."

"Kyle Rula was always farsighted in business affairs."

"The general explained it to me," Jesse said. "On Earth, gum arabic is used in soda drinks and diet food, also for cosmetics, medicine, and paint. Synthetic varieties are less resilient, so natural gum arabic is important. Is that what it means to be blessed by Dolvia? That resources are available beyond what others can muster? Are you blessed the same?"

"Jesse, why so curious?"

"Just wondering," she shrugged. "Instead of sending gum arabic through the wormhole, the Bryant cartel wants the resin diverted to their enterprises. Did Carline ever speak of it?"

"She never talked business with me, only that I should marry well. But you should focus on Paris and a place next to Petra Mitterand. What could be better?"

A few hours later, Jesse hugged me several times before she boarded the wormhole yacht for her new adventure. Jesse was gone, absent from my dreamscape, as it was said.

I was standing in readiness for the Urbyd shuttle. Dr. Spinelli was assigned to my same row for shuttle seating. "Serendipity," Spinelli said. "I can show you the bone fragments and arboreal gastropods that established the Uburu digs epoch, just to pass the time."

The general joined us suddenly there in the docking bay. "Kelly, you will want to sit down for this."

"General Hartley, please, no more gifts. Your generosity is too much." I carried remembrances from him for Brianna.

But then I saw the public comtech over his shoulder. An Arrivi woman wearing a sky-blue burka stood in the plaza outside the governor's house in Cylay. Demonstrators who were in the square to face the cameras and shout slogans seemed to back away from her. Karen doused herself with gasoline from a gallon can and struck a match.

"No! No!" I cried out in the Stargate Junction public area. "No! Wait!" I shouted, reaching to stop her.

The whoosh of flames across her burka quickly ate the fabric with a yellow-orange conflagration. Her skeleton crumpled in a black heap while billows of gray smoke darkened the sunny plaza. "Karen is gone," the general said. "That's a replay of this morning's events. Her remains have already been collected by the convent residents."

"What the Sam Hill?" a waiting passenger demanded in a strident voice. "People torch themselves on this planet? In protest to what?"

Dr. Spinelli quickly led him to the line of people waiting to board.

"But why?" I asked the general. "We were just—"

"The fault is not yours. Patrick was cruel while she was here."

So many new influences had been revealed to me as a result of seeing om, but not this. Not my mother's intentions; not her shortened presence in my life. Or perhaps I never looked at her and never sought her kind word or her advice. She was a veiled presence in service and nothing more. "So, suicide was the cause," I said. "Depression and the loss of hope."

"Death by fire carries the same honor for Karen as for Kyle Rula," the general said in a soft voice. "Her act was in protest to Rabbenu Ely's oppressive rule."

"Karen was not political," I said, careful to not look at him.

"She was unwilling to continue under oppressive rule," General Hartley easily articulated. "As with Kyle Rula and Karima Le, the same as with Marcy who was rabbenu's wife. The tribes do not lend their mantel to Rabbenu Ely."

"That's your spin for the offworld media?"

"Immolation is not so simple to accomplish," he said. "A painful death. Karen focuses attention on the struggle for home rule and forces the journalists to ask why."

"But we know why."

"We know Karen was wife to Joey Osborn," he reasoned evenly, "and mother to Patrick whom she had just visited. She protests the order of impunity and the imbalanced securities exchange, especially their move to gain monopoly of the gum arabic trade."

I only shrugged, still looking away. I knew the truth. "Karen knew nothing of the trade in resin. She was without hope."

"And now she has great honor," the general returned. "Would you like to remain here a few days? Just until the shock passes."

"Thank you, no. I need to go home."

His hug was gentle but also stiff. The expansive warm chest was offered as a token, and he smelled of vanilla and lemon. I was done with hugs then. They passed out of my life as easily as Jesse had. I could not meet the general's eyes, fearful of seeing om there.

"Dr. Spinelli," Hartley said. "If you don't mind, our young guest has sustained a shock."

"No trouble at all," the older man said. His manner changed seamlessly, sharing chi while he guided me onboard. He was silent and reading during the shuttle trip, just as though Dr. Spinelli knew what was needed. He was most gracious when silent.

I regretted my judging nature, standing on the sidelines, always numbering the mistakes of others that I had sidestepped. Always wondering what my life would be like had I been offered opportunities like Jesse or even Bernice. But like Carline, I looked to my mentors for approval—General Hartley or Jesse, Hakulupe Le or Brianna Miller. When had I returned the light of pride in Karen's eyes? When had I felt bolstered by her praise?

In the noisy quiet of the shuttle to the transport, I took out a notepad and began to write.

We disembarked in Urbyd. The terminal was clean and flooded with chilled air. Borabean guards stood with cynical eyes and long beards. I wore the sky-blue burka during a customs check, and we stepped outside. Dr. Spinelli reacted to the gravity and heat, and I was stressed as well. Two days must pass before we could travel with the diplomatic courier to Cylay, so we were escorted by men in gala-bias and carrying karkars to a hotel in the Royal Square. Streets were wide with square intersections. I saw no beggars or free-ranging domestic animals; and no offal smell, only heated adobe and cooking odors. The hotel was a designated resting place for intra-tribal negotiators. Our presence was tolerated by Borabeans due to the shuttle schedule. Ten days earlier, Aristides had been greeted in Cylay when the shuttle landed there in its turn.

Early the next morning, Dr. Spinelli and I went down to the beach near Ananke's palace, strolling outside to better acclimate to the heat. Officers followed us but kept a polite distance on the high dune, so I removed my burka for a short time. I wore a glassy and flat peridot gem set in a binding cord on my upper arm. I had pur-chased the decoration in the Urbyd Royal Square, frankly surprised that the souks there knew our customs and offered the service.

"Anything can be bought in Urbyd," Dr. Spinelli had said after he'd paid with several oblu.

At the beach, the defensive wall of the palace stretched along the wide cove, gleaming in the morning sun. The domes of reli-gious buildings were visible over the rampart, a pleasant view from the water, I was certain, or from the two promontory points that guarded the cove. The air was dry and smelled of the dunes and the ocean, all at the same time. A steady wind blew, drawing moisture from my eyes and skin. This breeze never lessened, it was claimed, but came from the east in another season instead of the south, carry-ing moist cooling air from the plateau beyond the Borabean dunes.

The glory of the ocean was everything I had hoped and more, so many colors with salt water dancing and spraying and misting.

Green swells rushed forward with a comforting hiss and receded together like a tribal dance. Frothy water lifted sand and pebbles, and the hiss was a purr of pleasure. We sat on the beach mesmerized by the rhythm of the roiling waves. Long streamers of my hair came loose, lifted by the ocean breeze caressing my skin.

Nettom hovered at the distant horizon, lazing in Nettki's domain. "So strange to me, Dr. Spinelli," I said. "Borabean have our same sky and communion with two moons. We all live on Dolvia's body, but they fail to discern her. Rather, they see other gods."

"Bydquii is said to be the more charming of the brother gods," Dr. Spinelli said. His eyes were teasing under the bushy eyebrows. "Not stronger, unless charm wins more favors. The Iamida River flows into his body by choice."

"But it flows across the land of Aequii, his brother," I added, reciting the little about Borabean myths that I knew, "who had seven sons."

Dr. Spinelli nodded his approval and finished the lesson. "They represent a litter from a single mating. Iamida's journey is a testing, and joining with Bydquii the reward."

We stood to walk to the hotel, but I turned back. Streamers of hair tickled my face, obscuring my view. I pushed them behind one ear. The ocean hiss sounded louder, a whisper calling to me. *Don't desert me today,* it seemed to say. *Kelly with the auburn hair.* The hissing waves pronounced my name.

"What is it?" Dr. Spinelli asked.

"Nothing, really. It's so easy to ascribe a personality to the ocean."

I had restless dreams those nights. I dreamt of swimming, racing across the veld, spying on Borabean militia from a moonlit crest, waiting for my goulep, waiting for Sarah. Then I was swimming again, clamping down on rodent prey, basking under the oleastra bush, waiting, always waiting.

An image rose, like a map. I knew the positions of each gualarep; on the veld, on the flats, on Uburu land. In communion and singing, they were littermates connected by scent and shared sensation. Know me, I begged, know that I am here. In my dreams, I raced through Siibabean leaf debris, my sightline close to the ground, my marbled hide swept clean by dew, accompanied by yapping ketiwhelps.

Early the next morning, Dr. Spinelli and I shared a ride with a Consortium courier in a transport helicopter to Cylay. I yawned and watched the passing dunes dramatically lit by the angling sun. On another day I would have devoured the sight with my eyes and shared the images with Edwina. But today I thought that the dunes were lit thus each morning and would be again tomorrow morning. My casual viewing meant little. I was tired of traveling and was glad to seek rest in my own bed.

In Cylay, I said my goodbyes to Dr. Spinelli who had been so kind. He gallantly kissed my hand offered from under the burka's folds and left in an ECCAV taxi. It was Sarah, wearing a burka, who waited to greet me. Not one from the leadership group, only Sarah.

"Hiki, Kelly Osborn," she said. "Welcome to the song."

"Sarah, you know me. Why so formal?"

She only smiled behind the facial panel and shouldered my small pack. We rode to the convent near the Consortium barracks in a taxi with one window broken and no air-conditioning. The driver was Cylahi but not a person known to me. He eyed our decorated veils, probably wondering at the rich women who traveled offworld and rode around in taxis.

"Edna and Edwina are ecstatic," Sarah said. "Brian welcomes you."

"Sarah, I have been offworld before. This is not my first disembarkment."

"But you return as a member of the song."

"And what does that mean?"

The taxi stopped on the street corner, waiting in the heat. Sarah paid the driver, and we got out in front of the convent gate where ragged women immediately approached begging for alms. Students came to the gate with baskets of bread to distribute, distracting the women while we entered.

Sarah greeted the students by name; she seemed to know everybody. I saw her then as her gualarep viewed her; seemingly monumental from a ground-level point of view, walking and smiling at me as we traversed the savannah. I received, finally, an initiation into a tradition long available to me. That sensation of waiting returned, always waiting. Images from my dreams recurred, or were they continuously there? I felt dizzy and weak in the knees, which was a typical acclimation complaint. But the images came   swimming, racing, spying, and waiting. Basking while I wait for my familiar to greet me. Singing and waiting on the body of Dolvia.

Sarah stepped to my side. "Welcome to the song," she repeated. "We need your strength. For the struggle ahead, we must bind together and sing in unison."

"Sarah, how long have you participated in the song?"

"Since Edwina's first hatching, when we built the savannah convent."

"All this time? How many are submitted?"

"Gualareps mostly commune with their own," she said. "They find it distressing that humans kill each other. To participate, a person must be selected, always in her familiar's dreamscape, even sacrificing family ties."

"How many?"

"Seventeen among the convent ministers and eight soldiers."

We were grinning, more than from the effects of the acclimation pill. "I embrace my duty in communion with gualareps," I said. "Duty is all."

PART THREE

It was in the days when Colonel Sector led
Known to all as Milo-pilo
Sheeks-Cylom to Cicero had fled
And there bore the general's twin sons
The generous blessings of Dolvia

Carl Hartley to Urbyd rode
Named for Dacupitte's mother's husband
Carl's eyes were blue, his heart was cold
The same as Ananke the Usurper
Whose wealth was grand beyond all reason

Cylay groaned under weight of Ely's rule
And the savannah was a desert
While in Somule, Kailyhi's stronghold
For the Feast we Arrivi gathered
And for to sing the praises of Dacupitte

SEVENTEEN

from Hershel Henry

AN OFFICIAL EVENT WAS PLANNED FOR THAT EVENING AT STAR-gate Junction, a debutante ball. I waited over a highball in the too-bright bar for the provincial pageant to get underway. I lit a menthol. A bartender rushed over, claiming that smoking was prohibited. And this was their idea of class? The pinnacle of Westend society? The cramped promenade showed aging Company tooling and retro-neon trim. The pleasure suites were dank and the women unchecked. Give head only, I had insisted, no penetration.

Cellphone use was intermittent, and the EAM stations were mostly in public cafés where you took a number and waited and paid by the minute. What was next? Dial-up? I needed to tolerate a brace of artificial days on this tin can to acclimate and learn the dialects before we disembarked on Dolvia. I had drawn a bald assignment, meaning no technical support, and mine was a three-year stint. I swallowed my drink, licking the untextured ice.

On the news program, a Cicero resident named Mrs. Shaw was opining as to why the tribal people resisted their governor's rule. The interview was staged in Two Forks on a different planet, situated in a studio with a static cityscape behind the chairs. "Rabbenu Ely is bolstered by Putuki cronies and offworld cartel interests," Mrs. Shaw claimed, rock steady before the cameras. "His mineral rights contracts must be nullified so the people can gain home rule. Arrivi want a new rabbenu selected by free and open election."

"Mr. Henry?" a voice asked behind me. I turned on my stool. "Are you Hershel Henry?"

I stood to shake hands. "John Milan, a pleasure." A rugged and trim field reporter, Milan had a sterling reputation with even a Pulitzer to his name.

"Australian, right?" he asked, glancing over my weathered features.

"Uh, yah."

"A desert overrun by brown snakes as I recall," he said. "Undertook some volunteer snake patrol, did you?"

"As a kid. Lizard hunting, scuba diving. I did some surfing too."

"Sit down," Milan said. "I can join you."

We ordered drinks and watched the comtech for a moment. "This expert Mrs. Shaw lives on Cicero," I observed to perhaps impress the senior man. "An expatriate of Dolvia. What can she hope to accomplish?"

"Media coverage."

"But why?"

He showed a dry grin. "Who, what, where, when, and why, huh? All the good questions. They want to break Ely's stranglehold on export licenses. Deregulation, however, would also end the tribal monopoly on gum arabic and oleastra oil, a big sacrifice for them." He sighed and shook his head. "A better story is about the managers returning from the mining explosion in the asteroid belt."

"I noticed there was no news segment on the mining incident."

"The Company slammed a lid on interviews," Milan said bitterly, "and the press got no permits for the asteroid belt."

"How many sites are they mining?"

"Several. Our only real gauge of the industry size is the demand for more conscripts. Still, we don't know how long workers survive the harsh conditions."

"Couldn't we ask questions and make a noise?"

"On what evidence?" he said.

"Complicity from the Consortium officials with the conscript traffic."

"Westend is a small playing field," he bit out as he watched me greedily lick the untextured ice in my glass. "You need Consortium access for any news that's not Company news." I was crunching the ice cube in the back of my mouth. "You know that ice was Company piss six hours ago," he added.

I didn't let it bother me, making a show of running my tongue over my front teeth. "A benefit from my betters, huh?"

He looked away. "This story needs fresh blood. Somebody with the idealism and energy to—"

"To what?"

"To shrug off the hypocrisy."

I tried not to fawn. "You've seen a lot, huh?"

"Several seasons, since before Karl Wyley's forces bottled up the savannah. Set aside all that research now. Nothing you learned from the media is true."

"But . . . but you—"

"That's right. Nothing you have heard me say is true."

John Milan finished his drink in one long swallow, then ordered another. "I arrived here with my camera and film jacket." With a forefinger, he coldly thumped the equipment-filled vest I wore. "Ready to set the record straight. The avenging voice of objective sanity, right?"

"I certainly meant no—"

"Stop sniveling. Tribesmen don't admire sniveling. And offer the Arrivi nothing; that's considered disrespectful. Demand what you came for, what you can secure no place else. Then you enter their system of debt and can barter with them."

"Yes, sir."

John Milan stared at me for a moment. "Whatever." He chugged the fresh drink and stood. "Your education begins right now."

"Where are we going?"

"You're about to meet a great man, General Hartley. Forget your constructed ideas; this is not romance. This is the future of Westend."

"Yes, sir."

"And stop with the suck-up."

"Yes, sir. Sorry, sir."

John led me to the military section of Stargate Junction. We entered a teak-paneled office staffed with Consortium officers, then passed through to a brighter executive office where several secretaries spoke quietly into headsets and watched two-way monitors. An older woman in a gray silk business suit approached us.

"Mr. Milan," she said as she shook hands. "The general is running perhaps ten minutes behind schedule. Go into the briefing room if you would like."

"What is the chance, Mildred," John asked as we crossed to another set of doors, "of securing some of the general's time? Just a few moments."

"I can ask," Mildred said with a brittle smile and opened the door to usher us through.

I saw four rows of seats that faced a podium with a speaker's stand. A row of flags stood behind, all from the nations in the group of aligned planets. A tech booth was in the back with video equipment and bright lights. Consortium journalists and some Earth reporters talked together while standing among the best seats. One stood quickly, and John shook his hand. John waved briefly to several others.

Three Company men wearing mandarin suit jackets with round white collars were seated together in the second row of the folding chairs. One stood and bowed stiffly. John returned an equally deep bow with his arms at his side. We took seats farther back. "We can learn nothing here," John whispered to me. "Nothing is said in front of Company men. And don't bring up the human trafficking in conscripts. You'll burn too many bridges. My bridges, carefully constructed."

"Yah, sure," I said, uncertain at his sense of caution.

A dark-haired Consortium journalist, one of only three women in the room, approached us. "Regan Villines, meet Hershel Henry, newly arrived from Earth." We shook hands. She was sinewy and tough with a furrow of suspicion across her brow.

"So the rumors of your retirement are true?" she asked John dryly.

"You only wish."

"They just completed the military briefing," she said. "We're guessing New Shanghai. Care to give odds?"

"A better choice than Cylay on Dolvia," John said. "The streets there are hot and dry."

"And stinking." Villines bent over John's shoulder, and they traded whispered secrets. Her bosom was more than adequate. This guy gets around, I was thinking.

An easel on the small speaker's podium displayed an aerial map of Dolvia's savannah and coastline. Urbyd was indicated in red, situated in a broad cove at the ocean's edge, rather like the wide mouth of a stingray. The inland towns of Cylay and Somule were located on the map. Neutral hospitals and academy sites were designated with blue. The map had little detail; no munitions depots or military staging areas were displayed.

The savannah was fallow, troubled with drought. Arrivi families had retreated to defensive positions near Mekucoo land. And closer to the Borabean boundary, a narrow strip of Uburu mesas meandered between the combatant forces. The mesas were a miniscule area of real estate compared to the expansive desert, a speck on an insignificant planet, used as a testing ground for Consortium troops and officers—and junior journalists. Dolvia was worthy only for its Westend proximity to Stargate Junction and the possibility of finding meteor fragments for industry-grade silicide. Once exchange rates were more in balance and fortunes grew at a standard rate, Dolvia societies would slip back into obscurity where they belonged.

For now though, there was a tribal conflict to cover. Kenru's Uburu militia had nibbled away at the Borabean outposts along the dunes. Karl Wyley's guerillas had staged assaults on military compounds and furnaces for silicide refinery, mostly Company sites.

Borabean had taken to squabbling among the factions, mostly over control of the silicide deposits and who owned what section of the rolling dunes. Mullah Anaxagoras of the Gora clan was set to work his way toward the capital, recruiting family men from decimated nomad groups as he approached Urbyd in a challenge to Ananke, himself a usurper. Ananke's effectiveness in negotiating offworld rights for mineral wealth was curtailed by his domestic power struggle, or so the media coverage had defined events.

There was another exit behind the podium. I saw a door open as Mildred and two military attaches entered and waited stoically. Mildred nodded vaguely to John.

"We're in," he whispered to me.

Reporters settled into seats; some took out recorders and notepads. I watched Regan Villines make her way back to her seat. John met my admiring glance with an arched eyebrow.

General Hartley entered and stepped onto the podium wearing the dress uniform correct for the debutante ball. His big frame carried a mature man's weight. His brushed-back hair was thinning and streaked with gray. He tapped the microphone to test the sound and faked a smile.

"Good evening; to some that would be good afternoon. Today I can announce that the securities exchange at New Shanghai on Cicero will open its doors in four days. The ceremony was set for sooner, but we encouraged the Consortium officials to push back events so reporters like yourselves have a couple days to acclimate."

He looked around at the press corps, who covered their remarks with coughs and grunts.

"The Company already has a center for the stock exchange in place," the general continued. "And the Consortium has a similar trading floor, uh, nearby. We expect brisk opening trades and some peripheral events for celebration." The exchange anticipated first-time public trading of commodities, especially peridot and other semiprecious gems, gold and nickel, and gum arabic, but not the silicide found under the Borabean dunes. The Company treaty with the Borabeans demanded exclusive rights of export.

"Many of you are traveling to Cicero for the first time, so—"

"Sir, if I may ask—" one reporter interrupted as he briefly raised a hand. "Why on Cicero and not Dolvia? Isn't the Arrivi savannah the source of most of the commodities offered on the new exchange?"

"You can travel to Dolvia if you want. There is a small stock exchange center in Cylay."

"But not in Urbyd?" another reporter quickly asked.

"I am told Borabean are planning to join the exchange but are distracted just now with, um, other concerns."

"You mean, to find the silicide?" one reporter called out. There were chuckles among the gathered reporters and crew.

The general smiled, very accommodating. "So check your supplies of meloquine," he said, "and AC adapters. Ground commissary requests are managed by the Consortium embassy. That is all." General Hartley gathered his few papers and turned to step down but remembered a final item. "We invite you to attend the debutante ball already underway in the promenade. You must dance with each of the young ladies, of course."

"Will you disembark for the meetings?" a reporter called out.

"Somebody needs to mind the store." General Hartley left with his attachés walking behind. Several reporters approached Mildred with handshakes and written requests. She met John's eye through the crowd and nodded vaguely toward the door.

"Come on," John said. He climbed over the folding chairs to break out of the crowd and rush the same door where General Hartley had exited. I followed hurriedly, a graceless bolting action. "Hey!" one reporter called out. "That's not fair!"

Mildred only shrugged and indicated the other exit, very secretary-like.

We entered a narrow corridor with blank walls and Chinese-style tooling on the baseboards. Dancing cranes were hand-painted on the tiles, widely spaced and each different from the other. Several walkways branched off, leading to unmarked security doors with Chinese inscriptions overhead. A stoic Hardhand corporal gestured we should move forward. "Weapons and recorders," he said, indicating the table. He watched a monitor as we dropped our hardware.

He could see the fillings in my teeth, I was thinking.

He opened the door behind him and nodded to a carbon copy of himself. We were passed through another hallway to a tastefully decorated apartment. A dark-haired woman, perhaps age twenty, put down her drink glass and crossed to shake John's hand. She was big-boned and trim, as tall as me, and dressed for the night's event. Her hair was pulled up, and she wore a yellow ball gown that exposed her shoulders and arms. Long white gloves and a dance card were set aside.

"Jesse, how are you?" John Milan asked.

"Fine. My father is just finishing."

"This is—"

"Hershel Henry," she interrupted, offering her hand. "Just arrived from Australia. Do you intend to write an exposé about living conditions in New Shanghai?"

"We were hoping in Somule," John answered for me. "Or the fortress."

"Why Somule when all the Westend players will be in New Shanghai?"

Just then General Hartley entered from the other room. "John," he said, shaking hands. "And your protégé, uh, Henry isn't it?"

"Hershel Henry, Daddy." My name sounded like music from her lips.

"Yes, of course. Is there coffee, dear?"

"Naturally there's coffee. There's always coffee." She went into the kitchen area.

I stepped to the map of Dolvia laid out on a table, textured and true to scale. "A general's map," I said. "The Uburu mesa elevations are not much higher than the savannah buttes. And here's the Canyon of Buttes, which was not indicated on your briefing map."

"You have an eye for topography," the general said. "And can you sketch?"

I grabbed a pencil from a desk and drew the outline of Earth's continent of Europe on the back of a used envelope. I extended the line drawing to Asia Minor and more.

The general barely glanced at the page. "Be seated," he offered. "To the best of my knowledge, John, you have no jump back number."

"Everybody's trying to get rid of me," John said. "And your secrets, general. I might as well retire, as much information as I get." General Hartley only chuckled. Jesse returned with steaming mugs and condiments on a tray. The general watched as I accepted the drink from her hand.

"How soon do you expect Anaxagoras will move on Urbyd?" John asked.

"What do you need, John?" the general asked, taking back the agenda. "We have little time here."

"Permission to enter Somule and beyond."

"Beyond Somule is only grazeland. Your better route is into Borabean land."

John squinted. This was new information. "The shuttle for Cylay leaves tomorrow."

"There are many shuttles," the general said. "Perhaps you can do us both a favor. Speak with Anaxagoras about his armistice with Rabbenu Ely. As you know, my officers were expelled from his khanate. But he has a taste for being interviewed by Softcheeks."

John sat back with twinkling eyes. "The great Anaxagoras."

"You may earn another journalism award." The general's eyes also glistened. He was accustomed to getting his way. "We ask that you travel with considerable luggage, as befits a Softcheeks," he added. "Satellite dish, too many camcorders. And take your young friend."

John looked at me. I only shrugged.

"What dialects do you know?" General Hartley asked me.

"English and French, and I can read some Chinese script as long as it's not philosophy; too hard."

"Is reading Chinese the test for who travels through the wormhole?"

I showed my best buddy grin. "Certainly a plus for the application."

The general showed a hooded look, appraising and cynical, but shrugged it off. "Henry's going to be a great help," he told John wryly. "Perhaps Henry can sketch landmarks on the Borabean dunes and write a short communiqué for my eyes only."

"Whatever is needed," I agreed.

General Hartley sipped from his mug and looked at his watch. "Well," he said and stood. "I'm slated to present one of the debutantes." He looked across the room at his daughter, gracing her with a full moment of his attention, and left by another door. I saw two corporals snap to attention in the hall.

"Busy man," I said.

Jesse stepped closer; I caught the faint scent of lemon and vanilla. "The general wanted me to extend the invitation," she said. "This coming out includes twenty-two debutantes, the largest group under Consortium rule. Won't you attend? With Mr. Henry, of course."

"A pleasant duty," John said. "But tell me, what's the story here?"

"I don't give interviews. You should show your friend the language tapes in our EAM library. He needs to catch up on Arrivi dialects."

"What is it?" John insisted. "A new offensive?"

"The only one being offensive here is you."

I chuckled. Jesse had gotten in the last word.

I went to change into formal clothes. I entered the promenade alone, crowded by then with uniformed Consortium personnel of both genders, with merchants and lawyers of many ethnic groups, a few couples, and several ladies like Jesse whose father or uncles served on active duty. I also saw waiting along the wall several women who were hired for the evening, a common gesture on long-distance transports. I joined John Milan who pulled at his stiff collar.

The music was piped in. The food was cafeteria quality with plastic forks and spoons. There was a central staircase leading to several business suites. The debutantes were announced, and each sixteen-year-old strolled down the steps on an officer's arm. The display was not commanding, more like a distraction from the closer conversation groups.

Regan Villines sat over drinks with two Hardhand executives. She waved, signaling we should join her. "Carl Hartley, the general's son, and Patrick Osborn who advises the Bryant cartel," she said by way of introductions. They stood to shake hands, members of the group known as the Junction Boys. We settled in for drinks while Regan indicated various dignitaries in the crowd, chief among them Aristides, the Abydian negotiator. He was tall and dry with a full beard under the kaffiyeh secured with a double-binding agal. His sharp eyes saw everything.

"You must dance with each debutante," Regan teased in a whisper. "It's part of the political theater."

Across the way Jesse talked with two colonels in dress tunics and white gloves. She laughed at one's remark, her bright face shining under the dark hair. Without prompting, Regan added, "It's just announced. Jesse Hartley will jump back when the wormhole yacht arrives again. She's set to take a Paris position as an agent for Somule Gems while her brother advises Company executives here. An interesting dichotomy."

The general descended the staircase with an older and plump debutante on his arm. Carl and Patrick stood to undertake their dancing duties, lending themselves to the evening's theater. I excused myself from the table group and went back into the bar where the comtech blared Consortium news.

Later, Jesse entered the bar area on the general's arm, just in case I had assumed she had arrived with a beau. General Hartley was courteous to each petitioner while Jesse served in her role as the general's daughter. I turned and hunched over my drink.

It wasn't but a few minutes later when she came over to me. "Hershel Henry," she said at my side. I caught that same scent of lemon and vanilla. "Shall I introduce you to these dignitaries?"

She was being transparent. I could yield a little. "Allow me to buy you a drink."

"A sip of champagne perhaps."

While the bartender served, I ventured, "I must take your advice and access the library tapes. The dialects are not so difficult, reminiscent of Latin."

"Arrivi can have several words for a single object," she said, "as if designating it through a series of changes."

"Netta, kari, cylay, and om."

"You have a language gift," Jesse said with an impressed look. I found myself hoping her look was more than just good manners. "Have you investigated Borabean?"

"Ah, not yet."

"It's a smaller language," she said, "stilted by ideologue phrases used by the muezzins, the preachers in their temples. Foreign words have crept in, mostly at ocean harbors. And government officials are often fluent in English. Their vocabulary must grow or collapse, cannibalized like Parisian French."

I just wanted her to keep talking. "And Chinese is too difficult for some crossover?"

"In Westend, Chinese is the language of secrecy."

General Hartley joined us. "How do you rate our ball?"

"Very pleasant."

"The general met my mother at a similar ball," Jesse offered with a grin.

I shrugged. "Perhaps I can meet someone special tonight."

Jesse signaled the debutante General Hartley had escorted into the hall, and she came forward. "Kelly is sister to Patrick Osborn. You should meet him."

"I've met him already, actually. And your son Carl, sir," I added to the general.

He only nodded. I turned to the young girl. "Shall we?"

I led Kelly out of the bar area onto the dance floor. I danced with several overdressed girls, but Kelly was by far the oldest and least trained in dance. The general embraced this duty with gusto, red-faced and towering over the trembling young women. Jesse danced with the journalists and with Carl and Patrick, but with no

Borabean in attendance. By their choice, I was thinking, her being gehenna and all.

Finally, she returned to me. "I don't find your name on my dance card."

"Your skill at the dance far exceeds mine," I pleaded.

She pretended to inspect the tiny gold-trimmed card. "Hershel Henry, Hershel Henry. No, not here at all." She knew the music in her voice troubled me.

"Quit now. Just come along."

I kept her separate from me, in her own dance space, while we moved among the others. Her perfume held steady against the varieties of men's cologne smudged on her from dance partners. I avoided her eyes; the confidence and secret intentions were not for my rubric. Our paths would diverge in a few days. When the music stopped, I led her back to Carl's side and walked away, my knees mechanical and creaking with each step.

I occupied the next several days at Stargate Junction with the language exercises Jesse had suggested. John's time was given over to Regan Villines. I saw him at some meals when he just groaned and rubbed his face. Jesse kept the debutante Kelly close to the general and had time for me only during public encounters. Each of her glances was noted and numbered, and the musical tones in her voice left late-night tinkling noises in my ear. I forgot about the conscript traffic, a story I could not publish even if I could secure the truth. More long hours were spent learning Borabean and Arrivi, anything to distract the mind.

The wormhole yacht arrived and disgorged more Company technicians along with the rich sons of Middle Eastern sheiks who were on industry tours. Later, the yacht stood ready for departure again. Jesse hugged her Dolviet friend several times before she stopped to shake my hand as a farewell. "I will be working in Paris mostly," she said, "if you ever travel that way."

"I will keep it in mind."

Days later we reported with our luggage to the boarding area where a shuttle would take us to the Borabean city. While we waited to board, I took a ribbing from John and Regan about my surfboard.

"Urbyd is an ocean port, right?" I asked. "Oceans have surf. Think about it, virgin surf."

Chinese Blackshirts and some traditionally dressed Arabs from Earth stood by, also waiting to board and whispering together. "They call you ridiculous with that thing," Regan said, indicating the surfboard.

"They wear tablecloths on their heads."

Before our seating numbers were called, Kelly Osborn sustained the news of a self-torching in the Cylay public square, apparently a relative of hers. Dr. Spinelli shepherded her onto the shuttle, and we finally boarded, headed for Dolvia's surface.

Company executives filled the seats. Blank porcelain faces and the panda logo emblazoned on their jacket pockets. They whispered together in Chinese, the language of secrecy. John and I had decided between us to keep quiet so that I could understand them, at least in part. I had explained to John that the written script was uniform whereas the dialects were multifarious and mixed with tangent languages and Buddhist phrases.

"You have acclimation pills?" John asked from his seat beside me.

"I'm all set."

"And the surfboard?" he asked acidly.

"Ah, stowed away."

"Start with the pills now so you get used to them. We have an audience with Ananke the Usurper. Hartley engineered it. You cannot be high and grinning during the talks."

"Yah, sure."

John gave me a long look, as if thinking this young pup was surely smug. "I only wish I knew," he said in a worried tone, "what Hartley has up his sleeve. All these seasons and I never penetrated the inner circle." A feeling of disquiet came over me. This desert-experienced veteran was worried, so then what to anticipate?

"Things will be fine," Milan told me distractedly, "just fine."

"Yah, sure."

We disembarked in Urbyd with the usual complaints of discomfort. I had lived in artificial gravity several months by then but was surprised at my limitations. My legs felt bound in concrete, then suddenly full of rolling water.

Borabean officials were not so very friendly. Regan Villines was forcibly confined to the hotel complex and press club. Borabean women working in the street bazaar as meydani, with big rumps and faint mustaches, turned away from her. Meydani could have been punished, it was true, for any public courtesy toward gehenna. No matter, Regan was set for travel to Cylay and glad for the travel, lingering only for unfinished business with John Milan.

Ananke's palace extended more than a kilometer, constructed by a former mullah who was overthrown due to oppressive taxes levied to support his ambitious construction projects. Our rooms looked out on the ocean from a high colonnade balcony dressed with sheer flowing curtains, not our usual press quarters in a sterile hotel with a public pool and public workout room.

Ananke and the ruling Abydian clan took as their emblem the pincer scarab. Beetle effigies were everywhere, even on the bedposts and tooled as marching armies into the doorjambs. The beetle was the familiar creature of some honored leader from centuries before. A pair of oversized bronze beetles, like laudan statues, wore earrings of lapis and jade. Their ineffectual wings were textured and partly raised. They had bulging and round faceted eyes and artificial ears added as anchors for decorative hangings.

On the third day of our visit, John and I were shown into Khalif Ananke's presence. He was seated in a palace garden with many attendants waiting at a respectful distance. The khalif seemed unfocused and stroked his beard. Several stacks of official papers were piled on the narrow table on his right. Large grouse with iridescent feathers strolled near an artificial bubbling pond stocked with fantail koi. From somewhere, brittle music played on string instruments and cymbals. Two Borabean women led us forward for an audience with the khalif. They wore flowing and form-revealing serge of subdued colors. It had been explained how this was an insult to us, being presented by females. Without a battery of armed forces to create a presence near the palace, we journalists could not attain greater status.

John touched his hand to his chest when he bowed low. I did the same. Three advisors, each wearing galabias and kaffiyehs of white linen, drew near Ananke. "Khalif Ananke," John said in Borabean. "You honor us with the gift of your time."

"John Milan," one advisor said in English. He was Aristides, who had been at Stargate Junction for the conference negotiation. "What news from Stargate Junction?"

"What can I add to your report and Tuang Cho's report?" John asked.

"Your perspective," Aristides gestured casually.

"Stargate Junction," John said, "has expanded but not fast enough, a true bottleneck. Cargo storage space is purchased only at a premium. Trafficking in conscripts for asteroid mining crowds out other concerns." I stared at John. Why mention conscripts here when he pushed against the story at Stargate Junction?

"The Consortium has legions of trained workers that they withhold," Aristides complained.

"Perhaps if conditions for asteroid mining improved, as you have provided with silicide mining, more workers from Cicero would be enticed by the pay rate."

"Or nations on Cicero could mandate indentured service to the state," Aristides said, "without competition."

"In the democracies on Earth, we believe competition in commerce is healthy," John returned. Aristides barely blinked. "Incidentally, Khalif Ananke," John said, again using Borabean, "may I present a protégé, Hershel Henry. He wants to see the desert."

I bowed again while touching my chest with fingertips.

"And what can 'ershel 'enry learn that you have not already discovered?" Aristides asked in English. His language skills were more than adequate. He slurred my name on purpose.

John shrugged. "Another perspective."

Ananke smiled behind the hand stroking his beard.

"And our reason," Aristides probed, "for allowing you to pass through our land?"

"Earth corporations with R&D capital," John returned easily, "place a high premium on personal contact. They follow current events closely. You understand, local executives must account for their invested millions in order to maintain their titles."

"You question our accounting?" Aristides asked.

"Not at all. I am here to reinforce it."

So bribes were paid and equipment assembled, too much equipment as part of General Hartley's plan. It was a couple of days, though, before we could get underway. To fill the time, Aristides led us down to view their trading floor, a high-ceiling limestone room decorated with beetle effigies, where three seated Borabean watched four screens and the big-board overhead. Modern technology overlaid a more ancient culture. The equipment was not much, no more than a single accounting house in Perth maintained. John tried to be positive, praising their quick advancement in the commodities market.

Carl Hartley, the general's son, joined us from a side office. His eyes were bloodshot and his gestures manic, the acclimation pill's effect, I was thinking. "We have secured an informant for the gum arabic trade," he boasted. "We'll grab their thunder soon enough.

Fragmented deals, first buys, followed by an apparent sell-off to keep the price down. When deregulation is finalized, we'll be ready. The Arrivi traders won't know what hit them." His grin was both dark and bright, seeming to shimmer in the harsh overhead lighting.

Carl invited us to drinks and dinner. John haltingly agreed, and we left, after bows to Aristides who talked on the side with his ministers. In the hallway, John spoke in low tones. "Don't get involved with Carl. He has some dirty appetites, dirty even for this crowd." I assumed John meant abuse of the acclimation pill that destroyed the liver.

So later, Carl and Patrick visited our quarters in the palace, dressed for the evening. Patrick lingered on the balcony overlooking the ocean, his look envious. "You have a great suite here. What do you have that Ananke wants?"

I only shrugged.

"Ready?" John asked from inside the suite. Patrick gestured that I should leave first and followed graciously. I wondered at Patrick's manner and why he was in Urbyd. Had he attended the Arrivi funeral of his mother who had torched herself in Cylay? It had run on the comtech news all week that Karen was mother to Patrick Osborn of the Junction Boys. She had torched herself in protest to Rabbenu Ely's rule, one of a series of immolations carried out in front of the governor's mansion. Patrick didn't even wear the arm amulet that indicated mourning.

Dressed alike in dark business suits, we exited the care of the khalif's suspicious guard and entered the Royal Square outside the palace. Statues of Alousha the spiritual redeemer and his followers loomed from the temple edifices. Insect emblems designating the various clans took a backseat in the sculptural display.

The coffeehouses were crowded with loud-talking salesmen of every ilk. The kids who entered to play video games were channeled to a different section. At the Rendezvous Bar outside the Peoples' Inn, weary but hopeful Earth-born grafters gathered at day's end. "Try the Kiam gin," one suggested to his bar mate. "You can get it only here and in Cylay."

There were Consortium arms dealers from Cicero. I also saw Junction bankers offering alluring lines of credit, Korean carmakers hawking the people's car, Swiss engineers expert in retooling aging manufacturing concerns, Israelis confident they could irrigate the spreading sand dunes, tobacco barons seeking a market with fewer bothersome health regulations, and the ubiquitous oil dogs trading and re-trading various grades of fuel held in reserves.

One man stood at the bar telling stories to the crowd about scuba diving and described the sheer drop-off of the continental shelf beyond Urbyd's bay. He was Softcheeks and had recently featured in a comtech story about the needed technical skills that Borabeans lacked. From his accent, I figured he was Russian or Ukrainian. His English, peppered with colorful metaphors, was learned in the classroom.

I went to the men's room, immaculate with two attendants who offered warm towels and a shave. On my way back to the table, I came across Steve Swanweil in the bar. "Mr. Henry," he said as if surprised. "I have been seeking an opportunity to speak. How are your land legs?"

"Getting stronger."

"Yes, well. May I suggest lunch tomorrow? We could exchange ideas."

"What ideas?"

"There are only twelve men you need to know here in Westend," Swanweil said. "A couple of generals, a couple of revolutionaries, and the rest are businessmen."

"The circle of elites? Pushing out the competition?"

Swanweil seemed to shimmer, maybe due to his slicked back hair brilliant under the lights. "The constricted trade routes suppress competition. Anarchy is the real nightmare. Liquidity is the first casualty of revolution."

"I thought innocent lives were the first casualties."

"Conflicts are undertaken in the name of innocents."

"So . . . twelve men and two women?" I ventured. Swanweil raised his eyebrows. "Brianna Miller who controls the treasure of Kyle Rula and Mrs. Shaw with the pharmaceutical patents," I added.

He made a sour face, odd on his handsome features. "Those patents are Earth-originated. Because of the R&D grant structure, the wait for market generics is too long. Just look what happened with the flu vaccine that had to be made locally. And the treasure you mention is not what people claim. These women . . . only an inconvenience. So, about two o'clock tomorrow, common standard time?" He smiled graciously.

"Tomorrow is a full day," I hedged. "But join us for dinner now. Carl and Patrick are waiting."

"I have a commitment, sorry."

Carl suddenly joined us. "Mr. Henry, I thought you were lost."

"You know Steve Swanweil."

"Surely, we were just—" Carl began.

"Can't," Steve interrupted. "Need to go. I was just being friendly with our new media friend." He swallowed his drink, then shook hands and left alone.

"What's with him?" I asked, but Carl said nothing.

Black tea and Campari were served at a sunny plaza café, and later we had dinner in a geisha house. An endless stream of courses were brought in by painted and demure Chinese-descent women. The meal was laced with constant offers to fill a small cup with rice vodka. Interestingly, the Company men had little contact with the women from the desert clans but mostly with the Han Chinese courtesans.

A Borabean man joined us, older and stout with a bloated face and bulbous nose. He was Asmach, supposedly a great warrior from earlier military campaigns. He was encouraged to drink and to boast while Carl goaded him. During thus-and-so battle, Asmach had fired his weapon until the barrel melted. Slashed this way with his knife, then that way. Asmach fondled the serving women before he belched and slobbered. Carl laughed. Patrick did the same.

John Milan turned darkly. "Carl only calls Asmach here to humiliate him," John whispered. "Carl doesn't have one-tenth Asmach's former courage. He doesn't know the meaning of integrity."

Carl excused himself before the fish course, absent some twenty minutes. Asmach was drunk and John brooding darkly. Patrick was attentive to a painted geisha server. I went out to clear my head and find a quiet moment. In the hall, I overhead voices and knew they were Carl and Steve Swanweil. Odd, they had barely spoken at the bar. I heard more voices speaking Chinese. Wan Su asked if the deal was struck, could they go forward with the plans? Swanweil assured him that all was prepared. Be confident of their support.

What was prepared, I wondered? I hurried back to our dinner. Carl returned before the tapioca had gone runny. Asmach was the worse for drink and nodding out. Once our group exited the geisha house, Patrick sulked on the side while Asmach took his leave. "Now let's have some real fun," Carl suggested energetically.

John immediately refused. "I have appointments in the morning. I can't be muddle-headed."

"Come on," Carl encouraged. "Spend a couple of hours."

"Another time," John said.

"Well, Henry, that leaves you," Carl said, ignoring his good friend.

"I want to try the surf," I said. "That means rising with the sun. Sorry."

Patrick and Carl left in an ECCAV. John and I walked back to the palace. Dolvia's two moons hovered overhead like uneven headlights from an old Buick; one amber and one tinged with red. I looked up several times while we stepped along a broad sidewalk near the square. "What's with you?" John said. "Drunk on sake or dizzy from the pill?"

"Why are the moons different colors?"

"A simple refraction of light, I should think." John was in a foul temper. He preferred the company of Regan Villines, I was thinking.

"What is Carl's story?" I asked.

"You didn't hear this from me," John said. "Young boys; he pulls them off the street and forces them."

"That's tolerated here?"

"An influx of rural populations, some desperate for food. You know how it works."

"And Patrick?"

John shrugged slightly. "Maybe he was first used by Carl, then brought along. Made to watch, made to participate. What fun without a resounder, huh?"

"Patrick could leave."

"And go where? Patrick chose this life. He has no other ties."

Not too many hours later with the sun barely up, I took my surfboard down to the water's edge. I watched the surf for some time while a steady wind off the water robbed moisture from my eyes and skin. I ventured into a rolling breaker with few underwater formations. The water and air temperatures were both eighty-five degrees but tolerable in the dry climate. I saw no fat waves that day and no tubes. I enjoyed several upright rides, quickly tucking back to catch the next crest. Good exercise for acclimating to the weather, I was thinking.

John Milan waited ashore with two Borabean men. I came out of the foam carrying the board underarm and approached them wearing trunks only. The greeting was made by touching fingers to chest. The Borabean had dark beards and draped kaffiyehs over their tunics with pantaloons and boots.

"These are Aensilus and Lynus," John said in English. "They are assigned to you."

"Not too much trouble, I hope."

They said nothing. Lynus seemed embarrassed at the sight of my bare chest.

"They want to know," John said, "what is the purpose of surfing?"

"Want to have a go?" I stood the board on end. Dripping saltwater flashed their way.

"Borabean don't like to get wet," John explained.

"Yah, sure," I said. "The purpose, huh? Surfing on virgin waves is great sport."

"It produces nothing," Lynus said in halting English. "What honor?"

"It's difficult to achieve, and I'm good at it. Besides, it's fun."

We walked together back to the palace entrance. The two men bowed again and left around the side. "They're not palace personnel?"

"From the desert tribes," John said. "And leave that damned thing here."

"Did you see the breakers? I can't wait for heavier weather."

That afternoon we rode in open vehicles, like lightweight jeeps I guess, but without independent suspension to be sure, to view the warehouse section that held furnaces for refining silicide. The campus entrance had minor security. Banners with clan insignia were displayed—a scarab, a triskelion, a three-headed snake, and others. Fewer than a hundred Borabean were assembled there, all men. Three squat silos waited to hold raw materials, never used because the silicide was at the ocean bottom. A square house with smokestacks, nestled out of the ocean breeze and behind the silos, was the location of the furnaces, looking small and old world with a redbrick façade. The empty parking lot looked even more wrong. In a flash of understanding, I realized that the buildings had been constructed from a foreign fund, following a known model for manufacture rather than the current needs in Urbyd.

John Milan was chatting with Aristides, so I wandered to a barrier that defined the edge of a high bank overlooking the Borabean Ocean. This view of open water contrasted sharply with the protected cove that fronted the palace. Cliffs warrened with bird nests rose high above the blue and green froth. Twisted and stunted trees like cypress formed blanched clusters along the cliff top, ancient and riddled with holes, a breeding place for parrots and wombats, I was thinking. Sea harpy nests were nestled on the backside of the clusters, out of the wind.

Below me, the roiling waves crashed against wicked rock formations. The cliffs led inland, then sharply out again, shaping a wedge of water with minimal beach area and no anchorage. I was certain riptides and maelstroms were common in the narrows there. Beyond the far shore, a dredge was anchored in unsettled water, deeper water; the exploration site for ocean-deposited silicide.

Two traditionally dressed Borabeans stood down the way, along with a child. Three offworld men were talking near the barrier, dressed in pantaloons and fatigue jackets, their backs arched against the steady ocean breeze. The foreign leader broke from his group and approached me. "Softcheeks reporter?" he asked offhandedly.

"Scuba diver?" I returned with equal indifference.

"I did some work for Borabean. I'm Capt—" He shook his head slightly. "Jessup Chandliss." He reached to shake hands.

"What's the drop-off angle at the shelf?" I asked.

Curiosity entered the Russian's look. "Just seventeen degrees and nearly twice the height of the cliffs. Full of cross-currents and toothy monsters."

"Do you have a submersible?"

He shook his head no. "Any deepwater experience for you?"

I shrugged. "With wormhole travel, my endurance has vanished. There's no local talent? An ocean always has—"

"A foreign group called Striiduc has made contact. Borabean are ingrown though. They only accepted me from a lack of skills." Chandliss smirked. "Their lack of skills."

"So I read the situation."

"Care to have a go?"

I shook my head no. "I'm scheduled to travel inland."

The Borabean who had been standing by the railing approached, and I realized that they were women under the flowing kaffiyehs. One wore a western business suit, and the other wore kid boots and a patterned sarong. Why were they posing as men? Why were they on the silo campus?

Chandliss noticed my surprised look. "May I present Brianna Miller of the Arrivi?" he said. She reached to shake hands, another surprise. "We apologize for this guise," she said in English. "The kaffiyehs were provided by the campus guard, in fact, as protection against the wind." I only nodded, not believing her. The two soldiers, who looked Russian like Chandliss, took up bodyguard positions facing the silos, poised for trouble.

"And this is Dulcinea from the Uburu tribe," Chandliss said. "They are conducting an industry tour, like yourself."

She held a hand high with her palm up and averted her look. "Hiki, Hershel Henry."

Dulcinea was probably accustomed to stares from strangers, from any man who caught a glimpse of her features. Not effervescent and spilling charm like Jesse Hartley, but smoldering and luscious like one imagined from a mythic harem or an adventure story with magical creatures and breezes that whispered secrets in the mist.

"Nu delaya," Brianna spoke sharply.

The child, who was no more than eight, touched my hand before Brianna could prevent the contact. I saw question in her upturned face and felt the cold fingers entwined with mine. They all stared at me, so I knelt before her. Her features were Asian, maybe Tibetan, with sunken cheekbones and small eyes.

"And what is your name?" I asked in Arrivi.

"Cleo," she said simply. "Your brother has restless energy and thinks of you often."

"My brother?" I looked at the others before turning back to her. "I'm not sure what you mean." She only blinked and stared, so I stood with a shrug.

Dulcinea released a deep sigh like she had been holding her breath. Brianna Miller showed a false smile and turned to Chandliss. "We should go." They guided the child away, not toward the silos but following the breezy path alongside the railing.

"Friends of yours?" I asked Jessup Chandliss.

"We came through the wormhole together, all except the beauty. She's native-born."

"And they brought a child on an industry tour?"

"Not my lookout," he shrugged. "Do you have family on Dolvia?"

"I had brothers in Australia, but they're gone now. Some time ago, in fact."

Chandliss nodded with unfocused eyes. "Well, when you're back this way, ask for me at Rendezvous Bar. We can do some exploring under the sea."

We shook hands again. "Well met," I said.

He left with his comrades, following the same path the women had taken. What an odd encounter, I thought, but maybe not so odd in this newly rich province trying to embrace Earth industry. Chandliss's type was all over Westend—probably ripped from his native lands by insurrection or conquest, leaving a decimated family and no career options. Chandliss must have come adventuring to where his skill set was unique and demanded top dollar, with no reason to make the return trip.

John Milan joined me just as an ocean breeze kicked up again. "Was yours a good adventure?" he asked bitingly.

I only grinned.

EIGHTEEN

WE ASSEMBLED AT THE PALACE'S WESTERN GATE WITH MADQUII wranglers who were paid a premium to guide us into their stretch of desert. Lynus and Aensilus, carrying shoulder-slung karkars, looked over the considerable luggage and shot watchful glances my way as I managed cameras and personal gear.

"You can use that thing?" John Milan asked. I snapped a couple of frames of him. "Candid shots are best," he insisted, "and none of that best-lighting crap. The man within his culture, not a fabricated pose for your idea of what Pulitzer needs."

"Pulitzer who?"

He only scowled. "You do ride sigpywa?"

"That would be the armor-plated centipede?"

John laughed, relishing my future days of discomfort. As tall as a Volkswagen and thrice as long, the Borabean beast of burden had hundreds of feathery legs tucked underneath and a long row of horns, like grouped rhino horns, on either side of her rounded back. She was not constructed by nature as a pack animal but could tolerate desert travel due to the ability to store water in her oily wormy body under the rounded plates, like an armadillo. Bora-bean packing methods included webbed nets that secured bundles among the many short horns.

Some larger sigpywa were halter-trained and accepted riders. The troop looked ridiculous though. Six bearded men were seated astraddle and single file, each grasping the nearest horn. Over the long hours of trekking across the dunes, there was no chance to doze without the danger of falling.

Amid the throng, one sigpywa keened and struggled against her harness. With a high squeal, she lifted the front half of her body and flailed her many feet. Double mouth pincers worked desperately. The bound equipment spilled onto the ground toppling a nearby stall. Bazaari complained with big gestures. Her handler whipped her mercilessly with a thorny club. The plate on her shoulder was split and oozed an amber substance that resembled honey, with an odd smell like heated and scented butter. She settled again and reloading began.

During the beating, Lynus had made a step forward, but Aensi-lus had touched his forearm in warning. I saw his eyes burn hot when he turned away.

I was made to climb onto a sigpywa's back behind John Milan and two Borabeans. The sitting position was unnatural and hard on the kidneys. I leaned forward grasping two horns until I got the hang of riding in rhythm with her gait. Lynus watched with humor and joined Aensilus, who chose to walk.

Later that day while we were taking up a dune trail leading away from Urbyd, I heard those two talking in Arrivi, something about how sigpywa had souls. What honor in abuse? Mostly it was interesting that they chose Arrivi words for their private talk.

When we camped that night, Dolvia's two moons hovered overhead, bathing the sand dunes in cool reflected light, sort of a bluish-yellow. Our camp was awash in a singular hard-edged hue with none of the colorful display I had seen in the city. But then, there was little ocean moisture in the air to refract the light.

The wind held steady though. I wondered how far inland the breeze imposed itself.

I left the tent carrying a jar of lanolin taken from my pack and walked among the groups of men. Some watched suspiciously, perhaps wondering where my assigned escort was. I approached the corral, hoping I would be able to identify the abused sigpywa. And that she would not bite me with those pinchers. I moved alongside the pen, straining to catch sight of her shoulder welts. The horned centipedes writhed over each other like a can of worms, disturbed in the close confinement by an unwelcome presence. The odor of heated butter came to me, and a quiet sucking and slurping noise. I did not want to know from what source.

Then I saw them on the side. Aensilus held the sigpywa's harness while Lynus steadied her and applied a gummy paste. He needed to insert his hand under the separated plate to reach the wound. They saw me and stood with dark looks. I shrugged and held out the jar of lanolin. They exchanged wry smiles before Lynus returned to his work. So I went back to the corral to fetch a bucket of water.

The following day I trashed the acclimation pills and chose to walk as my escort did. Within an hour, Aensilus brought up a galabia and kaffiyeh. They chuckled while I struggled with the agal. We three passed the tolerant sigpywa walking in a long line. John Milan glowered from his twisted perch.

It was late morning with the sun beating down and the wind battering our backs when we skirted a shrine of sorts. Behind it, several blanched skulls of children rested in the sand, somehow secured there. With morbid curiosity I craned my neck to see more.

Lynus came alongside and indicated I should stare ahead. "Just keep walking."

"What is it?" I asked in English.

"A sacrifice to Aequii's sons. Children of the enemy buried alive."

My gag response rose involuntarily. Sweat broke out on my forehead and upper lip as I struggled to keep my face straight. Lynus's face was stern but not toward me. "Only those of the Gora clan indulge this useless ritual."

"But how can they?"

"What to expect from a people who send their children onto the battlefield with death shrouds in their packs?"

"Your people?"

Lynus walked ahead. I knew what I had seen was not unique in the universe. In Africa where I had completed four tours for the foreign press, villages had been massacred and the victims mutilated as a statement of untempered power. In tribal areas where a central government held the people in little regard, with a shaky judiciary and suppressed media, the brutal acts of self-important men went unpunished. No public outcry, no media campaign for justice, no formal charges to pursue the offenders. My regard for Khalif Ananke dipped, and my anxiety for my personal safety soared.

On the third day, we entered a Gora encampment where tribal leaders were submitted to Anaxagoras. The wind had died down thankfully, and the dry air smelled of fuel oil. Their emblem, displayed on spacious fourteen-pole canvas tents, was the triskelion that resembled a three-legged octopus. The triskelion was a mythic creature and familiar to Iamida, the grandfather spirit. This was a military camp with mechanized artillery; few women and children were present. I saw a fuel depot that included a long line of Cicero-built off-road ECCAVs. Why was heavy ordnance stationed so far inside secure territory? And in which direction did it travel?

Our interview with Anaxagoras took place during the cool evening. John and I were shown into a tent war room where suspicious officers stood behind the leader. A big map drawn on oiled paper was spread out there, showing the city of Urbyd and designated encampments on the surrounding dunes that had few features. Anaxagoras's beard was long and full. He had a flat nose and wore several showy pieces of gold. A gold triskelion with ruby eyes hung on a chain over his rotund chest. I had read that the Gora clan controlled rich gold mines near Uburu land, although those mines were mostly played out.

John and I sat cross-legged some distance from the place of honor and were served olives and a greasy paste, their version of hummus, on bread patties. "Eat it," John said from the side of his mouth. I bit into the soft tortilla and nearly gagged, but smiled and managed to swallow some. The lesser emirs looked me up and down.

"John Milan," Anaxagoras said in English. "So good to see you again. I trust your journey into our poor khanate was not too tiring."

"Khalif Anaxagoras," John said, bowing slightly with his fingertips on his chest. I mimicked his gesture. "So kind of you to make the gift of your time. My assistant will take a few photos while we talk."

His assistant? I fooled with the camera awhile until they relaxed and ignored my monkey moves to gain the best angle. Then I photographed everything in the tent; I was mostly impressed with the opulence of Anaxagoras's livery. His officers and prize horses even wore gold-embossed triskelions.

"And how fares General Hartley and his lovely daughter Jesse?" Anaxagoras asked.

"Jesse has jumped back, as surely you know."

"To manage gum arabic contracts for the treasure of Kyle Rula," the emir said as he fingered multicolored olives in a bowl at his side.

"Jesse Hartley has taken a position as an agent for Somule Gems," John said.

How was it that at the mention of Jesse's name my heart skipped a beat? And why did this desert emir care? Because of the treasure of Kyle Rula? Their further talk centered on the new securities exchange and what to expect with the trading activity of each commodity. Anaxagoras expected little.

John Milan would have another chance to talk with Anaxagoras the following morning before we traveled through the khanates to Uburu land to board Consortium helicopters for Cylay. I suspected our extended desert trek had given Anaxagoras an opportunity to move his command location before content from John's interview was made public. I wasn't invited to the second interview, and I wondered what advantage John was seeking. Some under-the-table service to secure a comfortable retirement?

Our journey beyond the Gora encampment that started after noonday was rough going and plagued with incidents, making the earlier trek seem like a picnic. The first night a ketiwhelp pack prowled and nipped at the corralled sigpywa. When the night air was quiet again, one wrangler called out to Aensilus and nudged his friend.

"Was Shorttail among the ketiwhelps?" There was a story among them about how Aensilus had gotten lost on the savannah and led to water by a short-tailed ketiwhelp.

"Not just anyone can talk to ketiwhelp," the wrangler claimed as they strolled past Aensilus.

"More to the point, what do the ketiwhelp have to say?" asked the other.

"Follow the butterflies," they chided. "Follow, follow." The two laughed roughly and glanced back at Aensilus. My impression was that the soldiers in this khanate were corrupt and loyal to military spoils. For more of the same, they would enact brutal oppression, even toward their own, all in the name of Alousha the redeemer.

Rivers will conduct sound for long distances. Dunes, by contrast, tend to misdirect or absorb sound. So I was curious why I kept hearing pounding noises that evening: regular intervals of metal scraping metal like a press in a factory. I was walking among the tents trying to identify the direction of the activity when Aensilus joined me. "You can be less obvious."

"What is that?"

"Conscripts dig for silicide at night and sleep during the hot hours of the day."

"Conscripts on the savannah?"

"Gora dunes are not the savannah," Aensilus said sharply. "We're still one day's travel from the savannah. Just go back to your place." His look directed me more than his words.

Late the next afternoon, Anaxagoras's men on horseback escorted our company and equipment to the edge of his stretch of dunes. We entered a rocky salt flats where the sigpywa traversed the cutting stones gingerly, their bodies rocking side to side. I stood atop the last sandy ridge shading my eyes and staring back to identify the silicide digs. Only a tall metal catwalk was visible from my position. Aensilus grabbed my elbow and drew me roughly toward the lumbering sigpywa.

Everybody walked in the dry heat. I actually missed the steady breeze that had troubled our first days of this adventure. A tall dust column swirled erratically across our path ahead. "Tunanin," Lynus said beside me. "An ancestor surveys the land before the rains."

"Yah, sure," I shrugged, watching the unimpressive swirl.

"Yah, sure," Aensilus repeated the English syllables. They grinned together.

"May I ask a question?" I said in Arrivi. They both stared, surprised I had picked up any dialect, I was thinking. Offworld journalists seldom made the effort. "Aequii is an ancient god," I postulated in halting Arrivi. "And Alousha is a closer redeemer with opposing values. Which is more powerful?"

The two friends paused, considering my question. "You will come," Lynus said simply.

We set aside karkars for a time and raced ahead of the caravan while John Milan scowled from his place near the sigpywa. We hunted rock lizard all afternoon, but the karkars were deemed unsportsmanlike. None of my frequent questions were answered; this was more of a sports outing. I got handy with the knotted net and homemade dart gun.

"This is fun, yes?" Aensilus asked in halting English.

I had allowed my beard to grow. The sun-bleached stubble and hair were blond against my tan skin. Aensilus wondered at my silvery hair. He pulled a few strands and rubbed them between his fingers, shaking his head. Lynus provided a tin of insect repellent, like a shoe polish can. "It's best to keep your hair dark. You're an easy target now."

"Ah, melinga," I said.

"Yah, sure," he mimicked, and they laughed again.

The paste stank to high heaven when I put some in my hair, but it worked instantly. Later while we walked long hours in the burning sun, Lynus provided a swatch of burlap and said to stow it, to keep it off my skin until the rains.

"Netta sends away moisture," he explained. "Today you need your sweat."

In the cool evening we approached camp with our catch slung over our shoulders. "Do Arrivi own sigpywa?" I asked my companions.

"The poor things are imported from across the Borabean ocean," Aensilus said. "They breed quickly though. Better than horses."

Lynus asked in Arrivi, "The women of Pair-ass, they have perfumed hairless thighs?"

"Ample enough," I nodded.

"And their bosoms?"

"Quite adequate."

"And very white?" Aensilus asked.

"Why do you ask about Paris?"

"My brother," Lynus said with a grin. "He claims the women there are demanding sex all hours of the day." I only blinked. "Must be exhausting," he added.

I dropped my lizard prize near the campfire and gestured the Gora wranglers should roast the tail and legs. They glanced at Aensilus for confirmation and produced big belt knives to remove the scaly hide. Not even a grunted thank-you came my way.

John Milan only smirked. "Going native on us, are you, Henry?"

We were camped on some flats that led to a rock field with Uburu mesas on the horizon sitting dark with the late afternoon sun behind them. I was ready to be done with cross-country treks. At my side, Lynus tensed. He and Aensilus looked left. I strained to glimpse whatever was there but could discern nothing. Aensilus gestured to the head wrangler.

"Wait here," Lynus told me. He and Aensilus walked left, leaving me to swallow the insult of exclusion. I recognized that feeling of abandonment from childhood when my three older brothers had tormented me with jeers and insults. Fear and physical limitations had been my daily companion while I had tried to keep up with their rough-and-tumble play. I ruminated on memories of standing on the cliff edge over the limestone quarry while a brother in the water below called for me to jump, and the two brothers behind denigrated my bravery. I had my grandfather's name and my mother's favor, so they seemed to form a tight group with no entry for me.

But they were gone now, lingering only in my memory. My half-brother, younger than me by a decade, was taking university classes in Melbourne with an interest in pure science, the kind that took years of study and a lifetime of research. He was a serious bloke, carrying the legacy of a large family lost to tragic happenstance.

While I sat alone by the fire, one Gora handed me a bone of roasted lizard meat. From his place at the primary fire, John Milan called back. "The gang of three has dwindled to one, huh?" The wranglers did not bother to hide their grins.

I left the fire and wandered over to the corralled animals. From the oleastra bushes on the side came a short hiss, followed by another. Aensilus crouched there. Good thing he wasn't an assassin, I thought, or I would be dead. We ducked behind the sparse cover.

"You will come." He didn't wait for an answer but scurried over the rise.

In a wadi under partial moonlight, Lynus waited in the company of a large reptile. I stopped short. She was not so different from the one we had roasted but seven times larger. "She won't rob the desert of one tonight," Aensilus whispered and led me forward.

Lynus was much entertained by my wide-eyed stare. "Meet Edwina, a gualarep originally from Cicero."

"Ka, ka, ka, ka," the marbled and golden gualarep articulated. Her tongue rolled sideways from a wide-open mouth.

"She thinks you don't like her," Aensilus said.

This the one? came the question as if from a woman. I only stared harder.

Lynus shrugged. "It is seen."

What Cleo thinking? she wondered.

"Hey," I asked. "What's going on here? This animal talks?"

This animal talks? she mimicked. *Yah, sure,* she added.

The two Borabeans laughed but stifled their voices and glanced up at the rise. "You must greet her," Lynus claimed. "Sit cross-legged on the ground."

"Me?" I asked.

"No, the gecko in your pocket," Lynus said.

"Ka, ka, ka, ka, ka," the gualarep articulated as a laugh.

Aensilus pushed on my shoulder strongly, and I sat in the dirt. Edwina's head lifted and the fleshy and forked tongue flashed at regular intervals. A slurping noise pulled in my scent and tested my nerve. Saliva sprayed on my chin before she drew back. "Oh, man!" I complained, wiping the gunk with my sleeve. The men covered their mouths to stifle the sound of their laughter.

She approached again, only slightly hesitating when I drew back. She stepped over my lap strongly rubbing me with her flanks, first one way then back across. I was nearly pushed over. She stepped away then and was barely discernible in the moonlight with her golden hide against the sand dunes. "What on Earth?" I asked.

"Not Earth," Aensilus said. "Dolvia's embrace."

"Ka, ka, ka, ka, ka," and Edwina was gone in the night. Her speed was astonishing.

I stood and wiped my chin. "What was that all about?"

"So you Softcheeks don't murder Edwina thinking she is al-li-ga-tor," Lynus explained. "They are . . . what Softcheeks word? Guala-reps are en-dan-gered." He raised his eyebrows as if asking if that was correct.

"Endangered, yes," I said.

He only grunted.

Those nights I had restless dreams and from a troubling point of view. I raced across chaparral lands with my sightline not two feet off the ground. I hunted prairie dog and addax and surprised the prey in late night ambushes, clamping down with my big mouth. I tasted fur wet with pulsating blood. I found a tall warrior who sat while I rubbed against him in greeting. His orange hair fell in long dreadlocks. *Ka, ka, ka, ka, ka.*

Over several hours of the next day, we moved slowly. Any excuse would stop the column. I observed new Borabean coming up to change places with some who then left. Each signified on Aensilus before taking his leave. Also, the heavy packs we had dragged across the desert were greatly lightened. "What is this?" I asked Lynus.

"These Gora leave to join their families. These others guide us into the Madquii clan."

"Where the father of Aensilus leads?"

Lynus watched my face for a moment. "I embrace Cleo's word about you. It's good that you have disembarked." Smile lines showed on his tan face, so different from his manner in Urbyd. "What do you see?" he solicited as we walked along in the dry heat.

"In Urbyd," I shrugged, "there exists a veneer of modern culture on a mosaic of competing ancient beliefs. A thin overlay, no deeper than the amber and rose-colored tint on the moons."

Lynus squinted with question, maybe not following my words.

"The clans are fragmented," I shrugged, trying to keep my words factual. "The emirs allow Anaxagoras to grow fat. His heavy artillery is headed for Urbyd. The distraction with silicide and the new trading exchange gives him opportunity to move on Ananke. Tribal factions allow him the prize to weaken Company contracts. Then he himself will later be deposed by another emir, further destabilizing central power."

"Maneuvers we learned from the Company," Lynus said.

"After which Aensilus's father will cross the desert in a grassroots movement and enter Urbyd triumphant."

"Grass-roots?"

"Ah, it's just a saying," I said. "Like an upswelling among the people. Aegiv's rule is so much better?"

"Gora silicide deposits will soon be na-tion-al-ized," Lynus said. "Also the gold mines. Before horses and sigpywa, each khanate was contained within its own world. Most were ruled by so-cial-lis-tic vote. A good word, yes? We call it home rule. One day home rule will be for everybody."

"Everybody? Also the women?"

"Well, ah," he said with a sigh. "One battle at a time."

John Milan had diarrhea and a fever. During our afternoon rest stop, he was seated inside a pup tent with the flaps thrown back and glowered at me. "So, Lawrence of Dolvia," he complained snidely. "That lizard meat should have made you double over with stomach cramps."

I only shrugged.

"The young are so smug," he claimed. His body odor was daunting.

I searched around beyond the campsite and found some wet clay where colorful parrots had gathered to fill their bellies. I returned with a double fistful while Lynus watched me with a suspicious squint. He followed me to the pup tent where John sat groaning. I pushed in past the flap and the odor. "Here, eat some of this clay. It will neutralize the acid in your stomach."

"Clay? You want me to eat dirt?" He glanced up at Lynus loitering just outside.

"Not a cure," I said, "but to relieve the burning."

"Next you'll want me to drink urine."

Lynus chuckled. "Urine is a fine remedy for spider bite."

"Well," I shrugged, "that depends on whose urine and which spider."

John pushed away my hand holding the clay. "Not an exact science?"

I forced a smile and dumped the clay near the flap. Lynus shrugged, and we left John to his own methods of finding relief.

We walked a couple more hours to reach a sizeable encampment. The Madquii clan took as their emblem the three-headed snake. They had no horses and little artillery. Emaciated free-roaming erriv munched the dry gypsum weed. Our sigpywa were penned with feed and water some distance from the settlement. John Milan, dehydrated and stinking, was led into the tent area by two wranglers who reflexively pulled away from his unwashed self. Once he was gone, the packs were unlashed to reveal rows of automatics and portable EAMs interspersed with camera equipment and the unused HGEAM. Aensilus met my look.

"I feel so used," I said.

Lynus's wife and child came up for the greeting. Alaise was her name; she wore a head chador, and her gaze was lowered. His son was plump with dark straight hair. Lynus seemed ecstatic to see them and walked away arm in arm.

"Come," Aensilus said to me. "You must greet Father."

Outside a tent not unlike those around it, two bearded older siblings hugged Aensilus and slapped his back. They were Aeton and Aeolis, and they gifted Aensilus a gold pendant on a leather strap. The jewelry showed a stylized butterfly with black-tipped wings, delicate and not weighty like Anaxagoras's jewelry. Aensilus was more embarrassed than grateful. His siblings laughed.

Aegiv had gray in his beard and crafty eyes, a traditional leader who kept the desert ways. I suspected he knew no English. Aensilus led me to him near the tent where Aegiv was splashing water on his face from a shallow bowl. He took the handcloth offered by a tall and brutal-looking guard.

"Hershel Henry, Father," Aensilus said in Borabean. "He's the one."

I bowed, touching fingertips to chest.

Aegiv looked me up and down. His sons waited.

Aegiv rolled his eyes then. They all relaxed as if some weighty question was answered. He noticed the butterfly pendant and chuckled with the older two siblings. Aegiv stepped past me to finger the gift and bear-hug his youngest, the son who had brought Softcheeks to the family tent. The brothers went inside. Aensilus gestured I should follow and entered with his father's big arm over his shoulders.

Aegiv's wife, a rotund and hairy Borabean woman of a certain age, sported a sizable gold armband in the shape of a three-headed snake. Aensilus greeted his mother. The men sat on thin pallets while she served tea and olives. "The Softcheeks John Milan also travels with us," Aensilus offered in Borabean. "He's, uh, washing up for the evening meal." He glanced at his mother. "There's no need to prepare extra." The brothers shook their heads. I understood suddenly that John's discomfort had been engineered, but why was I still healthy?

"And the supplies?" Aegiv asked. Aensilus glanced cautiously at me. "Our new friend has some Borabean," he offered, ignoring his father's question. "And mansa Arrivi. Edwina likes him though."

"Edwina has a taste for young men," Aegiv claimed.

"Lynus should leave tomorrow," Aensilus claimed in a serious tone. "John Milan's condition serves as an excuse to move directly into Uburu land."

"All has been prepared," Aegiv said. "I wish that you could linger though."

Aensilus acknowledged honor from his father. He related the tale of how the pink Softcheeks had surfed upright on Bydqui's waves. They stared with dark squints and laughed together heartily.

Asmach entered the tent, stalking like a desert sheik in the old legends. I leaned forward to glimpse a black warhorse outside wearing a tan saddle with silver tooling, managed by a groom who was clearly overmatched. Asmach wore a kaffiyeh and agal; ammunition belts also crisscrossed his chest. He was armed with a karkar and holstered pistol, as well as a showy belt knife in a sheath. His face was bloated and red as it had been at the geisha house in Urbyd, but his presence was not diminished by signs of too much drink. Aegiv stood for a greeting, and they two soon left with arms over shoulders.

I squinted and watched Aensilus with a questioning look. "So many secrets," I said.

"Would it surprise you to know that Anaxagoras is my father's cousin?" Aensilus asked. "By marriage, not blood."

"Will Aegiv support the Goras march on Urbyd?"

Aensilus shook his head. "King Ananke is a blood cousin." He and the brothers laughed again, revealing deeply cut laugh lines above their beards.

We left the sigpywa with the Madquii. Riding all day in a narrow wagon drawn by a sure-footed erriv heifer, John fought malaria chills amid our stashed camera equipment, most of it never opened. Lynus's wife managed the reins and tended to John's needs. Her son had stayed behind with an uncle. The rest of us walked, venturing into Uburu flatlands interspersed with squat mesas, some terraced to support farming.

My beard was itchy and dark from the insect paste. My kaffi-yeh had been laundered by Alaise, also my trousers. I was twelve pounds lighter and muscled from the days of exertion. I was grateful for the adventure and my good tribal contacts but glad to soon benefit from Consortium technical support.

The savannah rains were pending. I could smell water and verdant earth ready to sprout new crops. In a wooded area with many low shrubs, we came to a stream that trickled noisily among some boulders. We stopped in the late afternoon, allowing the erriv to drink while the call came to camp here and wait for connections with Colonel Sector's troops. The men relaxed, and several even chose to bathe there, unhurried in unstructured personal errands.

The immediate area led to mammoth old-growth trees called mida and a frame house with erriv pens constructed from split rails. "They're like forest ash in my home country," I said to Lynus. "A variety of eucalyptus trees."

"You-ca—" Lynus pursed his lips.

"We'll go with forest ash. A hardwood, right?"

"All fresh water flows into the Iamida River, the grandfather spirit. He flows into Bydquii at the cove of Abydian. Iamida lingers here on his journey, however, because he loves these trees called mida. We never cut them but use the wood of fallen members sometimes."

I nodded. "Mida trees, loved by Iamida."

The two-story home made of rich building materials gave this valley an old-world flavor, overbuilt and secure. The wife and daughters of the resident family stayed out of sight, though, while the idle soldiers filled the barnyard. In a nearby open pasture, prairie grass and something called razor grass waved in the sunlight.

"It's beautiful here," I said to Lynus. "So different from the dunes."

"The buildings were constructed by an Abydian ancestor," Lynus said, "who was shipbuilder to the king before Ananke. He settled here with an Uburu wife and used his skills shaping mida wood. This type of house is found no place else."

Several Arrivi dressed alike in pantaloons and sleeveless shirts came through the brush and joined our traveling group. Presently, three Consortium helicopters arrived from a narrow gorge of oversized ferns and vining hyacinths. They settled on the level pasture before some men in uniforms and three women could join our group. John Milan, stiff and emptied of appetite, shook hands with the leader, and they walked left, ready for the report.

The women went directly to the wife of Lynus, apparently old friends.

I wandered through the camp, watching and counting munitions. I leaned with my back against the rail fence that penned the erriv alongside the outbuildings of the big house. Women labored in the backyard in the cool hours, most likely preparing a meal or doing laundry. They stayed out of sight of the gathering militia troops. I had my notebook out and was notating the number of trucks and munitions. A small hand protruded through the railing, gingerly reaching for my second pen in my pants pocket. I grabbed the wrist firmly and twisted to see who was sneaking around. A twelve-year-old with brown eyes and blanched skin stared at me without fear or contrition. She reminded me of a French girl I once knew, but what French child would accompany the militia?

"Nu delaya," a girlish voice said from my other side. I released the girl's wrist and turned to confront the one who spoke with such confidence. It was a younger girl, the Tibetan kid who I had seen with Brianna Miller and Dulcinea at the Urbyd railing that overlooked the sea. Cleo was her name, also showing no compunction; two pickpockets who had no fear of punishment.

"She says you're special," the first pickpocket said. "She says you're the agent of karsci, that you will make the record."

I kept my voice calm with the naughty girls. "I met Cleo before, but what is your name?" Her face was hard and appraising. "I will offer no bribe," I added.

"Do you even know what is karsci?" she asked in a hard tone.

"A sudden change within a season."

"Each person changes," the French girl said, "and we're all different the next day."

"Something to look forward to," I said. "Don't you have chores to complete?"

I felt Cleo intertwine her fingers with mine, a similar gesture to when we had met in Urbyd. I knelt so our noses were level and registered the worry in her gaze. The French girl spoke up again. "She says that you will tolerate karsci, and you will serve the tribes a long time."

"Are you reading her mind?"

"She likes you, but I don't so much."

"And who do you like?"

She thought about that for a long moment. "Milo-pilo," she answered finally. I didn't know who that was.

Lynus brought forward one who had auburn hair and glasses, wearing a decorated Arrivi gown with a long skirt and carrying a rucksack. She wore a large peridot gem on the round muscle of one arm, secured with a simple cord, the Arrivi symbol of mourning for a lost loved one. "This is Kelly Osborn, cousin to Rularim," Lynus said.

We both stared. "Ah, we met at Stargate Junction," I said.

She held one hand high with the palm upward. "Hiki, Mr. Henry," she said. "Melinga."

"Melinga. I am honored to view the spirit in your face."

Lynus was satisfied with that. He turned on his heel and left while Kelly encouraged the girls to return to the backyard where the women labored. When we were alone, Kelly said, "I have asked to greet you again so you can learn."

"Learn what?"

"Tribal logic."

"Things seem, uh, fairly straightforward," I frowned. "And what access do debutantes have to tribal knowledge?"

"I am cousin to Brianna Miller," Kelly confided. "I belong here, or rather on Mekucoo land next to Kecouroo. I attended the Junction ball as Jesse's friend. We must embrace these opportunities to live large." She pulled two chapbooks from her skirt pocket and handed them to me. "Read these. They will provide a better context for events."

I looked over the covers. "What events?"

She smirked, and the angling sunlight glinted on her wire-rimmed glasses. "Just read them." She retreated to where the other women waited for her. The chapbooks were small with simple glue binding, published by a local company. I thumbed through one and stopped at a page with a tribal chant.

> Dacupitte and Karlyhi make plans
> Still good in om
> Dacupitte visits each clan
> And plants his seed, anon

Promised to she of Somule Gems
But siring sons on all lands
The favorite of Edwina, and even
Dulcinea smiles at him alone
This father of legions waiting to rule

I looked up to see Lynus staring down his nose at me. "Chi cylay," he said. I didn't know what the phrase meant, but I pocketed the chapbooks and followed him toward the open pasture.

Near the noisy choppers, John Milan turned to say his good-byes. He shook my hand and boarded a chopper in the company of Consortium officers. He carried my digital images on a disc along with his interview with Anaxagoras and what he had learned from talking with the officers. He looked back, showing me a dark smirk, before working the seat straps.

NINETEEN

AS NIGHT CLOSED IN, THE CAMPFIRES DOTTING THE GORGE between the mesas were kept low, but the feeling was electric. Several clutches of militia had filtered in over the past hours, some native and some Consortium. Tents were erected, and the military squads gathered in loose ethnic groups. At the fires, the men and some women talked and laughed and shared provisions. At one fire, an older and crippled Cylahi man offered a chant about Dacupitte, the famous warrior with long dreadlocks. Building his reputation with fireside spin.

Pete had defended Brianna Miller, went the story, when Rabbenu Ely called her a whore and raised his hand. Pete had risked his life, their lives, to stand up to this old accusation. Everybody in the gathering heard Mark's chant. It had rhythm and cadence in Arrivi but translated poorly.

Hand raised, the pounding slap
Sounding down the limestone causeway
Accusing "Whore of the Company"!
Daughter of unrequited love
Rabbenu Ely never knew her

Surprised that two warriors
Chose to shield arisen Rularim
Mekucoo knife at his throat
Ely may die in his own house
Because he never knew her

Dacupitte, his successor
Risked himself and gained his place
Hence Ely is marked with kant
The tribes Ely can no longer lead
And all because he never knew her

Near the main fire, one burly Hardhand recruit challenged Mark who had offered the chant. A fight circle quickly formed, and bets were placed all around. Lounging Siibabean warriors, black and muscled, approached with karkars and ammo belts, relaxed in their own cohort. A testing was coming, the pecking order reinforced.

A Hardhand officer barreled in, the legendary General Shaw. I knew him from Company wanted posters. He was big and older with a care-lined face, wearing fatigues but not a specific uniform. He caught the Consortium soldier's offending arm raised in midair and twisted it back so hard I suspected his shoulder was wrenched.

"Call the soldiers together by the fire," Shaw instructed the duty officer. The former general spoke quietly with Mark, who only squinted and nodded. Shaw turned back to the soldier who was one of his own troops.

"So you want a fight? Fine, we can have a fight."

Shaw addressed the gathered warriors and soldiers. "Take your first lesson in tribal defense. This is Mark, the scholar who was hamstrung decades ago by Siibabean." The dark warriors on the side coughed and grinned, handsome and healthy with faces of open camaraderie.

"Give me your belt knife," Shaw instructed. Mark complied grudgingly. Mike Shaw turned so the gathered company could hear his words. "Mark, you must not harm this man. Do I have your word on it?"

Mark scowled and nodded. Mike Shaw gestured impatiently that the soldier should step forward. The Hardhand looked at his buddies, then hitched his belt and swaggered. The freshly disembarked soldiers laughed and hooted, an easy contest.

Shaw actually offered Mark's knife to the Hardhand. "Kill Mark with it."

The soldiers and warriors sent up a loud cheer. The combatants circled with bent knees and tense shoulders and soon fell into a wrestler's embrace. Mark pushed the Hardhand off balance, twisting his arm to recapture the knife. He threw the bigger man onto the ground and placed the sharp edge at his throat.

"Nu delaya!" Shaw called out.

Nobody moved as blood stained the soldier's uniform collar. Mark glanced into the crowd at a tall Cylahi with an implacable face, the famous Karl Wyley, before pushing the soldier hard so that he rolled onto the smoldering fire. The soldier's buddies helped the scorched man to his feet while Mike Shaw signified on Mark who sheathed his knife.

"Remember this," Shaw said in a ringing voice. "No matter the quality of your training, you have not yet killed to defend your families. You have not found a reason to become a lethal weapon, whereas these ones well know that reason."

He gestured to the Cylahi standing among the Siibabean. "Karlyhi, send out the one Omiibuk."

Karl Wyley shrugged. Or Karlyhi; I must learn to use their words and definitions.

A dark and muscled woman wearing fatigues from the clutch of Karlyhi pushed passed the gathered men and eagerly entered the fire's circle. Her hair was a close-trimmed nap and her skin glistened blue-black, exotic and dangerous. The warriors hid their grins.

The soldiers howled with excitation. Mike Shaw spoke to the duty officer. "Which is your best man for hand-to-hand combat?" The soldiers pushed forward a burly Cicero man who was a favorite among them. They laughed and slapped each other's backs. Bets were doubled; these were slow learners.

Shaw spoke to Omiibuk. "Give me your belt knife." She grudgingly complied. "You must not harm this man," he admonished. She only stared the general down.

Mike Shaw turned to the soldier. "Kill her," he said and stepped back.

"Can't we just wrestle around first?" the soldier asked, playing to the crowd who cheered. He and Omiibuk circled for a moment, crouched low with shoulders hunched. The soldier made a couple of half-hearted feints her way while the soldiers called for gang rape. Omiibuk shrugged him off and threatened the cheering soldiers in the circle.

Her opponent came at her from behind, grasping her elbows to hold her for the others to taunt. Omiibuk easily tripped him and threw him over her shoulder. She produced a sharp blade from her boot and quickly slashed across his cheek, causing a bleeder that would scar.

The Cicero soldier reached for her in anger, exposing many open places for her to wound. She inflicted light touches where she could have killed, meant to return the taunting. Omiibuk stepped back and allowed him to roar with frustration. She jerked across his space again, cutting his forearm deeply.

He grabbed the wound and glared at her with red-rimmed eyes. "Why you little—"

"Nu delaya," Mike Shaw called out, but the soldier lunged and stumbled. Omiibuk only pushed him down from behind. She turned to his jeering buddies, signifying on the greater threat. Karlyhi stepped into the circle and grabbed her raised arm to secure the knife. She jerked around, her blood still up, but saw who it was. Their gazes locked; anger turned to play before he set her free. Omiibuk strutted past the soldiers, counting coup, and exited the circle of firelight. Her mock-combat with Karlyhi would resume later, I was thinking.

Mike Shaw helped the humiliated soldier to stand. "Take your second lesson, soldiers of the Consortium. Anything you touch on this planet can kill you, even the cavern water."

He and Karlyhi walked quickly toward the command tent, leaving the morale cleanup for the duty officer. As they passed by me, I heard the general say, "I should have guessed Omiibuk carries two knives."

Karlyhi only chuckled.

It was late by the time they remembered me and my report. Colonel Sector, with his crisp uniform and showy mustache, stood with Lynus, now dressed in the uniform of the clutch of Kenru. We entered the command tent where Mike Shaw and Karlyhi stood talking. A scrolled map was open on the table, secured with tallow bowls, and some stacked munitions. The tent smelled of sweat and the mineral oil used for cleaning weapons.

"General Shaw," Colonel Sector said, "meet Hershel Henry who traveled recently with John Milan."

Mike Shaw shook my hand. He had an iron grip. "General Shaw?"

"Retired. How's your stomach?" he asked as the colonel took the seat of honor. Lynus made a snorting sound. General Shaw stepped back and waited on the side. Colonel Sector was in charge here.

"Why not take me out of commission as well?" I asked. "I can use John Milan's same equipment."

"Precisely," the colonel said. "John Milan saw what Aensilus wanted him to see. You saw what Dolvia would have you know."

"I don't feel blessed."

They waited, a tight group that had weathered many battles together. I tossed my notebook on the table, and the colonel flipped through it. There was no writing on the pages, only sketches of desert encampments with a north–south grid and overhead constellations. At the bottom of each drawing, using their clan emblems, was a count of how many from different groups lingered at specific locations. And the armaments they carried were indicated by stylized drawings. Colonel Sector easily understood what he was reviewing.

Another page showed an org chart with clan affiliations. The facing page had a drawing of Asmach dressed as he arrived in Aegiv's tent. Sector turned back to the notations about the Gora camp. Karlyhi pointed at one star configuration on the page and met Sector's glance. The constellations were not for location so much as for marking the season.

"So—" the colonel said. "A reporter who does no writing. That seems odd."

"I disembarked sixteen days ago. I've not been to Arrivi land. I thought to wait for the writing until I had something to say."

The colonel searched around the desktop before he rooted through his pack. He found a similar notepad, unused, and tossed it to me. "Continue with your drawings. We will review these. You have camera and film and—"

"I'm good," I said and nodded a couple of times.

"You are attached to our group now," Colonel Sector said. "Lynus will return to Madquii land soon, so you can travel with my staff." Mike Shaw showed me a level gaze. Lynus stood tall, perhaps proud that our trip had produced good results.

In the early morning hours, I walked up the gorge a piece, a stroll in the dappled sunlight. I washed my few extra garments in the stream and laid them on the boulder to dry in a patch of sunlight. I rested on a boulder there, looking over more pages of the chapbooks filled with tribal chants about a holy woman who overflew the savannah on the wings of a Murmurey bird, or a welfare minister too beautiful to bear who arrived with help just as a warrior was dying. Sugar-sweet romantic claptrap like the Ballad of Asmach the Warrior.

> Trained in the old ways, tempered by battle
> Friend and foe to Abydian, well nigh of respect
> Asmach made the gold mine truce
> Bringing peace to the mesas of Uburu
> His family lost, his soldiers sacrificed
> He fought nonetheless, clinging to tradition
> And forged a name worthy of this evening's
> Song and a warrior's emulation, anon.

A rich and calming sensation came over me and the sound of water rushing over stones. I turned suddenly and saw the guala-rep; a big head with hinged jaws, green hide, and swirling lines of bark-brown. I had been told they could modulate their hide color.

"Edwina?" I asked. "You gave me a scare." She opened her mouth and allowed the fleshy and forked tongue to lull on one side, her canines and saliva showing. "Very attractive."

"That's Edna, you numbskull."

Kelly Osborn stood down the way. She picked some footholds over the stony path and joined me. "On her left side by the leg. A long scar. Edna was once gored by a bull."

"Edna?" I repeated.

"Ka, ka, ka, ka," the big rep articulated.

"What's she saying?"

"You know already." Kelly saw my questioning look. "Dolvia's gift."

"Yah, sure." I nodded, unsure of her meaning. "Watershed events."

She stared with sunlight glinting off her wire-rimmed glasses. "The watershed of karsci. It's all in the chapbooks."

"I have them," I said. I stood and brushed specks of dirt from my pantaloons. "I have not completed them."

"Not the law, I know," she shrugged. "We have college people compiling the rulings now. The chants are from an oral tradition, a living culture."

"These chants? This is romantic rubbish," I claimed, showing another false smile. "Cyrus who ate the beating hearts of his enemies? Rularim who flies on Murmurey wings?"

"It's the truth! More true than you can know!"

"I cannot report this. I would be jeered out of the press corp."

"You Softcheeks know nothing," she said, suddenly angry. "You don't learn! Why are you even here?"

"Ka, ka, ka, ka," said the gualarep.

How I wanted to strike her, to slap the freckles right off her cheek. "Look, I don't have to listen—"

Suddenly a big knife was at my throat from behind, and a tribesman's strong arm across my chest. He had black straight hair and black eyes with lethal intent.

Lynus stood behind him. "Nu delaya! Rufus!"

"Ka, ka, ka, ka," the rep said again.

Lynus and the angry man stood staring for a moment before he pushed me into the stream. Lynus signified on him, holding a hand high, palm up. "Kelly is covered by me. Would I make a problem for my brother?"

Rufus did not blink as he focused on me. Power was centered in his abdomen and bright flashing anger. "Edwina likes him," Lynus added as though that claim carried weight.

I sloshed backwards in the water, but Rufus sheathed his belt knife.

It must have been the shock of the cold water and the naked knife. I thought I saw tongues of flame reach out behind him. The hot white flashes became a glowing aura, along with a rustling sound like warriors stirring in the bush. I shook off an odd smell, like burning tree bark. He silently led Kelly away, and I was glad to see her go.

Lynus stared down at me. "What!" I said. I hadn't sought any of this.

"Get out of the water. You must greet Edna."

"Yah, sure." Then I heard a giggle.

Yah, sure, repeated in a woman's voice. She entered the stream and walked over me, rubbing me with her flanks like she was claiming a possession. "Ka, ka, ka, ka, ka," she articulated.

"Quit now," I protested. "I'll never get clean."

Quit now, living is all.

"Kelly is the betrothed of Rufus," Lynus said, offering me a hand up to the bank. "He has no sense of humor about her. Except for Edna, Henry the jour na list would be bleeding your soul now into Iamida's chi."

"Ka, ka, ka, ka, ka," she articulated as though that was good fun.

"Edna spoke to Rufus?"

"Yeessss?" Lynus returned as though I should know.

"And you heard her?"

"Yeessss?"

I wiped the dripping water from my chin. "Watershed events for sure."

Suddenly I knew in my mind where Edwina waited in company with Karlyhi not a hundred meters away. And others: a Cylahi scout on the ridge, another at our far flank where Arrivi land stretched out. But more, a cadence of images with rhythm and light. On the bright savannah, a yearling clutch of gualareps chased ketiwhelp. An adult female sunned herself near an outcropping, her eyes troubled by flittering yellow-winged butterflies. A goulep talked with elders in a village, the children gathered in a long line staring in awe at her gualarep.

It was like a map with connected points at varying distances, or a video with discursive images in various saturations of color. The rhythm was like a song: a low chant and a tingling melody. And within the remote viewing, beyond the others and standing on a ridge, a woman in a sky-blue burka communed with an old male rep. Brian was his name. I knew his name was Brian. His memories were older and different than theirs, his song discordant. How could I know that? And who was that woman?

Kat, came the answer.

The images vanished, and I was suddenly back where I stood with Lynus, tilting off balance for a moment, my head spinning with vertigo. I looked down at Edna.

"Ka, ka, ka, ka, ka," she articulated.

Lynus was called away by two soldiers. I sighed and changed into my dry clothes, warmed by the sunny boulders. I rolled the pantaloons into a soggy bundle. I spent the hour with Edna, and we wandered farther into the gorge between two squat mesas.

So this was the song, the famous singing of desert animals lauded in the chapbook of chants. And I was accepted by the two primary gualareps, sisters who were mothers to many others. I hungered for those images that were a mental map for locations of troops and scouts, and possibly the enemy.

I remembered once I had been lost within the station we managed in Australia. The voices of my brothers echoed in my head with their jeers and taunts, but my ears heard only the wind and distant call of a dingo. Feelings of abandonment warred with self-hatred and the knowing that I would be punished when they found me.

"Ka," Edna said.

"You saw that? You saw what was in my mind?"

Edna shook her sizable head in a wide arch. She led me off the trail and behind an outcropping where she waited, tense and watching.

"What is it, Edna?" I asked. "Snakes? Are there snakes by the cool stream?"

She shook her head up and down, like exaggerated nodding, except that was not her message. "You want me to crouch in the bushes? Really?"

I looked around, suspecting some new prank. I didn't much like how prankish she and Edwina were. I saw Kelly just then, running up the trail we had just left, so I crouched to conceal my presence.

Kelly looked behind before she scrambled off the trail, unaware of us. Two breaths later Rufus sauntered by, easily following the signs to turn off the trail after her.

"A lover's spat?" I asked Edna with a chuckle.

We waited in the shade while a field mouse with oversized ears poked around in the underbrush to find a meal. Too small as prey for Edna, I guessed.

I received images of tree branches and bare arms reaching for a stronger hold. Displaced lemurs chattered loudly and climbed to higher perches. A tiny owl turned his head and stared. I saw an Arrivi skirt below me and bare legs with feet in sandals. I realized I saw the world from the point of view of Kelly, who must have climbed one of the big midas in the gorge. A red spider calmly traversed her leg as though it was part of the tree branch. Fighting tears, Kelly drew breath in painful gasps and swallowed hard. From her perch, she saw Rufus come loping through the brush, looking left and right.

Beside me in the gorge, Edna opened her mouth wide, allowing her tongue to lull to one side, an unattractive gesture, and tensely flicked her tail.

Within the remote viewing, I saw Rufus stop at the base of the tree and light a kari root cigarette with a utility match. "Kelly?" he said without looking up. "I know you're up there. Come down now, and I can walk with you back to the camp."

Kelly was still breathing in uncomfortable gulps. "I have no place there."

He spoke evenly as he exhaled the smoke. "A place has been made for you."

"Only from Brianna's word," she shouted down. "You don't even like me. You don't like my hair, or my glasses, or my choices."

"And that's why you cut your hair, to prove I don't want you? Not to emulate Brianna's hair? But to show . . . to make a showing that I don't seek you for . . . for anything."

In the gorge, I turned to Edna. "This is wrong. We shouldn't—"

She licked my chin quickly with her big tongue and then the side of my face. "Oh, just quit." I wiped the gunk from my chin while Edna and I waited. I sat heavily to take the pressure off my knees.

The images of sitting in the wide branches of a tree returned. Kelly called down while kari root smoke wafted up to her. "What do you seek?"

"Tell me that it's true," Rufus said her from below. "You cut your hair to punish me."

"You boast of my auburn hair to the warriors."

"I never needed to. They saw for themselves."

"But you were . . . expanded because of my hair. And what about me? What of me, Kelly? Nothing of me in the boast, only . . . only what you supposed was there."

Rufus stubbed out the kari root and stowed the remainder in his belt. "I have not spent the hours with you, I understand that now. Will you come down?"

"No." After a pause, she added, "What of me do you like?"

"I cannot say."

"Nothing, you mean." Kelly saw through the leaves that Rufus was exploring the trunk, seeking an easy route into the branches.

"I cannot say," he said as though he was stalling. "If I say, you will cut them off."

Kelly burst into tears again.

"Stop that now," he said, "and come down." She sobbed and seemed to catch her breath in painful gasps. Rufus continued, "If I say what I like, you must promise in advance to not destroy what I name."

"So you can boast to the others."

"There's no boast in this."

"What?"

"Promise you won't stop or hide or change or mutilate it?" Rufus called up.

"What?"

"Promise."

"I won't change if you won't boast," she said in a softer tone.

"Fair enough," Rufus said. "Come down now."

"Tell me first."

Rufus waited again, most likely trying to convince himself there was another solution, but perhaps he could not think of one. "I like what you write, most of it. The warriors care little for chants that don't name them personally. So to boast of your writing would get me nothing. So you see, there's no reason for you to stop writing or change to punish me. Is that enough?"

"You like the writing, some of it?"

"Very much."

"Which parts?"

"The parts not about you or me," Rufus said impatiently. "You must never make public what transpires between us alone. That's not for anybody, only for us."

"But nothing has transpired."

"Much has happened; you just push it away."

"I'm trying to find a reason," she whined. "I search and wait and you never—"

"Kelly, the feeling has always been there, but you're too fearful to see."

"See what?"

"Just come down."

"Go away. I'm still angry at you."

"I cannot return to the camp without you," Rufus said.

"You would lose face?"

"I'm trying here!" He sighed and tried a new tack. "Our connection already exists. If I return to camp without you, then something private between us is made public. We must return together."

"What something?"

"Come down and I will show you."

"Tell me."

"Kelly, trust me that in time all will be secure and correct before the others and . . . comfortable for you. You must rest within my knowledge of this."

"There is no rest in knowledge not shared."

"I know you, that you will perform your duty," Rufus said. "Trust that I will provide, and strive no more against what we have."

"But we have nothing."

"Come down, and we shall begin to build something."

"No, go away. I hate you."

"You do not have anger like Brianna's anger or even like Sheeks-Cylom," Rufus said. "You see each person who's present and greet him with honor. Mark spoke of it yesterday, how you made the greeting to each warrior when you arrived at Mayschool."

Kelly's breathing had settled. She craned her neck to see the warrior through the leaves and branches. "Mark spoke to you about me? What honor to you for my actions?"

"If I say, you won't ruin your place out of spite? Or write it in your poems?"

"You are silent because of my poems?"

"Perhaps I did not know that I must speak. I understand now, and I will perf—"

"Perform this task as part of a warrior's duty?"

"If you want to see it that way."

"Go away."

"That's it! I'm done with talking now. You force me into this act."

"No! Go away!"

"I have no choice," Rufus insisted. "You see how we are connected. Because you're so stubborn, my behavior must change. When your actions are right, then I can act correctly among the warriors."

"Go away! I hate you!"

Rufus secured the karkar strap across his chest and began to climb the tree.

The images ended abruptly. I blinked in the shade by the stream and spun around with vertigo. "Now?" I asked Edna. "Now you stop sharing?"

"Ka," she articulated real loud, like a command. She broke cover and sidled to the trail. She spun around and looked at me. "Ka," she said.

"Yah, sure. I'm coming." I stepped onto the trail with my bundle of clothes. "We were just getting to the good part," I complained as I followed her back to camp. She seemed in a hurry to escape her indiscreet spying.

Lynus was coming quickly in our direction, carrying my camera bag. "You will come," Lynus said, gesturing over his head, and turned on his heel to lead the way.

"Now what?" I asked as we rushed to join him.

He thrust the camera bag at me. "Is this all you need? For jour-na-lism? Do you need more pieces?"

"Ah, no, it's all here. What news?"

"Southeast Arrivi have been massacred," Lynus reported. "We can take you there. You will make the reporting."

"A village nearby. Massacred by whom?"

"Women and children alone on the land. Hurry! The chopper won't wait for you."

We rushed to the pasture and scrambled onboard a four-passenger stinger with the motor already humming and the blades slowly rotating. Two larger choppers were loaded with Colonel Sector's Consortium troops. I had dropped my clothes bundle in the pasture and was squished with my camera bag on my lap between Lynus and Colonel Sector. Across from us sat Karlyhi and Mike Shaw. Siize and Siiloba sat on the floor with their feet on the running boards outside. Each cradled an oversized and wicked-looking karkar with long projectiles on a ribbon that led to a secure munitions box.

Karlyhi saw me glancing around. "Gora don't linger," he said without expression. "The danger is low."

"Southeast Arrivi had rice farming for a few seasons," Colonel Sector told me over the engine noise, "but the crop was tainted and the paddies destroyed. We staked them to a new herd of erriv, and the men were bringing in the heifers. They have only two guala-reps that traveled with the men."

"So the village was exposed," I guessed. "A Company trick."

The three men in leadership gave me similar dark stares, a piercing focus that nearly unnerved me. "Destroy a village at your rear," I shouted, "before marching in the other direction. The people are demoralized and whatever troops arrive are made busy with the cleanup."

Karlyhi looked at Mike Shaw. "Anaxagoras marches on Urbyd."

The former general stared out over the head of Siiloba. While we sat in relative silence, Mike looked me up and down, his face hard and eyes appraising.

"But wait," I said. "If he's digging for silicide by his camp, why would Anaxagoras abandon the position and march west?"

Karlyhi only smirked. "Goras trusted the Company to locate the silicide. So they dig . . . and dig and dig."

"The diggers were sent to the wrong place," I guessed. "And now they won't trust Company advice again. Do you know where the silicide is?"

"We now know where it isn't," Karlyhi said. Siize and Siiloba both chuckled.

Colonel Sector's voice was loud in my ear, making me jolt. "We'll do a reconnoiter after we drop these passengers," he told Karlyhi. "The general can join my squad, if he still has an interest in field-work."

Karlyhi's eyes showed humor, looking at Mike Shaw who held his face still. Siize and Siiloba were both grinning.

The ride seemed short to traverse a distance that would take more than a day on foot. We overflew the trashed and smoldering village near a single stand of acacias. There must be old water underground there to support even this many families. The house fires had been contained, and some Arrivi had arrived to search among the wounded.

We scrambled out of the stinger, and the Siibabean brothers returned to their guard stations for the ride back, supposedly to ferry in more Arrivi. Another polished stinger was there, newly landed and just cooling. Wow, two command helicopters at this remote village.

Colonel Sector and Mike Shaw headed for the hovering transport choppers that carried Sector's men and climbed aboard. When they left, the turbulence settled, and I wiped gritty sand from my eyelids. Warriors approached Karlyhi to report and point left, claiming they had found a trail of discarded loot from the retreating Goras. Karlyhi walked away with them.

Lynus and I approached three men, one with his back to us and long dreadlocks caked with dirt. He turned, showing blue eyes staring from a face smudged with soot. A pilot stood at his side, and the third warrior was Asmach, who had traveled through Borabean land on horseback. The pinnacle of Arrivi militia leadership, I was thinking.

Lynus signified on Dacupitte. "A reporter to make the record," he quickly explained.

Dacupitte spared us a minute of his time, eyeing me with appraisal before he spoke to Lynus. "Take him through the village. Photograph everything." Pete and Asmach followed Karlyhi's steps to find the trail of retreat.

I pulled out the digital camera and checked for focus and the angle of light. We made our way among the damaged huts. The village men huddled in small groups holding a few household items or searched the deserted huts for missing family members. The path of surprise and resistance was easy to discern. I looked into one adobe hut that I assumed was a bush clinic. A white man was dead on the floor, his face and arms mutilated with knives, wounds inflicted before he died. The lenses of his thick glasses were splattered with blood spray and the wires bent.

"Dr. Ingram," Lynus said. "The Softcheeks doctor sent to study lingering disease."

In the yard, Kyros rabbe Sudl worked among the grieving men while Orin rabbe Murd's wranglers corralled the newly arrived erriv. I learned all their names later, after we decided which photos were good for the media.

Dulcinea and Kenru, Uburu leaders who were neighbors, as Lynus whispered in my ear, went to Kyros with their condolences. Dulcinea's forehead was wrinkled and her eyes red-rimmed. Her striking looks were not marred by the expression though. At Dulcinea's approach, Kyros stood tall with a tear-stained face. The self-inflicted cuts of grievous loss were fresh on his arms and midriff. Many among his group bled from similar cuts, an honored custom of mourning. Dulcinea kept her head bowed and raised a hand high with her palm upward. I captured a series of images from this moment between them.

I focused on the destruction and even switched cameras to use black and white and feel some distance from the carnage. We followed the path of the fighting toward a field over a rise, perhaps the trashed rice patties. The women had fought hard and kept together, apparently retreating left to high ground, leaving fighters with guns at hidden stations. Many Gora were dead and stripped of their weapons, by which group I could not tell.

We walked the path of pursuit and reached a narrow field where Arrivi bodies rested at odd angles, women and children and fewer desert-dressed warriors. Several broken karkars were visible, so the women must have run out of bullets and used them as clubs.

I took a step forward to get a better angle, but Karlyhi held out a strong arm to block my advance. "Not for you."

"He must make the record," Lynus claimed.

"Wait for those who grieve."

A few veiled village women waited on the edge of the killing field, wailing and clucking in distress and under veils. Another woman scrambled forward from a just-landed helicopter, followed by two more. She stopped near us and pulled off her veil. It was Brianna Miller dressed in a business suit, apparently just arrived from Cylay.

Dacupitte and Asmach offered explanations to her, and Pete touched her arm. Maybe he meant to guide her away from the killing field. She pulled away from him, flailing her arm to avoid contact.

"You are not the boss of me."

Pete stood tall and leaned back, the orange dreadlocks swishing past his shoulder, but he kept his hands at his sides. Brianna stalked in our direction, directing an angry glance over her shoulder at Pete. Asmach watched with his mouth open. Did any of these people get along?

The few village women gathered around Brianna, clucking and wailing. Brianna approached the field entrance where we stood. Karlyhi strong-armed her as he had stopped me. "You must not enter," he whispered. Karlyhi saw her face, and his eyes grew large before he released her.

I readied my camera, determined to follow if she searched the bodies. The sun beat down, and heat radiated from the ground in wavy patterns. Brianna resolutely walked among the bodies, and others who had hesitated now followed, stepping on soil soaked with blood. Mostly women moved in, with my stumbling steps close behind.

The village women had killed Gora fighters as their last acts. The karkars next to some bodies were smeared with blood. A couple of village women had been captured and butchered with knives. Their breasts had been sliced off and their bowels unraveled. A few had been bound and blinded with sharpened sticks, their skin stripped away while they could still cry out in pain and while the children watched in terror.

I heard the camera click and click again. My throat constricted and my stomach turned. I could barely see through my moist eyelids.

Brianna fell to her knees beside one woman who was Bibi Le, bare-chested from ripped clothes, with many bullet wounds, and clutching a murdered child as their blood mingled in the soft dirt. I photographed the pocket of her torn skirt holding a notepad that I was later told was the truancy book. Next to her, Brianna Miller heaved in painful sobs. I knelt and clicked away with the camera. Here I knew what my work could accomplish, the agent of karsci.

How could Dolvia allow this?

Insects buzzed around. A faint apparition danced before my clouded eyes. I lowered the camera and wiped moisture from my cheeks with a gritty palm. With the sun behind her, the holy woman Kat, dressed in shimmering pale blue, stood over Brianna who brushed her own cheeks, blinking in the sun to see Kat. "Who did this?" Brianna whispered.

"Anaxagoras, the rival of Aegiv."

"This is not the warrior way. The children. The torture."

"He did it for blood."

Brianna straightened her spine. The business suit was soiled with tribal blood. Her voice was low, barely a grumble. "We shall give him more blood than he knows."

Kat dipped her fingertips into the drying pool near Bibi Le. "You are baptized in blood." She poked those two fingers into Brianna's mouth. The taste must have been bitter and salty, and mixed with gritty dirt. A few drops colored her chin.

"Hold onto this moment, Brianna," Kat admonished. "You will need its deep wellspring of strength." Kat touched Brianna's forehead where the muscles drew up in anguish and left a bloody crooked mark there. "All those who follow you will bear this mark. You are the body politic now. Your fortune is our fortune."

Kat's her cool shadow fell across my face and shoulders. "You must rise now," she told Brianna. "These ones wait for you."

I remembered to use the camera. I photographed Kelly seated across from me and next to the body of someone's auntie. I felt sunlight on my forehead again and twisted to look back, but Kat was gone. I heard insects doing their work in the bright afternoon. A Murmurey flew overhead with a plaintive cry, flowing a large shadow across the scene of carnage.

I saw Kelly pick up a karkar. Using her skirt hem as a cleaning tool, she polished the carriage. Methodically as though in solitude, Kelly held the automatic to her shoulder to test the sight. She searched the ground for ammunition and resolutely loaded each projectile as if naming them and calling on them for success. I captured a series of images of her actions.

Brianna reached for the closest idle weapon, a karkar of Consortium design. Its weight looked comfortable in her hands. The smooth and sun-warmed barrel extended from the metal stock resting securely against her suit jacket. This was concrete.

She brushed dirt from the gun, inspecting each part. I heard countless metal snaps while the women who sat among the bodies prepared themselves and their weapons. The Arrivi women balanced the heavy stocks of the guns on the ground as crutches to painfully stand. Their burkas and long skirts were soaked with family blood. I turned this way and that, using the sun's light to capture determination on some of the exposed faces and the deliberate gestures of gathering strength.

Omiibuk picked her way among the bodies and stood before Brianna, her black skin shimmering in the unforgiving light. Kelly came to her side without a veil, the karkar barrel resting on her forearm. "Seven Arrivi children," Omiibuk reported. "Buried alive near the tracks of retreating Gora, a sacrifice to Aequii's seven sons.

The signature of Anaxagoras the butcher. Also, the two sons of Kyros rabbe Sudl are missing."

"Perhaps they ran away," Kelly said.

"Better they are dead than to run away," Omiibuk returned.

"Perhaps they were out hunting and will return."

"Perhaps they were taken," Omiibuk said in a harsh voice. "To be abused and raised Borabean."

"They're too old," Brianna said.

"For humiliation of the enemy," Omiibuk said, "For public harm, the sons of Kyros are the correct age and blood."

"Gora would do this thing?" Kelly said.

Omiibuk shrugged. "What to expect from people who send their own children onto the battlefield with death shrouds?" She spat in the blood-soaked dirt. "Also the conscripts are sacrificed. Where Gora were digging for silicide in the dunes, the equipment is trashed and the bodies of the conscripts dumped down the shaft."

"How many?" I asked.

"Does it matter?" Omiibuk said. Her eyes were pulled in tight slits like a dozing cat. "We knew of sixteen men and three women. Probably all of them dead."

I tasted bile in my throat. Others coughed and shuffled their feet. Brianna sighed heavily and looked again at Bibi Le's mutilated body. "This is for you."

My legs were stiff and my arms heavy. The sunlit horror lingered in my nostrils with a coppery tang. I inhaled the hot and pungent air deeply so I would never forget. I employed the camera without thinking about my motions, focused on decisions made among the group.

I photographed Brianna as she leaned on the sturdy weapon and stood, gaining her full height, centered and unforgiving. She shouldered the karkar and took the first resolute steps out of the killing field. Kelly walked behind, joined by many others who moved without being instructed. They walked straight to Karlyhi.

I photographed Karlyhi and Brianna in her blood-smeared suit standing together in silence. There was no need to speak. Brianna's angry look reinforced his tribal logic. Kenru came up from the side with Orin rabbe Murd. Trickles of blood had dried on Orin's arms from his self-inflicted wounds of grief.

"What's that on your face?" Orin asked, pointing to Brianna.

It was Kelly who answered. "The mark of Rularim. We all should wear one." She reached out to a bloody fencepost and smeared the gore before stroking her thumb across her own forehead to place a similar mark. Kelly turned to display the mark to the women behind, who reached to do the same.

Orin reported to Karlyhi. "Kyros is kenoma now. He will wander for a time in emptiness." They all took his meaning, a stricken warrior.

"Chi cylay," someone said beside me. Omiibuk put a hand on my upper arm and roughly encouraged me to come with her. "You will make a record of the Gora sacrifice of innocents. This way."

I was mostly pushed by Omiibuk to a place near the acacias where the heads of seven children were visible in an uneven line. Under Omiibuk's hateful look, I stepped forward to photograph the ugly scene: seven macabre graves with the heads exposed, hair gritty with dirt and eyes glazed white.

"These two are not Arrivi," Omiibuk said, "but from the clutch of Cleo Datong."

I heard Rufus speak behind me while I made a record of each sacrificed child. "That's what comes of bringing orphans to the desert."

Omiibuk's voice was hard. "They had no life where they were. Now their names will live on in our chants—Saed and Ankos of the clutch of Cleo Datong."

The leaders had all made their way to this place, quiet and angry, gathering strength for what must come next. Dulcinea the Uburu and her uncle Kenru stood with Kyros Kenoma. Kelly Osborn stood with Brianna Miller and Orin rabbe Murd, with many more behind. Dacupitte, Asmach, and Rufus lingered near Karlyhi, who was flanked by Siize and Siiloba, the brothers of Omiibuk.

"There should be a day of atonement," Kenru offered. "Time to grieve."

"The dead are dead," Karlyhi returned. "We will rob the desert of many Gora."

"We need a plan," Orin said.

"Tell your plan on the road," Brianna said. "This army moves now."

BE CERTAIN TO PICK UP

HOME RULE

THE NEXT BOOK IN THE SERIES

EXCERPT

I'M KELLY OSBORN, AND I WAS PART OF THE BATTLE OF IAMIDA shores. I was nineteen and assigned to stay with the children of those in leadership since there was no time to evacuate. As the betrothed of Rufus, I was to watch over Colonel Sector's girls and the other children in the village schoolroom.

Our station was overrun by Borabean warriors of the Gora clan. We heard them outside our hiding place; running footsteps and bursts of gunfire, the sound so different from a karkar's report. My heart was beating too fast, and I felt 12-year-old Millie trembling next to me, not knowing if we would be dragged onto the street for rape or hacking off our arms. Tears marked Millie's face as she huddled with her sister Anna.

The door was flung open. A bearded man in galabia and boots stood with a lowered gun and a bloody knife. In my memory, the blinding sun behind him was tinged blood red. His dark eyes surveyed us, assessing what treasure he had found. The children whimpered and hugged the walls. A knot formed in my throat. Sweat moistened the hair at my temples.

The Gora man slung the weapon's strap over his shoulder and reached for Millie and her sister. He cuffed Millie by the neck of her tunic and dragged them outside, clinging to each other and limp against his rough gestures.

"Kelly, Kelly," Millie cried. "Help us!"

I bolted after him. I had a large kitchen knife and nothing else. But it was wrong what he was doing, just plain wrong. Before he was aware of my move, I sliced across his liver from behind. His back arched, and he reached behind blindly, but I jumped away. I jabbed under his ribs with my graceless knife where he was exposed due to his own gesture. Thrust in and up, as we had learned from Omiibuk. His brow furled as he stared at me. He looked down at his galabia quickly soaked with blood.

He still grasped Millie's tunic when his knees buckled, and he collapsed in the doorway. The girls were pulled down on top of him, but they screamed and scrambled away. I wasn't actually thinking, I mean, forming thoughts. I remember kneeling beside the body before I balanced his automatic across his round shoulder. The girls gathered behind me. I pulled off my glasses smeared with blood and worked the trigger many times, sending a spray of bullets. Millie grabbed plastic ammo clips from the fallen and handed them to me to fit into the weapon. Tat-tat-tat-tat. I saw bearded men fall and did not care that I wounded them from behind; I was uncaring about that.

Finally, the gun was empty, the long barrel hot and smoking.

NAMES

used in The Body Politic

NOTE: *listed by last name (where available) and designated by status when first introduced; places and terms listed separately*

Aegiv – leader of Borabean Madquii clan, father to Aeolis, Aeton and Aensilus

Aensilus – youngest of Aegiv's sons, friend to Lynus

Alaise – Borabean wife to Lynus

Ananke – Borabean ruler in days of Brianna Miller

Anaxagoras – leader of Borabean Gora clan

Aristides – Abydian minister in Urbyd

Asmach – Borabean hero

Dr. Henry Beecham – hospital administrator after Dr. Abercrombie

Bibi Le – Southeast Arrivi married to Kyros Rabbe Sudl, mother to Kristos and Karry and two daughters

Brian – second adult male Gualarep imported from Cicero

Carline Bryant – sister to Joey Osborn and half-sister to Dacupitte, married to Sean Bryant of the Cylay Bryant cartel

Sean Bryant – a cartel founder and sweatshop operator, husband to Carline Bryant, brothers Daniel and Patrick

Cara – Mekucoo prince and companion to Cyrus

Captain Jessup Chandliss – Russian officer who migrated to Dolvia to serve as a scuba diver

Daniel Chin – Company executive, boss to Tuang Cho and Wan Su

Tuang Cho – Company executive and friend to Daniel Chin

Cochin – seafaring tribe beyond the Borabean who sought contracts with the Company for work as miners on asteroids

Cyrus – 1) Mekucoo warrior scarred from Company torture, 2) wild Gualarep on Siibabean land

Dacupitte – (pronounced dac-you-pit-tea) Mekucoo for "he who waits with angry eyes", their name for Hamish (Pete), the illegitimate son of Hamish Nordhagen and Heather Osborn, raised by Kecouroo

Ahmed Datong – member of clutch who remained on earth and worked with Somule Gems in China

Ankos Datong – male Earth orphan and member of the clutch of Cleo

Bernice Datong – oldest of the clutch of Cleo, agent for Somule Gems at Stargate Junction

Camille Datong – pickpocket from the clutch of Cleo brought from Earth to Dolvia

Claire Datong – middle girl of the clutch of Cleo

Cleo Datong – rescued member of clutch of Cleo Datong

Dominic Datong – member of the clutch of Cleo

Leah Datong – leader of the clutch of Cleo

Rosalyn Datong– quartermaster of the clutch of Cleo

Saed Datong – male Earth orphan and member of the clutch of Cleo

Dulcinea – Uburu woman and friend to Brianna, later wife of Aeolis then Kyros Rabbe Sudl

Frank Duerr – Cicero-born civil authority in Somule and Cylay

Edna – one of two female Gualareps submitted to Dr. Greensboro, later to Hakulupe Le

Edwina – one of two female Gualareps submitted to Dr. Greensboro, later to Kecouroo

Rabbenu Ely – Arrivi leader, a former revolutionary follower of Mula

Dr. Edna Edwina Greensboro – bush clinic research doctor, also known as Sheeks-Cylom, later wife to General Shaw, sons Eugene and Larry (You-Gene)

Hakulupe Le – wife to Colonel Sector, mother to Millie, Anna and Michael Peter

Hamilcar – common tribal name for Colonel Hartley, taken from Hanthudilciage which means talking-head

Billie Hartley – General Hartley's wife, mother to Carl, Heather and Jesse

Carl Hartley – son to General Hartley, one of Junction boys

Heather Hartley – General oldest daughter, named after Heather Osborn

Jesse Hartley – youngest child of Colonel and Mrs. Hartley

General Eugene Hartley – Consortium officer stationed on the orbiting transport, wife Billie

Hershel Henry – Australian born journalist, friend to John Milan in the last days of Rabbenu Ely

Dr. Ingram – Softcheeks doctor who studied the result of infection in southeast Arrivi village

Karima Le – oldest sister of Arim, sometimes called May, married to Haku Rabbe Murd

Karlyhi – Cylahi refugee picked up by Dr. Greensboro

Karry – older son of Kyros Rabbe Sudl held captive by Borabean Goras

Karisma – last son of Dacupitte (Pete) by Brianna Miller, raised by
Dulcinea

Kat – youngest of Haku Rabbe Murd and Karima Le's four children,
named for her dead aunt, later a holy woman

Katelupe Le – second oldest sister of Arim, sometimes called Terry,
later known as Terry the martyr and unfortunate mother to
Hakulupe Le

Kecouroo – daughter to Cyrus by his first wife, raised with Dacupitte,
niece to Cara, a bush clinic school teacher

Kenru – Uburu leader, son to Kecouroo and uncle to Dulcinea

Klistina Le – third-born sister of Arim, sometimes called Tina,
Brianna Miller's mother

Kristos – younger son of Kyros Rabbe Sudl held captive by Borabean
Goras

Kyle Le – youngest sister of Arim, sometimes called Kyle Rula or
Rularim, also as a businessperson called Kyle Rabbe Arim, a goulep
blessed with second sight. Wife of Cyrus and mother to Lynus and
Rufus

Kyros – mother to Cyrus

Kyros Kenoma – later name for Kyros Rabbe Sudl

Lynus – son of Cyrus and Kyle Rula, brother to Rufus, married to
Borabean Alaise

Captain Billie Manenowski – Consortium officer, married to Vera,
daughter Marsha

Marcy – Cylahi mulatto and one of Lucy's kids, wife to Rabbenu Ely

Mark – last of Lucy's kids, hamstrung by Siibabean, composer of chants

Martina – Martin Sumuki's oldest daughter, scarred on her eye by a
former fungus growth, also known as Lula

John Milan – Softcheeks journalist in the days of the Uburu refugee
crisis

Mildred – office manager to General Hartley

Brian Miller – hero of the Company refinery battle, father to Brianna Miller by Klistina Le, a sister of Arim

Brianna Miller – daughter to Brian Miller and Klistina Le of Arim, the second Rularim

Dr. Pierre Mitterand – French research doctor completing his residency on Dolvia

Moab – Uburu hero and short-time husband to Kecouroo in the days of Cyrus the Ketiwhelp killer

Haku Rabbe Murd – Arrivi cattle rancher, blind and obese with old napalm burns on his face and neck, husband to Karima Le of Arim, father to Orin

Len Rabbe Murd – younger son of Orin and brother to Hakki, a securities exchange clerk and newspaper printer

Orin Rabbe Murd – oldest son of Haku Rabbe Murd and Karima Le of Arim, father of Hakki and Len

Spindel Rabbe Murd – brother to Haku, killed on the road in the days of Martin Sumuki

Hamish Nordhagen – transport crewmember, father of Dacupitte by Heather Osborn

Omiibuk – wife of Karlyhi, brothers Siize and Siiloba

Oria – mythological Arrivi warrior present in many tribal chants

Oriika – Dolviet holy woman in the days of Martin Sumuki

Oroc -- mythological Uburu warrior present in many tribal chants

Heather Osborn – wife to colonist Carl Osborn, mother to Joey and Carline Osborn and Dacupitte (called Pete), later wife to Brian Miller

Joey Osborn – oldest child of Carl and Heather Osborn, brother to Carline, half-brother to Dacupitte (called Pete)

Karen Osborn – Joey's wife and mother to Kelly and Patrick

Kelly Osborn – chapbook poet, later wife to Rufus

Patrick Osborn – Company junior executive, one of the Junction Boys

Otieno – Striiduc ambassador seeking mining contracts from the Company

Pete – nickname for Dacupitte, illegitimate son of Heather Osborn and Hamish Nordhagen

Petra Mitterand – niece of Pierre Mitterand who inherited his estate

Ralph – Cicero-born male Gualarep, Mike Shaw's pet

Dr. Richardson – resident doctor at New Shanghai hospital with a heroin habit

Rufus – younger son of Cyrus and Kyle Rula, brother to Lynus

Rularim – latter-day name for Kyle Le

Sarah – goulep and welfare minister, friend to Vera and Karen

Colonel Milo Sector – Consortium officer married to Hakulupe Le, children Millie, Anna and Michael Peter

General Michael Peter Shaw – Cicero born Consortium officer, married to Dr. Greensboro, sons Eugene and Larry (You-Gene)

Sheeks-Cylom – native name for Dr. Greensboro first given her by Karlyhi, meaning ghostly Softcheeks

Siize – Siibabean brother to Omiibuk and Siiloba

Siiloba – Siibabean brother to Omiibuk and Siize

Dr. Spinelli – archeologist at Uburu digs

Wan Su – Company executive with Tuang Cho

Kyros Rabbe Sudl – Southeast Arrivi, married to Bibi Le, sons Kristos and Karry, later known as Kyros Kenoma

Ben Sumuki – tribal doctor and nephew to Martina

Martin Sumuki – Putuki officer at Tri-City Bank Corp in the days of Brian Miller

Steve Swanweil – Bryant cartel employee with connections to the Company

Terry the martyr – Katelupe Le, second oldest sister of Arim

Vera – wife to Captain Manenowski, mother to Marsha

Regan Villines – Softcheeks journalist and friend to John Milan

TERMS

used in The Body Politic

NOTE: *Character names are listed separately*

Abydian – Borabean ruling clan with beetle sigil, includes Ananke and Aristides

Acclimation pill – Company-issue stimulant for newly disembarking executives who experience difficulty with Dolvia's climate

Aequii – ancient Borabean god and brother to ocean god Bydquii

Airbus – an imported Consortium bus in three sections, the driver's cab, the patient section and a truckbed

Air-lift – elevator in Bioshpere and transport

Alousha – recent Borabean god in competition with Aequii and Bydquii

Arrivi – Dolviet tribe who own land and herd erriv. Their women wear full body veils with facial panels

Baktu – male Uburu garment consisting of a colorful wrap-around from waist to knees

Bald – freightate term for a person who live among the tribes without technical support

Beecham Place – later name for savannah hospital started by Dr. Abercrombie

Blackshirts – Company enforcers, some Han-Chinese and some former conscripts

Biosphere – Company built station on Cicero

Borabean – tribe living next tot he ocean north of Uburu land

Burka – required Arrivi body veil with facial panel

Bydquii – ancient Borabean god and brother to Aequii

Canyon of Buttes – Dolviet cluster of buttes within a canyon west of the savannah, a sacred area for Arrivi

Cenzea – air laden with carbon monoxide on Uburu land near the digs

Chador – Softcheeks term for the Arrivi burka with facial panel

Chikiocahi – the middle Softcheeks plane, within Dolviet spiritual viewing, which embodies the social self, also called the chi

Chi Cylay – tribal slang for "pay attention"

Cicero – Westend planet nearest Dolvia, a member of the Consortium

Company – Han-Chinese Earth corporation with mining interests in Westend

Company logo – an off-black and eggshell white image of the long extinct Chinese giant panda roundly sitting with one paw on its knee, superimposed over a circle of mandarin yellow rimmed with royal purple

Comtech – linked screens that broadcast Company sanctioned news in public areas throughout the transport system plus at Stargate Junction

Consortium – loosely formed federation of domestic governments on the four inhabitable planets of the tri-star system in Westend which includes Dolvia and Cicero

Cylay – 1) the capital city of Dolvia's savannah region, 2) one of four Mekucoo seasons when forces spread out from the source

Cylahi – poor Dolviet tribe who wear few clothes and fashion gold jewelry for a trade

Digit cohort – tribal children fitted with artificial arms after mutilated by Borabean

Dolvia – small planet with two moons, a ring of rain forests at its equator, plus an arid savannah region that includes the cities of Cylay and Somule

EAM – extra-atmosphere modem, a tabletop computer screen for communicating via satellite or directly with the transport. EAM-12 is text only, EAM-50 has video-conferencing

ECCAV – enclosed cross-country air-conditioned vehicle, the Consortium car

Ely – a house-and-hearth certificate demanded by ordinance of Rabbenu Ely in Cylay.

Erriv – Arrivi cattle with row of horns along the crest of the skull and neck

Eve of the Hunt – night before the Ketiwhelp hunt

Feast of Oria – Arrivi high holiday that takes place after the rains

Flats of Arim – geo-thermal section of the savannah that includes geysers, bubbling mud pools and mineral springs, originally owned by Len Rabbe Arim, Kyle Le's father

Fortress of Arim – manmade cave dug into the caldera wall above the flats and used as a hiding place by Kyle Le and Heather Osborn

Freightate – transport slang

Gefolge – Striiduc and Cochin miners who follow smogens, or adventurers

Gehenna – Borabean term for people of all other tribes, meaning "not us"

Gora – warring clan of Borabean with triskelion as their sigil

Goulep – persona non grata ostracized by her own tribe

Gualarep – marble-hide reptile originally from Cicero which can regulate it colors, identify by scent, and throw its thoughts

Hai – Arrivi word for yes

Hamstrung – Siibabean war tactic wherein the warrior's ancle tendons are slashed crippling him for life

Han-Chinese – Earth minority group who comprise the elite pool of Company executives

Hardhand – Dolviet term for disembarking colonists who set up small trade businesses in Cylay and Somule

Heartstone – Edna's word for empathetic pain for another's suffering

HGEAM – holographic extra-atmosphere moden that projected a deep-view image of the speaker

Hiki – an Arrivi greeting

Jump back – freightate for the return to Earth through the worm hole

Junction Boys – Westend educated economists including Carl Hartley and Patrick Osborn

Kam – Mekucoo penny, a copper twist

Kant – a lack of kari, no growth or reinforcement from Dolvia

Kari – one of four Mekucoo seasons when new growth presents itself

Kari root – medicinal herb that Dolviet men smoke as a cigarette

Kariom – Dolviet gray lungfish that hibernates in the riverbank until the ran comes, once worshipped as a god

Karkar – tribal automatic weapon, literally "stuck in kari"

Karsci – sudden shift of events with a season

Ketiwhelp – four-legged furry omnivores that plague Arrivi cattle

Kiam gin – imported alcoholic drink

Low-fic – short wave communications apparatus

Lucy's kids – eighteen mulatto Cylahi children, including Tommy and Marcy, sired by transport conscripts who Lucy Kempler takes in after their mothers die of dysentery

Madquii – clan of Borabean with three-headed snake as their sigil, led by Aegiv the lawgiver with three sons Aeton, Aeolis and Aensilus

Maser – medicinal laser used for sealing cleansed wounds

Mayschool – common name for the Karima Le of Arim and Murd Memorial College

Mekucoo – Dolviet tribe renown as Ketiwhelp killers

Melinga – Dolviet greeting, literally "may Dolvia embrace you"

Mercy seat – Mekucoo ideal taken from Earth culture, a peaceful gathering where all parties gain something

Meydani – women who owned stalls in the native bazaars to barter goods

Mida trees – forest ash, a form of eucalyptus trees lining the Iamida River on Uburu land

Murmurey bird – large flesh eater that nests year-round on the savannah

Netta – 1) a symbiotic balance of sulfur over silica, superheated for decades by subterranean geysers and spewed out the vents before the cooling rains to be captured on natural burlap, most often harvested by Arrivi women, 2) the longest of four Mekucoo seasons when the savannah is dormant, 3) a dry balance

Nettki – female Dolviet moon that never rises to a zenith but hovers continually at the horizon

Nettom – male Dolviet moon that passes overhead before sinking into Nettki's sky

New Shanghai – city on Cicero where Carline Bryant and extended family lived

Nu delaya – Mekucoo command to wait

Oblu – Mekucoo quarter, a silver twist

Okiioc – fibrous stalk, a staple in Siibabean diet that helps prevent cataracts and build strong teeth

Oleastra – wild olive shrubs on the savannah

Om – shortest of four Mekucoo seasons when all is made known

Onchocerciasis – river blindness caused when an internal colony of mites breeds and clouds the eyes with larvae

Putuki – Dolviet tribe who are mostly businessmen or domestic workers

Rabbenu – (pronounced ray-ben-you) a title of high honor reserved for the elected Arrivi leader

Regent – Company leader

"Rob the desert of one"   to attempt a foolish act that will kill you before the desert can

Second sight – the ability to discern more than is apparent

Sigpywa – oversized imported centipedes used as beast of burden by Borabean

Silicide – a form of silicone created in the absence of oxygen (as part of a meteor shower) and found in deposits on Madquii land and the flats of Arim

Siibabean – traditional Mekucoo enemies, tall and lean with perfect teeth, who wear a halo headdress of Murmurey feathers

Smogens – miners from Striiduc and Cochin, men who go adventuring

Softcheeks – a Dolviet term for Earthlings including Company executives

Somule – the Dolvia savannah city closest to the flats of Arim

Somule Gems – major Westend company to grow out of the treasure of Kyle Rula

Souk – a woman who worked in a stall in the native bazaars to barter goods

Stargate Junction – the space station at Westend's worm hole entrance

Striiduc – land of miners and sailors beyond the Borabean

Tektite – meteor stone found all over the savannah and said to enhance native skills of telepathy or skills of second sight

Travel number – permission to jump back to Earth by way of Company shipping routes through the worm hole

Treasure of Kyle Rula – a chest containing peridot and topaz gems and Cylahi gold jewelry plus some natural netta that had been offered over time as bribes to Captain Ellis to ensure Katelupe Le's relative health in the Company prison

"Three planes of Softcheeks" – within second sight, how Earthlings but not Hardhands appear to Dolviets

Tunanin – dust columns on the savannah, ancestral spirit who survey the land before the rains

Two Forks – a Cicero city where Mike Shaw's parents had a farm

Tzu – Company-made laser gun

Uburu – a northern mountain tribe forced onto the savannah when their crops are burned

Uburu digs – archeologist site visited by Softcheeks scientists

Unblessed ones – residents of Cylay slums who lived in conditions so grim, they were unblessed by Dolvia

Urbyd – Borabean capital city

Westend – a space quadrant beyond the wormhole and loosely ruled by the Consortium

Worm hole – the connecting time-compressed space anomaly between Earth's solar system and Westend

ABOUT
THE AUTHOR

STELLA ATRIUM IS A CYNICAL SEPTUAGENARIAN. SHE HAS SPENT a lifetime exploring female characters for real world reactions to obstacles. Often pushed into submissive and non-verbal roles, women really live in a world of networking among aunties, cousins, wives of husbands, convenient friends and neighbors. This rich world is largely unexplored.

"I grew up with all brothers, so I knew about women from stories and from school. What I found at school wasn't anything like in the stories, so I set out to learn why."

If you enjoyed *The Body Politic*, leave a reader review on Amazon or Goodreads. Visit Stella's website to order book 3, *Home Rule,* at stellaatrium.com.